innocence

by the same author

Five Mile House
Ordinary Monsters
The Wilderness

innocence

a novel by

karen novak

BLOOMSBURY

Published by Bloomsbury Publishing, New York and London
Distributed to the trade by Holtzbrinck Publishers

All papers used by Bloomsbury Publishing are natural, recyclable products made from wood grown in well-managed forests. The manufacturing processes conform to the environmental regulations of the country of origin.

Library of Congress Cataloging-in-Publication data has been applied for.

First published in the United States by Bloomsbury in 2003
This paperback edition published in 2004

Paperback ISBN 1-58234-435-3

1 3 5 7 9 10 8 6 4 2

Typeset by Hewer Text Ltd, Edinburgh
Printed in the United States of America by Quebecor World Fairfield

For Shannon

acknowledgments

This novel has been blessed with many good friends. Thank you, as always, to my agent, Elizabeth Sheinkman. You are, quite simply, the best. Karen Rinaldi, your faith astounds me. Lara Carrigan, your editorial wisdom has been a gift. Everyone at Bloomsbury has been wonderful from day one.

To my fellow sufferers of Writers' Disease: Thanks for taking my phone calls, for reading, advising, and indulging my anxieties. Lorraine Berry, your discernment lifted the veil – not to mention you are an amazing editor. Nancy Hanner, whose grace and quiet strength I have leaned on mightily. Shannon Hetz, who lent me too much of her time, her patience, and her front door. C. J. Kershner, it was fun to watch you read; thanks for your help. Elisabeth Lindsay, you are an inspiration. Kristan Ryan, I know an angel when I meet one. Amy Small-McKinney, your poet's sensibilities helped define this book's soul. See you all at Chenago.

Tamara Hendley, no words can express how much I appreciate your contributions as a friend and reader. Steve Heilman, you know, at least I hope you do. Deborah Jeffery, long-lost twin sister, thanks – in every color imaginable. Deborah Morrison, yeah, yeah, yeah – I'm going to be there any minute now. Ann Arbor or bust. Thank you to Sars for coining Merciless TV, and a shout-out of admiration for the writers at televisionwithoutpity.com.

And finally, to the young woman in Frederick Busch's Living Writers class at Colgate, who, flustered though she may have been, took the risk of telling me she thought Leslie Stone was inadequate as a mother, this book is your fault. Bless you. And Mr. Busch, apparently I owe you yet another one.

Barry. KC. Robyn. You are my life.

What is a good man but a bad man's teacher?
What is a bad man but a good man's job?
If you do not understand this, you will get lost,
However intelligent you are.
It is the great secret.

– Lao-tzu, *Tao Te Ching*
Chapter 27
Translation by Stephen Mitchell

. . . let no one know that you have a little bird who tells you
everything.

– Hans Christian Andersen, "The Nightingale"
Translation by H. P. Paull

through the looking glass

I waited until evening, that twilight moment when the pavement was the same shade as the sky. I wore the dress with the long skirt and the lace collar, tiny white flowers printed on chiffon the color of dusk that made me nearly invisible against the fading day. A white plastic headband I bought at the drugstore held back my hair. The headband pinched hard at the back of my ears, but I wanted that pulled-together effect. White high-heeled pumps. A small white handbag. Gardenia perfume. I might have been the vice president of the PTA, sent to drum up support for the next school levy. No one could have guessed my real business. No one could have guessed my handbag held a gun.

I was in a neighborhood of frost-heaved sidewalks, elm-arched streets, and rows of tiny bungalows that had become fashionable again. A gaggle of young girls in rumpled school uniforms was making use of the last light, playing double Dutch on the sidewalk. *A my name is Alice. My husband's name is Al. We live in Alabama and we all eat Ants. B my name is Betty* . . . One of the girls turning the rope puffed up her cheeks and blew a strand of hair from her face. She gave me a wary glance as I passed. I was a stranger, and she was of the generation taught to be watchful of the strange. *C my name is Cindy* . . . I smiled at the jump-rope girl; the jump-rope girl did not smile back.

I found the Carse house. A short, straight walkway bisected the tiny lawn. Yellow mums, moon colored at this late hour, bunched up against rounded yews in the mulched beds on either side of the front steps. Heavy-limbed clematis sagged on wires wound around each of the columns supporting the roof over the porch. The porch light wasn't on; the windows were curtained and dark. I paused for a moment, took a couple of good, deep breaths, and forced myself to focus on being present. Flexible. *Okay. All right.* I climbed up out of shade into shadow.

The front door held a glass panel that ran nearly the door's entire length. The glass was oval like an elongated lens, and the interior was hung with venetian blinds. These were shuttered tight. No sound from within, no television or radio. No hint of a lamp. It didn't matter. I knew he was home. I knew he was waiting; I'd kept him waiting. I wanted him a little frustrated, a little afraid. Like me.

I rang the bell. I rang again. A minute or more passed and then I heard footsteps approach. A light came on behind the blinds. Fingers, one bandaged, parted the slats. Above me the porch light snapped on, bright yellow-white. I smiled, trying to look harmless. I was not who he wanted to see. He cracked the door an inch. I have learned to tell much about a person from the way he opens a door.

"Yes?" he said. He had a hesitant voice, deep and roughened. His breath smelled flat and yeasty. He'd been drinking. Another smell, an acrid, acetonelike odor, seemed to hover behind him.

"Mr. Carse? Theodore Carse?"

"Yes." He was only partially visible. A middle-aged man with thick, dark hair. He looked average. Ordinary. They always do. In all my years as a cop, I never encountered a walking atrocity that came wrapped in anything other than mediocrity. It took me until my last day, my last moment on the force to understand that the banality itself was a disguise. It was how they got close. I was no longer a cop, but some instincts are not as easily cast aside as employment. No matter what I was doing, I was always on the job. Right then, my instincts were fixed on Theodore Carse, who was peering at me through the door with distrust equal to my own. He was wearing a white dress shirt buttoned to his neck. I could see his throat work as he swallowed, the frown lines around his mouth, the watery gleam of his eyes. *Wait,* I felt myself pulling back from the judgment, being hauled back, really, by the sudden gunshot-sharp memory of what could happen when fear got the better of my reason. *Wait until you know for sure.*

I smiled at him. "I'm a friend, a family friend of Sara Bateson. I'd guess you'd say I'm here on her behalf."

"I was expecting Mrs. Bateson."

I bit my tongue in order not to instruct Mr. Carse on the damnably sad limits of expectation and instead offered him a sympathetic nod. "I understand you had an appointment with Sara. It was my idea to come in her place. This was so upsetting for her the first time, well, I'm sure you can imagine, and here, she's found the courage, after all these years, to have her daughter declared legally – "

"Don't say it. Please, don't. Vanessa may still be alive."

"Yes, I know that is what you believe. I know about your phone calls. I thought it would be best if I took a look at what you'd found before anything makes this even harder for Sara." Up to that point, nothing I had said was a lie.

He lowered his head, wagging it in regret. "I recognized it would be upsetting to hear these things again after so much time. I tried to be respectful. I tried to be delicate." The door opened a bit more. "That's why I had to call her. This information I've obtained? It seemed the only decent thing was to give it to the family first, that way they could decide how to proceed. If the police or the press got hold of it – "

"I agree. I feel the same way. You see, I am – I was Vanessa Bateson's godmother, Mr. Carse. Like you, I have only the family's best interests at heart." I sensed the shift in my posture; I've been told that I have a tendency to lean into my lies, as though daring the listener to call me on them. I fixed my eyes on his face as he appraised me up and down.

"You look familiar."

"I do?"

"Yes, you do."

"I don't know why I would."

"What's your name, again?"

A my name is . . . "Alice. Alice Liddell. You can telephone Sara if you want to check this out with her."

He ran his hand along the edge of the door as though gauging its sharpness. "I have been trying to call her for the past two hours. We were supposed to meet at three-thirty. I didn't know what had become of her."

"She's at my place. You can reach her there." I recited the phone number at my office and hoped Sara Bateson, who was waiting at my desk, was as good an actress as I needed her to be.

"I think I'll do that. Not that I don't believe what you're telling me." He cleared his throat and pulled the door wide and stepped back. "You needn't stand out there in the cold, Miss Liddell."

It hadn't seemed cold to me, but since I was in, I decided not to contradict him. I went into the house where the smell – fingernail polish? – was quite strong. "I hope I'm not disturbing your and Mrs. Carse's dinner."

"There is no Mrs. Carse," he said as he showed me into the front room. He turned on the table lamps, first on one side of the sofa, then the other, before explaining that the telephone was in the kitchen, waving his hand in the direction of a closed door. He invited me to sit; I thanked him but refused the invitation. He asked me if I wanted something to drink, some coffee? A beer? As long as he was going to the kitchen, anyway. I declined and repeated the phone number. He repeated it back and then, still repeating it, he crossed the room and pushed through the door that swung into the kitchen.

Seconds later I could hear his voice, muffled from behind the door. This is what I had hoped for, an opportunity to survey the room and glean a sense of the man from his surroundings. The furniture seemed old, the sort you inherited when your parents died, as they had inherited it from theirs. The room was claustrophobic in its tidiness. Not a magazine or newspaper lying about on the end tables banking the sofa. No water rings on the coffee table. No photographs on the mantel. No sweater or quilt tossed on the arm of the straight-backed chairs. No mail on the large leather-topped desk. Built-in bookshelves on either side of the fireplace held what looked to be an older set of encyclopedia, big numbered volumes with blue spines and gold lettering. The lower shelves were filled with other sets of identically bound books. On the very bottom shelves I could also make out the open, paper-ridged spines of the sort of scrapbooks you get from photo supply shops. I had bought the same kind when I was a kid.

It wasn't the mortuary sterility of the room that bothered me. The symmetry I had noticed in the yard had been carried to an oppressive extreme inside the house. Each lamp, each chair, each framed botanical print on the wall had a mate set equidistant from an imagined center. The wall-sized mirror over the fireplace only doubled the doubling. Absolute balance made me dizzy, because the need for symmetry was a sign. Imposed symmetry was always a sign. And that smell. What was that?

Carse's voice had grown louder, not angered, but pleading: Mrs.

Bateson had disappointed him; he thought he'd proved himself trustworthy. Sara was doing a good job. I had told her to keep him occupied for as long as possible, let him think he was persuading her participation in whatever game he was playing. It was then I noticed the metal wastebasket beneath the desk. I did the divided attention trick I'd picked up early in life; I tuned half my awareness to monitoring the cadence of Carse's words, listening for that rise and fall conversations tend to take just before good-byes get said. The other half of me went to work.

I slid the wastebasket out toward the light. The white plastic bag lining the can was empty, but the acetone smell was stronger. I lifted the bag, pulling it away from the sides, away from the bottom of the can. I knew how it went when a mind was unable to contend with the avalanching disorder of life. You could end up seeing dozens of things that weren't even there while, at the same instant, going willfully blind before the very truth you were bullying yourself to uncover. In the resulting hubbub of the interior shouting matches, mistakes got made. And sure enough, in the bottom of the wastebasket was a detail he had missed. The discarded blade from an X-Acto knife had gotten wedged in the seam where the bottom of the can met the walls. A rim of brown sludge clung to the cutting side of the triangular blade. I touched it. Rubber cement. Spongy, not quite dry. He had been working on something when I arrived. That's why the delay before coming to the door, why the smell was still so strong. I dropped the plastic bag back into place and eased the wastebasket back under the desk. I remembered the scrapbooks on the bookshelf. *What are you collecting, Mr. Carse?*

I drifted toward the fireplace in what would appear as idle curiosity to the casual observer. I scanned the bookshelves, a perfectly civil bit of nosiness, and as I reached for one of the scrapbooks, I could not help but register the titles of the other volumes, the significance in those titles: a complete set of the Oz stories, *Narnia, Charlie and the Chocolate Factory, The Stories of Hans Christian Andersen* – a grown man with nothing but children's books? – and, damn it, *Alice in Wonderland. Alice Liddell.* I glanced at the kitchen door. Damn it. He knew. He knew the moment I used the name. He was playing with me, too.

I heard Carse, his voice strained, almost shouting, "I understand, I understand, I'll show her exactly what I was going to show you." I heard the receiver slammed back into the cradle. Was that for effect? Had he even made the call – or had he been pretending, right along with me? I hurried to the sofa, sat down in the corner up against the armrest, crossed my legs at the ankles, held the handbag hard against my diaphragm. The chiffon of my skirt was still settling as he came back into the room.

"Did Sara clear up your concerns?" I asked, working the catch on the handbag with my thumb.

"Yes. And no." He was agitated. He paced before the sofa, uncertain, grinding the fist of one hand into the palm of the other. He slowed and then tilted his head. "You look so familiar to me. Weren't you the one who dealt with the press when Vanessa disappeared?"

He was trying to see how much I already knew. Carse had me figured out. He wasn't about to give me any information, Sara's blessings or not. So why test me? I looked at the spines of the scrapbooks.

I pointed to the bookshelves. "Do you collect stamps?"

He looked over his shoulder as though he had no idea what I was talking about, and then he laughed in a broken chuckle meant to convey he found no humor in my feint. "No. Not stamps."

It wasn't a feint. "Children, then?"

"Pardon me?"

"Those are children's books."

"I thought you meant something else. I don't know if I'd call it a collection."

"You have an rather extensive library there."

"They were given to me when I was very young, but I've read them. Several times. I'm particularly fond of the Lewis Carroll." He gave me a smug little you-are-in-check grin.

"Me, too." *All right, I concede. You caught me, Mr. Carse, but that grin has to go.* I opened the handbag and slipped my hand around the grip of the .32, preparing to employ the fail-safe defense strategy of my childhood: When losing, pick up the board and throw the pieces. "Mr. Carse, did you kill Vanessa Bateson?"

"What?"

"You heard me."

He acted as though he hadn't, and for several seconds he stood staring at me as though time in his universe – or mine – had stopped. He gave his head a slight shake as though the question itself had finally made impact. His bandaged hand went to his mouth as though he were going to be sick; his eyes grew big with understanding. "Is that why she sent you?" he whispered. "Is that what she thinks?" He crumpled into one of the straight-backed chairs and rocked himself back and forth. "Oh, dear God. I only wanted to help Vanessa. Whatever could have caused . . . me? Hurt a – whatever could have made her think . . ."

He was broken, bereft, his face slack with confusion. I watched him, waiting while my instincts ran analysis, ready to intercept and restrain the blast of adrenaline that might get me moving on decisions I wasn't aware I'd made. But what came through was only a sinking weariness and pity, sour and soiled tasting on my tongue. I was the larger threat in this room, and realizing that only made the weariness heavier. I let go of the gun, snapped the handbag shut, but kept my thumb on the latch. I trusted my readings of anyone only so far – and that included my readings of myself.

He rocked, his forearms against his thighs, head down. "Does Sara Bateson really believe that? Why on earth would she think such a thing?" He sounded near sobbing.

"Mr. Carse, you start calling to say you have heretofore undisclosed information about her child, a child who disappeared eight years ago. You tell her not to go to the police. Who else would do that? Who else would have such information and not volunteer it earlier? Who else would have a vested interest in the continued torturing of the woman?"

"Torturing her? By wanting to help her find her daughter? No one knows what happened to that girl. How can Mrs. Bateson have her declared dead? Just like that. Sign the forms, and poof, problem solved. She may still be alive. You know that, don't you? I'm the only one who seems to want the girl to still be alive."

"You are most certainly not alone in that desire, but you must – "

"Look!" He bounded upward, propelled by an urgency so intense that I feared for half a second that I'd read him wrong. He went to the bookshelf and yanked out one of the scrapbooks. "This is why I called her. This is what I wanted her to see."

He planted himself on the couch next to me, too close, his knees brushing mine. The intimacy was a huge shift out of the stiffly formal behavior he'd been demonstrating, but it seemed as though he was unaware of the sudden collapsing of distance between us. He opened the album, not on the coffee table but between us so that the pebbled fake leather of the book's black cover fell onto my thighs. The album was wedge shaped and bulging due to the number of pages he'd forced into it. Those pages had been divided into sections, each section labeled with a tab, each tab bearing the name of a child. A lot of the names I recognized from either the press or my own involvement in their cases. He'd been at this awhile; ten names in this book and half a dozen equally crammed scrapbooks still on the shelf. He was tapping on the tab labeled "Vanessa Bateson," but I was reading the one three levels below it. *Oh, Amy, you're here too?*

And at the mere sight of her name the fragile partition between the present and past burst open. In an instant, I dropped through time; it was four years earlier and it was all happening again. The August heat, the children dying, one after another, shot and stomped and dropped from windows until I could take it no more. But more presented itself when I walked into that hotel room and found Amy among the video cameras, four years old and basically ripped in half from the inside out. With that my mind rent itself free from having to coexist with my life. The next thing I know, I'm in Interview Room 2 at the station house. I've locked myself in the cage with the suspect. My weapon is drawn, and it seems the most sensible thing in the world to get rid of the monster. So I shot him and he died, thus preventing anyone from ever determining if he had indeed been the one responsible for Amy's death. I was acquitted by reason of insanity and hospitalized for the good of all. I eventually regained myself, but the price had been steep. My release meant that those forces that had driven me to fire the gun had been released with me. They followed me home from the hospital and now followed me everywhere.

"See?" Carse said, turning to Vanessa's section. "I've saved everything, everything I could find. This front part is the newspaper stories. See, I have the very first one: 'Ten-Year-Old Missing in – '" He read several paragraphs aloud from the yellowed rectangle of newsprint. I tried to listen but I already knew the story. I'd heard it more times than I believed possible. It was how they all began, the *Once upon a time* of my work. He then moved on to his handwritten transcripts from newscasts and a nationally televised crime show that devoted an episode to the search for

Vanessa. Finally came the inevitable pages of his own notes and diagrams, his theoretical connections among suspects and those never suspected, probable explanations and implausible causes. "I wanted to show this to Mrs. Bateson, to make sure she's considered all the possibilities. The police get so busy, and there are so many children missing, how could they focus on one child sufficiently? I'm not criticizing. I'm a realist. I understand it can't be done."

"What can't be done, Mr. Carse?"

"The police can't give one child their full attention long enough to make a difference."

"You might be surprised at how long one child can hold a cop's attention." I ran my finger along the tabs. "You seem to be focusing on several yourself."

"Somebody needs to. Somebody needs to keep the options open, to keep processing and reprocessing the information, in order to prevent tragedies like this." He turned past his notes to a clean page with only one clipping mounted in the center. It was a school portrait of a pigtailed ten-year-old with crooked teeth and her mother's eyes. Vanessa's obituary. Sara told me it had taken her a week to compose it – another mile marker along the spiraling path in the woman's private wasteland. Part eulogy, part statement of surrender, the piece stated the situation in language as plain and steel-plated as the resolve it took to write it. "Vanessa Leigh Bateson who was taken from this world by circumstances yet unknown . . ." Two days after the piece ran, Theodore Carse had placed his first call to Sara.

"How can she do it? How can she give up on her child?"

"So that's why you called her? The legal declaration – "

"I didn't want her to give up. Not yet. Not now. If she would only take a look at these notes."

"Letting Vanessa go is not the same thing as wanting her gone."

"But what kind of mother just gives up?"

"One who has given everything she has and now just wants some peace. Let her do what she needs to do. Leave her alone."

"But this is my life's work. I'm trying to help. Somebody has to help."

Man, oh, man. Which part of this was sadder? What he was doing or my taking it away from him? And which was the more dangerous? "Mr.

Carse, I'm sure you meant no harm, but I must warn you that you are opening yourself up to immense legal difficulties. Harassment charges at the very least, not to mention a civil suit based on the pain you are causing Mrs. Bateson. I will recommend that Sara file a restraining order against your having any further contact with her. I also highly recommend that you not attempt to contact any of the other families you think you might be *helping*. You aren't helping. You can't."

"How do you know that?"

"Mr. Carse, do you understand what I just told you? You are already over the line."

His face altered, sort of downshifted in a subtle frown, and his voice dropped into a darker pitch. "So you're a lawyer? You've come here to threaten a decent man trying to do a little bit of good in this shit-filthy world?"

The handbag was open before I thought about it. "I'm not a lawyer, and I'm not making threats, only telling you the way this is going to work. Here" – I reached into the handbag, gently pushing aside the .32 – "this is me." I dug one of my business cards out from the pocket in which I shoved my license. He took the card. I left the bag open, balanced on my leg, gripping the rim so he couldn't see the trembling in my fingers.

"You are a detective?"

I shrugged. "People hire me to find answers to their questions. Most of those questions involve their kids. More often than not, no one likes the answers I find. That's how I know you can't help."

"Have you been looking for Vanessa? Is that how you know Sara Bateson. Can you use these – "

"I'm familiar with the history; I read the papers, too. But I'm associated with the case only because when you told Mrs. Bateson not to go to the police, she needed someone to evaluate the situation. She called me because I specialize in missing kids."

He looked up from the card and blinked at me. "We want the same thing."

I felt a distinct chill in the room now. "No, Mr. Carse, we do not want the same thing."

His eyes narrowed. "Well, that's true. I do it because it's right. I don't wait for someone to offer me money." He bolted to his feet, making toward the desk so quickly that the album tipped and fell closed, the entire weight dropping in my lap. The impact of the album knocked my handbag to the floor. The gun slid onto the carpet. I shoved aside the album and dove for the weapon. In doing so, I took my eyes off Carse. Split second. Split second was all it took. When I looked back he had an X-Acto knife gripped in his hand, and he was coming back toward me.

No. I jerked upright, stood, and pointed the gun at him. "Stop, Carse." But he didn't stop, he kept coming back around the edge of the couch. I steadied my aim, left hand supporting right wrist – "Stop now." He turned then, stooping forward, ignoring me. He threw open the album. He turned to Vanessa's section and with long, swift strokes of the knife, he cut the pages free.

"Here," he said without looking at me, "these are for Sara Bateson. Make her look at them. Tell her I said to be sure she's considered every possibility that I have." He held out the pages, waiting for me to take them. His breath was ragged with fury.

I, on the other hand, was not breathing at all. I forced the gun to lower. Forced myself to inhale.

"Take them," he said. He still would not look at me.

I made my left hand move forward and take the sheaf of pages. My right hand held on to the gun grip like it was an exposed root on the cliff side from which I felt myself slipping. I willed the gun farther downward, pointing it at the floor. My voice sounded like it was coming from outside my head. "One more phone call to Sara Bateson, one letter, hell, you even think about thinking about getting in touch with her, and I'll have you up on charges. And then you can be in the paper. Do we understand each other, Mr. Carse?"

His shoulders slumped a bit and he shook his head. "I'm sorry," he said to the book as he began to page through the other sections in his collection of lost kids.

I kicked the handbag so that it lay closer and I could bend down enough to grab it without taking my eyes off Carse. Then I tucked the pages under my arm and began to back up slowly, making my way toward the door.

He was still turning pages. "I wanted only to help."

"Then leave Mrs. Bateson alone."

He lifted his head slowly, tilted it and stared at me, then the page, then me again. "That's where I know you from. Amy. You were the one who – "

But my hand was on the doorknob and then I was outside and hurrying down the steps, down the walkway, down the sidewalk in the full darkness of night. I saw one of the little girls from earlier. She was still jumping rope, alone in the blue-white round of a street lamp. The *scuff-thump* of her school shoes was beating nearly as fast as my heart. I didn't want to frighten her, so I slowed my steps. When I got close enough I said, "Sweetheart?" She looked at me without losing her rhythm, her pigtails bounced on her shoulders. I pointed at Carse's house. "You stay away from him. You tell your friends. Stay away from him. Okay? Promise?" She kept jumping but smiled with a wide mouth full of crooked teeth. "Good," I said, continuing on for all of ten steps before I realized who I'd seen. "Vanessa?" I spun back around. The jump rope lay coiled at the edge of the sidewalk. The girl was gone. They are always gone.

I remembered the gun was still in my hand. *L my name is Leslie . . . Yeah, this is me.*

a n o m a l y

It was nearly eight o'clock when I pulled into the parking garage nearest my building. My office was in the north wing of a three-story granite behemoth that had once housed the Reeves Academy, a private school for the children of the rich. The school had shut down in the late 1970s after an embezzlement scandal cost it what few students still attended. The building had been sold to developers, who turned the classrooms and dormitories into offices. Above the front entrance, a large bronze crest was set into the stone. The ornamentation on the crest, long since darkened by the blacky-green patina of age, was that of a lion's head crowned with a garland of laurel. Arched over the lion was the phrase *Omnia mutantur, nos et mutamur in illis* – All things are changing, and we are changing with them. I knew the translation only because it appeared on the brochure the leasing company, Reeves Management, sent out. It appeared on the lease as well. And on each rent receipt. Apparently, somebody had tired of being asked.

The lion glared down on me and the sheaf of papers I was carrying as I climbed the entrance steps in my stocking feet. The high heels had given me blisters; I'd taken the shoes off halfway to the office. My stockings were now ruined – after two blocks of sidewalk – to the point my toes were poking out of a web of nylon strands. I'd taken off the headband as well, not surprised to see – in the light over the entry – the smudge of blood on my fingertip from where I'd been rubbing my scalp. I held my fingers up as if to show the lion how badly the day had gone. Decades of rain had run through the Roman lettering of the motto, through the veins of the laurel leaves, through the lion's mane, and down onto the granite, pulling along strands of metallic discoloration to stain the rock in such a fashion that it appeared the crest was sending out roots. That age-old effort to fasten on to something larger than oneself and gain permanence.

"Enough with the *omnia mutantur*, already, huh?" I said to lion just as Carlos, the Reeves's latest victim of doorman duty, opened the door to let me in.

"Absolutely," Carlos said back, thinking I had been speaking to him. *Absolutely*, I had learned, was Carlos's response to every query or statement. You doing good today? *Absolutely*. Think it might rain? *Absolutely*. Meteor going to crash into the planet this afternoon? *Absolutely*. I'd yet to figure out if this was because Carlos was simply distracted by his studies – his counter was always piled with thick textbooks – or if it was his way of saying he was tired of us tenants who offered little more than barely disguised declarative statements for his affirmation. I never asked outright; I could guess the response either way.

He unbuttoned his uniform, an ill-fitting navy jacket with an embroidered lion crest on the breast pocket. "You have a visitor upstairs."

"Mrs. Bateson? Yes. I know."

"Wanted to make sure you expected her."

"I appreciate that."

"Absolutely."

I checked my mailbox in the lobby and then made for the north stairs. The Reeves still felt like a school, what with its long, echoing hallways and stairwells. When I was here at night, which was frequently, I had that same shivery trespassing sensation as when the janitor would let me in after hours back at Swifton Woods Elementary to fetch a forgotten homework assignment or lunchbox. A school building was a space designed to conduct the movement of life. To be inside a public place devoid of public was like wandering through a graveyard. You noticed most what wasn't there. The implication was that you shouldn't be there either.

My not-quite-ex-husband had protested mightily when I decided to install myself here. After the hospital, after everything I'd been through, Greg felt that the unwieldy associations of isolating myself in another old building was the last thing my limping psyche needed to negotiate. He worried aloud about my rounding a corner to find phantoms hovering in the shadows. My argument that those phantoms were already in my head and therefore wherever I happened to be did little to quiet his fears, and for weeks after I moved my business into the Reeves, he sent me brochures from brightly lit modern offices that reminded me of self-service storage facilities. He'd finally given up when I convinced him that if I were going to have to see ghosts, it was a comfort to have them appear where at least one might expect them.

But they weren't ghosts at all. Many of the children I saw had been found alive, but their experiences had forced them into new configurations of themselves. The ghosts of what *was,* then? Maybe. It didn't matter. I didn't believe in ghosts. I wished I could have. It would have made everything so much easier. You could talk about ghosts, you could tell stories about them and make the listener see what you saw, too. But ghost was too easy an answer here, a dismissal, really. A reprieve I didn't deserve. These children I kept seeing weren't answers in themselves but questions I couldn't figure out how to ask. Each one a glint of light off a hard, dark truth so removed that by the time I saw them, their images, like the light of stars, had already been traveling toward me for eons. I understood that the visions weren't real. These apparitions were my mind superimposing its sorrow on the already sorrowful world. It was this sorrow and the unpredictable but inevitable arrival of the next apparition that had forced me to push my daughters out of my immediate orbit into the stable system of their father's custody. I couldn't protect them from everything, but I could protect them from me. The things I saw. The things I might do about what I'd seen.

I felt one coming. As I hauled myself up the worn stairs, I would not have been at all surprised to have passed a specter on the way down. I kept looking for someone, or something. I felt watched, but I saw no one. Still, I stopped at each landing and checked. The first two floors of the Reeves held expansive suites of offices while the third floor, what had once been the dormitories, comprised small, individual offices behind doors with numbers painted on their frosted glass inserts. These were set around a ballroom-sized open area that the developers had furnished with chairs and a couch. We shared it as a common reception area, the offices being too cramped for such niceties. The offices were converted dorm rooms, squat shoeboxlike spaces – just enough for a desk and a few filing cabinets. We each had one window, one ceiling fixture, one phone jack, one electric outlet on each wall.

I crossed the reception area toward the only door with light diffusing through the glass. The polished hardwood floor felt cool and smooth beneath my feet. The air held a lovely just-brewed-coffee aroma, but that might have been wishful thinking on my part. I was also indulging, as I opened my office door, the wishful thought that the meeting I was about to have with Sara Bateson was already over and I was on my way home to a bathtub of hot water and an icy glass with about three fingers of scotch.

"It must feel good, what you do," Sara said as I came in. She was looking at the bulletin board on the wall beside my desk. I used it to tack up the photographs I'd been given. Prospective and newer clients always make the same assumption, that these photographs were my successes, children happy to be found, the families my work had reunited. I didn't correct that assumption unless asked, and they usually didn't ask until they'd figured it out for themselves. These were the *befores* and sometimes the *never agains*. I put them up so that the families who had provided them would know I had not allowed myself to forget. I did not keep photographs of my daughters here. Keeping Molly and Emma safe meant keeping them away from me and what I did.

"I have good days," I said as I laid the handbag on my desk, and noticed the FULL light on the answering machine blinking furiously. *You gave Carse your card, idiot.* "This wasn't one of them."

She turned and smiled at me with the sort of kindness that comes from hard-won empathy. How had she managed to hold on to that? Kindness had been one of the first luxuries I'd ditched in order to maintain altitude. I'd seen that kindness in Sara's *before* picture in Carse's pages, before losing Vanessa had put the circles under her eyes, had dulled and grayed her hair, had added the extra pounds that weighed down on her, the burden of her grief made manifest. "The day wasn't that good for me, either," she said. She ducked her chin at the papers in my hand. "Did he really have something?"

I shook my head. "Theodore Carse had nothing to do with Vanessa's disappearance. He doesn't know any more about it than what he could glean from the press. I've looked through his stuff. He has theories, but then everyone has theories. If you want, we can talk about them."

"No point in that, is there?"

"In my opinion, no."

"So he won't contact me anymore?"

16

The red light on the answering machine was blinking like a warning. *My life's work.* "I'm not sure."

Sara lowered herself back into the chair and spread her hands over the scribbled calendar pad on my desktop. She stared down at the expanse of days her fingers had covered. "I waited until she was eighteen, when she would have been eighteen, when I would have had to – you know? – anyway. I kept thinking that if it was the wrong thing to do, if Vanessa was still on earth somewhere, I'd sense it; she'd fight me doing this. I'd feel her fighting. God knows that child fought me on every bedtime, every bite of vegetable, every . . . I just believed I'd feel her if she were still here. And when I signed the forms, I felt nothing. Nothing. And that was all right. It was like being told that what I'd done was all right. Then I start getting these phone calls and this man I don't know is yelling at me that I've given up on my daughter too soon." She lifted her head and looked at me. "Have I?"

Some questions no human being should try to answer. Instead, I offered her facts of self-defense. "You can't let this guy in your head, Sara. Theodore Carse is interested only in Theodore Carse. He wants to be a hero in someone else's story because he can't be the hero in his own. That makes him a dangerous man. Not today, not tomorrow maybe, but the day is coming when he's going to have to find one of these kids, and the only sure way of doing that is to become the guy who takes them. I'm going to make a few calls and get him checked out more thoroughly, get him on a few lists with a few of my friends. You are going to take out a restraining order and change your phone number and then promise me, promise yourself, promise Vanessa that if Carse or anyone else tries to exploit you or the memory of your child ever again, you will have that person punished every which way the law will allow."

Sara nodded with a shallow dip of her jaw that told me she'd barely heard my instructions. She was anticipating Carse's next phone call, the cruelty of his accusations, and the strange relief of hearing them from a voice outside her own. I went around the desk and swiveled the chair so she had no choice but to face me. I lowered myself to my knees, sitting on my heels, looking up into her sad, kind eyes.

"Don't talk to him, Sara. Don't let him talk to you." Outright begging.

"No. I won't."

She probably believed herself when she said it, but what I heard was surrender. She was beginning a journey straight into the disaster she thought she'd earned. I could do nothing to stop it; she'd been waiting for this a long time. I leaned against the desk, almost sick with fatigue. "Do you want these pages Carse gave me?" I slid them onto the desk where she could see them.

"I don't think so." She flipped through them with indifference. "I have basically the same thing back at home." She stared down at me. "How much do I owe you for this?"

After I called down to ask Carlos to grab a taxi – *Absolutely* – for the woman, I took Sara Bateson's check, gave her a receipt, and showed her to the door. It occurred to me that she might have been insulted by the immediate thud of the dead bolt locking behind, but I didn't care. I went to the window and lowered the shade before lifting the bulletin board from its hook so I could get to the wall safe. I dialed the combination, had the door open before I took the .32 from the handbag and removed the clip. The gun went on the shelf, the ammo back in the box, as my hands began to shake – the beginnings of the burn-off. Merely taking the thing out into the light pumped me full of premonitory energies – terror and rage – that I could not acknowledge, let alone feel, until I had the weapon back in the safe. I understood, on some intuitive level, that this self-induced prohibition against self-awareness had something to do with my hallucinations, from Vanessa jumping rope all the way back to Amy's voice in my ear four years earlier, not to mention the dozens of boys and girls in between them. In an attempt to pretend some control over the phenomenon, I'd been keeping records of these tricks of vision. I took the bookkeeper's ledger out of the safe and turned to where I'd tucked the ballpoint pen in the spine. I wrote the particulars of seeing Vanessa and the quality of the experience: aural and visual, how long it lasted, how long it took me to recognize the identity of the apparition. The events were getting stronger, sustaining themselves in three dimensions for minutes at a time. When the hallucinations had started, Amy had come to me as just a voice. Tonight Vanessa had existed three dimensionally at a distance and I approached her. This strengthening was a mystery and with it came an equally strengthening apprehension of who I'd see next.

The predictability of the pattern was hardly a comfort because I saw only those children who weren't coming back.

I closed the ledger and put it, along with Sara Bateson's check, in the safe. Shut the door. Spun the dial. In the ticking of the slowing spin I thought I heard something, a louder tapping sound. I leaned toward the safe, listened, turned the dial left and right. I couldn't reproduce it. What couldn't be deliberately reproduced was anomaly. Anomaly was to be ignored. For as long as possible. That was the first rule of science.

I raised the bulletin board and slid it along the wall, trying to catch the hanger on the hook. Difficult because I was still shaking. The pictures jostled about so close to my face that the images melded into a soft, colorful blur as though these children and their smiling families were returning to the dreamlike fog from which they'd taken shape. The dream that I was going to do good for them somehow. I hadn't exactly chosen this work. In the calming of the turbulence following my breakdown, I had drifted into a purpose: I needed to find what was lost. More important, in locating lost family members, I would never have to doubt the reality of what I was searching for. Or so I thought. Besides, I had background in family mediation. I had friends on the police force. I had experience. What I also had was a reputation, and it was, I discovered, my reputation that drew many would-be clients to my door. I was, as one of them put it, "willing to make things right." I explained, as always, that what I had done was make a massive, awful mistake.

But he killed that little girl, Amy. You got the right guy.

That was never proved. And either way, it wouldn't matter.

Hell, I'd love to have pulled the trigger on that scum. In fact, if you find the creep my daughter calls her boyfriend with her, you have my permission –

You need to leave. Now.

Humans ran away for reasons, and often those reasons presented themselves on the other side of my desk, teary-eyed and pleading for a second chance to affect the inhuman reign of suffocation, intimidation, or vengeance they called love. These types were usually easy to identify. When the whole of the client's intent seemed to be convincing me how much the missing was adored and needed to be found, my interior alarms tripped. I'd bet those same ardent rationales had been presented to the

19

missing prior to their escape. Beware the love that has to explain itself. I turned down these jobs on the spot, silently hoping as I did so that the escapee had run somewhere safe, although I couldn't say where that would be.

It became evident that the cases I was most comfortable accepting were the heartbreakers, the ones I feared would end badly when I began them, the ones in which I would look not for those who had absented themselves by choice but for those who had been taken. To be taken you had to be small. And so I ended up looking mostly for kids. Kids taken by drugs or gangs. Kids taken by vindictive spouses. Kids taken by grieving relatives. Kids taken by demons masquerading as neighbors. Kids who had been taken by the unknown, vanishing into so much nothing from playgrounds and backyards and front porches and libraries and malls and supermarket parking lots. Kids taken so long ago everyone else had given up looking. I had searched for kids who I later discovered had never existed. I had searched for kids who I soon found out were not lost in the usual sense but had met fates the mother or father could not accept. It was delicate, careful, monstrous work. When you were looking for someone's stolen child, you were looking to return order to a collapsed world. You were, in essence, trying to put salt water back in the sea and mountain peaks back in the sky. The sun back in daytime, the moon back in night. The planets back in their orbits. God back in heaven. Everyone and everything back where it was supposed to be. And you were the only one who knew, from the outset, that no matter what you found, going back was impossible. No such thing as a *simple* case of a missing kid.

And there I was, my arms full of missing kids. The hanger on the bulletin board finally grabbed the hook. I was guiding the board back against the wall when the tapping sound began again. But not from the safe. It was outside. Not tapping. Footsteps. Quick, light footsteps moving in circles. It was a kid, a kid running around the perimeter of the reception area.

I whispered her name. "Vanessa?" The footsteps stopped. I let the board fall against the wall; the hanger caught off level, the board shifted, settling at a slant. I reached for the phone on my desk, my hands quaking so I could barely hold on to the receiver, let alone punch in the three digits that would ring Carlos's desk. I watched the blinking message light on the answering machine. Finally, he picked up.

"Door," he said.

"Hey. It's Leslie. Upstairs? You know?"

"Absolutely."

"Carlos, is anyone here with kids tonight? Have you seen any kids running around?"

"Naw. No kids. Not tonight."

"You're sure?"

"Abso – you all right up there, Ms. Stone?"

"I'm great. Fine. I thought I heard something. Some kids."

He laughed. "Well, they tell me the Reeves is haunted."

"Show me some place that isn't." I hung up the receiver, clumsily, clattering it back onto its base. I listened then. Still quiet. I interlocked my hands to keep them from shaking themselves free from my body. I couldn't get a deep breath, and that was making me lightheaded. I sat down in my desk chair, took hold of the chair arms, and held on. Waiting. The silence extended into minutes; my heart began to slow. The shaking slacked off. I could feel my lungs start to expand more fully. Hot, almost feverish, I felt perspiration dampening the back of my neck. The systems were resetting, I was coming down and out the other side into an all-encompassing exhaustion. Sleep. I wanted nothing more than to sleep. Phillip, in our closing arguments, had said that no man was ever going to fuck me better than fear. He was tired of competing. Lawyers. Always with the last word.

I realized I was staring at Carse's pages spread over my desk. I straightened the pages, aligning the edges. If Sara had wanted them, I'd have made copies for her. It was important to keep the originals here, maintain the paper trail, in the event – *be wrong, be wrong* – Carse took it to the next level. I pulled a fresh manila folder from my bottom drawer and printed "Carse, Theodore" on the tab. The pages had to be folded to fit into the plastic bag I was using to preserve whatever prints might be evident. I sealed the sliding lock on the bag, slipped it in the folder, then swiveled the chair to open the horizontal file cabinet beneath the window behind the desk. I opened the drawer with too much force; the window shade snapped up on the roller, winding itself nearly to the top of the window. It did that occasionally and never failed to startle. My nerves did the lurch and flutter. I wanted to get done. I wanted to go home. I cursed the window and focused on the alphabetics of the files. Dozens of thickly stuffed folders, labels protruding like little headstones, each with a name I'd written.

We want the same thing.

No, we do not. This is different. I'm different. I'm –

The protest slammed shut on the sound coming from behind me. The running again. It was on the far side of the reception area and heading around toward my door, slowing, slowing. Stop. *Don't turn around.*

The knock was soft, almost an apology. A rapping at the wood on the edge of the glass, it set the pane to rattling ever so slightly. *Don't turn around.* Anomaly. Ignore it. The knock sounded again. A bit more insistent.

"Vanessa, I cannot help you," I said. Sometimes admitting my failures aloud dissolved the illusions of ectoplasm my guilt and regret had summoned. I focused my eyes on the window behind my desk, on the reflection of the door hanging in the glass like a portal into night. Quiet. But I sensed it wasn't over; it wasn't going to be bought off that easily this time. On that realization, the banging began. The door was being pounded by fists, kicked. Pause. The doorknob turned one way then the other. The pounding began again. *Make it stop.*

I stood up and faced the door. My body felt sluggish, awkward, as though my limbs had been filled with sand, so heavy I wasn't certain I could move. "I cannot help you!" My shouting seemed only to infuriate it. It began flailing against the glass. I saw the shadowy shapes of the arms, the fist as it impacted against the frosted pane. *It's going to come through the door.* "Stop!" And my legs that couldn't function a second before were bounding forward. I wrenched the dead bolt open and yanked the door wide. "Just stop!"

The shadow-deep expanse of the reception area yawned before me. No figure or human form. No enraged child. No one. Still, I picked up a familiar fragrance, a jasmine-and-lilac-scented cologne that was popular when I was a girl. We all wore it that summer.

What was the point of these carnival spook house tactics I kept conjuring against myself? It wasn't as if I couldn't remember that perfume. I remembered that summer too well. "What do you want me to do?" My voice, too loud, bounced back on itself, ricocheting around the exposed brick and darkened doors and skylight panes. "I can't do anything about it now." I stood there, staring into the emptiness, immobile, as the echo of my argument died away – I don't know how long. Then the softest puff of warm air, a bubble-gum-perfumed breath, touched my face. A sigh. Disappointment. I heard disappointment, and then I heard the slight squeak of leather soles turning on the polished floorboards. The footsteps moved away from me, slowly, across the reception area to the stairs where they began their descent.

I listened until the footfall faded beyond my hearing. I closed the door, slid to my knees. *The Carse thing has me worked up. The scrapbooks reminded me. That, and I'm tired. I am very tired.* I rested my forehead against the door, eyes closed, surrendering to the dull tug of drowsiness. *Get up and go home, Leslie.* But I couldn't. I was nearing sleep when the footsteps came back. I could feel them vibrating up through the wood and into my skull. The knock was slow, almost hesitant. Again. We were going to do it again.

I flattened my palms against the door, holding it shut. "Go away." I said. "It's too late. I cannot help you." The knob turned. I realized I'd forgotten to engage the dead bolt; the door opened, pressing against my body with growing force.

"Go away."

The voice was a familiar quiver of curiosity and concern. I recognized it but didn't trust the recognition.

"Mom? It's me."

"Molly?"

"You okay?"

"Yeah. I'm fine." I began pulling myself to up to my feet, opening the door as I went. Afraid of the answers, Molly wasn't about to ask me anything about who I had been sending away or why I was down on the floor. I volunteered information. "A stupid old mouse has been running around in here the past couple of days. I thought I'd finally cornered it." And that's how fairy tales were born.

"Oh," my daughter said, regarding me with the same expression one might wear upon finding that yet another unexploded nuclear device had landed in her garden. It would be funny if it weren't so frightening. "Maybe you should get a trap or something." She stood on the threshold in standard Molly-wear, jeans, running shoes, hooded sweater zipped to her chin; she was waiting not so much for an invitation to enter as the all clear. Her hair was wind tossed into a tumble of dark tangles about her too-pale face. Her cheeks were flushed scarlet and her blue eyes – more the color of sadness than sky – were huge and sparked, high alert. Almost as tall as I was, she held my gaze, unblinking, as though trying to tell me something that the Defiance Clause in the Thirteen-Year-Olds' Union Contract would not allow her to put into words. Obviously, I wasn't the first scary thing that had happened to her today. My mind downshifted into worry, pulling me back to the one reality I never questioned: the necessity of my daughters' well-being.

I motioned her to come in. "Is your dad waiting downstairs?"

She took a giant step forward. "No. He's at home with Em, I guess."

"He's still in Swifton? How did you get here?"

"I took the train. Then I walked."

"You walked? Alone? That's almost six miles. Your father let you – "

"He didn't know. But I left a note."

I looked at the frantic flashing of the answering machine. *Full. Full. Full.*

Molly followed me to the desk. "He looks pissed," she said, pointing at the machine.

"Sweetheart, you are about to learn a whole new meaning to the word." I picked up the receiver, handed it to her, and then hit Greg's button on the speed dial. "And when he's done with you, I get my turn."

"Hi, Dad," she said and scrunched her eyes shut in preparation. "Yeah – I'm fine – I just got here. I'm with Mom – I'm – I told you that in the note – " At that she abandoned her defense. Her shoulders slumped and she listened, nodding. "Okay," she said and handed the phone back to me. "I'm grounded."

"I should think so," I said, putting the phone to my ear.

"What I told her," said Greg, his voice thin with fury and relief, "is that the planet lacked the necessary gravity to ground her sufficiently. And goddamn it, Leslie, why carry a cell phone if you never turn it on?"

"Hey, I was working. It wasn't like I knew what she was planning. Do we need to go over the term *custody* again."

"Don't," Molly said, and I heard what she meant: Don't fight; don't be crazy; don't put me in the middle of it. Just don't.

But it was already done. "Are you all right?" I asked Greg.

"I am now. How about you?"

"Long day, and I'm expecting a long sleepless night of imagining what could have happened here."

He started chuckling. "Maybe this weekend we can compare nightmare notes. She covered the bases, Les. Made after-school arrangements for Emma, took a lasagna out of the freezer so we'd have something for dinner – what was so important?"

"You're asking me?"

"That's what her note says: 'Em at Rita's. Gone to city. Have to see Mom. Important.' "

"You needed to see me?" I eyed my daughter with the same reluctant pride I had heard in her father's laughter. "You were going to see me in two days."

"This is business," she said and sat herself in one of the chairs on the client's side of the desk.

I sat down in my chair. "I'll bring her back to Swifton tomorrow. She'll miss a couple more hours of school, but – "

"I can't go back to school. Ever."

"Greg –"

"Dad doesn't know about it. Not yet."

"Leslie, what's going on?"

"I'm not sure. I'll fill you in later." I hung up the telephone. "Okay, Molly. Spill it."

She pulled down the zipper on her sweater and withdrew an envelope she'd tucked against her chest. She pushed the envelope across the desk. "Two hundred and thirty-seven dollars and sixteen cents. I had more, but I had to pay for the train ticket."

"What's it for?" I asked, trying not to let the cash become an addendum to my imaginings of Molly alone on the streets.

"That's almost a whole day, isn't it? What you charge for a day?"

"Molly?"

"I want to hire you."

c o u n t e r c l o c k w i s e
1 8

Down in the yard you can hear him working. The *thwack-thud* of the ax as it strikes what is left of the tree. He likes to joke about how the lightning bolt only made the old oak tougher than it had been. The shock had turned it into some kind of living stone. That's why it's taken nearly three summers to bring it down. "Like hacking through granite," he says.

You hope he cannot hear you in the attic. That would be impossible, of course. But you are prying up one of the flooring planks, and the nails squeal so as they come free of the joist. It seems like the loudest sound in the universe. The heat isn't helping. It's so hot up here. Your Sunday school blouse is stuck to the perspiration soaking your back and chest, sweat rolls down your thighs into the cuffs of your knee socks. Your hands are wet; they keep slipping from the crowbar. Your back hurts from the effort.

At last, the board comes away. Kneel beside the opening and force the package into the void you have opened. It hits with a dull thump. Try not to think about what is making that sound. Get the board back in place, line up the nails over the holes, and tap them gently back down. Sunlight from the vent sparkles on the pennies in your loafers. Brand-new 1975 pennies. Dad gave them to you last week for these new shoes. And now, you have betrayed him. Or protected him. You aren't sure. You're not sure of anything except that you would give anything to not know what you now know. But that's what you get for being a bad daughter. Listening where you shouldn't be listening, seeing what you were never meant to see.

He can't ever find out what you've done. No one can. You take the penknife from your skirt pocket and carve the letters of your name: LESLIE. Add a date, three years earlier, June 21, 1973, your twelfth birthday. The week before lightning hit the oak tree and he told you the tree house was unsafe and you discovered the attic made an adequate substitute. You are fifteen now and have learned much about this attic, the way the house carries all its sound upward. He used to tell you that your bedtime prayers rose of their own accord the way all things warm and light rose toward heaven. You are now pretty sure where all those appeals for blessing ended up. Every prayer, every wish you've ever spoken has risen only to be trapped in the attic along with everything else: the hard words of your parents' shouting and the whispered phone calls your sisters made late at night and the drone of the everyday living until it all got mixed up together. The words cooled, dimmed, and disappeared unacknowledged. Your prayers had never even left the house. That explained a lot.

Sit back. Study the carving. This will work. If he finds it, he'll think it sweet. A memento of you, his youngest. His princess. You get up to leave. You can never come up here again.

On the other side of the attic is your mother's old dressing table. You've been using it as your desk. It has a broken drawer, and the edge of the oval mirror is cracked from where she hit it when she was throwing shoes and bottles right before she left. You are looking at yourself, your faraway reflection. You look like you always have. You look like she did as a girl. You look like a stranger to yourself.

want and need

"Hire me?"

Molly nodded. "For one day – or as much of a day as this will get." She sucked her upper lip behind her lower teeth, determination personified, and leaned forward to push the envelope closer to me. "Unless, you know, I can pay you back later."

I wanted to grab her hand, grab her whole being, hug her hard, but she would have been insulted by the gesture. "Well, you know, Mol, I do offer an outstanding discount for family members. What's up?"

She frowned. "If I hire you, I mean, if I pay you, you have to keep what I tell you secret, right? You have to keep it confidential."

"You're thinking of lawyers, sweetheart. My work has rules. I could lose my license if I kept certain information secret. As your mother, however, I am not quite so bound by – "

"Maybe I need a lawyer. Can I talk to your friend Phillip?" She always said it like that – *your friend Phillip* – enunciating his name as though she were trying to flick something distasteful off her tongue.

"Phillip and I aren't in touch anymore, remember?" A week ago, forcing that concession from me would have made her grin ear to ear in righteous vindication. This evening it only deepened the thought lines across her brow. I was beginning to worry. "Molly?"

"Do you know any other lawyers?"

"Forget the lawyers. Tell me."

Her face worked as she considered her options. "Do you remember Lydia?" I could hear her choosing the words.

"Lydia Parrish?" Sweet, coltish, blond child with scary good manners. "Of course I remember her." Her friendship with Molly had made Greg's move to Swifton seem worth the upheaval. The girls had bonded over stories of their parents' collective marital failures. "She's your best friend."

That earned the patented, adolescent eye roll of derision. "Was. Back in fifth grade, Mom. Things are different now. Eighth grade is different. We're into different kinds of stuff. We haven't hung out together in a long time."

"So this is about Lydia?"

More consideration of possible responses and then finally, "No one can find her. She's, like, disappeared. I wanted you to sort of look around some."

"Did she run away?"

"That's what everyone is saying."

"I didn't ask about everyone. What do you think?"

"I think we need to find her."

"Who is *we?*"

"Everyone. You know, everyone who cares." Molly lifted her fist to her mouth and chewed at the edge of her thumb. That was all she was going to give me on that.

"I agree. We need to find her. What does this have to do with you, though? Why don't you want to go back to school?"

Her eyes shifted down toward the floor. She sighed. "This is my fault."

"Lydia's being gone is your fault?"

She nodded. "It will probably be in the newspaper tomorrow, not my name, but everybody at school knows what happened and, well, you know, they'll figure out fast enough that it was me." Her fist clenched and she shook her head hard, forbidding the tears that had edged into her eyes.

"*What* was you?"

"I really don't want to talk about it right now. So, you know, back off." She pressed her shoulders forward and hunkered down in the chair. She was mad at herself for already telling me more than she had wanted. The child was frightened and tired and confused, but the child was my child, and when she said back off, she meant *back off.*

The direct path shut down, I tried another. "You hungry?"

"No. Sorta."

"What's say we head on over to my place so I can get out of this goofy dress. We'll call out for pizza."

"Okay." She gave me a smirk. "I wasn't going to say anything, but you do look kinda –"

"I was supposed to look kinda. We'll go to the apartment, have a little pepperoni, a little rest, and maybe you'll feel like talking a little more."

"Not if you can't keep it confidential."

"I cannot hold on to information if someone's in trouble or hurt. That would be wrong, and you know it."

"If you can't keep it a secret, then I can't tell you."

"If you didn't want to tell me, Molly, you wouldn't have walked six miles in the dark. You would not have given me your life savings."

She stood, snatched up the envelope with her money, and fixed me with a look of irrevocable will. "I want to, but I can't."

It was my father's curse realized; I'd gotten one just like me.

Molly disappeared into the bedroom she and her sister shared when they stayed at the apartment with me. I took a quick shower. At ten-thirty, dressed in our pajamas, we ate pizza and fudge-ripple ice cream straight from the carton while Molly watched the last half hour of *Eden,* a show she declared herself addicted to. I watched Molly as she talked over the television, trying to explain to me what was happening on-screen.

"Okay, this Jasmeena girl, in the blue bikini? She's new, but she's a superbitch."

"Language, Mol."

"Well, she is. You can't believe a word she says."

Eden was another one of the new hyperreality shows, a concept that was rising out of the ashes of plain old reality programming. Hyper-reality, as I understood it, shared the basic structure of the genre's previous incarnation in that a group of high-strung narcissists were confined by some elaborate means with the sole purpose of screwing one another over on their way to the big cash prize. The difference was that HR programs were seeded with professional reality players: attractive, uninhibited human specimens who gave good TV. The popular players developed fan bases, followings that guaranteed them participation in other games on other networks. Even I recognized a couple of the players on *Eden.* The rules of this game were tied to the creation myth from which it took its name. The near-to-naked players wandered the grounds of a lush private estate. Each week one or more of them were randomly selected and approached by the appropriately snakelike host to choose between Want and Need. If they chose Want, a substantial amount of cash was added to their individual winnings. If they chose Need, the group received a Gift from the Gods: food, booze, word from the outside world. The object was to keep the others from learning how much you were gaining while at the same time trying to convince them that you were responsible for the sudden appearance of unexpected good fortune. If found out – or believed – to have chosen personal profit too often, you'd most likely be expelled via the Good/Evil vote in the end-of-show Judgment Hour, and your winnings would be divided equally among those who remained. The time between these judgments was spent on the sexual escapades and backstabbing that could launch long-term careers in the genre. Molly, assuming ignorance on my part, set about explaining the basic reality strategy of trying to secretly team up with others in the game. Without taking her eyes off the show, she then started outlining, hands gesturing flowchart organization in the air, the Byzantine complexities of these self-serving alliances, and I went into the "Uh-huh. Yeah? Hmmm" maternal pretense of listening while I tried to interpret the pretzel knot in the rest of her body language.

She was sitting cross-legged beside me on the couch, one arm hooked around her knee, so that she was pulling herself forward, so far forward that she was nearly folded in half. It was a posture of both eagerness and self-defense. Her freshly washed hair hung wet and lank alongside her cheeks, and all I could really see of her face was the end of her nose and the reflected TV light gleaming off her teeth as she spoke. The show took a commercial break and, as the broadcast switched signals, the screen dimmed; Molly dimmed with it. She was in midprediction for the outcome of that night's Judgment Hour when the first commercial came up: the teaser for the eleven o'clock local news that would follow. Molly flinched and then froze. I turned my attention back to the set. Film of students milling about the grounds of Swifton Woods Junior High played out on the screen as the announcer said something about five students being held on suspicion of sexually assaulting a fellow student.

Everyone knows it was me. "Molly?"

She didn't acknowledge my questioning tone. She unknotted her limbs, stood up, and padded off to her room. The door shut behind her. Want and Need? No choices here. I got up and followed her. I tried to. She'd locked the door.

"Hey, Mol?" I drummed my fingers a couple times against the wood. "Can I come in?" I was leveling my voice in an attempt to sound the exact opposite of panicked. When she didn't answer, I reached for the metal skewer I kept on top of the door frame. The skewer was the emergency key – stuck through the hole in the knob, it would release the lock. I waited to use it, hoping she'd relent and unlock it herself. "Molly, please."

"I'm not going to talk about it."

"Sweetheart, if something has happened to you . . ." The words hovered around my head, an idea that I dared not allow entrance. Instead I stared at the skewer's chrome-plated, angled point. I imagined one could do some real damage with it. I started to imagine the faceless thug who may have touched my child. For sanity's sake, I shunted my whole self into numbness. "Molly. Sweetheart – "

"I'm not the one they're talking about." Her voice was calm; the measured quality from earlier had returned, as though her mind had adopted that same enfolded stance as her body had adopted on the couch, her words curling up around herself to defend the vulnerability in her middle. We were both terrified of what the other might say. "If that's what you are thinking. It wasn't me."

"I don't know what I'm supposed to think. You won't tell me what's going on. Then the news says there's been an assault at your school and the story alone has you running out of the room. If this is not about you, why did you run – " Oh. "Lydia. It was Lydia, wasn't it?"

"We have to find her."

"What the hell happened?"

"Go watch it on TV. They'll tell you."

"I'd rather you told me." I hoped for at least another refusal. Not a word. "I'll go watch, but I'm only going to have more questions." On that threat, I walked back to living room, leaned against the wall, as far from the television as I could get, and waited. The flicker of bluish white from the screen gave the room an Ice Age luster. My furniture was old, a hodgepodge of rescued castoffs from family, pieces Greg had no use for when we separated. My grandmother's quilt was folded over the arm of my sister's unwanted recliner. My mother's dishes were in the sink. Molly and Em's schoolwork on the fridge. It was my apartment – double-bolted and chain-locked security – and I felt only dread, as though I'd stumbled into a snare. Not as an intruder, but as prey trapped in an inescapable space as the radiant box across from me continued to disgorge the images that would eventually drown me in ice-colored light. I didn't want to watch, but I had no choice.

The reporter spoke over the same loop of film used in the teaser. Details were sketchy, mercifully vague, but the impression left behind was brutal. The reporter had learned, in spite of efforts to keep the story quiet, that earlier that morning, five male eighth graders at Swifton Woods Junior High had been taken into custody pending investigation of allegations that they had sexually assaulted a fellow classmate during a party at the victim's home. The party had taken place the previous weekend, and the incident might have gone undiscovered if a staff member at the school had not overheard the victim confiding *quote* in an extremely agitated manner *unquote* with another, as yet unidentified student. Of greatest concern at the moment was the disappearance of the victim, who, like the others involved, would not be identified by the media unless authorities requested the identification as part of a search.

A click sounded off to my right. The bedroom door opened and Molly stood there, her arms crossed over her chest, stiff shouldered, her jaw set, a sentinel in daisy-printed flannel pajamas. "That's why I can't go back."

. . . another, as yet unidentified student. "You were talking to Lydia?" *Everyone knows it was me.* "You're the one the teacher overheard?"

"We have to find her."

"I should say so. But it's very likely she'll turn up on her own, maybe by the time we get – "

"No, she won't."

Don't argue with the child; comfort her. "Tomorrow when I take you back, I'll make some calls. I'll at least find out what there is to know. How about that?"

"Thanks, Mom."

"Will you tell me what Lydia told you?"

"No."

"Molly, you're going to have to talk about it eventually, you're going to have to tell the police – "

"If they ask me, I will."

"You can't wait to be asked. If you want to help Lydia – "

"I'm not trying to help Lydia. I'm trying to help the guys." She drew herself up to her full height. "They didn't do anything, Mom."

Of course, she needed to believe that. These boys must have been her friends, but the events, even in the foggy state of allegation, had a gravity stronger than the pull of friendship. I lowered my voice. "Then explain this, sweetheart. If nothing happened, why would Lydia run away?"

"Oh, something happened, but it wasn't the guys' fault. Lydia Parrish is a slut."

"Molly – "

"Well, she is. And I don't think she ran away. I think someone's hiding her."

"Why would anyone do that?"

"Because it was Lydia's fault, and they don't want anyone to find out."

"Molly, no matter what's gone down in a person's past, if she's been assaulted – "

"You don't understand, Mom. I know what I'm talking about." She turned her back on me. "I was there." The door slammed shut behind her.

The phone rang. Even after this time apart, I recognized the caller by the frantic undertones in the ring. I picked up the receiver. "Hey, Greg."

"Were you watching the news?"

1 7

If you are going to do this, then you'd better do it now. The rope on the attic door is a braid of deep blue satin cords, the end tied with a tassel your mother saved from an old lamp. It looks prettier, she'd said, than the shank of old wash line your father put in. You used to have to jump up to grab it. Now, you barely raise up on your toes. The panel opens easily, the steps unfold, descending under their own weight. You catch the first riser before the ends collide with the floor and ease the whole thing to a silent connection between where you are now and where you need to be. The package is clutched to your chest. You can almost feel your heart beat through it.

Hurry up the steps. The attic is always shadow dense at best, but not too bad this time of day. The vents let in enough light for your purposes. You don't dare pull the string for the overhead bulb. He might see it, a white-yellow brightness, slanting through the cornice vents. Not that it would trouble him; he knows you long ago took over the attic to replace the privacy afforded by the tree house. But today you can't risk his suspicion over anything. It's his job to be suspicious.

You have to get busy. He will be coming inside soon, and he might hear something. Sound travels in this house. You gently lay the package down. Quiet. Take up the crowbar. Choose a place to begin. It is so hot up here. Ignore it. Hurry.

Down in the yard you can hear him working.

proof

Greg didn't know any more than I did. He'd been so swept up in trying to locate Molly that he'd disregarded, plain had not heard, any information that didn't relate to the present emergency. I didn't volunteer Molly's exiting comment about being there because in part I didn't know what she meant and in part because I didn't want to believe she meant it. Mostly, I didn't tell him because it would mean finding out he had allowed her to go to this so-called party, and then I would have to kill him. I was too tired for that.

By the time Greg and I had finished alternately reassuring and terrifying ourselves with admissions of how little we knew about our daughter, Molly had fallen asleep, the bedroom lights still on and the blankets tossed over her head so that I couldn't see her face. I folded back the bedding so that she could breathe better and brushed her hair from her eyes. She was on her belly, her arms pulled under her. It didn't look comfortable, but her back was rising and falling in steady rhythm with her toothpaste-scented breaths.

"I didn't tell your dad," I said, drawing close to her ear. "But he's going to find out, Molly. If you were there, you have to tell." I kissed her cheek and tasted tears. I smoothed her sheets and went to the door. I hit the switch. Out of the darkness came Molly's sob-hoarse voice.

"Leave the lights on."

I didn't even make the effort to get in bed; sleep was going to be impossible. I wandered around the apartment fighting off useless impulses: call the authorities in Swifton and attempt to worm information out of them; shake Molly awake and make her talk; call Greg back and pick a fight so I could scream out my fear at someone who was as scared as I was; call Phillip, after six weeks of silence, and ask him to come over and hold me down so that I could scream. None of those options seemed workable – or sane – but the appeal in each was undeniable. I needed something, anything to get away from the absurd little singsong memory cycling through my head like the tinny musical tease on a jack-in-the-box; *what goes around comes around to what goes around comes around to . . .*

I planted myself in front of the computer for an hour, researching what I could off the Internet, but as the story was just breaking, nothing was up yet. It was too early for the on-line versions of the morning papers and the search engines would have come up empty on the current events – even if I'd had the courage to type in + "Assault" + "Swifton." That little exercise would have been like playing a slot machine that promised to pay out in broken glass, razor blades, and stories I'd spent a lifetime trying to forget all bound up in a single word: *Nightingale*. It had started right after I turned twelve, right after the storm that took out our oak tree. Three straight summers. 1973. '74. '75. Little girls taken from their beds, raped, and then released to wander dazed until found. The one suspect finally taken into custody had to be let go due to lack of evidence. He then vanished, but not before one final assault. Eleven girls total. I had known them all. I was willing to bet that if I were to type "Nightingales" into the search prompt I would get exactly the same information that I had archived in my notebook at the time it was happening. The names of the girls. Details of the crimes. Increasingly frequent newspaper articles reminding citizens of necessary safety precautions. Stories of the protesters picketing my father's office. Letters to the editor demanding he call in the FBI or state troopers or whoever it would take to "protect our children." I would lay good money on the probability that the first hit would be that terrible piece by Margaret Wexham that earned her a Pulitzer and christened my ravaged friends under their media-friendly collective noun. I still remembered enough of her withering assessments of my father's procedural incompetence interwoven with appropriate lines from Hans Christian Andersen's "Nightingale" parable of pretense versus truth. I had no need to see the words again. I couldn't afford that particular windfall at this particular moment. It was best to walk away. Besides, the sound of my fingers on the keyboard had become too reminiscent of the earlier, disembodied knocking of vanished schoolgirls on my office door.

I shut down the computer. I had only one recourse left, the outlet I'd discovered early in the weeks of wandering in a sleepless fog after I decided – against everyone's advice – to go off the medication. Bread. When sleep abandoned me, I made bread. Anadama, Cuban, ryes, braided challahs, pumpernickels, and whole wheats, depending on what I had in the kitchen at the time. Instead of ferns or spider plants, I kept and fed a crock of sourdough starter. In the morning, on my way to work, I would leave the still warm loaves, bagged in brown paper, at the doors of some of my elderly neighbors, whom I imagined not so much grateful as suspicious. Perhaps to the point of never eating a bite of what I'd left them. That would be fine with me. I never ate it myself. I didn't exactly want bread; I wanted the experience of transformation. To make bread was to change the physical reality of the world with your own hands, and the part of the world I was trying to change was not exactly the source of nurturing sustenance.

Right then I wanted to change my daughter's mind, and if Molly awoke to the rich aromas of a freshly baked cinnamon loaf, and if I could offer it to my daughter, sliced, battered, and grilled up as her favorite French toast for breakfast, she might revise her view of me as the untrustworthy but necessary ally. She might feel safe enough to transcend the bruised strangeness between us and find a modicum of comfort in my company. In that comfort, she might be more willing to talk. I wanted my daughter's trust, and I was willing to bribe her to get it. She'd suspect what I was up to from the instant the first scent of cinnamon hit her nose; I'd used this tactic before. But it was worth a shot.

I went to the kitchen, turned the oven to 375 degrees, and hauled out the bowls, the board, the pans; measured out the flour and salt; poured milk into a saucepan to scald as the half stick of butter melted into it. I tested the warmth of the tap water on my wrist before adding it to the teaspoon of sugar in the measuring cup. I then dumped the yeast granules from the envelope into the sugar water bath and began my watch. Proof, it was called, this five-minute test of the yeast's viability. The mushroom-colored granules settled on the bottom of the cup. Minuscule bubbles of carbon dioxide broke at the surface as the warmth woke the little beasties

and they started devouring the sugar. The bubbles strengthened expo-
nentially, creating a froth that exploded – mushroom clouded – in the
chaotic, blooming aftermath of unbridled life. I loved that, in a Dr.
Frankenstein *It's alive!* sort of fashion. It reminded me of the aha moment
in an investigation when the proliferation of data suddenly reached
critical mass and the mind could generate not only ideas but also sense
from those ideas. Out of that sense, real solutions might coalesce. Proof of
the mind's viability, if you will. Proof of my mind's viability, to be specific.

I mixed the milk and butter and yeast with as much flour as it could
hold and turned out the raggedy mass of dough onto the board to knead it
until it felt like elasticized silk. I then rounded the dough and plopped it in
an oiled mixing bowl to rise. While that was taking place, I cleaned up the
spilled flour and puddles of buttery milk. I washed bowls and pans. It was
after four o'clock when I punched the dough down, divided it in half, and
shaped the loaves into rectangles. These I brushed with melted butter,
sprinkled with a mixture of cinnamon and sugar, and then rolled so the
sugared spice would swirl through each slice. The loaves went into pans to
rise again before baking.

Nothing else to do but wait, I sat on the floor, my back against the
almost too hot oven, holding my knees to my chest. Flour dusted my
pajama pants. The kitchen smelled doughy and sweet. I closed my eyes
and allowed myself to indulge a full appreciation of my fatigue. It wasn't
sleep, but it was close.

I heard her come into the kitchen, but I didn't open my eyes. Two can
play the pretend-to-sleep game. She padded over to the oven and, sighing,
slid down to sit next to me, her body close, leaning into mine. Her
labored, wet-sounding breaths told me she'd been crying again. When she
laid her head against my shoulder, I gave up the game and shifted so that I
could get my arm around her. I pulled her close, resting my head against
hers. Through the yeast and the cinnamon, I could smell her, the warm,
perspirey scent of recent sleep and something else, perfume? My old
perfume? Where could she have found that? I hadn't worn it since I was
fifteen – my eyes snapped open. My arm was out, muscles flexed, hugging
the shoulder of a child who wasn't there.

I scrambled to my feet and backed away from the oven. "Molly?" The
kitchen was empty. The bread loaves rising and rounding the dish towel

that covered them. Nothing out of place. I walked, forbidding myself to break into the run my body wanted, down to Molly's bedroom. The lights were still on. She was deep-sleep diving under the covers. I could hear her snoring softly, but I had to make sure she was really there. I pulled the blankets back quickly with enough force that it roused her.

She yawned, rubbed at her eyes, and squinted up at me. "What's wrong?" Before I could say anything, the alert uncertainty in her face dulled before what she'd obviously remembered. She wriggled her head back up to the pillow. "Is something wrong, Mom?"

Breathe. Smile. Don't scare her. "Just checking on you." I made a great show of shaking out the blankets and let them fall back over her. "It bothers me when you get tangled up and buried like that."

She wasn't buying it. "Are you all right?"

"Of course." I took the opening. "I'd be much more all right if I had a clearer picture – "

"Please, Mom."

"Please, Molly."

She yawned again. "You smell like cinnamon."

"French toast for breakfast. Homemade."

She shook her head back and forth against the pillow. "I don't eat bread anymore. It makes you fat."

"Does not."

"Does too."

So much for bribery. "Go back to sleep, Mol." I reached out to touch her cheek and she withdrew from me with a jerk. I lowered my hand to a safe distance. "I'll see you in the morning, then."

She arched her neck and saw the soft blue light in the window behind her. "Looks like morning now."

"You still have a couple hours. Get some sleep."

"You could take the bread out to Dad and Em. They'll eat it."

"Thanks, I may do that." I turned to go. "Lights on or off."

"Off, I guess. Mom, will you do me a favor?"

Build me a fortress on the far side of the moon. Forge me a shield of impenetrable strength. Turn the world backward until time undoes this terrible thing I can't bear to tell you. "Sure, sweetheart. I'll do whatever I can."

43

"If you see Lydia, will you tell me?"

My fingers on the light switch, I looked back over my shoulder. "What do you mean, if I *see* Lydia?"

"You know. How you see things?"

"I'm not sure – "

"Dad explained it to us a long time ago. That's the reason, one of the reasons you don't want to live with us. Because you hear things, you see stuff – people, kids, who are, you know, lost, and it kind of freaks everyone out."

"Oh, he explained that, did he?"

"Don't get mad. He said it isn't your fault. That's part of how you figure stuff out. You can't help it if your imagination kind of *leaks* to the outside."

"He said my imagination leaks?" *Christ, Greg.* "Whatever my imagination may be up to, understand it's not that I don't want to live with you and Em – "

"Just tell me if you see Lydia. I'd want to know."

I could have opted for leverage here, set up an I-tell-you-if-you-tell-me deal, but she was asking me to let her know if I thought her friend was lost beyond retrieval. She needed the reassurance of my answers more than I needed whatever information might have hidden in hers. "If I see her – "

"Promise?"

"Promise, but I don't think I will. Bad as this is, bad as what little I know sounds, it doesn't feel like that sort of situation. She'll be back." I switched off the light.

"I hope you're right."

Me, too, I thought, but didn't say it. Instead I wished her a couple more hours of rest. Then I went to the kitchen where the loaves had risen too much and were beginning to droop over the sides of the pans. The bread would be yeasty, full of cavernous air pockets. It was ruined, but I shoved the pans in the oven anyway to complete the process: killing the yeast and drying out the gluten-walled chambers formed by their short but productive lives. A loaf of bread was nothing but the airy skeletal remains of an alien presence. A sad thing, really. But the baking had to be done, it was required by the equation set forth in every monster story out there: You had to destroy your creation before your creation destroyed you.

44

m o l l y

She pulls the blankets back over her head, stretching the sheets taut, battening herself down in the darkness. Still, she cannot escape the smell of cinnamon. Her mother's footsteps cycle up and down the hall. Mom is pacing the way she does when she's worried, which makes Molly worry about what Mom might try next to get more information. Whatever it is, it won't work. Molly has to keep to her plan, no matter what anybody might do or say, no matter how much they may come to hate her.

Lydia already hates her. She has told Molly this fact straight out several times in angry whispers, but during the fight, she said it over and over, her voice growing until she was shouting. The sound echoed around the girls' washroom, smashing against the tile and steel and glass back into Molly's head. It wasn't a normal part of their usual fighting, one of those hand grenades of words they tossed because they knew it would hurt. She heard the cold burn in Lydia's voice. *I. Hate. You.* Lydia meant it this time, and Molly knew then that Lydia was capable of real damage. Not physical – well, maybe, she'd seen what Lydia could do when really pissed – but if Lydia could, through the force of her hatred, push Molly right out of existence as though Molly had never been born, she would.

It wasn't like they chose each other. Everyone assumed they *should* be friends. It wasn't because they were the only new kids in Mrs. Zeigler's class that autumn. Swifton Woods Elementary had tons of new kids every year. And it wasn't because both sets of their parents had separated. Most of the kids she knew had been through at least one divorce. That your parents couldn't live together forever wasn't that big a deal, really, or at least that's what the lady said during the weekly Families in Transition group that the guidance counselor had forced them to attend. Molly and Lydia had arrived late to their first session when the other kids were already into the project of the day: making banana splits. The lady – "Call me Wanda, honey" – at the front of the room was going on and on about how sometimes good things come from splitting stuff up. Molly and Lydia had looked at each and begun to giggle. From then on, when they went to FIT, they'd sit off by themselves, nudge each other, and roll their eyes at the stupid things Call-Me-Wanda-Honey would say. But what had locked Molly and Lydia into the friendship box had been the other kids' wariness of them. No one ever joined them at their lunch table or in the library. No one invited them to play after school. It was as though they were being quarantined the way oddly acting animals get caged separately. Whispers followed them everywhere. The whole town seemed to know that their mothers had returned to Swifton Woods to hide out from their pasts. Lydia's mom for reasons of a tragic romantic intrigue in Paris, and Molly's mom because she'd gone crazy and killed a guy.

For all that everyone at Swifton Woods Elementary thought they might have had in common, Molly isn't sure now that she even liked Lydia – ever. What she liked was Lydia's family. And if being Lydia's friend was the necessary price of getting to hang out at Lydia's house, that wasn't so bad. It meant getting away from the chaos of her own home. At Lydia's, the furniture matched and everything was clean. Instead of TV or the screech of power tools or the sound of people yelling, they had music. Both Mrs. Parrish – Amanda, she insisted Molly call her – and Lydia played the piano. Molly couldn't contribute more than the *boom-de-a-da* part of "Heart and Soul," but Amanda, who was as beautiful as a movie star, would sit with her to show her how to one-finger her way through the melodies of Molly's favorite songs. When the piano wasn't in use, they had classical music or jazz on the stereo, and Molly had learned to identify certain composers simply by the style of their music. Amanda also taught Molly how to needlepoint and how to trick flower bulbs into blooming by keeping them dark and cold in the cellar so that you could have tulips and daffodils in January. Amanda Parrish made the family meals – even pizza – from scratch, often calling the girls from their homework to come in and help with the chopping, mixing, shaping of dinner. Neil Parrish, tall, suntanned, and handsome, would come in around six o'clock. He would call Molly *mademoiselle* and kiss her hand. Everyone, even Lydia and Molly if they wanted, would have a glass of wine while they caught up on one another's day, saying all sorts of funny, sophisticated things as they slipped from French into English and back again. Neil would pause to translate this word or that for Molly, or quiz her on a word from the last evening. She tried hard to remember because it made her happy when he would raise his glass and *salut* her. Lydia would get jealous and declare herself the only true Francophone in the room as she laughed and mocked them on their horrible American pronunciations.

According to Lydia, Neil had been in France on business when he met her mother at a cocktail party. They'd fallen instantly in love. Amanda was still married to Lydia's real dad, so Neil and Amanda never acted on their feelings until her father became sick, and everyone knew he was going to die. Here the story would change depending upon Lydia's mood. Sometimes she'd say that her father had nobly given Amanda permission to seek the comfort of Neil's affections, as he had been aware of their friendship from the beginning. Sometimes Lydia would say that it was learning of the affair that was the last blow; it was the shock of that knowledge that killed him. When she was in one of her vicious rages, she'd accuse Neil or Amanda or both of them of conspiring in her father's outright murder. Other times, she'd get pensive and dreamy and wonder if Neil was in fact her real father. Molly loved all these versions, envied Lydia her ability to change the ending to suit her current frame of mind. Molly never told her story. It was neither romantic nor sophisticated, and it always ended with memories of her mother in the hospital, slouched in a chair, her head so full of drugs she couldn't even remember Molly's name. Molly liked to pretend these memories were only dreams, frightening but without any real substance. The more she was with the Parrishes, the easier that pretending became.

In the beginning, Lydia was pretending, too. She seemed to like having Molly around. Molly was her project, the way the flower bulbs were Amanda's. They'd spend hours up in Lydia's antique-furnished bedroom, trying on different outfits as Lydia labored to uncover Molly's "personal style" as prescribed by the magazines they borrowed from Amanda. The bed would be heaped with piles of fancy sweaters and pleated skirts with labels in languages Molly didn't recognize. Lydia would braid and curl and barrette Molly's untamable hair. She brushed shades of eye shadow on Molly's lids only after she'd okayed this brown or that violet with the

47

current issue of *Vogue* or *Cosmopolitan*. She fingered gloss onto Molly's lips, holding the tissue for her to blot the excess. Then she'd make Molly walk with her eyes closed to the full-length oval-shaped mirror for the unveiling. Neither of them was ever happy with the results.

Lydia, when she was feeling patient, would say Molly's beauty was a "mystery" waiting to be solved, and she'd coo what sounded like encouragement *en français* as she dragged Molly back to her private bathroom to wash her face. Other times, Lydia would drag her hands through her own princess-perfect tumble of blond curls and swear that Molly didn't even *want* to be pretty. She'd take the magazines, go flounce down on her bed, and start reading the sex articles aloud until Molly told her to shut up.

The problem, Molly understood, was that she could not be Lydia. Lydia's body was on fast-forward. By the end of fifth grade she had hips and breasts, during that summer she got her first period. Always taller than Molly, Lydia was shooting skyward, all gazelle leg and dancer grace. But Lydia was also angry most of the time, too. She seemed especially angry at Molly for not keeping up, as though Lydia had awakened to find herself too big for the playhouse where Molly remained safe from the teasing and dirty talk at the municipal swimming pool. It was more than a lag between them. It was a betrayal. But Lydia's anger, like everything else about Lydia, changed. Within the first month of the new school year, she discovered that with her new body came power. The boys melted before her and the girls copied her every move. Molly, who was being distanced from Lydia by her growing horde of admirers, would watch groups of teachers watch Lydia walk down the hall. They would stare for a moment, make eye contact with one another, shake their heads, and turn away. No matter how secretive the teachers thought their appraisal was, Molly knew that Lydia was aware of their eyes. It showed in her smile. The more her awareness of the effect she had grew, the more Lydia went from being regular old bossy to being flat-out mean. And Molly became her favorite target.

The very last time she spent the night at Lydia's house was toward the end of September in their sixth-grade year. She had been suspicious from the moment Lydia passed her the scribbled invitation in the hall after their math classes. What could she want? Lydia hardly spoke to her at school anymore and was less and less available when Molly tried to call on the phone. Uncertain, Molly went anyway. That night, however, Lydia almost seemed like the person she remembered, giggly and talkative, confiding to Molly her opinions of the other kids in the class and then making her promise not to tell. They stayed up very late, propped up on the pillows in Lydia's bed. Molly kept yawning, drifting toward sleep, but Lydia would prod her and keep talking. Sleep finally won out.

Molly had no idea what time it was when she woke up – or how long she'd been asleep. Lydia's bedroom was dark. Lydia wasn't in the bed, but Molly could hear her in the bathroom. It sounded like she was having trouble breathing.

"Lydia?" she called, trying to keep her voice down. "Lydia, are you okay?" When she didn't answer, Molly got out of bed, nearly tripping on the hem of her nightgown, and went to the bathroom door. A weak flicker of light shone at the edges of the door. Candles? Molly knocked softly; the door inched open on the impact of her fist. "Lydia?" She pushed the door open farther and peeked inside.

Molly caught only a glimpse. Lydia had her back to the door. She was naked. She must have sensed the intrusion, because she whipped her head around to see Molly and when she did she picked up a water glass and heaved it. Molly pulled the door shut and felt the glass hit and shatter in the spot where a second before her face had been, as her eyes were adjusting to the light, as she was starting to see.

Molly ran back to the bed. She got under the covers and did the only thing she knew how to do when people went crazy: She pretended to be asleep. She felt sick to her stomach, and her mind was already attempting to undo the flash of memorized image before her eyes. She clutched the sheets to her chin and scrunched her eyes shut tight, trying to steady her breath, trying not to tremble when, how many minutes, hours later, she heard the bathroom door open. Lydia crawled into bed next to her and snuggled up close, wrapping her fingers about Molly's wrist. Lydia smelled like sweat and soap.

Lydia whispered. "Promise you'll be my friend?"

Molly swallowed. "What were you doing?"

"I need you to be my friend. Promise you'll be my friend no matter what?"

"Why wouldn't I be your friend?"

"Promise me, Molly."

"Okay. I promise."

"And you won't tell anyone my secrets?" She tightened her grip on Molly's wrist.

"I don't know what your secrets are. All right – stop it; that hurts. I won't say anything. I promise."

"If you really, really promise, I'll tell you the truth about how my father died." She lifted her head so that she could speak directly into Molly's ear. She talked for a long time, whispers without intonation. When she finished, the light in the room was the milky gray on the outer edge of daybreak. Lydia rolled away and got up again. "If you don't believe me, come see. I'll prove it." She headed back toward the bathroom.

Molly didn't follow Lydia. She didn't want to see any more than she already had. She'd pulled the quilts over her head and hidden there in Lydia's room until it was safe to go home.

But honestly, it feels as though she's never left, as though she's been hiding there in that same place under the covers for three years now until this morning at her mother's apartment when the hiding has to end. What Lydia has done makes hiding any longer impossible. Promise or no promise. Molly curls her fingers over the binding and gets ready to shove back the blankets, already squinting against what she expects to be the painful brightness of day.

1 6

From your bedroom window you watch him work the ax. He hefts a thick slice of trunk onto the hacked-up surface of the oak's stump, wedges his feet into the valleys between the humped gnarl of the roots, raises the ax, lets it fall. *Thwack-thud.* The blade sinks deep into the section of trunk, splitting it clean. The secret, he says, is to let gravity do the work, to get a good arc in your swing and let the blade fall. It will come down true and straight because that is the easiest thing for it to do. Path of least resistance, he calls it. He knows what he's doing.

Take up the pen and write your final entry:

> *Dear Dad,*
> *I'm so sorry.*
> *L.*

You put the hat in the scrapbook and shut the whole thing flat as possible while wrapping it round and round with masking tape to hold it shut. You try not to think too much about what you're doing. You think instead of what you can wrap the book up in so that it won't make a noise when it hits the ceiling board. There's that old Bugs Bunny beach towel at the bottom of the linen closet. That will work. And then maybe you should put it all in one of the plastic bags you saved from the mall. In case it starts to smell.

Once the package is wrapped and sealed, you take it and the crowbar out into the hallway, which seems to telescope in length. You walk faster, trying to stay ahead of your fear. But it's gaining. If you are going to do this thing, then you'd better do it now.

s w i f t o n

General wisdom holds that you can't go home again, but as I see it, you can never really get away. Home has a black hole, a zero point at its center that holds you in an inescapable orbit, reducing the universe to a binary set of locations: Wherever you are, you either are or you are not at home. And as Molly and I drove past the SWIFTON WOODS WELCOMES YOU sign on the edge of town, the poles guiding my sense of emotional navigation switched and distances came undone; I was moving backward, watching time spool itself back onto the spindle as though the woman I had become was unraveling herself until I was, again, the girl who had decided to leave. Every week I returned to Swifton to visit my daughters in the house where I grew up, and on the instant of arriving, I was the daughter desperate again to take off. Home was, for me, the most forceful reminder that I had no home.

The changes to the town since I'd left only amplified my sense of foreign loyalties. Swifton – no one called it Swifton Woods anymore – was a minor city now, indistinguishable from the other minor cities that crept and bulked along side the highway like ravenous alien blobs. Suburban sprawl choked out the fields and forests I had once relied on to serve as a moat between the life I'd built and the one I'd disowned. The woods of Swifton Woods were gone long before my birth, stripped away early in the last century for corn and alfalfa and dairy stock. A half century later, at the end of the Second World War, the grain and grazing lands began to be stripped for houses and shopping centers. Not everything changed; the swifts, those colonies of small, dark birds for which the wooded area had been named, continued to thrive. My grandparents, who had felled their fair share of trees, had talked about watching the massive flocks gather over the woods at dusk, soaring against the stars on their swallow-curved wings. One by one, the birds breeding that season dive-bombed – cyclone spirals – down into the treetops, down into the hollows, holes, and caves in which they nested with their young. The others, thousands of them, remained aloft for the whole of the night, circling over the forest like a denser form of darkness.

Breeding and serious storms were the only forces that brought the swifts to rest; these birds were built for flying and as such did everything – eat, drink, preen, mate, sleep – on the wing. Therefore they weren't particularly disturbed when the trees disappeared and the hillside caverns closed. They simply set up their nurseries in the structures that arose where the trees had been: inside chimneys, in the crumbled-out crevices of exterior walls, in the concave shelters of the *e*'s, *a*'s, *s*'s, and *g*'s in the large, lighted lettering of store signs. I remembered running out of the grocery store when I was very young, my hands covering my head, terrified of being hit by a bird on the way up.

Swifts didn't take off. They jumped from a perch, wings spread, falling six or eight feet, until they'd gained sufficient air pressure to push off. The fledglings weren't always the best judge of distance. Not to mention the never-ending shower of defecation for which we earned, from our high school athletic rivals, the unfortunate but inevitable nickname of Shiton Woulds – as in Shiton Woulds if They Coulds. We always figured it could have been worse; the town founders could have taken a liking to another of the local aviary residents: a cousin of the swift, the goatsucker.

The spring of 1976, when I was fifteen, the Chamber of Commerce hired a firm to scrub and disinfect the business district of downtown in preparation for the bicentennial festivities. The firm did such a superior job, Swifton put them on a yearly contract. Rumor had it the firm was not only washing up after the swifts but also removing unhatched eggs from their nests and leaving piles of poisoned grain in convenient stations. Whether or not that was true, we noted a slow attrition in the number of birds. Nevertheless, the declining population of swifts didn't seem to matter because over the decades, the residents of Swifton had developed habits of defense that had become something of a regional culture. Those habits were still evident as Molly and I made our way through the chilled but sunny brightness of downtown that morning. We lurched along in the slow-mo samba of gas, gas, brake through the lighted intersections, waiting as young mothers hurried through the crosswalks, tilting open umbrellas over their babies' carriages and strollers. Older women window-shopped, protecting their recently rinsed and styled hair with clear plastic rain bonnets that tied beneath their chins. Men chatted at the corners, absently adjusting the bill on their caps or holding folded newspaper to their scalps. Kids were still employing the tried-and-true method of my youth: When entering or exiting a Swifton building, check the sky and don't dawdle.

Molly looked swift-ready. She'd slunk way down in her seat, the hood of her sweater pulled close to her face, her hands shielding her forehead. She was trying not to be seen by those on the sidewalk, trying not to be seen by me. She had spoken no more than a dozen sentences since we left the city almost two hours earlier. Each one only in response to my questioning, all variations on the no-I-won't motif of our earlier conversations. To avoid talking to me during the drive, she'd busied herself in tuning the radio to find stations playing one of the songs she liked, which when found would cause her to crank up the volume to just this side of painful. That was all right. She thought she was feigning stoicism through the music. She had yet to reckon the problems inherent with being a child of the generation that had succored social revolution on acid rock. By the time I'd reached Molly's age, I'd already been enjoined to have sympathy for the devil. I wasn't the least put off by her electronically enhanced teenybopper noise. The songs themselves – overblown ballads of lone-liness and unrequited love, digitized throbs of defiance you could dance to – were betraying her but not to anything I had not already imagined. I remembered being thirteen and the gauntlet of emotional razor wire that was the eighth grade. Much of what she felt she wouldn't tell me; she believed I couldn't understand. It broke my heart twice over: once for her exquisite sense of isolation and once for the institutionalized hymns of another normal part of growing up used to justify that anguish to the ones who were feeling it.

Normal until a few days ago. I caught her watching me, her eyes full of wary assessment. "Can't you go any faster?"

"Not unless you want me to drive *over* the other cars."

The idea was meant as a joke; she didn't laugh. "We could have gone the back way."

"That takes even longer."

"But we can go faster on Old Quarry."

"Yes, we can, but anything over fifteen miles per hour and the potholes on Old Quarry will snap my axles."

"They fixed the potholes last week."

I could imagine Greg already pacing the driveway wondering what was keeping us. "We've got only a few more minutes, Molly."

Her face narrowed. "We could stop for ice cream at the Dairy. I'll buy."

"Ice cream?" I swallowed my laugh; the bribee had become the briber. "It's not even ten o'clock in the morning" – *She's offering you something* – "but you're buying, huh?"

She nodded faintly.

"The back way it is." I made a left turn at the next intersection and threaded the residential streets, passing the houses that became more run down the closer we got to Old Quarry Road. At that intersection the houses gave way to empty, rocky lots staked with signs announcing coming development of projects like the Old Quarry Plaza and the Old Quarry Promenade. Old Quarry Road, which had the official title of the Martin Quarry–Swifton Woods Turnpike, had originally been the sole artery to the entire area. Like most back roads, it was named for the places it connected. The Quarry end of the road was about twelve miles to the south, where back in the early 1900s, as local legend had it, would-be gentleman farmer Silas Martin was outraged – simply outraged – to find that one of the pastures he'd purchased, on the advice of his nonfarming son, was nothing more than twenty-five acres of bare, untillable rock. Martin had demanded the cost of the useless acreage be excluded from the total price of the sixty-acre parcel. Turned out that twenty-five acres was a solid hunk of granite ranging between seventy-five and one hundred twenty-five feet deep. Turned out that Silas Martin was, when in the city, the owner of a firm that built the monuments and mausoleums for the city's distinguished, honored, and wealthy dead. Turned out Martin's son, while certainly not a farmer, had studied geology at Harvard. So the Martin Quarry, from which the family made millions and which was the source of most of the foundation stones of Swifton's original buildings, was acquired for nothing. How much of this was historical fact? I'd never cared enough to go looking, but the story served only to exemplify the bedrock of

Swifton's primary faith: We were cursed by the abundance of our blessings.

Old Quarry Road, even when repaired just as Molly had promised, was two lanes of bump and grind through what was left of the undeveloped countryside, a suspension-shimmying hill-and-dale thrill ride that rolled with the fields, past the barns and houses of those who had yet to sell. Some of these places were still being worked by proud folks getting by on subsistence farming, growing their own food, raising cows for their own use, maybe renting a booth at the Swifton Farmers' Market or maintaining a roadside produce stand. They may have been rich on paper, but they were farmers. To let the land languish would have been a sin. These working farms were few and growing fewer; the alfalfa and corn fields around Swifton lay increasingly fallow, as year by year their owners watched the value of their land increase by simple laws of scarcity versus demand. Many parlayed their growing wealth into early retirements, travel tours, and educations for their children's children. The younger families tried their hand at esoteric niche crops like heirloom seeds or baby vegetables for gourmet kitchens, herb gardening, hydroponics, or like Lydia's family, whose property we were passing, wine making.

The sign at the end of their drive read OLD QUARRY VINEYARD EST. 1999, NEIL AND AMANDA PARRISH. The Parrish house sat way back from the road, a wraparound veranda offering grand views of the surrounding vineyard: row after row of grapevines laid out at angles to the road like a paranoid's idea of effective fencing. It was getting near harvest; the vines, heavy with fruit, drooped against the wire supports to which they were pinioned. Like acres of orderly crucifixions. Children. For a second. It was only for a second.

The suddenness of that image, row upon row of crucified children, sent a seizure of cold through my chest. I didn't realize I had stopped the car, that I had stopped and was staring at the vineyard until Molly touched my arm. I could feel the fear coming through her fingers.

"You see something, Mom?"

See wasn't the word. "No." I turned and smiled, tried to smile, too big and bright, a cheery little lie. "Honest. Let's go get that ice cream."

"I don't want any." She looked down and shuddered. Her shoulders fell. Surrender. "The party was at Lydia's house, you know."

We were stopped on the downside of a hill and anyone cresting behind us wouldn't have time to stop, but I was afraid if we were to start moving, the moment would vanish. "And you were there?"

Nod. "Do I have to tell?"

"The police will want to question everyone who was at the party. If you really want to help your friends, then yes, you have to tell. You tell exactly what happened as truthfully as you can."

"But with Lydia gone, I'm saying the same thing the guys are saying, you know? I don't see how that would help. Lydia needs to tell it."

"And you think Lydia's version is going to be the same as the boys'?"

"Yes. She's slutty, but she's not mean. To them. She wouldn't want the guys to get in trouble. She wouldn't lie."

"I have to ask again, why would she run away?" The peaks of the gables on the Parrish home were just visible from this angle on the hill. I checked the rearview mirror; we had to get going. I let my foot ease off the brake pedal and gravity pulled us into an accelerating downward coast. "If she knows they're in trouble, why would she make herself unavailable? Running away would make more sense if she knew her story wasn't going to line up with theirs, if she were hurt and not sure what to do about it."

"I told you I don't think she ran away."

"Molly, sweetheart, do you know what sexual assault is?"

"What's that supposed to mean?"

"It means that maybe you didn't understand what you were seeing."

"Didn't understand what I was seeing? Didn't understand that Lydia and the other girls were drunk to the point of puking by the time the guys, by the time I got there –"

"Other girls?"

"Yes, other girls."

Ask. You have to ask. "Are you one of the *other* girls?"

"No." Her head was turned, leaning against the window; she seemed to be watching her reflection in the side-view mirror. "But no one's talking about the other girls yet. Because the guys are trying to keep them out of it. They would have protected Lydia, too. No one was supposed to know. It was Lydia who started taking her clothes off. It was Lydia who started undressing the other girls." She pulled the hood of her sweater closer to her face. "There wasn't any, you know, I mean nothing happened. I mean, the girls were dancing and touching each other, but Lydia was telling them what to do. They were copying the video to the song – well, you wouldn't know it. The girls were laughing like they were just goofing off. The guys were kind of freaked out, standing around watching this, and then suddenly Lydia started daring them to touch her, to well, you know – God, she was so drunk she could barely stand up. When nobody moved, she went over and grabbed this one guy's hand and made him touch her, and then she got another one of the guys to kiss her. It got real quiet, everyone kind of looking at each other, and then the guys got out of there; in less than a minute everyone was gone and that was it."

"That was it?"

Again with the nod.

"Nothing more than that? The boys didn't go back later?"

"No. They went to another guy's house."

"And you saw all of this?"

"Yes."

"Hmmm. I don't know where the assault thing is coming from, but you still need to talk to the authorities. They will cross-reference the details, and your statement can only go to corroborate the boys' – "

"But then they'll know, Mom."

"Know what, Molly? What are you so afraid of?"

She closed her eyes as though trying to hold the tears in. "I was at the party, but I wasn't exactly invited."

"What – "

"I was watching, okay? No one knew I was there. I was standing at the window, watching. And then at school, we were in the rest room, and Lydia started in on me, like she always does, calling me a fucking lunatic just like" – my daughter shot me a look of immeasurable agony – "and I sort of started yelling at her about what the boys were saying. But that was a lie. The boys hadn't said anything. To me, at least. Some teacher overheard us and went to the principal, and the principal went to the police. Nobody was supposed to know. And now everyone does and Lydia's disappeared and it's my fault."

"Oh, baby – "

"Don't." She pulled herself closer to the car door as though in fear I might try to touch her. "Don't be nice."

59

"It's going to be all right, Molly."

"I don't think so."

"We'll get through it."

"*We?* What are *we* going to do?"

The car had coasted almost halfway up the next hill. Gravity working against us now, we were slowing back to a stop. I pressed my foot against the accelerator and we began crawling upward again. "You are going to tell the truth, and me, I'm going to find Lydia."

We passed the Dairy, what the locals called the general store–ice cream stand–gas station run by the Masterson family out of their musty old house on the site of their defunct dairy farm. At the Dairy, Old Quarry Road forked, one branch going off to either side of the Masterson property. The left branch, trundling off to the northwest, became Swifton-Brank, and the right, curving back toward town, became Jackdaw Road. Ours was the first house on Jackdaw – or the last, depending on which direction you were headed.

I pulled into the drive, a smooth band of freshly sealed asphalt. The odor of tar and oil was thick. One of the first things Greg had seen to, when he struck the deal with my sisters, was getting the driveway paved. It was a long driveway. My grandfather had built at the rear of the property; the house was a good quarter mile from the road. When the weather was dry, any vehicle had raised an aurora of dust in the air. I'd tried to talk Greg out of the pavement. The dust was nice, I explained; it was good to be able to tell when someone was coming. Greg's two-word response to this and any other argument against his changes was simply "resale value."

For resale value, Greg had taken to mowing a swath of beach in the long grasses beside the algae-scummed pond my sisters and I had named Lake Yuck. He'd talked about getting a circulating pump installed to discourage mosquitoes, clear the scum, and make the pond more attractive for swimming. As we rolled past, I was happy to see another summer had passed without a pump. What would Lake Yuck be without the yuck?

Emma's bike was lying on its side up against the hedge of yews that boxed off the front lawn. Molly pointed at the bike and said, "That was there when I left yesterday." Her voice was soft with amazed gratitude, as though she had been surprised by a landmark in a place she felt lost. "There's Dad."

Greg was at the end of the drive, hauling plastic bags of peat moss out of the back of his truck and stacking them in the small barn we called the garage. Beside the garage was a group of sapling trees waiting to be planted, their roots bound in balls of burlap. He heard us approach, looked up, and waved with a single sweep of his gloved hand, then headed toward us, wiping his forehead against the rolled sleeve of his flannel shirt. He hadn't shaved; his hair was a couple weeks past needing a cut. His jeans were ripped at one knee and the lower pant leg was stained in dark red; he'd caught himself on something. Knowing the man as I did, knowing how he relied on converting helplessness into the numbness of physical work, I doubted he was even aware he'd injured himself.

Molly was out of the car before we'd stopped. Greg reached out to grab her, but head down, she avoided his grasp and ran for the house.

"Finally putting in your orchard?" I said, nodding at the tangle of trees as I got out of the car.

"Apples, some pears." He was watching the house where the screen door still bounced behind Molly's vanishing. He turned back to me. "I kept Emma home from school."

"Her tummy?"

"You know how she is when things get, um, tense. Paper this morning says there were other girls involved. Is Molly okay?"

"Yes. And no."

He sagged against the implication. His face, worn by the weather in his years on construction sites and by the emotional storms of his life with me, revealed the fear he thought he held private. The subtle shift in the line of his mouth, the ridges along his brow as his features pulled down in worry. He'd felt overwhelmed often in marriage, that I knew, but for the first time, he wasn't certain he could handle being a parent. The idea he was about to fail at one of the last things he was sure of appeared to be crushing his heart. "She told me she had a baby-sitting job that afternoon. She took her bike and – "

"Greg, you can't blame – "

"How bad is it?"

I shook my head. I had no words, but I could tell from the sinking light in his eyes that he'd understood well enough. We might be able to uncouple, but we'd never unmate. Part of us, the best and the worst and the rest of us, had gotten tangled together in a life once removed; that life, walking around in the tender shell of a thirteen-year-old girl, was hurting in a way we couldn't help. It was a pain beyond language. I walked over to Greg and put my arms around him. A moment later he returned the embrace, stiff-armed for a few seconds before he buried his head against my neck. And there we stood, holding each other in mutual acknowledgment of our limitations, pretending not to feel like strangers.

15

The window near his desk is open; the breeze comes in cool and you can hear the faraway booming of bitterns calling one another as they hide in the rushes at the edge of the water. You've seen them, necks stiff, bills lifted skyward, swaying like the grasses they are attempting to disappear into. You have no such camouflage. If he comes in here now, you are caught.

You listen to the muffled rhythms of the ax, counting each beat like the tick of a second hand on a slow-moving clock. The keys jumble and clank, in spite of your attempts to quiet them, as you locate the small one that unlocks the desk's bottom drawer. It will be in here. This is where he keeps important things.

The envelope in the drawer is bulky. You lift it, comparing the weight with the envelope you brought in with you. Shake yours a bit so the bulk is similarly displaced throughout the brown paper.

You switch the envelopes, close the drawer, lock it. Shove the envelope up the front of your shirt. The paper sticks to your sweating skin. Hurry. Out of his office. Lock it as he would. Tiptoe to the coat closet in the foyer and slip his key ring back in his jacket.

Tiptoe back up the stairs, back into your bedroom. You slide the envelope out from under your shirt and open the clasp. The hat, an orange baseball cap, is in a plastic zip-lock bag. You want to be rid of it, rid of the whole thing. You have to decide and decide quick. Once decided you can't ever go back.

You let the decision fall according to the gravity of what you need. He's your father and you, who have lost so much, cannot lose him, too. From your bedroom window you watch him work the ax.

telling

"She shouldn't be in there alone." Greg stood in the foyer near the closed French doors. Behind the doors, through the veil of sheers over the mullioned glass, our daughter sat at the end of the dining room table, her hands folded before her, her head down as though in prayer. Andrea Burnham, the detective the Swifton police sent over in response to my call, sat next to Molly. Detective Burnham was a youthful woman with a broad freckled face under a mass of rust-colored corkscrew curls. Her glasses were thick and dark-rimmed; those and the complete lack of makeup gave her the appearance of a shy, studious girl. She wore a gray gabardine pantsuit that showed the freckles on her neck and upper chest. Her chin was resting in her hands, her elbows on her knees, in effect making her smaller than Molly, whose statement was being taken on the tape recorder set up between them. Burnham handed her a legal pad and Molly started drawing or writing. We couldn't hear the detective's questions or Molly's answers, only the low, hesitant break and hum of their voices. Greg had positioned himself near the doors, and I was expecting him, at any moment, to press his ear directly to the glass.

He peered into the room again. "We should have called an attorney."

"Greg, she's a witness. She doesn't need an attorney. She just needs to tell them what she saw." I sat on the stairs, refolding the newspaper so that I could read through the story again. So far, Molly's version of the events had been only validated by the local press.

"Why can't we be in the room?"

"Because we can't. She'll edit herself to protect us from the information. That's what kids do; they protect themselves by protecting their parents."

"Yeah, I suppose."

"We'll be able to read the statement."

"It would be easier to hear it. Less real, you know." He looked down at his boots. "Why couldn't she tell me?"

"Too much to lose. It was less of a risk to tell me."

He glanced up. "But she did tell you. She ran away to tell you."

"Exactly. She didn't call me. She didn't wait forty-eight hours to see me. Molly got on a train and got the information as far away from you and Emma as she could get it. Protecting herself from what you might think of her for being at the party in the first place, for spying – " *What goes around comes around . . .*

"Les?" Greg had somehow rematerialized, hunkered down in front of me, his eyes searching mine. "You blanked out."

"No, I didn't. I'm tired. Problems sleeping last night. It was nothing." We'd reached a sort of unspoken détente for dealing with these moments. I didn't argue with his concern over the minutiae of my behavior; he didn't argue with my insistence that every little thing was fine. "Don't worry. Just a bit of *leakage* from the old imagination, I guess."

"Ah, yes."

"That was the best you could do?"

"Well, I couldn't think of any other way to explain the concept of a psychotic break to them. How should I handle it when Emma asks why you want to stay away from us?" His question held no sarcasm, no sharp edges at all, and I felt ashamed for my earlier assumption of hostility. But not too ashamed; the current situation had no doubt fostered much of his gentility. Greg, whether he would admit it or not, hated the unpredictability of my forever short-circuiting mental states, but then no more than I myself hated the sizzle of phantom sparks and faint whiffs of nonexistent ozone.

"This ongoing obligation to come up with a reasonable explanation for my unreasonable life is exhausting."

"So is never being able to stand down from the red alert level of vigilance." His expression softened. "Okay, let's not do this right now."

"How about let's not do this ever again?"

He extended his hand. "Deal." We shook on it, laughing at the knowledge the agreement would never last. Our laughter was cut short by Emma's pleading from the top of the stairs.

"Why do I have to stay up here?"

I leaned backward to look at her, a nine-year-old girl in a rumpled pink nightshirt, upside down. "You're sick enough to stay home from school? You stay in bed."

She pulled one of her dark pigtails further askew. "I'm bored."

"Then you're feeling better."

"So can I come down?"

"Sure. Get dressed and we'll take you to school."

She rubbed the bottom of one bare foot over the top of the other. "My stomach still hurts."

"Then get back in bed."

"I'm hungry."

"I'll poach you a couple eggs."

"Ew."

"Too bad. Poached eggs are what people with stomachaches eat."

"Dad let me have oatmeal cookies for breakfast."

I straightened. My vision swam and sparked. "Back to bed or back to school. Choose."

"This sucks." She stomped off to her bedroom.

"Indeed it does." I sneered at Greg. "Cookies?"

"They were *oatmeal* cookies." He sighed. "I know. I know. I couldn't do the hard-ass, dark-room-and-weak-tea bit with Emma this morning. Damn it, Les, *my* stomach hurts. I wanted someone to feel better – even if it meant cookies for breakfast."

"Got anything in a chocolate chip?" I smiled and reached out to push his hair off his forehead. "And maybe a big ol' glass of single malt to dunk them in?"

He had almost realized it was safe to smile back when the French doors burst open. Molly shot out of the dining room, caromed off the foyer wall as she grabbed her sweater, and without looking at us, plowed out the front door. Detective Burnham came into the foyer a minute later. She held the tape recorder and the legal pad. "I'll have this transcribed and bring it back. Molly can take a look at it. See if she wants to add anything."

Greg stood up. "You think she's left something out?"

Burnham shook her head and her curls bounced. "Not intentionally. But she's very embarrassed and I get the feeling she's hedging on details. She doesn't want to get anyone in trouble, and now that it looks like charges are being pressed – "

67

"Charges?" I stood as well, leaning on the banister. "Lydia turned up?"

"Nope. No sign of Lydia. Yet."

"Who's pressing charges, then?"

Burnham pointed at the newspaper I'd left lying on the stairs. "You've seen the reports. Other girls were involved. Some of the families are quite upset."

"Upset about what? Molly said nothing happened."

"Nothing? There was fondling, kissing. The girls were inebriated and therefore arguably unable to defend themselves. That is sexual assault. The degree has yet to be established."

"Molly swears Lydia instigated – "

"That's what the boys are swearing, as well. A, we have no Lydia, and B, the boys are in a whole mess of trouble – of course this is not going to be their fault. Mrs. Stone, I know who you are – " She grinned and adjusted her lenses so that she was looking at me over the top of the rims. – "What I meant to say was that I know of your background. This 'Lydia instigated it' should come as no surprise to you. What's always the first defense of the attackers in a gang rape? 'The victim led us on; the victim wanted it.' How else to justify standing around and watching another human being brutalized while you wait your turn?"

I kept my voice low. "This was an adolescent game of show-and-tell. Underage drinking? You got it. Bad judgment? Absolutely. Coercion? Maybe. But gang rape? Come on. If you're going to go with an argument of forced contact, the boys have as much a claim to violation as any of the girls."

"Says who?"

"Says Molly." Greg took a step toward the woman, who held up her hand indicating he should stop where he was.

"She's your daughter; of course, you believe her, Mr. Stone."

"And you don't?"

"Helplessness is a terrible thing. It can change what we see, what we remember seeing." She turned to me. "You know how witnesses get tangled up in their memories. Look, I don't think for an instant Molly is lying, but it strikes me as damn suspicious that every one of these kids is telling the exact same story with the exact same language."

"Maybe because what they're telling you is the truth," I said and crossed my arms over my middle, holding myself back.

"Maybe because they're telling me a truth they've rehearsed. Maybe, just maybe, Molly has adopted the rehearsed truth because she wasn't where she claims to remember being during the assault."

"What are you suggesting?" Greg's voice had gone flat with dread.

"Like I said before. Helplessness is a terrible thing. Hard to admit, you know?"

"Christ." Greg stared at me.

I wagged my head. "Until Molly tells us otherwise, it happened as she says it happened."

Burnham offered me a sigh and a hopeful smile. I recognized the expression from the dozens of times I'd offered the same to other shock-stricken parents. I recognized as well the sad lack of any authentic optimism behind it. "Be prepared for her story to change. I realize this is difficult. We can only hope Lydia turns up soon."

Preferring my anger to her resignation, I upped the ante in my daughter's favor. "Molly is of the opinion that Lydia is in hiding."

"Oh, the scenario is far more dramatic than that. According to Molly, Lydia isn't hiding, she's being hidden, against her will." Seen and raised.

"That's ridiculous." Greg narrowed his eyes. "Who would do that?"

Burnham beat me to the answer. "I think the implication is that the family is preventing the girl from coming forward with a less than attractive truth."

"That would be the implication." I felt my fists tighten. "At least the obvious implication. Perhaps someone should look into the possibility. I mean if we're really interested in testing Molly's story." Called.

"Mrs. Stone, I'm on your side here. More important, I'm on Molly's side." She pushed her glasses back up her nose, the magnification made her eyes huge. "Down at the station, my desk is up against the wall where they hang the pictures of the previous chiefs. So your father's portrait watches me work."

"And that is supposed tell me what?"

"Nothing, really – except I've read up on the Nightingale case, studied the evidence, his files and . . . again, nothing really. You know, we still consider it open, ongoing? We've reworked the evidence as technology has made new methods available. Your father didn't have facilities that we take for granted now. No one can blame him for that. I have a great deal of respect for his work in bringing the case down as far as he did. He caught a lousy break. But still, his is a great example of a good, persistent investigation. A great example I intend to follow." She didn't wait for my response but turned for the door. "Tell Molly that I'll be back in a couple hours with the transcript." She raised her hand over her shoulder in farewell and let herself out.

Greg exhaled. "What do we do? Do we come straight out and ask Molly if she was –" He rubbed his mouth as though he were trying to erase the words before they got into the world.

"No. We don't ask; we listen. And we are careful around Andrea Burnham. That reference to the Nightingale thing? Not good."

"But she seems all right. She seems to really care about Molly – "

"I don't like her. Too sure of herself."

"Funny. I was about to say she reminded me of" – he caught my warning flash of a glare – "someone I used to know."

The water was getting close to a boil; I poured a teaspoon of white vinegar into the pot. The acid kept the egg whites from spreading. My mother taught me how to poach eggs. It was one of the few memories I had of her that was not a conjured-up fiction founded on a photograph or a co-opted experience from my sisters' stories. A real memory, a moment with the woman I could actually summon forth on command. It was only a few days before she left us. I was almost five and sitting on the counter, in my bathing suit and sandals. I was lumpy with mosquito bites and covered with pink blotches of dried calamine. She had her hair up in a knot held in place by a leather band with a stick that slid through it. The leather was stamped with tiny yellow stars. Her ears were pierced with gold hoops. She was wearing a cotton nightgown and she smelled like the medicated powder she sometimes sprinkled on me after a bath. Her eyes were red from crying. It was dark outside, and she was showing me how to poach an egg. Measuring the vinegar in a spoon like it was cough syrup. Pinch of salt. Cracking the egg into a teacup. *Those egg contraptions are a waste of time . . .* I watched her watching the pot come to a boil. *A big boil, until it looks like the water is going to jump out of the pot, see?* She took the long-handled slotted spoon and began to stir the boiling water. *Stir hard, until it makes an empty place in the middle and then slip the egg into the middle of the empty place.* She removed the pot from the scarlet coils of the burner and placed it on a cool burner next to me. The cooking egg spun round and round the slowing vortex of steaming water. *The spinning keeps the egg together long enough for the heat to firm it up in a nice shape.* She set the timer – *it takes seven minutes* – and stood next to me at the counter as together we watched the spinning egg come to a stop and rest, cooking, at the bottom of the pot. I remember how her falling tears dripped and rippled across the surface of the scalding pool of water.

I watched the eggs chase each other around the bottom of the saucepan, then set the timer to the seven-minute mark. Through the kitchen window, I could see Molly, her back to me, sitting with her legs pulled tight to her chest on the weathered oak stump in the middle of the backyard. Every so often her hood would billow away from her head and she'd huddle farther into herself. The windows – Greg had yet to get the storm panels up – rattled as the house was buffeted by the building gusts of wind. A low bank of clouds was rolling in from the east, dark, cold, and heavy like an autumnal high tide. As the cloud cover overtook the afternoon, it channeled the sunlight into long angles that poured over the fields of the wind-tossed grasses, over my sullen, frightened child in a luminous wash of ambered gold.

I rapped at the window, trying to get Molly's attention and motion her to come inside where it was warm. If she heard me, she had decided to ignore it – probably in order to maintain some semblance of privacy. Where did kids today go? It was then I saw the oak restored, rising again magically in the magic gold light, Molly rising with it on one of the platform floors of the tree house. In full summer, when the tree was choked with leaves, my sisters and I would hide for hours, each in her own little room of the Swiss Family Robinson extravaganza our father had built for us. We'd sequester ourselves to read or we'd meet in the big "upstairs" area to whisper critiques about Dad's new girlfriends and float theories about what they might be doing after we went to sleep. We'd have elf wars in which we'd fend off invading tribes (errant squirrels) with tiny green acorns we'd pluck from the branches; after we scared off the squirrels, we'd ping each other. As I grew older, the fairy tale fortress in the tree lost its glitter and became what it always had been, recycled boards and barnwood planks, scratchy ropes and rusty nail heads that snagged my sweaters. Still, I had loved to haul myself up the ladder lashed to the trunk. The only way to make sense of the world was somehow to get out of it. High up in the stout branches of that massive old tree, I found quiet and solitude and a soothing for the mysterious, aching loneliness that I was beginning to realize was the price of living among other people. So much the better when Denise and Joanne found they'd rather surrender to the mystery than wonder about it and left the tree to me alone. Then, when I was just about Molly's age, nature chose to shut down my sanctuary with a million-volt zap of finality, and I'd taken myself to the attic to continue my befuddled hermitage.

But now, where did kids around here go? To school. To malls. To parties, of course. I wished that Molly and Emma had a tree house, and I could lift them above the continual bombardment of noise that defined their world. I wished I could give them quiet. I wished I could have given them a childhood. But the big-branched trees of Swifton Woods were long gone, and I had hit what little bit of shelter they'd known with my million-volt breakdown. When I thought about it later – much later – lightning striking the oak tree that evening had sounded exactly like the gun I fired in the Interview Room. The results had been the same: Childhoods ended all around.

Molly unclasped her knees, stretched her legs out in front her, and shook them. She stood up and headed for the garage. I rapped at the window again. This time she turned around. She mimed steering unsteady handle bars and then pointed in the direction of the Dairy. Bike ride. Good idea. I tapped at my wrist, raised my finger to indicate one hour. She nodded and disappeared in the shadows of the barn; a few seconds later she was coasting down the incline ramp of the garage entrance, gaining some speed before pedaling away.

I finished up Emma's lunch tray: the eggs, saltines, and big glass of tepid water designed to make the most noxious offerings of the Swifton Woods Elementary School's cafeteria seem palatable by comparison. As much empathy as we felt for Em's anxiety-driven maladies, it had become clear that our attempts to provide reassurance though humoring her imaginary discomforts had further undermined her sense of security. When we'd finally caught on to the fact that *she* couldn't make out whether the stomachaches were real or not, and what she wanted from us was some indication of how worried she should be, we stopped worrying and treated her as though we were clued in to the ruse. The number and duration of stomachaches had decreased dramatically. One Monday morning last spring, when Em had surprised us by getting on the bus even though she didn't feel well because "school was easier than being sick," Greg and I had exchanged a few high-fives, after the last of which he didn't let go of my hand. We'd lived apart for a long time, but our desire for each other was still intricately cross wired, and although we were able to discipline old physical attractions, a moment of shared happiness, that most illicit and reckless of indulgences, made us horny as hell. Before we knew what was happening, we were kissing and halfway up the stairs to bed to celebratory sex, propelled by nostalgia and the overwhelming joy of having gotten one right. And then, as his fingers slid up the sides of my spine and around and under the edge of my bra, I had remembered we were separated and separation seemed, by definition, to preclude this sort of celebration. I had pulled away from him, laughing at my own weakness, reminding him we didn't do this anymore. He laughed and grabbed my wrist, pulling me upward, and reminded me there was nothing stopping us. I told him to let go. He let go. *Nothing stopping us but you.* As I tucked my shirt back in my jeans – *yeah, that's right, me* – I explained not wanting to undo the pleasant novelty of competency with another confusion-inducing mistake.

Getting our marriage back together would be a mistake?
  Greg, you don't really think going to bed is going to fix anything, do you?
  It would be a step in the right direction.
  If we're looking to plummet farther into disaster –
  Our marriage is a disaster?
  Greg, we aren't exactly married anymore.
  Whose fault is that –
  Greg –
  – and since when does being married or not play into your decisions of who you're going to –

And we were off. Greg on the stairs, me below him in the foyer, shouting invectives at each other, as though in some weird inverse of a Shakespearean balcony seduction. Only death was going to end our fighting. Fighting suited us better than sex, anyway. We understood fighting; the inevitable infliction of hurt was out in the open and undisguised. Besides, we both knew what to do after a fight. One of us left, and the other one was happy for the leaving. The advantage of the separation was that we tended to be careful of our timing; we fought when the girls weren't around as if trying to sell them on the benefits of the breakup. *See? No yelling. Isn't that better?*

Better. I could hear Emma singing to herself, a tuneless variation of one of the songs Molly had been pursuing on the radio in the car. She was sitting up in her bed, which was strewn with books – mostly preschool picture books and early readers she'd long outgrown. I set the tray on her lap and mirrored back the scrunched-up look of disgust she gave me in thanks for the meal. She poked at the eggs with the spoon. I felt her forehead and sat down on the edge of her bed.

"How much did you hear?"

She spooned the yolks over the whites. "Of what?"

"Of anything that might make you worry."

"I heard stuff at school, yesterday. On the bus, really."

"Anything you want to talk about?"

"Lydia Parrish ran away because she got caught having a sex party."

The incongruity of Emma's voice and those words had to ricochet around my head for a couple seconds before I could respond. "That's one way of putting it."

"Is it true?"

"Well, Lydia Parrish seems to have run away. And there was a party. And some sexual sort of things may have happened, but we're still trying to figure out exactly who did what."

"Oh." She crumbled a saltine over the destroyed eggs. "Is Molly okay?"

"Molly is sad and kind of angry, but I think she's okay. She will be."

Emma nodded. "I bet she's sad and angry 'cause of Tim Zinni."

"Tim Zinni?"

"It's part of a secret. I'm not supposed to tell."

"Hmmm." I picked up a saltine from the tray and broke it in half. "But Molly already told me Tim Zinni was at the party." I nibbled on the corner of the cracker as I tried to finesse my nine-year-old out of information she'd probably taken a blood oath to keep quiet. I recited the list as Molly had given it in the sudden confession of details she'd indulged Greg and me with right before Andrea Burnham had arrived. "It was Tim, Chad Hyatt, Mark Delacroix, Tyler Endicott, and Joey Pickering – is that right?"

"Those were the names everyone was saying on the bus yesterday. There were girls, too."

"Yes, I know about the girls. See? Not so big a secret."

"That's not the secret part."

"Em?"

She put the eggy spoon in the glass of water, rendering the last bit of the meal inedible. "I promised."

"It's important to keep your promises. It's also important that we help Molly." I stood up. "You think about it some more while I get you dessert."

"Dessert?" Her eyes widened and then shut down to slitted suspicion. "You already had cookies, didn't you?"

"I promised I wouldn't tell."

"Just think about it."

I was almost out of the room when she said, "Mom, I don't want to, ever . . ."

"Ever what, sweetheart."

"You know. Go to parties."

"I hear you. Back in a minute." I pulled Emma's door closed. Across the hall, the door to Molly's room, what had once been my room, was closed. Molly would be gone for another half hour minimum. I despised the idea of what I was about to do, but I was perfectly in my rights, concerned mother that I was. *A concerned mother who is also a professional investigator.* Bad enough that I was going to search her room, but I was going to do it in a such a manner that she'd never know I'd been in there. I wanted Molly's unquestioning trust, but more than that, for her sake, for my own, I needed to know the size of what she was up against, and a thirteen-year-old girl does not have a fully formed grasp of scale.

Was there such a thing as doing wrong for the right reason? The answer to that one I'd learned long ago, but my responsibilities to my daughter's well-being smudged the line between right and wrong to the same deep, stormy grays of the approaching weather above us. I opened Molly's door, trying to feel moral vindication in the fact that at least I'd taken a few seconds to debate the necessity of the trespass.

1 4

You hurry into the kitchen and start making lunch. Two sandwiches for him. Nothing for yourself. You dice leftover chicken from the dinner your sister Denise made, mix the chicken with chopped celery and mayo. You heap this onto slices of wheat toast topped with tomato and lettuce. Put out a bowl of potato chips and pour ice tea. He comes in, smelling of work and Old Spice cologne. He washes his hands at the sink and sits down at the table. "Pretty fancy. What's the special occasion?" You shrug because you can't tell him that lunch is the beginning of an apology for the betrayal, although you're not quite sure who has betrayed whom.

He asks why you aren't eating. Press your hand to your belly and frown. He frowns back and nods his head as though he understands. Ever since your mother took off, he's been left trying to convince you he understands the mysteries that you and your sisters have to live with. He takes a bite of the sandwich and winks at you. "This is great." You notice the bruises, deep bluish purple staining the entire ridge of knuckles on his right hand. Even though you know how he got them, you ask. "Oh, this?" He turns over his hand and considers the injury. "Must have slammed my hand into something." He doesn't lie. But he doesn't tell the truth, either. "Can't recall. Didn't hurt." You hope he's right, but you doubt it.

He mistakes your expression of revulsion for one of worry. "Really, Les, it doesn't hurt." He then says the tree is almost finished. He asks if you want to come out and help him stack wood. Sure, you tell him. After you clean up the kitchen and change your clothes – oh, and check to make sure you don't have any homework. About an hour, maybe.

"Forget it." He laughs. "In an hour I have to leave for work." The laughter dies out. "Could get busy tonight." He doesn't say any more than that – he doesn't talk about his job with you or Denise or Joanne. Still, you know what he means. You know more about it than he'd dare to imagine. He finishes his second sandwich, drains his glass of tea, letting a partially melted ice cube slide into his mouth. "Dat was verwy good, Pwinsess. Tanks." He smiles, then bites into the ice. Crunching ice sounds like breaking bone. You jump up and clear his plates, taking them to the sink to rinse. He tells you to come on out; you don't have to work, just come on out and keep him company. "All right," you say, turning the hot water on full blast. "Let me change my clothes."

He leaves the kitchen, letting the screen door bang. You watch through the steamy windows over the sink, the shape of him as he picks up the ax. *Go. Go now. You don't have much time.*

Turn off the taps and run to the living room. Lift the couch cushion and grab the envelope. Hurry. Hurry to the foyer, to the closet where he hangs his old leather jacket. You hear the jangle of metal as you turn the jacket toward you. A man of order, your father keeps things where he expects to find them: His keys are always in the right side pocket of this jacket with his wallet and his badge. Your fingers hit the key ring. Pull it out slow. Quiet. Three steps to the office door. Unlock it. You're in.

The window near his desk is open; the breeze comes in cool and you can hear the faraway booming of bitterns calling one another as they hide in the rushes at the edge of the water.

m o l l y

It's colder than she thought it would be, riding into the wind. Molly pedals down Old Quarry–Brank Road as fast as she can, not so much for the speed but because it feels so good to move. For the past week she has felt like the rubber band in one of the toy airplanes that Rita's brothers love so much; each minute of each day has got her twisted tighter and tighter to the point she's been sure that any second she's going to snap. Now it is unwinding in a numb frenzy through her legs. Faster. Faster. A bit faster still, and she's sure she's going to leave the earth. Take off like Elliot, the kid in *E.T.* Like Elvira Gulch in *Wizard of Oz*. She sees herself as the wicked witch on the bicycle, and her heart drops like Dorothy's house.

The edge of the paper bag from the Dairy is getting damp with sweat as she holds it, steering the bike with one hand. She had made her purchases quick as she could. She didn't want to be hanging around when the high school let out and the older teenagers started wheeling into the parking lot to spend the afternoon sitting on their car hoods, eating junk food and talking. Molly knows what they'll be talking about, laughing about; she doesn't yet know if her name has percolated the surface of the gossip. It is bound to happen soon, and she doesn't want to be pinned at the ice cream counter unable to avoid listening as someone says someone had told him it was some kid named Molly Stone whom the teacher at the junior high had overheard.

She reaches the Turnbull farm and steers onto the dirt drive, past the No Trespassing signs. The signs had gone up when the Turnbull family sold everything last spring to somebody who hadn't yet decided what to do with the place. She rides past the house, a shingled saltbox with boarded-up windows. The lawn is near knee-deep. The boxwood hedges are scraggly with untrimmed shoots and the flower beds thick with stinging nettles. Molly rides out behind the barn chained shut with padlocks, to Mrs. Turnbull's old greenhouse – broken and always open to wind and rain and girls looking for solitude.

Molly had discovered the greenhouse one June afternoon spent wandering with the intent of avoiding her chores back at home. She'd pedaled up the driveway to see where it went and had found the tiny greenhouse. More than half the glass panes were busted. The place where the door had been was empty. The interior was a mess of broken glass and shards of terra-cotta pots scattered on the low, warped wood shelving. It smelled of earth and mossy green growth. She'd hauled herself up to sit on the potting table, and sat there for an hour maybe, watching chipmunks forage among the rubbish on the fieldstone floor as far away the sump-pump call of the bitterns throbbed. Quiet and alone. Nothing more than that. Yet when she finally began the bike ride home, she'd felt like she'd stumbled into another universe, a place only she knew about – knowledge she had to protect. From whom she couldn't say.

Over the summer she has come here almost daily. Stopping at the Dairy for snacks or a soda, she brings along a book she is reading or her music or the journal she is trying to keep because it seems like an important, grown-up thing to do. She didn't write much, however, because writing filled her head with words, sounds, voices posing unsolvable riddles; what she really wanted was quiet. It was the only thing that seemed to soothe the bitternlike throb of emptiness in the middle of her heart.

She wants quiet today. More than anything, just a little quiet. An hour. That is long enough only to get to the greenhouse and get back. She doesn't want to risk being late, or worse, not being there at all when the policewoman comes back. They'd come looking for her. She couldn't risk them finding her here.

Molly dismounts from the bike and walks it onto the fieldstone floor. The tires shift and crunch the already broken glass. She leans the bike against the table and opens the bag: a couple cans of diet soda, string cheese, chocolate-covered pretzels, single-serving cups of applesauce, and batteries for the CD player. Some for now, some for later.

Molly is closing the bag, wondering how long the stuff will keep, when she hears the footsteps. Careful steps that nonetheless cause the glass to crunch beneath them. Molly closes her eyes. No.

The footsteps stop, inches away. The voice is soft, breathless from running.

"Molly? Come on, Molly. Don't be pissed, okay?"

Molly snaps her eyes open, snaps her head to glare at the intruder. "What is wrong with you? You're supposed to wait until it gets dark."

"I know." Lydia combs her mittened fingers through the dirty blond bangs protruding from the edge of her sweatshirt hood, flattening her hair against her forehead. "I saw you come up the driveway. It's scary in that house by myself. I don't like being by myself all night. There are noises and shit."

"It's only a couple more days, max." Molly hands the bag of food to Lydia. "This is only going to work if you stay missing long enough for them to be more worried about you than they are freaked out about what happened at the party."

"What if they find me before that?"

"They are *supposed* to find you, remember? You just can't make it easy for them. Like I said, Lydia, if they figure you're upset enough to run away they're going to go real easy on you no matter what."

"You're sure?"

"Yeah, I'm sure. It's really simple. You hang out in the house. They get more worried. They forget about the stupid party. My mom finds you. Everyone is happy. You don't have to do anything but not get found. I'll come by and leave stuff every day – but you have to wait until nighttime to come get it. The only way this doesn't work is if I get caught with you."

"Okay. I'll wait until no one can see me. Can I get some more candles or a bigger flashlight – and a blanket, maybe? It's colder than I thought it would be."

"I'll bring what I can; I did bring you more batteries for your stereo. I have to get going."

"It's so freaking scary, you know? And lonely. I want someone to talk to. Or TV. Or something."

"I know this is hard, but so far everything is going like we planned it. Just pretend – pretend it's like a big game of hide-and-seek. Remember how we used to play that up at your place? Pretend you found a great place to hide."

"Yeah, but for how long?"

Molly takes the handlebars of her bike and starts to walk away. "Like I said, a couple days. Three or four at the most."

"That long?"

"Probably not. I'm leaving clues all over the place."

"I hate hide-and-seek."

"Stay out of sight until my mom comes looking for you. No matter who shows up around here – it has to be my mom who finds you."

"I'll try. But Molly?"

"Yeah?"

"Why are you doing this for me?"

Molly shrugs. "Not sure." A less than honest answer. She steers the bike out of the greenhouse; left foot on the pedal, she gets the bike moving before lifting herself onto the seat. She knows that if she had told Lydia the whole plan, Lydia would probably kill her. For real. Molly heads for home without looking back.

ten thousand things
to remember

I started at the bed, moving systematically and with care. Under the mattress. Under the pillow. Behind the headboard. The bedroom of any thirteen-year-old girl was worthy of the sort of evaluation usually reserved for the interior chambers of the great pyramids; display and concealment shared equal importance in the design. Meaning had to be read in layers. Intruders were anticipated, so misdirection was every-where. Like an archaeologist or a thief, I had no idea of the value of what might be discovered, but I was driven by an overriding sense that there was something here to be found.

I ran my hand behind the glossy posters of singers and actors and hyperreality television shows she'd taped up over her butterfly-print wallpaper. I pulled books from her bookshelf and looked not only in but also under her jewelry box, the underside of it, the underside of the drawers in her bureau. Behind and between the dozens of beanbag animals she'd collected. Inside the pockets of the sweaters hanging in her closet, inside her shoes. The top shelf of the closet appeared in disarray. Two stacks of Molly's outgrown clothing, one on either side of the shelf, had tipped over into the middle as though the item that had held them in place was missing. This empty space on the closet shelf only amplified what I hadn't been able to locate.

Her desk drawers held pens and gum and bottles of glittery fingernail polish, letters I'd sent her from the hospital, birthday and Christmas cards, a couple of paperback novels in the bodice-ripping tradition that I'd prefer she not be reading, half-finished friendship bracelets in knotted rainbows of embroidery floss, birthday cake candles with burned wicks held together with a rubber band, a stapled sheaf of printed text that looked to be episode-by-episode recaps of the *Eden* show she'd been watching last night – countless artifacts of Molly's adolescent existence and not one clue as to what they might mean to her.

I closed the top two drawers, but the bottom one jammed a third of the way in. It had been shut completely and had opened easily enough a minute earlier. Something was blocking it. I pulled the drawer all the way out, expecting to find a wayward pair of socks. It wasn't socks. The envelope Molly had tried to tape underneath the drawer had pulled free and become wedged between the drawer runner and the floor. The seams of the envelope were close to ripping because it was stuffed so fat with papers, the whole of the accumulation held together with a rubber band. I dislodged the packet and in the process caught a loose edge on the flap, which tore almost completely free. She would know I'd found it, no way to cover my tracks. I might as well see what she was safekeeping in secret.

I worked the stretched-to-its-limits rubber band off the envelope. My heart cringed; I felt I was betraying what may have been the final shred of trust between Molly and me. I could almost hear the shriek of fury when she discovered what I'd done. Maybe, if I were careful enough, I could get everything back the way she had it . . . No such luck; the rubber band burst and the envelope spilled open, sending book pages, pieces torn from newspapers, magazines, index cards swirling in slow drift to the floor. I looked down at the pile of print fanning out at my feet. I recognized key words, bold print of headlines among the jumble: AMY. MURDER. INSANITY. No point reading any further, it was pretty clear what Molly had been collecting.

I tried to ignore the words as I bent down and began to stuff Molly's clippings back inside envelope. I tossed the envelope in the bottom drawer and nudged it. It slid smoothly shut. I understood why Molly had those clippings and why she'd hidden everything as well. It was a part of her life, too, a dangerous part that she could neither embrace nor disavow. We never talked about what had had happened. We couldn't yet.

Saddened again by my daughter's burdens, I sat down at her desk. Molly's efforts to cope had manifested in a high need for order. Her desk was always just so, with her schoolbooks piled in a neat pyramid stack. She'd covered each of them with brown paper cut from grocery bags and then decorated the covers with intricate zigzag patterns in sparkling, near-transparent ink. Each book, although done in a differing set of colors, was covered with the same design:

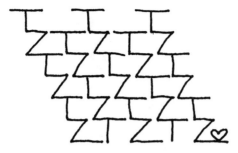

Had it not been for the tiny heart drawn at the bottom right corner on the cover of the top book, I might have dismissed Molly's Rosetta Stone as just another piece of rock. That little heart, tucked into the stair-step angle, changed the relationship of the lines. The zigzag pattern was made up of alternating *T*'s and *Z*'s. Tim Zinni. That was the big secret? Molly had a crush on her classmate? *I wasn't invited.* She had followed him to Lydia's party; that's why she was there. I'd have laid money on that one. My daughter, the stalker. No wonder she was so adamant about the boys' innocence – except, except, except: Her need to have Tim be innocent – or worse, her desire to impress him with her loyalty – might have motivated a deliberate revision of the facts. I'd found what I'd hoped I wouldn't. Molly had a reason to lie.

I checked my watch. She still had a good twenty minutes before she was due back. From the window I could see the grasses in the fields behind us bending before the wind. The sky had pulled itself so low that the bellied swell of the clouds threatened to graze our rooftop. Rain was coming and the cold of the wind was sure to blow Molly home sooner rather than later. A sturdy gust rolled across the field, flattening the grasses and whistling through the eaves of the roofline. Above me, in the attic, something fell with a thump. The wind had probably blown out one of the vent screens – steel mesh in a frame that fit over the slats of the vents to discourage entry of birds and insects. When the wind hit the house at a particular angle, it could knock the screen right out of its clips. Making certain the screen was in place had been my job after the big storms. It was during this chore that I was struck with idea of using the attic after the tree house became off limits.

Another thump sounded above me, followed by the heavy, rhythmic thud of someone walking from one end of the attic to the other. It sounded like Greg. He must have learned of the problem with the screens from my sisters – most likely from one of Denise's infamous lists of Ten Thousand Things to Remember. God knows I had never talked about this place with Greg except to try to talk him out of taking it on. But it was Greg's sort of deal: live here rent free in exchange for taking care of the place and watching the land values. When the prices peaked, he was to sell, and the profits would be split three ways among the families. Greg's idea of taking care of a place was to reinvent it along the lines in the do-it-yourself magazines he pored through: *I turned a three-bedroom ranch house into a five-story Victorian mansion.* I told him that his work would be eventually razed for some strip mall; he told me he found that appropriate.

He was putting the screen back in place. I could hear the aluminum frame squealing, metal sliding over metal, as he secured it back behind the clamps. Seemed silly to do it right then with the wind howling; maybe he was going to fasten them in more thoroughly. I looked out into the sky. Darker still. The side door on the garage hadn't been closed properly and so had blown wide open. The doorknob was banging against the garage siding. It had a way of doing that. I was thinking I'd better get in the car and go find Molly, when Greg appeared in the yard. He was pushing the wheelbarrow filled with bags of peat toward the garage. I looked up at the ceiling. Above me, the intermittent squeak and squeal stopped. Footsteps overhead. The squeaking noise began again. Not the screens. It was nails being pulled out of wood. Not in the right place. But close.

I stood up. I walked as calmly as I could from the dimness of Molly's bedroom, across the hall, and into Emma's room where she was drawing flowers on her forearm with a ballpoint pen.

"Do you hear that?" I asked her, pointing toward the ceiling where the footsteps were moving again, in a hurry now, directly over our heads. The squealing of nails started up. Searching. "Do you?"

"Hear what?" She didn't raise her eyes from the art project on her skin. "I thought about – "

"Later, Em."

"What about my dessert?"

"Later." I walked back into the hallway and looked up at the access panel to the attic. The cord pull with its faded tassel, now frayed and almost denuded of fringe, was swaying slightly as though caught in a draft of invading wind. I watched the back and forth of it slow, coming to a halt like the pendulum of a clock that had gone unwound. Outside of time, that's where I felt I'd stumbled, and in the cessation of the sequential forward motion of moments, the footsteps began again from the area over Emma's bed toward me. Stopping above where I stood. Waiting.

The doctors had offered me the scientific, psychological explanation of the whole ghost deal: Ghosts were the stories we would not or could not listen to; unable to speak and unwilling to be silenced, the stories manifested themselves externally in an attempt to force a confrontation with the unacceptable. That was why the ambivalence was always centered on belief in the haunting rather than on the significance of being haunted. To accept that significance would be to acknowledge and to acknowledge would be to know and to know might prove unbearable, so it is easier to get stuck in a debate over what we can believe of our experience. Well, the scientific was all fine and good fun until a moment such as the one I had fallen into – or out of – when my blood went to liquid nitrogen and my bones froze to a shatter-ready brittleness and I would have sworn I could see my own breath, iced as it was from the inside; that was if I could have made myself breathe.

How had I gotten from there to here? I didn't recall having walked an inch, and yet the cord was hanging directly before me, and I was reaching up, my hand closing above the tassel, shoulders tensing as I began to pull the panel open. Harder than I remembered. I had it open four or five inches when my arm was jerked upward by a forceful tug in the other direction. The panel smacked shut. I pulled again and met resistance, something pulling back. I wrapped both hands around the cord, leaned into the pull with my full weight, dragging the panel open. Six inches. Twelve. The cord snapped with violent upward yank, burning my hands and throwing me off balance. I landed in a heap on the floor, heard the panel slam, and turned quickly to see the last of the cord disappearing up through the brass grommet. The knot on the tassel stopped its progress. The knot rammed against the opening with increasing fury until whatever it was gave up the fight and allowed the cord to snake slowly back through the grommet until it was in the original position, swaying, tassel fringe shimmying ever so slightly. Bait.

We were in the dining room. Burnham had granted us spectator status as long as A, it was all right with Molly, and B, we didn't interrupt. The detective had arrived almost on Molly's heels, and Greg had shepherded them inside about two seconds before the downpour hit. I offered to make hot cocoa as though steaming mugs of chocolate would make this meeting benign, just a little chat among friends on a cold autumn afternoon. Greg and Molly had regarded me with similar expressions of dismay at the prospect of dragging this out further with absurd rituals of hospitality, but Burnham – probably trying to get a few minutes to talk to Molly outside my supervision – had said yes, hot cocoa would be grand.

So there we sat, in the brightness of the chandelier, each of us with an untouched mug brimming with cooling chocolate and swollen, soggy marshmallows, as we listened to the rain pelt the windows and watched Molly review her statement.

"That's everything." Molly handed the pages back to Andrea Burnham.

"You're sure there's nothing you want to add?"

"I'm sure." Molly's cheeks, nose, and chin were still crimson from the bike ride. The rest of her face was very pale, almost as pale as the ivory-colored turtleneck sweater she wore. She'd clipped her wind-whipped hair back in a thick ponytail at the base of her neck, stray tendrils clung damply at her temples and close to her ears. "Do I have to sign it or something?"

"You're not fourteen yet, so the law sees you as a child and therefore not accountable to things like signatures. But I can see you are a serious, thoughtful young lady; signing it is a good idea." Burnham took off her glasses and leaned closer to Molly. "As long as you understand that by signing this statement, you would be promising not only to me, but to everyone, your friends, Lydia, that this is the truth."

Greg sighed. "Damn right she understands that."

"Mr. Stone." Burnham fixed him with a warning stare. "Molly?"

"Yes. I understand."

Burnham nodded. "Okay. But before you sign off on this, I want you to take a look at something." She pulled a folded sheet of yellow legal paper from the file folder she'd brought the statement in. "Remember this? This is the picture you drew for me this morning when I asked you where you had been standing at the window over at the Parrish house."

Molly unfolded the paper. I couldn't see what was on it; Molly studied it for a while and then shrugged. "That's what I drew. That X right there? That's where I was."

"And you drew the window as best you could from what you remembered?"

"I'm not an artist or anything, but that's what I remember."

"You draw just fine." Burnham smiled at Molly. "But I have a question." She reached in the folder again and took out a black-and-white photograph, an eight-by-ten, and slid it over to Molly. "This is a picture of that window at Lydia's house."

"When was this taken?"

"That's not important right now, what's important is that you have the details down except for one. See?"

"The plants in the window?"

"Yeah. The plants. Plants hanging from the ceiling, plants on the shelves, plants on the floor. Lydia's family has a regular jungle going in that window."

"But you can see around them, through the leaves."

"Yep. And it would obviously make it a bit more difficult for someone inside the house to see out, don't you think? Kind of like a duck blind – "

Greg again. "Do you know what a duck blind is, Mol?"

"Shush." I put a finger to my lips.

"I know what a duck blind is." She lowered her head. "I hadn't thought about the plants."

"You didn't worry about whether the kids inside could see you?"

"Not really. They were busy. I was down low."

"That's right. You told me; you were hunched down by the sill. But what I want to know is were the plants there last weekend during the party?"

Molly raised her head and blinked a couple times. "No. There were no plants in the window last week. I don't remember plants being in the window."

89

"You're sure?"

Greg cleared his throat. "Memory can be tricky."

"Jeez, Dad, give me a chance. Yeah, I'm sure. I'd think I'd remember all those plants."

Burnham glanced up at Greg and me, her mouth set in a grim line of concern. "I'd think you'd remember them, too."

Molly's voice went up in pitch. "What does it matter if I remember plants or no plants, anyway? It's like you're not going to believe me or anybody else until you talk to Lydia – "

"And Lydia's being hidden away?"

"I don't know. It seems weird that she'd take off when her friends – "

"She left a note, Molly."

"She did?" My daughter knotted up her forehead in confusion. "I didn't know there was a note. Well, notes can be, you know, faked? Somebody could have forced her to write it." Molly stood up. "So do I have to sign something or what?"

"Let's hold off on that for a couple days. I'd like to arrange a videotaping of your statement."

"Do it again? Why? Don't you believe me?"

"What I believe, Molly, is that you are a good person who thinks she is helping some people she cares about very much. What I want is you to help yourself."

"I don't need help. Lydia is the one who needs help."

"So help her."

"I'm trying." Molly hit the table with her fists and then pushed away, storming out of the room, up the stairs.

Burnham looked at us. "She's your kid. What do you think?"

Greg leaned back in his chair and made a scoffing sound. "Oh, we're allowed to talk now?"

Burnham put her glasses back on. "I can only imagine how difficult this is for you."

"No, you can't," said Greg.

I shook my head at Greg; it would be a mistake for Burnham to think of both of us as antagonistic to her cause. "What's with the plants?"

The detective closed her eyes in thought. She was trying to gauge how much information she could give without damaging the quality of the information she hoped to collect. Assessments made, she opened her eyes. "We have some discrepancies in the statements. Each of the other kids, when asked the exact location of the party, each of them said something to the effect of the front room with 'all the plants in the window.' Molly is the only one to say differently."

"You think Molly's lying about being there?" Greg sounded relieved by the possibility of his daughter's dishonesty.

"It's not that easy," I answered for her. The name Tim Zinni buzzed like a stunned wasp bouncing around my brain. "If the detective here thought Molly was lying, she would have called her on it."

"As soon as the word came in from the principal of the junior high school, I went out to talk to Mr. and Mrs. Parrish about what was happening, to find out what they knew. This was before Lydia disappeared, before we'd taken any statements. No plants were in that window. Not a damn plant in the house."

"So she's telling the truth?" Greg's shoulders dropped.

"You might be a better judge of that." Burnham slid Molly's statement toward Greg. "What I know is that she's telling a story. The truth will emerge when we get all the stories told."

Greg sighed, reached across the table, and picked up the pages of Molly's statement. I watched his face as he began to read; I watched until I couldn't watch any longer. When I looked away, I met Andrea Burnham's gaze.

"What is your sense of this?" she asked quietly, smiling at me with the sort of compassionate pity that triggered the instant deployment of my iron-plated distrust.

"You asking the inadequate mother or the disgraced cop?"

Before Burnham could answer, Molly was shouting from the top of the stairs, "Who the fuck was in my bedroom?"

The detective's expression of pity slid into a grin of coconspiratorial appreciation. "Who went through the room? Mom or cop?"

"Does it matter?" I got up from the table, ready to go forestall Molly's indignation with a lecture on the etiquette of swearing when one has guests. "She's the daughter of both."

13

You fear you may drown inside your own mind. Information is suffocating. Words tumble and better one another against the feeble efforts of your own voice to dam up the cacophony: *shut up, shut up, shut up* . . . Panic is about to slip its moorings.

Exhausted, sick, you close the notebook. You can reread these newspaper articles, trace your drawing lines and circles only so many times – and you've been doing so for hours. You have tried and tried and are still trying to see what your father has seen, the shading of information that made him so sure. But you don't see it, and even if you could, what he has done would still be wrong. Wouldn't it?

And yet, after church, he changed out of his suit, put on his dungarees and his old flannel shirt, announced that he was going out to work on the tree as he's done almost every Sunday since the start of summer. It's as though nothing has changed. Maybe nothing has. Maybe this is the way things have always been, the *real* world he and your sisters keep telling you that you're not ready for. Is this what they felt when your mother left them behind and you were too young, too small for the reality of her leaving? Maybe this state of shock is only a sounding of the depths of your selfish preoccupation; maybe you should be grateful that the blindness of childhood has at last fallen away. Grateful or not, you can see now. The day is full of unforgiving light, and you fear your eyes will burn from the unrelenting clarity of everything. You will end up blind again, but this time you will know it.

The orange baseball cap. That's what they remembered, those who were able to remember. His face had been distorted by the stocking and their fear. So they remembered the hat. It was an odd color, they said, not the brilliant orange hunters used, but almost rust. Odd but surely not the only one. A person could drive to a store and buy one anywhere. And now there's an odd orange cap, odder still for the blood soaked into it, locked in your father's desk.

In a plastic bag. In a brown paper envelope. Evidence supplies like the ones he gave you, in good-natured solemnity, when you told him years ago that you wanted to be a cop, too, and you were helping with the investigation. You were twelve. He could not have known that one day you'd be investigating him. Neither could you.

You have to get rid of that hat. It's proof either way; you have to get rid of the hat – without your father realizing it's gone. Switch it. But with what? He's going to recognize any of your old softball caps or the ones he's bought you as souvenirs at ball games. And then you remember. *What goes around comes around. Buddy.* You go to the old toy chest at the foot of your bed. You use the chest now to store the clothes you've outgrown or worn through but love too much to add to the charity bins at church. Near the bottom you find the university sweatshirt that belonged to your mother, the one with the kangaroo pocket in front. Denise and Joanne wore it threadbare before they gave it to you. You remember only because you were wearing it on the night of the storm. Work your hand into the pocket. Sure enough, the hat is still there. Three years, nearly, and it's still there. The color is almost the same, isn't it? Not rust, coppery – but brighter. It will have to do.

Get a plastic zip-lock bag from your desk. Seal up the hat. Stick it in an envelope, lick the glued strip on the flap, put the brad through the hole, and spread the prongs to close it. You hope it looks right. Hope it sounds right as the plastic slips around the interior. Feels right in weight.

Go. Go now.

Halfway down the stairs, you hear the back door creak open. He hollers your name, "Les!"

Freeze. "Yeah?" Your voice sounds creakier than the hinges.

"You getting hungry? Want me to make you some lunch?"

"That's all right. I'll make us something."

"That would be great, Princess. I'll finish up this little bit and be in. Around ten minutes?"

"Sure."

The back door bangs shut and with it your ability to think. You dash the rest of the way down the stairs. No time. Hide it. The sofa in the front room no one uses. Under the cushions. Until he goes back outside.

You stop in the foyer and wipe the sweat from your hands on your skirt. Breathe. In. Out. Swallow. Move. You have a distinct sense that this is not you. You are watching yourself as you hurry into the kitchen and start making his lunch.

crushing for juice

Amanda Parrish had answered the phone with the tentative *hello?* of a woman who wanted desperately for her daughter to be on the other end of the line. When I told her it was me, Leslie Stone, she had paused before responding as though her mind had to once again process the fact of Lydia's absence. Ever the embodiment of graciousness, Amanda's first words, upon regaining her balance, had been of happiness to hear from me; it had been such a long time. I had agreed and then, in order to spare her the energy of feigning small talk, asked if she thought there might be anything I could do to help. She broke down for only a few seconds, then composed herself well enough to ask if there was anything *I* thought I could do.

And so she was waiting for me, sitting in one of the wicker rocking chairs on the veranda, when I drove up to the house. It was almost five o'clock, although the low, clouded sky made it seem much later. The wind-driven lashes of rain had slackened to a steady fall of sleet, which was thickening into snow. We'd get no accumulation; it was too warm for anything to stick to the ground, but the leaves and grape clusters of the vineyard were collecting the semicongealed ice crystals, making the fruit look like a jeweler's creation in the sweep of my headlights. I parked and turned off the engine. Amanda, in mud boots and a yellow rain slicker, came out to the car with an open umbrella to meet me.

"I apologize for the quagmire," she said as I stepped out of the car and into the rain-logged dirt of the yard. The chug of a tractor engine was just audible. She gazed out into the vineyard where the cone of a work lamp shone on a portion of the vines. "Poor Neil. The last thing he needs is to get stuck in the muck out there." A lone figure moved in and out of the lamplight. Every so often the blade of a knife would flash silver as he cut free bunches of grapes and tossed them into what must have been a bin of

97

some sort. Amanda sighed and motioned me toward the house. "Neil said to tell you he's sorry he can't come in to talk, but we have contracts for juice that have to get out."

"And it's easier to work than to deal with the crisis at hand?" I adjusted my pace to keep up with her long-legged stride.

"You know my husband."

"I know my husband."

She moved aside so that I might head up into the cover of the veranda first. "You and Greg are back together?"

"Not exactly."

"But you're still not – "

"No. Greg and I are, well – " In the distance I heard the tractor engine rev, maniacally ascending in pitch, as though trying to climb out of a pit. "We're stubborn. Neither of us wants to be the first to give up."

Amanda shook out her umbrella and leaned it against the chair she'd been sitting in. "Stubborn can be commendable." She sat down to remove her boots, and while she was doing so I peered into the front room through the big bay window. The view of the baby grand piano, the fireplace, the furnishings was unobstructed by curtains or shades, let alone foliage of any kind.

"Are you looking for the plants?" she said as she slipped her feet into moccasins. "I don't know why the boys say they remember plants in the window – Detective Burnham said they did. We got rid of the plants a month or so ago when Neil decided that we had enough flora to tend to outside the house." She opened the front door. "And we feared Lydia might have allergies."

I stepped into the softly lit entry hall. "Still, it's a rather large detail for five stories to get consistently wrong."

"I agree. But I'm thinking the boys might mean it as the room that used to have all the plants. It might be the way they remember the room."

"Which would mean they'd been here before."

"That's what it would mean. They're Lydia's friends. They were here often."

Inside, the house was warm and simply decorated. Amanda had music on the stereo, a classical piece of somber cello. She apologized for the odor of paint; they'd been repainting the entrance before – well, *before*. She then offered me a glass of wine, a taste of their most recent "experiment." When I declined, she showed me into the front room.

"A case of the cobbler's kids never having new shoes." Amanda laughed after apologizing, again, for the disarray. "Or rather the piano turner's kid always having a flat middle C." She invited me to take a seat on the couch in the bay of the window as she began to gather up the tuning forks and adjustment tools that lay on a pale chamois draped over the piano bench. "Not that anyone is playing it much these days, but since I'm kind of tied to the phone right now I thought I'd take the opportunity. It's something useful I can do." She hung her head.

I said nothing. Nothing I could say would have eased her despair. After a minute or so, she shook it off, looked up at me, and smiled. Brave and lovely even in sorrow. As though posing – I stopped myself there, aghast; I would have thought myself beyond such pettiness. When we were growing up, Amanda had been, beyond doubt, the prettiest girl in Swifton and therefore condemned to an instant envy-based dismissal by the ordinary girls such as myself. Ashamed as I was by the memory of that, I was even more ashamed by the persistence of the compare-and-compete impulse to the present moment. As if anyone could compete with the woman. The years may have etched intricate lines of conflicting emotions at the corners of her eyes and mouth, but the effect had only burnished her prettiness closer to beauty. She was wearing her chestnut-gold hair in a scalp-close crop that only a woman with such delicate features could pull off. Lean and angular, she still moved like the ballet student she'd been before running off to Paris at nineteen with a twice-her-age jazz pianist. She'd returned home at thirty with nine-year-old Lydia, Neil Parrish, and a skill for piano tuning, which she had since parlayed into a profitable little business. Worldly and elegant even at this moment of distress, Amanda in her mud-streaked jeans and oversized sweater, her face bare of makeup, looked like a grieving princess struck down in a fairy tale while I, in my jeans and sweater, felt like a just-discovered stowaway on the back of a potato truck.

"We miss having Molly around," Amanda said as she went back to organizing tuning forks in a velvet-lined case. "She was always such a good friend to Lydia."

"We miss seeing Lydia, too, but you know how fast kids change at this age." I caught, belatedly, the significance of the piano remark. "Lydia isn't playing the piano as much?"

"She isn't playing period." Amanda's voice broke. "She quit."

"Did she give you a reason?"

"Lydia doesn't give me reasons for anything she does."

"That's too bad." *Do what you came to do.* "You've heard nothing from her?"

Amanda sat down on the piano bench. "Only the note she left. It said we wouldn't understand and she didn't want everyone to be angry with her."

"Angry about what?"

"The party, I guess." She picked up a crooked-neck metal tool with a wooden handle and rolled it between her hands. "None of this was supposed to go public. We were going to deal with it ourselves, keep it quiet and sort it out among the families. And then that teacher overheard Lydia and whoever, so the girls had to press charges."

"From what I understand of the situation, no one should be pressing charges here."

"No? You may want to take that up with Andrea Burnham. We were told, the other girls' families were told, that if we did not press charges, Swifton's finest would have no choice but bring our daughters up on underage drinking. The Morrettys and the Bankses and Nora Jenkins have already filed. Donna Morretty called to let me know. She felt they had no other option. Better to have your child in court as a victim than as a delinquent, I suppose."

"You haven't filed?"

"With Lydia unavailable to verify things one way or the other? No. I don't want to jump to conclusions."

"Say you were to jump."

She laid the tool next to her on the bench. "Neil believes the kids are using Lydia as a scapegoat, because of her reputation. Yes, we are well aware of Lydia's reputation. Neil believes that since she's not around to argue the point, they invented this nonsense about her trying to orchestrate an orgy as a way of getting out of trouble. He thinks she heard about it, and that's why she ran away. She's hurt and embarrassed and frightened that she's going to be held accountable for something she did not do – but everyone is going to believe she did."

"That's Neil. What do you believe?"

"I believe Neil adores his stepdaughter." She bent forward, her elbows on her thighs, and pushed the heels of her palms into her eyes. "But to be honest? I believe those boys are not lying. I can see Lydia doing exactly what they describe."

"And that's why you're not pressing charges?"

"I don't know what happened to her, Leslie. She was always so sweet-tempered, so amenable, you know?"

She wanted reassurance that her memories of her own child were not false. "I remember Lydia coming to play at our place on the weekends when I was there. So very bright. All pleases and thank yous. I remember hoping some of it would rub off on Molly."

"Well, it rubbed off on something. One day my sweet little girl turned into someone I barely recognize. It wasn't overnight; it seemed like overnight, though. Puberty hit her earlier than her friends. That was hard. Being taller and older looking. The teasing she took was pretty brutal, but none of us gets out of childhood unscathed, right?" Behind her hands, Amanda tightened her lips into a slight smile; apparently she remembered her girlhood, too.

"No," I said, trying to make it sound like an apology, "none of us gets out unscathed."

Amanda didn't acknowledge my remark. She kept her eyes hidden. "At first I thought that hormones were the cause of her behavior; she just needed time to adjust to the physical changes. Or perhaps it was a delayed response to her father's death. Or a combination of the two. But over time, she became even more troubled. She stopped playing the piano. Her grades plummeted. She was screaming at us all the time. And she became extremely, to be blunt, sexual; we'd be out the grocery store or at the post office and Lydia would be giving men – adult men – a look of, well, you know that look. Sizing them up. It wasn't merely curiosity. Or even seductive. It was predatory. We finally had to admit that what was happening to Lydia was more than the onset of adolescence. We've since taken her to doctors – endocrinologists, psychologists, and pediatric psychiatrists. We've tried drugs. Nothing seems to calm her down for very long."

I wanted to comfort her, one mother to another, to tell Amanda that although she may have been way on the outskirts of normal, normal was what Lydia was. This sort of high-stakes acting out was part of growing up for some kids. But Amanda would have seen straight through it. She knew I would recognize the implications of what I was hearing. I couldn't quite gauge if she wanted to talk further or not, but we were in the middle of a mine field of information. Going back seemed no less hazardous than continuing forward. "Okay. A terrible question?"

Amanda lifted her face. "Can't be more terrible than the ones I've asked myself."

"Any chance Lydia has been traumatized?"

"You mean sexually?"

"Trauma is trauma. Her behavior, however, sounds consistent with the sort of thing you see in situations where there's been sexual assault."

Her expression darkened. "I'll give you the same answer I've given every doctor, every shrink, every social worker who has asked that question: Of course, she's been assaulted. She lives in a culture that hooks children up to a television tube and force-feeds them like veal calves until they're fattened up on artificial desires and have learned their sole purpose in life is to want whatever it is they're told to want."

I was taken aback by the shift in her tone. It struck me as odd that rather than the standard, even practiced reaction of horror or confusion or denial such a question generally drew, Amanda's reaction was to politicize her daughter's pain. Perhaps it was only a defensive stance cultivated after she had tired of the repetitive assault of the question itself. They must have been asked as many times as doctors they'd consulted. Yet her defenses were no match for the obvious. "It's an awful thing to consider," I said, withdrawing to a less provocative position of concern. "The last thing I wanted was to trouble you even more."

As I hoped, my backing up pulled her forward. "What troubles me is that when Lydia started reading at four years of age it was never chalked up to a library trauma, and her academic giftedness was never attributed to an assault by an overzealous teacher, but the child displays a precocious sensuality and suddenly, they want to strap Neil and me onto polygraph machines. You would not believe what they asked us."

"Yes, I would." *Push.* "Amanda, surely you realize that thirteen-year-old girls do not as a rule come on to adult men – "

"What planet are you living on, Leslie? Have you seen a music video? Have you seen any of that *Eden* show they're all devoted to? Innocence is dead."

"We're not talking about innocence; we're talking about basic adolescent development. Millions of kids Lydia's age watch television; they're curious, and maybe they're trying stuff we'd like to think they're not ready for, but not every one of them is out trawling the produce department at Mercer's for sex."

She straightened, glaring at me, appalled. "My God, Leslie."

"I'm sorry, that didn't come out right."

"I should hope not." She laced her fingers over her legs. "Besides, the sex is not that disturbing."

"No?"

"Well, you kind of have to expect sex from teenagers, don't you? Stars, moon, ocean, earth, sex. It's the way of the world. It's what we are. Children are our sex lives incarnate, right? But the gamesmanship? The maneuvering for power?"

"You think Lydia is maneuvering for power?"

"Worse, I think she's sees this as a game. That's what the party was about. The running away. None of what Lydia does has any meaning to her. It's just one move after another toward no purpose but to keep the game going. Power for its own sake."

I had a flash of a memory, my father teaching me to play chess, never once letting me win because *you only get better by playing someone better than you.* "Who does Lydia see as her opponent?"

"Pardon me?"

"In this game, who is Lydia playing against? You?"

She stiffened again. "We passed the polygraph. Neil and I, both. Twice."

"Amanda, I wasn't – " Even though I was.

"I want her to come home, Leslie." Her posture collapsed, spine, shoulders, head dropping, as though she were shattering in slow motion. "I want her to be all right."

"That's what we all want, so let's work on getting her home, okay?"

She sighed, nodded. "I can show you her room. It's a mess. The police went through her things after we called about the note. And of course,

103

Neil and I had already searched it ourselves. We didn't find anything. No drugs or . . . well, nothing, thank heavens."

"I'd be more interested in what you didn't find. Do you have any idea of what she took with her?"

"They asked about that, too. Her backpack – the one she uses for school – is gone. Clothing, I suppose – I didn't really take inventory of what wasn't there." She got up wearily. "Do you want to go look?" She assumed my response and headed out of the room. As I followed her past the piano, I reached out my index finger and depressed a couple of the white keys, hitting the narrow gap between them. No sound. I withdrew my hand. A gritty residue remained on my finger. It smelled like soil.

l y d i a

It's not so bad, not really. Except for the cold. And the dark. And the noises that she'd never hear if she weren't alone. Lydia adjusts the teddy bear she's using as a pillow and snuggles herself deeper into the doubled sleeping bags, one belonging to Molly, one her own, and focuses on the candle flames. She has the candles set up in the sooty fireplace; safer to keep the open flame contained – Molly's idea, again. The candles, an assortment of multiwicked pillar and scented waxes in glass jars, give off a cheery brightness but no warmth.

The candlelight is not bright enough to read by for very long without getting a headache, and she doesn't want to waste the flashlight batteries on a book. She puts the headphones back over her ears and turns up the volume. The sound of the DJ's voice is more of a comfort than the music. She is settling back into a state of semicomfort when something – a feeling, not a sound – something with tiny claws scuttles across the wood floor behind her. The sensation jerks her upright, her heart thudding. She rips the headphones off her head, grabs the flashlight, and arcs the beam around the empty room. It's a mouse, of course. It must be. She hopes it's a mouse and not a rat. Mice she can handle.

It probably wants the food that she's storing on the top shelf of one of the built-in bookcases. The shelves are away from where she's trying to sleep, but she fears she might have gotten potato chip crumbs or flecks of chocolate doughnut on the sleeping bag, between the sleeping bags, or, oh God, in the sleeping bags. The idea of little things crawling onto and into her cocoon as she sleeps unawares makes her stomach sick. She shoves herself out of the sleeping bags and leaps to her feet, shivering in the sudden chill as she brushes off whatever might be clinging to her sweater, her jeans, her hair. She then unzips the sleeping bags and shakes them out, away from the fireplace. Lays them flat and sweeps them down with her hand. She's gone through this process five times since nightfall.

Convinced she's cleaned the bags as well as she can, she rezips them, one inside the other, and scoots herself back inside, pulling them up tight around her neck. Her nose is running. The only thing she has for tissues is pages from the notebook she found at the bottom of her backpack. She'll ask Molly to bring her a box of Kleenex. And some toilet paper. The water in the Turnbull house is still working, but it runs only cold. She wants a shower. Her hair feels greasy and she smells bad. But she can hold out for a couple more days. Molly says it will only be a couple more days and nights. She has to trust Molly that this is the only way out. She has to trust Molly because, honestly, although she remembers how the party started, she has no idea – except for what Molly has told her – how it ended. She can't remember a thing.

She puts the headphones back on and turns up the music until it hurts.

cannibals

When I arrived back at the house, Greg was in the kitchen folding articles from a massive pile of laundry he had dumped on the table. Around him on the floor were a half dozen plastic laundry baskets in which he distributed the folded items according to owner and location. He was also drinking a beer – another one in what appeared to be a concerted effort to attain full-on drunkenness, judging from the number of empty long necks lined up on the counter behind him. Knowing Greg, the beer was an attempt to amplify the normal white noise tedium of household chores – anything to block the memory of Molly's statement, which his mind, like my own, would have been broadcasting on an infinite loop. I grabbed a beer for myself from the fridge and set about helping him.

The laundry was dryer warm and perfumed with the chemical spring of fabric softener. I picked up a wad of bath towel. An ant trundled out of one of the folds. I flicked it off; it landed on Greg's forearm. He crushed it between his thumb and forefinger. "At least he died a clean death." Greg swallowed back his laughter and wiped the ant remains on the breast pocket of his shirt.

"Nice."

"Like everything else today."

"You want to talk about it?"

"Not really." He flailed at my head with the washcloth he'd just folded. "You have snow in your hair."

"That's because it's snowing." I deflected the towel with my beer bottle.

"And you're drunk."

"That's because I've been drinking. How are Neil and Amanda holding up?"

"I'm not sure. Weird vibes. Molly may be on to something."

"They have Lydia locked in the basement?"

"No. But I looked around Lydia's bedroom and her bathroom and, going on what Amanda could tell me, Lydia left with what you'd expect: her backpack, a few clothes, a teddy bear she's fond of, a CD-radio headset thing – "

"Sounds like running away to me."

"But she also took books. Almost an entire shelf of paperbacks is gone."

"Always about the books with you, isn't it?"

"That was uncalled for."

"A joke, Les."

"Not funny, Greg. Nothing about that time was funny." I leaned over the laundry and picked up his beer bottle. "I'm cutting you off."

"I'll behave myself." He pulled the bottle out of my hand and gave me a sloppy, lopsided grin that couldn't quite disguise the anger behind it. "No more loony bin jokes."

"How reassuring."

"Tell me about Lydia's books."

Anything to change the subject. "If you're running away, the emphasis is generally on the *running*; you don't want to be hauling around twenty pounds of books with you, unless – "

"Unless you're anticipating having a lot of downtime with nothing to do," he said as shook out a place mat with fraying edges. His eyes met mine. "She's hiding out, waiting for this to blow over."

"That's what I'm thinking. She's somewhere close by keeping tabs on the chaos, waiting until it's safe to come in. I wouldn't be surprised if one of her little friends is helping her."

"Which only gives more credence to the idea that Lydia's responsible."

"Responsible? For what? She's thirteen."

"Yes, but it would mean the boys didn't – "

"And we're supposed to feel better?"

"The boys are only thirteen, too." He rolled up a pair of Emma's socks and tossed them into a basket. "We're not all monsters all the time. At least, the judge thought so." Another pair of socks bounced into the basket. Then another.

I tired of waiting. "Are you going to explain that?"

He squinted at me. "You didn't hear? It was on the news earlier – where are these ants coming from? Jesus." He crushed this one against the tabletop. "Anyway, the judge decided that pending a trial or whatever it is they end up doing, the boys were hardly a threat. He sent them home with their parents and told them to go back to school on Monday. So maybe as the word gets around, it will get back to Lydia and she'll turn up none the worse for wear and the whole mess will be forgotten."

"That would be great, but I don't think that is going to happen."

"Me neither." He took another drink. "Damn Nightingale case is going to bust open again, isn't it?"

"It usually does" – my turn to drink – "at the first hint of any sex crime around here, but only as a historical reference; there's no real connection."

He was shaking his head. "The other girls at the party? Nora Jenkins's daughter was one of them."

"Amanda told me."

"Nora Jenkins, Les? Her maiden name was Scott?"

"Janet Scott's sister?"

"Yep. And you have to assume that the sister of the last Nightingale is going to have an ax to grind."

What goes around comes around to . . . "Don't call them that. I hate that Nightingale crap. They weren't *birds*. They were little girls. They had their own names."

"I know, Les."

"Do you?" He was getting too close to what I did not want to talk about. I picked up Emma's filled laundry basket and headed for the stairs. I passed by the little den that had once been my father's office. Molly was seated at the assemble-it-yourself computer desk, her fingers tapping rapidly at the keyboard. The lights around her were off so that her face shone ghostlike in the pale glow of the monitor. If she sensed my presence, she gave no indication. I hauled the basket to the top of the stairs, stopped, and looked up at the attic panel. The tassel at the end of the cord hung motionless. No sound of footsteps or boards creaking. But I knew she was up there. I knew what she wanted.

"Janet? I would do anything to change it if I could, but it's over," I said, as though the sound of my adult voice might break through the icejam of childhood memories and allow time to flow forward once more. It didn't

109

work. I could still feel her waiting. In that expanding sense of her expectation, I began to pick up the light floral notes of the old perfume. Stronger here than in my kitchen or office, as though I had just spritzed some on my own wrists. My encounter with Theodore Carse had initiated processes that were gaining momentum, feeding off the energies of Lydia's disappearance. Damn right the Nightingale case was going to bust open again; it was busting open right then. Graves were being upended all about me, including my own. That's how it happened: Too many anomalies and you started to doubt your reading of the entire world. The stories fell apart. I had been to that place of utter stillness in the center of the chaotic nothing. I hoped never to go there again. I wouldn't have to if I could keep moving. Physical motion was the antidote; to put one foot in front of another was to necessitate the reinvention of order. I forced myself forward, step following step, moving back into myself as I moved toward my younger daughter's room.

Emma was on her belly, her feet on her pillow, her nose in a book. She raised her eyes as I came through the door, reading me like a weather report. "Are you tired, Mom?"

"Yes." I set the laundry basket next to her on the bed. "I need you to put this stuff away for me, okay?"

"More? I don't have any room left."

"That's so sad." I opened her closet door and turned on the overhead light. Greg apparently had been unable to part with the relics of our daughters' childhood, and so, like Molly's closet, Emma's shelves were packed with arching stacks of outgrown clothing and toys, held in place here by the keystone roll of Em's sleeping bag. The bar beneath the shelves, however, held mostly barren hangers. "Oh, look! You do have room. It's a miracle."

"I'll do it later."

"Now, please. Before it gets wrinkled."

She moaned the moan of the infinitely mistreated and climbed off the bed. When I left her she was trudging toward the closet and mumbling grievances. Feeling secure enough to risk complaining, that was a good sign. I closed the door to her disgusted announcement that she'd found an ant in her clothes.

Greg's voice sounded from the shadows at the other end of the hall.

"Rain earlier must have driven them in." He was sitting on the floor, his legs stretched out straight in front of him, his back against the wall near the guest room I used when I stayed over. His head bobbled a bit as it did when he'd had too much to drink, nodding in assent, as though he'd reached the state of inebriated grace in which he could agree with everyone about everything. "The ants." He nodded in approval of his theory.

"Did rain pretty hard there for a while."

"I'm sorry, Les. I should have known better than to drop the Nightingale – sorry, the Janet Scott – connection on you like that."

"I'm fine."

"I should have known that would upset you."

"Greg, look at me. I'm fine." I went over to where he sat and slid down the wall to sit next to him. "Any mention of the Nightingale thing is going to bother me. That can't be news to you."

"Nope."

"I just hate that word. So some writer finds out that Melissa Shapiro happens to have been reading 'The Emperor's Nightingale' on the night she was abducted. Next thing we know the press has this made-for-the-movies tag line to describe the assaults, and the girls are no longer *girls*; they're the Nightingales. The writer walks off with a paycheck and prizes for her artful culling of those little girls' trauma, and Swifton gets a jazzy code word that makes the horror easier to talk about."

"Not to mention how that article blasted your dad."

"Yeah, let's not mention that. Writers. Remember what they did to us? Fucking cannibals, each and every one of them."

"I'm glad you're not upset." He patted my knee.

"I'm not upset. I'm pissed off." I lifted his hand away from my leg.

"It was thirty years ago, Les."

"Thirty-two, and tell that to Janet Scott or Melissa Shapiro or any of the others. Tell that to the Swifton police who are still trying to make up for the fact the bastard walked. Make up for what it sees as an ancient family disgrace. That's what this thing with Lydia's party is really about, you know, it's about – "

"Your father screwing up. And that means it's about you."

"Why would you say that?" I had a sudden vision of Greg tearing out ceilings and finding cursed totems amid the clumping gray drifts of blown-in insulation.

"That's why you became a cop, right? To fix what he left broken? Catch the bad guys he couldn't. I mean, that's obvious even to a jerk like me." He gave me a slow, sad smile.

"You're not a jerk." I laid my palm against his cheek. "You're an idiot."

He nodded, his eye lids drooping. "I am a drunken idiot."

"Yeah, but a sweet drunken idiot. Go get some sleep."

"Okay." In trying to stand up, he worked his arm around my shoulder. "Come with me?"

"Not a good idea."

"We don't have to do anything."

"Mr. Stone, I've been to bed with you drunk before. If memory serves me, you won't be able to do anything."

"Maybe I've been practicing."

"Maybe that's an image I'd rather not have in my head."

"Tell you what, then" – he nuzzled my ear – "I'll grab my sleeping bag out of the closet and sleep on the floor in your room. That way, if you change your mind . . . What's the matter, Leslie?"

"You have a sleeping bag in your closet?"

"Is that a crime, officer?"

"Emma has a sleeping bag in her closet."

"Seemed to be a convenient place to keep them."

The large empty place on the shelf. The tumbled-down pile of clothes. "Then where is Molly's?"

"It was there last – " but before he could finish the thought, Molly was shouting down in the living room.

"Gross! Gross! Get them off of me! Oh, gross!"

We were on our feet and running, Greg close to pushing me down the stairs. Molly was in the dark of the den, jumping up and down, pointing at the computer. The monitor screen was alive with ants. They scurried about the lit screen like animated exclamation points with translucent wings. The wings were falling away from their bodies, raining down on the keyboard like fine slivers of ice.

"Okay, I'm sober now," said Greg as though sober were a swear word, and then he did swear. Repeatedly. He moved me aside to get to the table lamp, then switched on the bulb, clicking through to the brightest setting. My first inclination was to keep clicking on back to darkness; we'd have been better not seeing. The insects were emerging from a slight crevice at the top of the crown molding where it met the ceiling. Wave after wave, they heaved themselves out to drop the full height, some hitting the floor, some hitting the desktop. Those on the floor had fanned out and were trudging along the carpet, while those on the desktop were moving in streams toward the light of the monitor. Discarded wings drifted over and among the hundreds of tiny creeping bodies.

Emma screamed – a wholly appropriate response, I thought. She must have come down when Molly started shouting. She was behind us leaping from one bare foot to the other in panic. "I hate ants!"

"Not ants," said Greg wearily. "Termites. Swarmers."

"Whatever they are, kill them." Molly gestured wildly in her apparent frustration at our lack of action.

"Yeah. Kill 'em!" echoed Emma.

"They're as good as dead now." Greg bent down to peer at a struggling termite body. "They were looking for a place to start a new colony. That's what swarmers do, but they can't survive outside for more than a few minutes, an hour or so. It's awful late in the year for these guys to be showing up – and to come in from up there?"

"And yet, here they are." I brushed a scattering of wings to the floor. "What do we do?"

"Right now? We get the vacuum cleaner and start cleaning them up. Tomorrow I call in a pest guy, we track down the source, and then we figure out how we're going to come up with a couple thousand bucks to have them exterminated." He pulled himself to standing on the desk chair and ran his finger along the entry point, smashing termites beneath him as he passed. Molly and Emma let out simultaneous sounds of revulsion. He looked down on them and laughed. "I thought you wanted them dead."

"Joanne and Denise will have to help out with the money." I headed for the front closet where Greg kept the vacuum. "These are their termites, too."

"Good luck convincing them." Greg leaped down from the chair, landing unsteadily. "Your father should have pulled out the stump when he took down that oak."

"But the tree is on the other side of the house."

He wasn't listening to me. " – so, if they're coming in from up there it means, God help us, they've been in house long enough to eat their way up and over."

"Through the attic?" said Molly.

"Good guess. Let's go see what we can see."

I blocked his path with the vacuum cleaner. "Not tonight. We've got enough to contend with down here."

He stepped around me. "It will only take a minute."

"Can I come, too?" said Emma, already pulling him toward the stairs.

"I thought you hated ants."

"These aren't ants. You coming, Molly?"

"The only place I'm going is to take a shower. A very long, very hot shower."

"Oh, come on, Molly, please. We never get to go up – "

"No!" Too loud. Too abrupt. They halted in midstep, their heads swiveling slowly around to assess me. I pulled back. "Not tonight. It's too cold and too dark. No one needs to be going up there tonight. It will wait."

"Yeah. I suppose." Greg eyed me and then shrugged. "Those bugs have been up there awhile. Few more hours isn't going to hurt. Molly, go get the broom, and Em, for goodness sake, get some shoes on." The girls set off on their appointed missions, grateful for the excuse to flee. Greg, not taking his eyes off me, came back into the room and began uncoiling the vacuum's power cord.

"You don't want to be up there at night," I said.

He went to plug the cord into the socket at the base of the desk; it was full. He pulled the top plug and the computer clicked off, the monitor blinked and went black. "Noise," he said, our old habit of warning the girls about the coming roar.

I turned to watch the still emerging swarmers, wriggling, squeezing out from beneath the molding into an unavoidable free fall. It was as though the letters of all those articles in my notebook had become animate and were eating their way out of the secret, out into the light, telling my story against my will. Janet had apparently found the right place to look.

1 2

Forgive me.

You are in the backseat of the station wagon on your way home from church. The sun beating down on the unshaded parking lot at Swifton Presbyterian has made an oven out of the car, and so you ride with the windows down, the roaring wind tearing at your hair. Denise sits beside you. Joanne is up front with your father. He's taken off his coat and loosened his tie. His sleeves are rolled up and his elbow is out the window. Your sisters are laughing. You laugh with them, and because you are pretending, you laugh too loudly, bending forward, holding your belly, rocking back and forth. Denise tells you to mellow out, it wasn't *that* funny. You have to take her word for it because you have no idea what they were talking about. Your reception of the world is still fading in and out. You're working with a broken antenna, bent back on itself by the impact of new information, your head is stuck on a single signal and even that won't come in clearly. You won't let it. Blocking it with snowy, crunchy static, so that your father's voice remains faint, scratchy: *what goes around comes around, buddy.*

No turning it off. The knobs are lost. The plug is out of the wall. You attempt to distract yourself by going over again and again and again the articles in your notebook. The answer is in there. It must be. The notebook is not with you, of course, but you've read the words so often as to have committed each element of typography to memory. The stories are imprinted on your awareness so concretely that the physical act of reading them is now more a process of comparing what is on the page to what is in your head. And you need to compare, letter by letter, to see if, by chance, anything on either side has changed in such a way to make what your father has done make sense.

You lean against the door frame, close your eyes, the better to concentrate. The wind blasts past your face, filling your ears with a thousand whispers. You realize the static in your head is not the sound of emptiness but rather the sound of all available signals collapsed into one station. You play all the hits all the time. With effort you can isolate each. The words in your notebook take on voices, high-pitched and low, dipping in tone, rising to shrieks. The local articles scream in incandescent vowels – *rape, rape, rape, rape* – while the city papers drone on like drums about the run of unsolved assaults in the rural suburbs of Swifton Woods. You can hear the snipped condemnations of the famous Margaret Wexham who wrote the article for the famous magazine and turned your friends into nightingales. She uses big words, articulated with the same clickity-click as an IBM Selectric: *sexual objectification, tragic affectations, jurisdictional incompetence.* That article sounds like beetles scuttling about an empty can. The nightingale story itself, which you copied by hand from a library book on Hans Christian Andersen, reads itself over and over in your mother's voice, starting from the beginning before it gets to the end. Your mother always spoke with a hesitant thoughtfulness as though she feared someone uninvited might listen in and misinterpret her, a spy forever reminding you she had secrets she could not share. ". . . *it sounds prettily enough, and the melodies are all alike; yet there seems something wanting, I cannot exactly tell what.*"

In disentangling the voices, the jamming signal fails; your father thunders into your head, words as catastrophic as tidal waves. *What goes around comes around, buddy* . . . He raises his fist. Your eyes snap open before he can bring it down. Everything shatters back to a crackling disorder. You fear you may drown inside your own mind.

n i g h t

We stood at opposite ends of the staircase: Molly at the top, shiny faced and freshly scrubbed; me at the bottom, termite wings stuck to my socks and reeking of the pesticide I'd sprayed over everything. We were shouting over the sound of the vacuum Greg had been pushing compulsively around the lower floor, in an attempt to erase every last invader.

"I lent it to a friend."

"Which friend?"

"You don't know her."

"I still want a name."

"It's just a sleeping bag – it's not like I let someone borrow Emma."

"Exactly. So what's the big deal? Give me a name."

"Do you want a phone number, too? That way you can call her – except she won't be there; her family went camping this weekend, which is why she needed to borrow – "

"I'll take that phone number anyway."

"You won't get an answer."

"Oh, yes, I will. Eventually."

Greg, stretching the cord, wheeled the vacuum out into the foyer, the motor's brashness made even louder by the wood flooring. Molly shook her head at either me or the noise and stalked off toward her room. The vacuum motor cut out; Greg had pushed the thing one room too far and had yanked the plug. Taking it as a sign to quit, he began to reel in the slack, wrapping the cord around the caddy on the back of the vacuum.

"That's all of them." he said, keeping his eyes on figure-eight loops he was making. "Do you really think Lydia has her sleeping bag?"

"Yes, sir, I do."

"Why wouldn't she tell us?"

117

"Because she's scared we're going to say she had prior knowledge of Lydia's plan to run away and did nothing to stop her."

"Which would be why she felt so compelled to help find her?"

"Maybe. Or maybe Molly has known all along that Lydia's version of the party isn't going to play out as advertised."

"Or maybe it means she thought Lydia wanted to borrow her sleeping bag. Maybe she had no idea why the girl wanted it." He pushed the groove in the plug onto the cord, locking the plug in place. "It could be that simple. They are friends."

"They *were* friends, and nothing is simple with teenage girls."

He sighed in frustration. "We can hope, can't we?"

"Hell, yes; we can hope." I went back into the office to reboot the computer, planning to get on-line and check my messages. A scattering of tiny black bodies writhed wingless on the keyboard. I looked up. A fresh wave of swarmers was wriggling into the light. So much for hope.

I sat in the dark of what my sisters and I still called Mom's sewing room. None of us sewed, and for the longest time after she left, none of us dared to enter it in the silent, shared fantasy that at any moment, she'd put down her work and come out to see what we wanted for dinner. Since Greg and the girls moved in, the tiny space had become a combination guest room—storage closet for winter coats, broken appliances, and unused exercise equipment. On those nights I decided not to make the drive back to my apartment, it was where I stayed. The bed was little more than a cot, too soft and too small for the sort of stuporous thrashing about that I called sleep. It didn't help that the room's temperature was unpredictable. This night the radiator was disinterested in its purpose; the leggings and T-shirt I was wearing were barely adequate protection from the chill. Around two o'clock I moved the comforter and pillows to the floor, but termite memories crept on countless little legs across my mind. I couldn't bring myself to lie down.

I raised the shade on the window and, with the comforter wrapped around me, watched the almost full moon slipping through the dissipating cloud cover. My thoughts kept returning to Lydia, imagining her huddled in Molly's sleeping bag somewhere equally dark. She must have been cold, too. Was she as frightened for herself as we were for her? Or was the fear of the anticipated turmoil awaiting her back at home stronger than the emerging turmoil of being out there on her own? If I were Lydia, in these circumstances, how would I have defined safe? Well, we don't run away from places; we run away from people. The aloneness would be what I wanted, especially in these circumstances; the farther I got from other people the safer I'd feel. So if I were Lydia, I'd head away from Swifton, but not toward the city.

From the attic above me came a faint but furious scratching sound. Mice, was my immediate guess – we always had mice – but the sound downshifted in my perception from that of scratching to that of hundreds of thousands of tiny jaws munching steadily through the wood. Certain that the sound would keep evolving into more intimate threats, I decided to move on to more productive efforts. I got up and went downstairs to see what Greg had in the kitchen.

He hadn't restocked since my last late-night baking session, so the flour canister held the scant half cup I'd left behind a couple weeks earlier. No flour meant no bread, and I needed to bake. I stuck my bare feet into Greg's boots, put my coat on over my pajamas, and grabbed my keys for a dash to Mercer's twenty-four-hour grocery on the other end of Swifton.

I decided to take Greg's pickup. The quickest route to Mercer's was Old Quarry, and the way the moonlight glinted off the lawn made me suspect black ice on the roads. The truck was heavier, more secure on slick pavement, and besides it heated faster than my soda-can-on-wheels sedan. Shivering, I climbed behind the wheel, got the engine going, and shoved the temperature control lever to the highest setting. The radio blared to life; I lowered the volume before putting the truck into gear and starting down the driveway.

The radio was tuned to the local AM talk station Greg liked to listen to and yell invectives at. The host of the current show, *All Night Hot Talk,* was trying to interrupt the caller – on a bad cell phone connection – with a question. The caller kept on ranting in rapid-fire, breathless sentences against some issue that had caused him great personal offense. I was about to turn it off, but the phrase "junior high rapists" caught my attention.

". . . See, that's what I'm saying, Bob. These kids are out of control.

The parents don't do squat teaching them right from wrong and then you get these liberal jerkwad judges who pat the junior perverts on the head and say no biggie, you go back to your spoiled little lives and we'll pretend this never happened – "

"I hear you, man, but – in the interest of fair play – the judge didn't exactly let them off the hook. He simply said they weren't a risk and it was all right for them to go back to school while they were waiting for the – "

"I have daughters. Do you have daughters, Bob?"

"Yes, I – "

"Would you send your girls to school on Monday if you knew a dozen sex predators would be wandering the halls?"

"Well, of course not, but these *five* boys aren't what I'd call – "

"How do you think these kiddie porn kings get their start, Bob?"

"Point taken. So what do you suggest we do? Lock them up?"

"Hell, yeah, lock 'em up and then get a big old knife and – "

Enough. I smacked my hand against the radio controls until the sound went dead. Both hands back on the wheel, I held on tight and tried to concentrate on feeling the road conditions through the wheels' response to my braking and accelerating. By the time I'd reached the closed-for-the-night Dairy, the cab of the truck had heated thoroughly, but I was still shivering.

Driving Old Quarry in the dark was like working your way blindfolded along the knobby spine of an irritable beast; you went carefully, certain that at any second you'd be shrugged off into the roadside ditch. The brightness of the moon waxed and waned from behind the clouds, throwing a slow-motion strobe effect over the landscape. The wind gusted; I had to steer in compensation as I watched for the telltale sheen of ice on the asphalt. My mind, foggy edged with sleep deprivation, focused best as it could on driving and thus turned away from guarding the gates.

When I first spotted the small figure by the side of the road, illuminated by my headlights, I thought it was one of those spindly roadside saplings, a birch, maybe, with slender branches bent and motionless in a cage of ice. The human qualities became quickly apparent, and as I slowed to acknowledge the presence, I recognized her. It was Melissa Shapiro. The first victim. Her hair was in braided pigtails. She was wearing eyelet lace pajamas with sleeveless top and capri bottoms, and fuzzy slippers. It was what she had been wearing the night of her abduction. The wind did not rustle her clothing or her hair, and her image was unsteady, drained of color, as though I were looking at an old black-and-white newsreel. She stared at me staring back at her, and then she raised her right arm out parallel with the road, pointing back toward the direction from which I had come. I turned my head to try to see what she was pointing at. Only the dark of Old Quarry was behind me. When I turned back to Melissa, she was gone.

I thought about it for maybe thirty seconds before steering the truck through a three-point turn and heading back in the direction Melissa had indicated. I drove slowly, not yet knowing toward what. I was nearing the fork of Old Quarry and Jackdaw. At the Dairy, the solitary light over the store's entrance began to flicker. It went out completely for a moment and then flared, brighter than before, the way some bulbs do before they burn out for good. In the sudden and very white light stood Charlotte Crowell. Victim number two. The same old-photograph coloration. I recognized her by her Snoopy nightshirt and the cast on her arm. Even at this distance, I could feel her eyes on me. She pointed me toward Swifton-Brank. The bulb above her flickered again and went dark.

I drove on as directed. An oncoming car, the first one I'd seen, crested the top of the hill, high beams blazing. No matter how I flashed my lights, the driver didn't get the message or didn't care. I averted my eyes to avoid the momentary blinding and glanced toward the house I was passing to the right. Catherine Grimaldi, victim three, pointed me farther down the road.

I knew then that I was going to have to see them all. And one after another, in accelerating succession over the course of the next couple of miles, each of the Nightingales appeared: Donna Anderson on the veranda of the Applewoods' home; Rose McKnight beside a broken fence post; Kelly Ann Sevpulveda sitting beside a mailbox as Kimmy Tate pointed me toward Nicole Bartlett, who pointed me farther down Swifton-Brank to where I could already see Jennifer Norman and, beyond her, the faint glowing form of what would surely be Mandy Epelle. Grainy and gray scaled, like three-dimensional photographs from the album my subconscious maintained, each one a figment of my intuition, both an assistance and an accusation of betrayal from thirty years earlier, they were dressed in summer sleepwear, silently guiding me toward a place where their collective pasts crossed my present. I offered up the same old apologies. One for my father's failures. One for my own.

Mandy vanished before I'd passed her. I saw nothing ahead of me but the dark of the road, in the rearview mirror, more of the same. I kept going, however, because one girl was left. Janet, who had been so adamantly present over the past twenty-four hours, had yet to appear to me as the others had, and so I slowed the truck to a creeping roll for fear of missing her. The interior of the truck's cab had heated beyond comfort. I was sweating; I could feel the perspiration rolling down my back, my neck, between my breasts. I wanted to adjust the thermostat but couldn't seem to take my hands off the wheel. I wasn't breathing right, gulping air, but not getting any oxygen. Dizzy. Slow down. Stop.

The smell of perfume was sudden and engulfing, surging through the vents with a choking thickness. I started coughing, the taste of the alcohol and artificial flowers coiled around my tongue, down my throat. My eyes stung and teared. Certain I was going to be sick, I fumbled about the door for the window crank, found it, and hurried to get the window down. I leaned out into the cold fresh air. Breathing deeply, still coughing, I wiped the tears out of my eyes. My vision began to clear, and I glimpsed what at first I thought to be an ember floating in midair way off in the distance to my left. The emerging moon revealed the structure around the ember; it was a speck of light escaping from behind boarded windows of a house. I realized I'd stopped in front of the old Turnbull farm. It was supposed to be unoccupied at present, but someone had taken up residence. Squatters perhaps, or . . . *Aha.*

I put the truck in reverse, backed up to the driveway entrance, and made the turn past the No Trespassing/No Hunting signs. I rolled up almost to the house, then I parked and got out of the truck, easing the door closed. Quiet. I wanted to walk the rest of the way because if Lydia heard me coming, she might bolt.

l y d i a

A noise awakens her. She sits up. For the first few moments she doesn't know where she is, then it comes back quick enough. She listens. The larger candles are still burning in the fireplace; their light throws long, quivering shadows against the wall. From the back of the house comes the sound of shifting boards. Maybe it's the wind. Please, let it be the wind. But it isn't – unless wind has learned her name.

"Lydia? Sweetheart, are you in here?"

She doesn't answer. The owner of the voice is in the house now and moving toward her.

"Lydia? It's Leslie Stone. Molly's mom?" The owner of the voice comes into the room. Lydia hasn't seen her in a long time, but she's definitely Molly's mom. She's got on muddied work boots that are too big for her and a pea coat. Her hair is smooshed around like she just got out of bed and she is smiling kind of sad-like. She comes toward Lydia slowly and lowers herself to the sit on the floor. "You warm enough in here?"

Lydia shrugs.

"Have you had anything to eat?"

"Yes. I have plenty of food." She tilts her head toward her supplies.

"I'm glad to hear that. You have lots of folks worrying about you, you know?"

"I didn't want anyone to worry."

"Love and worry – almost impossible to separate those two. You ready to go home?"

Lydia looks down. This is the question Molly told her to expect, the one Molly told her how to answer. "Not really. I bet they're angry, aren't they?"

"Afraid is more what they're feeling," Mrs. Stone says, "and maybe a little angry because they don't like feeling afraid. But that will disappear the moment they know you're all right. Besides, we don't want to stay here, do we? It's freezing."

"Can I go to your house? Please. Just until morning. Then I'll call home."

"Hmmm. Going to my house does sound like a solid first step." Mrs. Stone stands up and holds out her hand. "Come on. I'll help you pack."

Lydia wrestles herself out of the sleeping bags, gets to her feet without help. Mrs. Stone pulls the sleeping bags apart and then gets on her knees to fold and roll Molly's. Lydia feels awkward standing there. The silence is awful. She has to say something, anything, to make the silence go away. "You were faster than I thought you'd be."

"Faster?" The woman cocks her head as though she didn't quite hear Lydia. When she does this, she looks exactly like Molly when Molly is thinking, only a lot older and more tired. "Faster how?"

"Finding me." The words are out of her mouth; Lydia realizes she's slipped. She pulls her fingers to her lips; Molly is going to be pissed. "I mean, I'm happy you found me so fast." That was worse. *Shut up, Lydia.*

Mrs. Stone scrunches up her forehead, puzzled, for a second. She stares at Molly's sleeping bag and then her face changes. She looks back up at Lydia, smiling even more sadly than the first time. "I'm happy I found you fast, too." Mrs. Stone sits back on her heels and crooks her finger, beckoning Lydia closer. "Sit with me."

Lydia, terrified she's ruined Molly's plans beyond repair, does as asked. She kneels in front of Molly's mom, copying her posture. "Is something wrong?"

"Many things, I think." Candlelight and shadow break across the woman's face, making it difficult to sort out her expression. "I want to ask you a question. The question is not nice, but I have to ask, and here in the middle of the night in a house where no one lives is probably the best place to do it. Whatever you tell me I will believe. Whatever you tell me I will take care of. You will not be alone with it any longer. Okay?"

Lydia is aware of her heart accelerating against her breastbone. "Okay."

Mrs. Stone nods. "What I know of the world tells me that more is going on in your life than anyone could guess. I think you are a girl with secrets. Some secrets are poison, Lydia, and that poison can make us sick inside ourselves. Some secrets make us do all sorts of things trying to get away from that sickness. Understand what I mean?"

When an adult asks if she has understood a concept, Lydia knows to give the only acceptable answer. "Yes, I understand."

"But it never works. Not for long, at any rate. You can't ever escape, because the secret is inside your own skin."

"Like when people drink too much?"

"Or make trouble for their friends."

"The party?"

"The party. So here's my not-nice question: Do you feel safe in your own house?"

"Safe?"

"Yes. Safe when you are with your mother? Your stepfather?"

"Neil? You mean is he *molesting* me?" Lydia starts to giggle with relief. "Is he touching me in *bad* ways?"

"I know you've been asked before."

Lydia tries to get her giggles under control. "All the doctors ask. And then they ask if it's my mom. Or a teacher. Or a neighbor. I tell them no, no, no." The giggles are starting to feel like anger. "Nobody is touching me. I have no brothers or sisters. I don't even have any pets. Nobody is touching me. Why won't anyone believe that?"

Mrs. Stone reaches over and takes Lydia's hands. "Listen, sweetheart. Look at me."

Lydia can't. She's embarrassed because her hands are dirty and her nails are so ratty looking from her chewing at them over the past couple days.

"Lydia? I said I would believe whatever you told me. If you say no one is touching you, then I believe no one is touching you."

Lydia looks up, tries to read the woman's expression. "Really?"

"Really." Mrs. Stone squeezes Lydia's hands and then releases them. She goes back to rolling up Molly's sleeping bag. "But I still think you are keeping secrets."

"I can't think of any," Lydia says as she crawls to the fireplace and begins to blow out the candles, one after another, until the room goes dark and thick with the smell of smoke.

125

11

Dr. McCafferty is at the pulpit. His black robe hides his belly; the purple satin of the sash around his neck deepens the green of his eyes. Behind him, on either side, are two large arrangements of flowers – roses, mums, stephanotis – everything in white, left over from a wedding or funeral. The sunshine pours in through the arched windows on your side of the sanctuary. Dr. McCafferty gazes about in silent preparation for the sermon. The congregation settles in, bracing itself. Out of church, he's a nice man, everyone's jolly uncle, but when he's trying to impress God, he's boring. Normally, the blandness of his delivery erodes your best intentions; you end up slouched against the hard wooden pew, forcing your yawns through your ears. Today is not normal. Normal is gone forever. You sit straight, wide-eyed, eager for his limpid syllables, attentive, hoping he will reveal the answer that you've been praying for since the service began. *What should I do? What should I do?*

You feel horribly ill. You haven't slept. You will never sleep again. Everything inside you feels swampy and stuck, like you are wading through the grasses on the muddy edge of Lake Yuck. He hasn't started speaking yet. What's he waiting for? He inhales and parts his lips – finally – but it is your mother's voice that creeps through the sanctuary.

"The story I am going to tell you happened a great many years ago, so it is well to hear it now before it is forgotten . . ."

Those words are from "The Emperor's Nightingale." You had to copy the story into your notes from a library book. You needed every word of the story to try to understand the terrible things being said about your father. To have your mother say them only made the words worse, as though it was your mother had found a new way to condemn him. You glance at Joanne and Denise and your father down toward the center of the pew. They don't seemed the least bit unnerved. They don't hear her.

127

Dr. McCafferty is gesturing – sharp, precise slicing movements, his mouth does not match the words you hear your mother saying. Concentrate on his mouth. Mom's voice fades and his takes over.

". . . and forgiveness is worthy of contemplation, especially in consideration of what we have endured as a community: While it is true that we are expected to be forgiving, the Bible instructs us that the Lord's forgiveness is dependent on the repentance of our sins . . ."

All right. This is church talk. This is what you expect. Okay. You relax, and instantly you lose him. Your mother is back.

" 'What is this? I know nothing of any nightingale. Is there such a bird in my empire? and even in my garden? I have never heard of it . . .'"

Stop. You pinch the skin on your inner wrist, twisting the flesh until your eyes water from the pain. Pain wakes you up.

"The Lord will forgive us anything, if asked, and ask we must, with real repentance in our hearts . . ."

And you are sorry, so very sorry. But you are not sure you are sorry for the right reason. Is that enough? You look again at your father and once more your mother's voice replaces that of the minister.

" 'Your imperial majesty,' he said, 'cannot believe everything contained in books; sometimes they are only fiction . . .'"

Bow your head. Stare at your hands.

" 'My excellent little nightingale,' said the courtier, 'I have the great pleasure of inviting you to a court festival this evening, where you will gain imperial favor by your charming song.'"

Close your eyes. Ask for forgiveness again. Her forgiveness. Maybe she will go away. She doesn't.

" 'My song sounds best in the green wood,' said the bird; but still she came willingly when she heard the emperor's wish . . ."

Please.

"She was now to remain at court, to have her own cage, with liberty to go out twice a day, once during the night. Twelve servants were appointed to attend her on these occasions, who each held her by a silken string fastened to her leg. There was certainly not much pleasure in this kind of flying."

Please. Stop.

". . . the emperor said the living nightingale ought to sing something.

But where was she? No one had noticed her when she flew out the open window, back to her own green woods."

You want to run, cover your ears and run from the church. Instead you sit very still, as though the words inside and around you are angry hornets, and anything you do now will only make them angrier.

". . . the barrels were worn, and it would be impossible to put in new ones without injuring the music. Now there was great sorrow, as the bird could only be allowed to play once a year; and even that was dangerous for the works inside it."

"It is indeed a form of death."

"Cold and pale lay the emperor in his royal bed; the whole court thought he was dead.

"All around the bed and peeping through the long velvet curtains, were a number of strange heads, some very ugly, and others lovely and gentle-looking. These were the emperor's good and bad deeds, which stared him in the face now Death sat at his heart."

"So you see, true forgiveness is a twofold event. It is both the death and resurrection that allow our ability to love one another, our very lives, to arise clean and healed. This is the forgiveness Christ came to teach us. Let us seek forgiveness not in order to have our sins forgotten. Rather, let us both ask and offer forgiveness in order to restore and thus remember, if only for a moment, the original innocence of our souls.

"Let us pray. Dear Heavenly Father, we beseech your forgiveness . . ."

You open your eyes. Where is your mother to finish the story? To tell the part where nightingale comes back and saves the emperor with its singing? You wait and wait, listen hard. She doesn't come. Dr. McCafferty drones on, asking and asking. How do you know when you've asked enough? You look over at your father; his hands are fisted on his knees, his forehead bent to meet them, praying as hard as he knows how. Look back at the altar. Dr. McCafferty's face is bloodied. His eyes swollen shut.

You cover your eyes with your palms, pressing in until the darkness glows. Your head fills with static. *Forgive me.*

s i g n s

"Move over," I whispered.

Greg, who even when we had shared a bed had never quite grasped the share part of the deal, grumbled sleepily and pulled himself over to the far edge of the mattress. A second later he shoved himself up on one elbow. "Leslie?"

"Yeah." I lay down beside him in the warmth he'd vacated and pulled the covers up to my chin. "I gave the guest room to Lydia."

"You found her? Neil and Amanda must be – "

"Haven't called them yet. It will wait until the morning. Lydia needs to rest a couple hours before this crap descends on her. And I need to think a bit longer before she goes back to them."

He lowered himself back to the pillow. "What aren't you telling me?"

"First? I'm getting the distinct impression that Molly was right about Lydia being hidden because Molly was the one hiding her."

"Did Lydia tell you that?"

"Lydia isn't saying much of anything, but it's looking like they hatched the Lydia-runs-away shtick as an excuse to get me involved."

"With the police and press already digging in, why would they want you involved?"

"They'll have to answer that one. Not that they will, of course. Not that it would make any sense if they did. But I'm going to find out. Molly wanted me to investigate Lydia's disappearance? She's got herself an investigation."

"Well, at least you did find Lydia. Now she can clear up what actually took place at that damn party." He patted around under the blankets until he found my forearm. "Good work, Detective."

"I'll remind you of your admiration when the shit starts flying every which way."

131

"Is it going to be that bad?"

"Truth?"

"No. Please lie." He laughed in resignation. "I've missed this, you know? Lying awake in the dark with you and worrying about the end of the world."

"Paranoia is *my* hobby." I turned on my side toward him. "You need to get a hobby of your own."

"I have a hobby." He turned to face me. "I collect signs of the coming apocalypse."

"Goodness, man, where do you keep them all?"

His hand closed around my arm and he brought my palm to his chest where I could feel his heart. The warmth of his body, the reality of his skin beneath my fingers began tripping switches I could have sworn I'd permanently disconnected where Greg was concerned. I don't know which one of us was the more surprised when I didn't resist his tentative kiss or the less tentative one that followed.

"Guess this would be one of those signs," I said.

"Yep. It would be the official closer, I would think."

"Promise?"

He shifted closer so I could feel how hard he was. "End of life as we know it."

"Life as we know it is overrated."

"It wasn't always that way. Or was it?"

"Greg – "

"Were you ever happy? Here? With me?"

I put my hand at the back of his neck and pulled his mouth to mine, letting him pull in my tongue as I threw my leg over his. I pulled my mouth away from his. We were breathing like we'd been rescued from the brink of suffocation. We stared at each other, our faces barely visible to each other in the thin veil of the dimming moon. I was certain his questioning expression mirrored my own.

"Answer me, Leslie. Were you happy? Ever?"

"I wanted to be," I said, as I drew my hands down the familiar topography of his shoulders, chest, and belly, every contour, each out-cropping of muscle and bone exactly as my fingers remembered it. This was how home was supposed to feel. "I don't know if I can do *happy*. But I wanted it."

"I wanted it, too." He trailed his fingers up under my T-shirt and along my spine. "I wanted to make you happy."

"My happiness is not your problem to solve."

"That's the thing, Les. I never saw you as a problem. A first-class pain in the ass, maybe, but never as a problem."

"You can lie better than that. But thank you." I slid my hand beneath the waistband of his shorts and took him in my hand. "So this is the end of the world, huh?"

"According to all the signs."

"If we're doomed anyway" – I rolled onto my back, bringing him on top of me – "we may as well burn the sucker down."

I slept for less than an hour, waking in the soft light of seven A.M. I disentangled my body from Greg's and got up. He shifted into the empty space I left behind. I watched him sleep, aware of an increasing tension around my heart. I couldn't tell if it was nostalgia, regret, or something more dangerous. I grabbed his robe from the hook on the back of the door.

In the hallway, I heard voices, low and serious, coming from Molly's room. Her door was closed. I checked the guest room; the cot was empty. Back at Molly's door, I rapped quietly with the back of my hand. The conversation stopped.

"Yeah?"

"I wanted to let Lydia know that I'm going to call her parents now."

The door inched open. Lydia appeared. She smelled of soap and shampoo. Her hair was combed and held back on each side by tiny butterfly clips. She was wearing Molly's clothes: khaki pants that showed her ankles and a sweater that barely reached her waist. "May I wait up here?"

"Sure." I looked over Lydia to make eye contact with Molly, who was sitting on the end of her bed. "But the running away stops now."

Molly gave me a wonderfully composed expression of complete and utter confusion, on which I closed the door. I headed downstairs to the phone. Behind me, I heard Lydia call out. "Thank you, Mrs. Stone."

Neil and Amanda were on our doorstep within ten minutes of my hanging up the phone. I had barely finished dressing when the doorbell started ringing interspersed by rounds of insistent knocking. The commotion woke Emma, who stood in the hall scratching her thigh and yawning questions as to what was going on. I instructed her to stay in her bedroom and then bounded down the stairs to get the door open before they broke through it.

Neil pushed past me. "Lydia?" He was wearing a parka more suited for an end of January cold snap than a crisp autumn frost. Probably the first thing he grabbed from the closet. His hair spiked upward, uncombed, and his glasses only magnified the dark circles under his eyes. "Where is she?"

"Calm down, Neil," said Amanda as she stamped the mud off her running shoes before coming in behind him. She was hugging herself, pulling the thin cardigan she wore closer to her shoulders. Her face was red from crying. "You don't want to overwhelm her."

"I just want to know she's all right."

Lydia appeared at the top of the stairs. "Yes. I am."

Neil caught his breath and Amanda started sobbing. They raced each other up the stairs, arms opening to engulf Lydia, who did not turn to meet them, but rather stood, her arms at her side, her head lowered in embarrassment. Greg stumbled out into the hallway, squeezed past the reunited family, and ambled down the stairs, looking back at them and grinning.

"I love happy endings." He sidled up beside me and kissed my cheek.

"It ain't over yet," I said, watching Neil and Amanda and trying to get a read on the body language as they kneeled, almost in supplication, embracing their stiff-postured and nonresponsive daughter. "We need to call Andrea Burnham," I announced in the general direction of the Parrish family. Only Lydia raised her eyes in response, staring at me with an expression that I could only categorize as wonder.

I cradled the phone to my ear, hunching my neck, and worked at making coffee while Burnham lectured me for waiting this long to get in touch with her. It was the standard "professional bitch-out," controlled in pitch and full of vague threats based more on the humiliation of my locating Lydia than on any real transgression of the law. Once her ego had blown itself out, the inherent detective need to know surfaced.

"The afternoon she went missing, we checked out the Turnbull place. First thing we did was a quick once-over of the abandoned and empties."

"But you were looking for her body."

"In situations such as this it is always a fear. Given the wording of her note, plus her parents' assessment of her mental condition, suicide was a real worry."

"It would have to be."

"Thank goodness it didn't turn out like that."

"Yes. Thank goodness."

"So are you going to tell me how you came into the information that she was out at the Turnbull place?"

The Nightingale girls told me. "Lucky guess."

"At four o'clock in the morning? That's some special kind of luck." She laughed. "Look, Leslie, I know your daughter is involved, but A, I don't have to tell you the hazards in withholding evidence, and B, I don't have to tell you that playing to Lydia's fears is no way to help Molly."

I sneered at the receiver. "No, you don't. On both points."

"Glad to hear it. I'll be out there shortly."

"We'll be waiting." I hung up the phone and turned to check the progress of the coffee maker. The water was still gurgling into the top of the filter contraption while coffee, dark and steaming, dripping into the pot from the other end. I inhaled the aroma, trying to breathe in enough caffeine to cut through the sludge of fatigue in my brain. I needed to be fully awake, because A, Molly needed an advocate, and B, Lydia needed rescuing from something I couldn't quite name, and C, Andrea Burnham needed to be deprived of the satisfaction of thinking she knew my child better than I did.

m o l l y

Lydia comes back into Molly's bedroom and flops down on the bed, rolls her eyes. "You'd think I'd been gone for years."

"What happened?" Molly thinks Lydia looks sick, all pale and puffy.

"They were really worried." Lydia blushes. "I guess they really did miss me."

"So are you going home with them now?"

"No. Your mom called the police. They want to talk to me, but she thinks the *grown-ups* should talk first."

"I told you that if she was the one who found you, she'd stay involved. She'll make sure that everyone understands nothing all that bad happened. This kind of stuff is important to her. Have you remembered anything yet?"

Lydia shakes her head and then takes up Molly's pillow, hugging it to her chest. "I remember what I'm supposed to say, though. I won't screw up on that again."

"Okay."

"You're not too pissed, are you?"

"No. It wasn't an awful mistake. I mean, Mom was going to figure it out sooner or later. I'll talk my way out of it somehow." Molly reaches under the bed and comes up with her mother's cell phone. "Got it."

"Your mom is going to see the number on her, you know, bill."

"Not for a while. We just can't chance that someone here listens in. If it becomes a problem, I'll tell her I made the call." Molly turns on the phone, listens for the dial tone, and punches in the numbers. "Not lying, am I? Ringing."

"It's too early to call."

"You want to talk to him or not?" A woman answers at the other end. She sounds suspicious. "Hi. Mrs. Zinni? My name is Molly Stone. I'm in a couple of Tim's classes at school. Yeah, hi. I was wondering if I could talk to Tim. I mean, if he is up yet." *About what?* "Oh, um, there's an English project we are supposed to be doing – a group project, right. And Tim was supposed to have part of it ready for us by, you know, Monday, and . . ." Molly wonders if Mrs. Zinni – if Lydia – can hear how nervous she is; she can barely hear her own voice over the rushing pulse in her head. She would never have been able to call Tim on her own. "Okay. Thanks." Molly presses the phone against her shoulder; she can feel herself shaking. "She's going to get him."

Lydia nods. "You do that well."

"What?"

"Make stuff up."

Molly's the one blushing now, but for different reasons. She puts the phone back to her ear. He comes on. *Molly?* His voice is thick as though he has a cold. "Hi. Tim? Hi. This is Molly. Hi. Can you hold on a second. Somebody wants to talk to you." Molly extends the phone to Lydia and whispers, "It sounds like he's been crying."

Lydia takes the phone. "Hey, Tim? It's me. I'm at Molly's house. We're waiting for the police right now. Yeah, I'm going to tell them exactly what happened. Then it will be done, right? Okay? Tim? Oh, God. I'm sorry. I'm sorry, oh don't . . ." Lydia begins to cry. "I just want you guys to be my friends again."

Molly gets up from the bed and goes over to the window. Frost flowers lace over the glass, and the world outside is edged in hazy white. The weathered gray of the old tree stump is sparkling with beads of melting frost, and for a second she imagines that these sparkles look like stars to the termite city just below the surface where millions of termite citizenry scurry around, blissfully unaware of the disaster about to befall them from the sky.

t i m

Lydia's weeping sinks into the nothing that has taken over Tim's body. Everything is okay, he hears himself tell her. It's all right. He knows his mother is listening in on the extension. That's all right with him, too. This is his new approach to everything: Whatever the world wants of him, it can have. If he doesn't give it up, they'll take it anyway. He keeps the phone to his ear until Lydia decides she's done talking. She says she's going to call the other guys. She says good-bye and hangs up.

Tim's mother comes into his room, smiling and wiping her eyes. "We're almost through this, honey."

"You think so?"

She nods. "Lydia's back. We'll be fine."

"All right." He becomes aware of the frantic beeping on the receiver still in his hand, the *please hang up* recording comes on. Tim does as the recording tells him and turns back to the computer on his desk. He goes back to the game, to distract himself and not think, but working the game controls is making his wrists hurt. He pulls the cuffs of his rugby shirt over the bruises the handcuffs left. The meaningless demons that inhabit the game shuffle about the monitor. He is supposed to cut them off, cut them down, cut them up with bullets and blades until the screen runs puke green with their mutant juices. The demons now seem familiar, as though their likenesses had been lifted directly from the nightmares from when he was little and certain that monsters were hiding under his bed. The demons' animated ugliness is terrifying, their shambling gait unstoppable. They keep coming. He shoots wildly without aiming, hitting nothing. They get him and he dies early, like a newbie, over and over again.

The phone rings. Tim, startled, jumps away from it. He forgot to turn it off. He knows he should be used to it by now. It's ringing all the time. His mother will pick it up as quick as she can. He won't answer because he's scared of who might be on the other end. It won't be his friends; the judge said the guys were not allowed to speak to each other. Instead, lawyers call. His parents' friends. People who aren't his parents' friends. People who want to yell at them or yell at him. His dad is going have the number changed to an unlisted one next week. Tim doubts it will help. The phone will keep ringing even if they rip the cords from the wall. Scared as he is of the callers, he's more scared of the fact he often doesn't know if the ringing is real or in his head.

He heard the phone ring the first time, in the middle of the night five days ago – could it be only five days ago? The ringing woke him and as he was falling back to sleep his father came into the room to tell him they had to go down to the police station. The police had heard about the party and wanted more information about the drinking. Tim's father asked him there in the bedroom and twice in the car if Tim had been drinking, too. No, Tim had said. And that was true.

"You keep on telling the truth." His father had hugged him after Detective Burnham said she needed to speak to Tim alone. She closed the door on the little conference room. She had him sit down and asked him questions. Tim told the truth, speaking loudly into the tape recorder to make sure it got every word.

The girls had been drinking before you and your friends arrived?

Yes. They had on music and were dancing and acting, you know, weird.

They were drunk?

Yeah, they were.

What did you and your friends do when you realized they were drunk?

I guess we just stood around watching them act stupid and kind of laughing at them.

How did they take that, you laughing at them?

I don't think they noticed until Lydia started getting angry. She started yelling at us and then came over and tried to hit us, kind of shove us around, but she kept falling over. We thought it was funny. She got this really weird look on her face and then . . .

And then what? I know this is hard to talk about, Tim, but like your dad said, you need to tell me what really happened.

Um. Lydia started, um, to take her clothes off. And then the other girls started, too. They were laughing and Lydia said she wanted to make a video. She started telling the girls how to dance and to, you know, touch each other.

Did you touch any of the girls? You need to say it out loud, Tim, so the recorder can pick it up.

Yes. I touched Lydia.

Where did you touch her?

He had been embarrassed because he couldn't remember the right name for that part of a girl's body and the names he could think of sounded dirty. So he'd pointed in the general direction of his own lap.

Her genitals. Again, Tim, you have to answer out loud.

Yes.

Yes, what?

I touched her, um, genitals. She dared me. I told her to go away, but she grabbed my hand and made me.

She made you?

Yeah.

You said she was falling down she was so drunk.

Almost falling down.

You're a big kid for thirteen. You play football?

Sometimes.

What I'm wondering is how a falling-down-drunk girl physically forces a stone-cold-sober athlete like yourself to do something he doesn't want to do?

I don't know.

It was the only honest answer he had; the lawyer told his parents that it was his honest answer that got him and the others arrested. Five days later, Tim still replays the party in his head looking for a better response to the detective's question, but his memory gets woozy with the unrealness of what happened. It's not dreamlike, because in his dreams, no matter how horrible or bizarre, he is always convinced the horrible or bizarre events are actually taking place. The party was different, and as it went from strange to stranger, Tim had felt like he did when he'd talked himself onto the Dead Man's Drop, a ride at a seaside amusement park his family had visited over the summer. After he'd seen the ride up close, the 315-foot tower from which riders were dropped in a ring of harnessed seats, after he'd heard the screams of the droppees, he'd decided that he did not really want to go on the thing – he only wanted to go home and tell the guys he'd done it. Problem was that Tim was certain they'd be able to tell he was lying, that something in his words or face would betray his chickening out. He'd then be a coward *and* a liar. The only solution was to do the deed.

He sweated out the hour-long wait in line, but when the ring began its slow ascent, he had the distinct sensation that he wasn't really doing this. He could feel his hands gripping the padded safety harness over his shoulders. He watched the park and the people in it, his mom and dad among them, growing smaller and smaller, as the beach and the sea beyond it grew large. There was no feeling of peril or thrill. In fact, when the seat finally came to a halt with a jarring thud that caused the other riders to whimper with dread, Tim felt only sad. He surveyed the line where the boundless blue of the sky met the boundless blue of the sea, expecting something. Nothing happened. He was suddenly sure they would be up there forever. Not stuck or trapped, just stopped. Then he heard a motor and the metallic clank of a release mechanism. The ring fell, his stomach went so far up into his throat he couldn't have made a sound if he wanted to. He was back on the ground in seconds. The harnesses released and the riders were free to go. He exited the ride on wobbly legs, met his parents, and they went to buy lunch. Later, when he told the guys about it, he still felt like a coward lying about what he'd done because, really, he had not been there when he did it.

The same way he wasn't there when Lydia, her eyes glassy but bright with a kind of cold-fired craziness, had taken his hand, squeezing his fingers so hard he felt the blood cut off. Embarrassed as he was for her nakedness, he found himself fascinated, his eyes would not rest in a safe place. He felt the others in the room watching him, expecting something. His body was starting to voice expectations in that pulsing language he had yet fully to decipher but could not ignore. The hugeness and confusion of the moment were making him angry, and the anger held him in check, unable to move.

"I dare you." The words, smelling of alcohol and sweat and the seashore, triggered a release mechanism in him. He gave in to her downward pull of his hand and let her make him do what he could only, just now, barely admit in secret to himself having wanted.

Tim realizes the memory is working on him in ways that make him feel both ashamed and powerful. He shuts his mind down and repeatedly hits the Replay button on the game control until the mutants begin to creep back into firing range.

l y d i a

Downstairs, the grown-ups are talking with the police. Her mom raises her voice every so often, but Lydia cannot make out what they're arguing about. Molly is at her desk, pretending to get caught up on her homework so Lydia can finish crying without being stared at. She blows her nose, extra loud, trying to get Molly's attention. Molly pretends not to notice.

"What are you working on?" She finally asks.

"Math. Story problems."

"Algebra?"

"Whatever."

"Do you need help?" Lydia says and then winces. She hopes Molly won't remember that her grades forced her out of the Advanced Math class.

"Not yet. I want to see how far I can get on my own. Oh – " She opens a desk drawer and takes out a bunch of papers. She folds them in half lengthwise and sails them like an airplane toward where Lydia is on the bed. The plane falls apart; the papers scatter. Molly groans at Lydia, and as the papers settle to the floor, they both break into giggles. Molly says, "Those are the *Eden* recaps from Merciless TV. I printed out the last one yesterday, so it's like everything you would have missed."

Lydia thanks her and scurries about the room retrieving the pages until she finds the episode she wasn't able to watch. She settles back on the bed to read. But the words blur; Lydia can't read the first line. Her stomach goes watery and she feels sweaty and weak. "Molly?"

Molly looks over her shoulder and her face grows tight with concern. "You okay?"

"I don't know if I can do this. If I could only remember something."

Molly comes over and sits next to her on the bed. She gives Lydia a quick hug. "I told you what happened. All you have to do is tell them what I told you."

"But how do you know what happened?"

Molly starts gathering up the pages that Lydia had left lying on the floor. "Do you want Tim to go to jail? The other guys?"

"Of course not."

"Then you are going to have to . . ." Molly's voice trails off and she points at the door as someone starts to knock. Before Molly can say anything, the door opens, and Mrs. Stone comes in to tell Lydia that they're waiting for her downstairs. Lydia pushes herself up from the bed and tries to ease past Mrs. Stone, who is giving Molly the universal you-are-so-busted stare of death. Before Lydia is out the door, however, Mrs. Stone wraps her arm about Lydia's shoulders. She closes the door on Molly without saying anything. She pulls Lydia close and begins to explain in quiet, careful words the terrible thing that's going to happen next.

10

You keep losing your place in time. It's as if the movie that is the world is jumping sprockets in the projector. One second you are crying in the dark of the kitchen, your chest aching from running, your pajama bottoms soaked to the knees with the algae-stained water from Lake Yuck. The next second you are buttoning your shirt cuffs to cover up the scratches on your arms. You have no memory of the minutes in between.

Check the clock. Church is four hours away. Your notebook is open on your bed. You glance at it and then back at the clock. Church is now two and a half hours away. How did that happen? The puzzlement is cut short by sounds from downstairs. Heavy footfall at the rear of the house, traveling toward the foyer, then on the stairs. He's back. Quick, turn off the lights. You hold your breath for fear he will hear you as he passes by your bedroom. The door to his closes.

Turn on the lights again. The darkness is too much like the missing chunks of time, an emptiness that echoes. If you look into the void too closely you will see the pictures that go with the noises you are trying not to hear. *What goes around comes around to what goes around comes around to . . .* what?

You go back to your notebook. Maybe you have the answer in here somewhere. Maybe if you looked harder, if you could make your mind work more clearly. You keep looking at the magazine article about the Nightingales, the last part where Margaret Wexham criticizes your father's work, accuses him of failing to care enough because the victims are girls. You reread it and reread it. Time slows down. The void brightens. The picture starts to focus. It's your father, and he is shouting, "What goes around comes around," and he is . . . the picture brightens too much, the film burns, leaving only a white blankness where it was moment ago dark. It is the white of sunlight on white walls. You are in church. Dr. McCafferty is at the pulpit.

my life's work

Detective Burnham insisted that she accompany Lydia and her parents to Swifton Medical where a Sexual Assault Response Team exam could be performed immediately. Amanda protested. She didn't see the point in a SART exam; the party had been more than a week ago. Lydia had showered and changed several times. Why should they subject her to that ordeal? What could they possibly find? It was Neil who finally convinced her: "Bruises don't wash off, Amanda."

With that, I went up to fetch their daughter from the cloister of Molly's room and tried to explain to her the necessity of the next step. Lydia's eyes grew huge and tears brimmed, but the girl was all cried out. She nodded her head in compliance. Greg collected Lydia's backpack and the sleeping bags as Burnham directed. She wanted to have those tested as well. Before they left, I extracted a promise from Amanda and Neil that they'd call as soon as possible to let me know how the exam went. I was about to head up to gently but thoroughly third-degree Molly about her part in Lydia's runaway scheme when a car horn rendition of "La Cucaracha" sounded outside. I looked out the sidelights of the front door to see a white van with foot-long wrought-iron ants welded along the roof, making it look like a giant motorized sugar cube at a picnic. The termite guy.

His name was William Watson, and he was carrying a black vinyl binder at least six inches thick. "Call me Bill," he said twice, once as he shook Greg's hand, once as he shook mine. Bill was a short, skinny man of about sixty with a well-trimmed salt-and-pepper beard and ears that were as gnarled and meaty as tree fungus. He listened to our tale of the previous night's insect horror with his eyes turned toward the floor, his head cocked as though he were a oncologist and our complaints might hold the first subtle signs of a malignancy larger than we were prepared to face. He then brought a stepladder into the front room, climbed up, and shone a flashlight into the crevice from where the swarmers had emerged. He poked at it, digging along the edge with a sharpened pencil, dislodging a few wingless bodies that fell dead to the floor.

He climbed down from the ladder. "You got termites," he said as he displayed a carcass impaled on the pencil point.

"Well, yes," said Greg, "that would be why we called you."

"Odd point of entry," Bill said with a certain consternation in his voice. Then he laughed. "But then termites aren't exactly your Einsteins of the insect kingdom. Cockroaches. They're your thinking man's bug."

"I don't like to think that much," said Greg.

"You ought to appreciate what you're up against. Roaches? Now, they're wily. Ants are persistent as hell. But termites are just plain stupid, and the stupid, because they don't know any better, tend to be tenacious. That's why a good termite extermination is going to take a two-year commitment minimum."

I wondered if I should collect these last few specimens to send along with the copies of the estimate I planned on mailing to Joanne and Denise. "How much is our two-year appreciation of their tenacity going to cost us?"

"How much is the long-term soundness and security of your home worth to you, Mrs. Stone?" He smiled and I heard cash registers. He took up the binder he'd set on the computer desk. "Allow me to show you the services my program delivers."

Greg and I sat side by side on the couch as Bill ran through his sales pitch, which was equal parts a grade-school science report on the life cycle of the *rhinotermitidae* and a hard-core statistician's wet dream. We studied corked vials containing specimens of the various stages of a termite's (aka white ant's) life, we examined sections of lumber in various stages of termite (from the Latin root *termes* or woodworm) destruction. And then came charts on effectiveness of termiticides (woodworm should not be confused with wormwood, a poisonous plant from which tonics have been produced to ward off worms of the digestive tract, not to mention it's the main ingredient of absinthe, a liqueur that'll kill you; that's a pesticide joke), comparisons of the differing termite control services out there (*rhinotermitidae* is the subterranean family of termite species, which total three thousand in number), and why Bill's was the best.

Forty-five minutes into the presentation, as I was about to ask Bill how large a check we would have write in order to make him stop talking, Greg stood up and said, "We're pretty sure they came in through the attic. Would you like to see the attic?" He didn't wait for Bill to respond one way or another; Greg just bolted for the stairs, making his escape.

Bill, convinced he had finalized the sale, grinned victoriously at me, put down the binder, and headed off after Greg. I heard the hinges of the access panel squeak open and the rattley roll of the steps in descent. I found I had a sudden and unexpected appetite for more information. I wanted to call Bill back for more deathless details on the social insects of the order *Isoptera;* I could spend the rest of my days buried in the pages of the binder as the *rhinotermitidae* happily devoured the walls around me.

Greg called from the top of the stairs. "You coming up, Les?"

Up. I had not been up in the attic since that Sunday in September more than thirty years earlier. No matter how – over the past forty-eight hours – my confusion and guilt had manifested themselves as Janet Scott's searching for the piece of evidence that would have spared her becoming part of a terrible story, it was clear that my stronger sense of self-defense was intent on keeping me out of the attic. It was the lesson of my illness, after all, that the past cannot be fixed, only survived and set free to be exactly what it was.

"You don't need me," I said, coming around the corner to the base of the stairs.

Bill, already in the attic, whistled and shouted, "Holy moly, would you look at this?"

Greg, assuming that my reluctance was Bill based, pressed his palms together in a silent plea. I shook my head. He frowned in disappointment before turning to climb the steps into the attic, head down, like a man on his way to the gallows. The act was for my benefit; he was trying to make me laugh. Greg believed in the power of positive momentum, and he was doing his best to keep the bedroom events of early this morning rolling forward. *You and Sisyphus, buddy.* I was afraid I was going to have to remind him of the difference between conciliatory and consoling.

I turned to go back and clean up yet more dead termites – and nearly ran headlong into Lydia. I caught my breath in surprise. She was still wearing the clothes she borrowed from Molly. Her hair was pulled back in a loose ponytail, and I could make out the yellow-green blur of a fading bruise on the side of her neck.

"Are you done at the hospital already, sweetheart?"

She blinked at me and sighed. Her breath had an acidic, metallic smell. Her skin was pale and damp with perspiration. She was running a fever; I could feel the heat radiating off her.

"Why don't you come sit down?"

She looked around the foyer, confused.

"Do your parents know that you're here?"

She didn't answer.

"Lydia? Sweetie? Are you okay?"

Her eyes fluttered and rolled up into her head; her knees buckled, falling forward. I reached out to catch her, my back braced and readied for the weight of her fainting body. My arms closed around her; Lydia disappeared. She'd not been there at all.

I straightened slowly. "But I felt her," I said aloud, arguing with the empty foyer. I could still feel her, a thick, sickly heat shrouded me like partially melted paraffin. I glanced up the stairs, remembering Molly's request: *If you see Lydia, will you tell me?* But was that Lydia? Or had the thing I kept in the attic co-opted a new form, something I could see and understand and not so readily dismiss as an old, irresolvable hurt? My intuition had made a connection between Lydia's situation and that of the Nightingale girls. And yet, the sense of looking directly at something I couldn't name, let alone determine the shape of, left me feeling lost.

On that thought, the air about me went dead and then fissured; I could hear the air cracking, ripping apart. It sounded electrical, like sparks; the sparking sound changed, broadening, splitting into trilling little giggles. Little girls laughing, hard, mocking, forced laughter, throughout the house. The laughter moved past me, up the stairs, and seemed to unify at the foot of the attic steps, the unified sound became a elongated, panicked warbling, the song of a frightened bird. Emma came out of her room, walked right through the center of the sound, and halfway down the stairs where she stopped, hands on her lips.

"Aren't you going to answer the phone?"

"The phone?" At the sound of my question, the birdsong shattered into the regular electronic bleating of the telephone. I stared at Emma who was obviously running her Mommy Disaster checklist. "Just on my way," I said way too cheerily and ran to catch the call in the kitchen.

It was Neil. I didn't have to ask; his voice had the empty flatness of shock. "We're pressing charges."

I thought of Lydia's apparition, how it vanished from my arms a few moments earlier. "I'm so sorry, Neil."

"Amanda's a wreck. Blaming herself. You know, I thought I was ready for the worst possible outcome. But, my God, Leslie" He stopped, I could hear him struggling to stay on the flatlands. "Well, she's got contusions inside her, internally, and the doctor found what looks like . . . oh, Jesus, teeth marks on her . . ." He didn't finish. I could hear his breathing and the busy drone of the emergency room behind it. Finally, he said, "I'd better go check on Amanda."

I made the usual useless noises about our family being available to help theirs any way we could. I don't think he heard me. He clicked off; I hung up my end of the line, ready to admit I'd been wrong in my suspicions of Neil, at least. Ready, but not quite able to voice that admission aloud. What if I were wrong about being wrong? Yes, but he had been the one to convince Amanda of the necessity of the SART procedure. But that might have been nothing more than a feint. Some feint, he wouldn't be able to protect himself by making evidence available. And so the vortex of doubt spun on. I was ashamed of my inability to stop it. How many times and to how many authorities did the man have to prove himself above reproach – yes, but had he proved it? – and didn't Lydia's sick and terrified apparition suggest the threat was ongoing? But she swears that no one is touching her – "Stop it," I said, commanding myself to cease the endless circling and get on with the next thankless task on my to-do list. I had to inform Molly that the hope she'd been holding on to, that she could get out of this unidentified, had sprung a disastrous leak. I grabbed a couple sodas and a bag of pretzels, and headed upstairs for a tea party with my daughter.

Greg and Bill, the termite guy, were on their way out the front door. Bill was lecturing on mud tubes and humidity factors and bait placement strategies. "Nothing in the attic," Greg said with the intonation of a B-movie zombie. "We have to take samples around the house now."

Bill took Greg by the elbow and pulled him outside. "See. Look there.

The mulch? That's exactly the sort of conducive environment I was worried about." The front door closed on Greg's mouthing *help me.*

The sight of the attic steps brought me up short. As unnerving as the hallucinations could be, I wasn't often frightened by them. They belonged to me, a private symbolic language for stories yet beyond words; I might have dreaded what stories the visions would eventually reveal but not the visions themselves. I feared the real that existed beyond my mind. The attic steps frightened me because they were real and always would be. What lay at the top of them would be real, as well: the realization that time had moved on but I had not. If it had been only me, I would have turned and left the house and kept going forever, but it wasn't only me. I made myself continue on up to the second floor.

To get to Molly's room, I had to squeeze through the narrow space left between the open stringer of the attic steps and the wall of the hallway. I held my breath and raised the sodas and pretzels over my head, trying not to let any part of the steps touch me. Successful – and chagrined by the continued need to evade what I already knew – I knocked on Molly's door. When she didn't answer, I opened the door. She wasn't there.

"Molly!" I hollered, trying to fill the sound of her name with the implication of all the misery that was going to come down on her young head if she had dared to leave the house.

"I'm up here." She was sitting on the edge of the attic floor, her stocking feet pulled up to her so that only the tips of her toes rested on the top riser of the attic steps. "Dad said it was okay."

Okay. I held out the soda as an offering, bribe. "Want to come down and talk?"

She ignored the invitation. "Was that phone call about Lydia?"

"Yes, it was. Come on down and – "

"I'd rather stay up here." Had she figured out that I would not come up after her? Or was she just hedging her bet that I was less likely to talk about certain things out here in the middle of the house? If it was the latter, she'd guessed wrong.

I lowered the soda can. "You know, you could have just asked me. I would have helped you without the whole Lydia running-away scam."

She shrugged. "If I'd said anything before she took off, I'd have had to explain how I knew what was wrong, and I don't want to do that. If she was gone, I was sure you'd come look for her and make sure she got the chance to tell her side of what happened to the right people. Because, you know, it's your job."

"You weren't sure I'd come out because *you* needed help?"

"Well, you always *see* other kids. Dad says you *see* these kids because you're worried about them. You never *see* Emma or me, do you?"

"Oh, baby – no, I don't see you or Emma. But I hope I never ever see you the way I see other kids. I don't ever want to be that worried about you."

She nodded but did not look convinced. "How is Lydia?"

"Things are not good."

"Oh. Is there going to be a court deal?"

"Maybe. If it goes to trial."

"If it does, will I have to, you know?"

"I would imagine so." I ventured a couple inches closer to the steps. I wanted to put my arms around her, small comfort though it would be. "If it comes to that, you're going to be an important witness."

Molly didn't say anything, just looked down at her knees.

"I am very, very worried about Lydia," I said, and Molly raised her eyes in question. "Yes. I saw her."

"When?"

"A little while ago, here in the house. You asked me to tell you, so I'm telling you. I saw Lydia. I'm afraid she's hurting bad."

"That's what you saw."

"That's the truth in what I saw. I want to know the truth in what you saw at the party."

"I've told you the truth. I told that police person. I can't change the story simply because you don't believe me. Anyway, now that Lydia is back, you have someone you have to believe."

"Believing isn't the issue, sweetheart. The problem is that Lydia's injuries suggest more went on at that house than either you or the boys or even Lydia is saying."

"Maybe she did stuff to herself," Molly said in a tone that sounded more authoritative than questioning. "She's weird like that."

I was about to ask Molly what exactly she meant by "weird," when the phone started ringing. After the third ring, Emma shouted from the kitchen, "Mom, that Carlos guy at your office place wants to know if you can come to the phone."

"Carlos?" I looked up at Molly, who smiled a bit, no doubt grateful for the interruption. I told her not to move, I'd be right back. I squeezed past the steps again to get the phone in Greg's room.

"Hey, Ms. Stone."

"Hey yourself. Is there a problem?"

"Not sure. But there's this guy who keeps coming round asking for you. The first time was last night around nine. I told him your office was closed, but he kept saying he had an appointment. I told him you'd left for the day, so then he tries to hustle by me and get up the stairs. I escorted his ass out the door. But he was back bright and early this morning. He's been in here like five times, and I've seen him pass by at least twice that many. Like he's pacing outside, waiting for you. He won't leave his name or a message. He keeps saying it's important he see you in person."

"What does he look like?"

"Real nondescript. Soft voice. Talks very formally."

"Medium everything? Thick, dark hair?"

"That's him. Absolutely."

Carse. He'd changed his mind about sharing and had come to collect his pages. *My life's work.* "When he comes in again, tell him I said that what he wants isn't at the Reeves, and that if he wants to speak to me to leave a number where I may reach him. If he does leave a number, call me back. If not – call me anyway."

"Absolutely. There he goes again, walking past the front door right now. He's really creeping me out."

"You and me both. I appreciate the heads-up."

He chuckled. "Remember it come Christmas."

"Absolutely."

We said good-bye. I sat on the edge of the unmade bed, staring at the tangle of sheets and comforters, the deeply shadowed folds where little things with teeth could hide undetected waiting for you to lie down, drowsy and vulnerable. I thought of Sara Bateson, her soft, pillowy shape, how she wouldn't begin to fight if Carse decided to punish her. A jolt of adrenaline hit my heart. I redialed the Reeves and got a busy signal. I then called the city police and asked them to go check on Carlos and Sara; I had reason to suspect they were in imminent danger. No, I didn't have the Bateson address with me, but she was the mother of Vanessa Bateson, if that helped. Yes, that Vanessa Bateson. I described Theodore Carse and warned he might be armed. They said they'd do what they could. I leaped to my feet and tried to remember where I'd dropped my keys. Downstairs.

Out in the hallway, Molly was shoving at the attic steps, attempting to get them to fold up again.

"What's wrong, Mom?"

"I have to go to my office for a while. I'll be back as soon as I can. I'm sorry."

"But what about – "

"I'm sorry, Molly," I half shouted at her as I loped down the stairs. I heard her harrumph behind me, "Yeah. Right."

I found my keys and sprinted for my car, which was blocked in by the termite van. I threw open the van door, hoping Bill had left the keys. He had not. I leaned on his horn. "La Cucaracha" blared repeatedly until Bill came tearing around the corner of the house, Greg right behind him.

"Move it!" I yelled, pointing at the van.

Greg grabbed me by the arm. "What the hell, Les – "

I didn't have time to explain something I couldn't have begun to explain anyway. Bill was backing up his van. I wrested myself out of Greg's grip and jumped in my car, shouting at Greg not to let Molly leave the house. The termite van was barely out of the way when I shifted into gear, my tires squealing as I hit the accelerator. I sped down the driveway, calculating times from Old Quarry to the highway, from the highway to the Reeves, already certain I wasn't going to make it fast enough. In the rearview mirror I could see Greg, staring down at the streaks of burnt rubber I'd left at his feet.

Once I was on Old Quarry, I wanted to see if I could reach Carlos. And after him, Greg, to have him make certain Molly was all right and that she understood this was an emergency. I reached over and opened the glove compartment, trying not to take my eyes off the road, and dug around for my cell phone, getting more frustrated by the second, sending maps and manuals scattering to the floor. And then I did take my eyes off the road to look. Where the hell was my phone?

m o l l y

Molly pushes the Dial button on her mother's cell phone, listens to the numbers beep as the call goes through. She is so nervous; the butterflies in her belly are flying around on steel-spiked wings. Mrs. Zinni answers, and Molly stammers through the reason she needs to talk to Tim again, if it's okay and she isn't bothering anyone because if it was a bad time, she could –

"I'll get him, Molly, dear. Hold on."

She decides to hang up but then undecides, because he'd know it was her anyway and she didn't want to seem geeky like that. Besides, this was important. He needed to know as soon as possible.

"Hello?"

"Hi, Tim. Me again. Molly?"

"Yeah. My mom said."

"How are you?"

"All right."

"That's good."

"You want something?"

"I called to tell you about Lydia. They took her to the hospital – "

"Is she all right?"

"She's all right. I meant they took her to look for signs that she had been, you know."

"And she's all right?"

"My mom says not really. They found something, and my mom says that Lydia's parents are going to be, you know, pressing charges."

Molly hears a gasp and then a softly breaking sob.

"All right," says Tim, his voice level. "Mom, it's all right."

Mrs. Zinni inhales deeply and says, "We're going to fight it, Tim. All the way."

"All right."

"You'll have your day in court, don't you worry, honey – "

"I thought you'd want to know." Molly doesn't say good-bye; she hangs up as Mrs. Zinni continues to reassure Tim. Molly hits the Power Off button on the phone, watching the usual *good-bye* animation before the shutdown. The screen goes dark. Funny about that. A person would never know what had appeared there a second earlier. And if she tried to explain it, she'd first have to believe she'd seen it herself. How could she do that, for certain, if she was the only one who saw it? It was easy to do for things like cell phones. Everyone had seen the little dancing telephone waving farewell while that dorky music played. But what if you were the only one who had seen something? Molly thinks about her mother seeing things. People believe her. They think she's crazy, but they believe she sees what she says she sees. Molly believes her mom saw Lydia. Why would she lie about it? More important, Mom not only believes she sees these things but also that these dreams or ghosts or whatever they are require Mom to do something on their behalf. *You know what you saw.* A shudder of something colder than cold shakes Molly's body. *You know what you saw.*

She says it aloud. "I know what I saw." For the first time since this started, she is beginning to believe.

the one left behind

The side street that was my usual shortcut to the Reeves had been closed
for repaving. I had to thread my way through the one ways and no left
turns downtown, so that when I finally got there, I came up on the back
side of the building. I double-parked beside a minivan. A bag lady in an
oversized man's parka and unbuckled rain boots was wheeling a wagon
full of empty bottles along the sidewalk. She pointed out that I wasn't
supposed to do that. I thanked her for her concern and began to run for
the front of the Reeves, fighting the blasts of wind that used the city streets
as corridors. It was colder than when I left; I wished I'd thought to grab a
jacket.

I rounded the corner and saw a patrol car. Then I saw Theodore Carse.
Two uniformed officers had corralled him against the rear bumper of
their vehicle. Carse, dressed far too nicely in a charcoal wool coat over a
gray suit and red tie, was speaking animatedly to one of the officers, his
gloved hands punching the air in emphasis. The other officer appeared to
be going through Carse's ID. Carse turned his head, saw me, and tried to
push through the officers.

"That's her," he said, nearly shouting, as I approached. "That's the
woman I'm here to see."

"I am also the woman who called the police," I said, catching my breath
by blowing the heated air into my chilled hands.

"Why did you do that? You were the one who asked me to come down
here. You said you needed my help."

"You are" – the officer who wasn't holding Carse's wallet consulted his
notepad – "Leslie Stone?"

I nodded. "Look, Carse, I don't understand why you think we have an
appointment. I did not call you. I never requested your help."

"You took my notes."

"You gave me your notes. You want them back?"

The officer with the notepad tilted his head, motioning me aside. "We got nothing here, ma'am, but a man with a mixed-up appointment calendar. He's not carrying a weapon. He's not making threats. He's walking round the block to keep warm; that doesn't quite make for loitering. We got to let him go about his business."

I looked up at the front entrance of the Reeves, where Carlos was standing holding the door halfway open. He snapped me a salute. I turned back to the officer. "I'm not sure that's a good idea."

"We've got no choice." The officer lowered his voice and said, "He's a weird duck, that's for certain." We both sneaked a peek at Carse, who had given up the argument and was now gazing at me. Anxious. Beseeching.

I glanced at the officer's notepad and saw Sara's name. "Did you get in touch with Mrs. Bateson?"

"Not me personally, but we have confirmation from the neighbor that she's out of town visiting relatives for a while. Said she's been under a lot of stress the past few days."

"And Carse would be one of the sources of that stress. Has anyone been out to physically check her house?"

"Not sure about that. All I got here is that the neighbor had been asked by Mrs. Bateson to look after the woman's pet cat."

"Was the neighbor male or female?"

"Doesn't say."

I looked over at Carse. A darkness opened in my mind, a cold sinkhole of certainty. "Get someone out to that house. Find out what her travel arrangements were. Find out if she actually showed up anywhere."

The officer squinted at me, as though trying to remember something. "Okay, I see where you're going with this, Ms. Stone. But according to the doorman, that Carse fellow has been hanging around here the entire morning."

"But we don't know what he was doing last night, or yesterday afternoon, do we?"

"I'll call it in, but you understand, we're damn tight on manpower, and I am going to have to let Carse walk 'cause – "

"Tell you what, I'll keep Carse here with me, keep him busy until you make sure Sara Bateson is safe and sound."

He raised the brim of his cap. "That could be hours."

"I'll be here." I took the pen from his hand and scribbled my office phone number at the bottom of the page. "Call me after you – you personally – have spoken to the woman. And then have Mrs. Bateson call me."

"Yes, ma'am – and maybe I can have the department's catering service send you over a nice little supper so that you don't get peckish during the wait."

"Oh, could you? That would be lovely."

He gave me a sideways smirk of disgust. He hitched his thumb at his partner, who handed back the wallet to Carse and headed for the passenger side of the patrol car, leaving Carse alone on the sidewalk, looking about in confusion. Officer Smirk gave Carse the once-over, no doubt cementing the man's description in his mind. "We'll be in touch," he said to the scene in general. "Weird ducks."

Complain as he might, I knew he'd follow through on Sara, not because of my suspicions but because of his own. The squad car pulled away. I went over to where Carse was waiting, trying not to grin.

"Give me your gloves."

"Pardon me?"

"Gloves."

"Ah. I understand." He took them off and handed them over. "You want me to leave fingerprints."

"Very good. So you probably won't require explanation for the reasons behind the rest of the rules."

"Rules? The officers searched me thoroughly; you have nothing to fear from me, Leslie – "

"That's rule number one: I am Mrs. Stone to you. We are not friends."

"We could be."

"Not in this life. Rule number two: You stay in front of me. You stop when I say stop. You sit when I say sit. Step out of my line of sight, step out of line period, and you will live to regret it in such a way that you will never be able to see your own scars. Rule three – "

"Remember rules one and two?"

"Well, at least we understand each other," I said as I gestured toward the front entrance. "Let's go."

He bent his head in submission – "Yes, Mrs. Stone" – and headed up the entrance walkway. My stomach did a queasy little lurch; I couldn't tell if it was in apprehension of what the afternoon might hold or a sick realization that, whether intended or not, I'd played myself right into Carse's fantasies. The difference didn't matter. I knew only that I did not want to spend a nanosecond longer than necessary with this person. I looked up at the lion as I climbed the stairs. Ice had formed along the features. The bronze snout glittered and dark icicles hung from its fangs.

Carlos met us at the door. He said nothing to Carse but fixed him with the sort of stare you got from big dogs behind chain link fences. "You need help with anything, Ms. Stone?" He had to raise his voice a bit to be heard over the fan of the space heater Reeves management had set up in the lobby. Noisy, but the heat was wonderful.

"Not at the moment." I pointed toward the stairs. "We'll be in my office."

Carlos looked at his wristwatch. "In about fifteen minutes, I'll be doing rounds on your floor. So I'll check in on you then. Maybe sooner."

"We'll be watching for you," Carse said with a smile.

"New rule: No talking to anyone."

"Yes, ma'am."

Carlos poked Carse in the shoulder. "I think the lady told you to zip it, asshole."

"Thank you, Carlos, but I've got everything under control, okay?"

"Absolutely, Ms. Stone. Just offering you some backup."

"This isn't your problem." I nudged Carse to get him moving. "See you in fifteen."

Carse started up the stairs; I stayed a couple of risers behind. At the first landing he paused and began to remove his overcoat. "It's too hot," he said with the petulant overtones of a child who believed himself to be wrongly disciplined.

"I'll carry it."

"I can manage to carry my own coat."

"I want to be able to see your hands." I extended my arm, and he dropped the heavy charcoal wool over it. It was warm with his body heat; it gave off an odor that held the faintest edge of rubber cement. I went through the coat pockets as we continued the climb. Empty.

162

We were almost to the third floor when Carse looked back at me and sighed. "I can't understand why you would lie to the police about calling me."

"No lie. I did not call you, Carse."

"Oh. I get it. Semantics. True, it was your secretary who called to say you needed to see me ASAP." He had reached the reception area at the top of the stairs. "But that is the same as you calling, isn't it?"

"Nice try." I came up behind him. "I don't have a secretary." I directed him across the center of the reception area toward my door. Being the weekend, the lights up here were off and the space was in shadow except for the trio of bright rectangular shafts from the skylights. Carse had stepped out of one shaft of sunlight and partially into another when he turned back to me.

"You don't have a secretary?"

"No." The confusion in his question finally convinced me the story wasn't a ploy.

"You really got a call?"

For a few seconds after I heard Sara Bateson say, "I called him," I thought she might be one of my visions, telling me what I'd just now figured out. When I saw Carse's reaction, his slow, backward withdrawal from the light, I knew she was no hallucination. As if in response to my granting her reality, Sara came forward out of the shadows. She was wearing the same flowered dress as when I last saw her. Her hair was mussed and her makeup was smeared as though we'd awakened her.

The queasiness in my stomach began to expand. "You called him here?"

She didn't acknowledge my question. When she raised the gun at Carse, her hands shook so that the weapon bucked about in front of her. "I've been waiting for you since yesterday."

"It couldn't have been you, Sara." Carse sounded more amazed than frightened. "After all the time we've spent on the phone, I think I would have recognized your voice."

"I thought of that. I did. So it was my friend – I had a neighbor lady call. It doesn't matter, does it?" She glanced at me. At least she knew someone else was there.

"Sara?" I let Carse's coat slide to the floor. I held my hands up, open

163

palms facing out – dual meanings in universal sign language: I carry nothing and stop where you are. "You don't want to do this." I took a couple steps toward her, testing; she did not take the gun off Carse. A couple steps closer. "You can't do Vanessa any good this way."

"I know." She nodded hard, and her breath caught, breaking almost into sobs.

Carse continued to back up; for every step he took away from her, Sara took two steps closer. "Don't move," I said to him, to both of them.

Carse halted, but Sara walked steadily forward. "I don't want to see anyone hurt anymore, Leslie. That's why I'm going to stop him." She was at a slight angle to me now. She was perspiring, blinking rapidly. I doubted she had ever fired as much as a cap gun. She was scared and tired, far beyond her limits. That made her infinitely more dangerous.

"I meant no harm. Please. Understand that."

I could hear the desperation in Carse's voice. He had gone rigid the way a prey animal does at the moment of attack as if to signal that it couldn't be killed as it was already dead. I didn't dare move, either. I didn't want to startle her or have her firing off wildly. "Sara Bateson, put the gun down. Right now."

"What you need to understand, Mr. Carse," she said as she raised the gun to her own temple, "is what it feels like to be the one left behind." She closed her eyes. Carse, acting on that instinct which focuses on the threat rather than the target, used the instant of Sara's distraction to grab at her gun hand as she squeezed the trigger. The bullet hit one of the office doors, shattering the glass. Sara dropped the gun and then sank to her knees. The back of her head was bleeding, wetting her hair and neck. I rushed to grab her before she fell over.

"Carse! Go get help. Call nine-one-one." He didn't move. I couldn't be certain he even heard me as he stood studying the fine spray of Sara's blood on his own skin.

9

And then you are running. You don't know where you are running to, only what you are running from. And yet, no matter how hard or fast you go, the garage seems to stay right behind you, as though it is chasing you, a hulking monster's head filled with gold light and the sound of breaking bone. The farther you get from it, the larger and louder it becomes. You don't look back out of fear it is right on your heels, the big front doors swung wide revealing a golden void behind a gate of gleaming teeth. *Run*.

Pebbles and sticks sting the soles of your bare feet. You hear yourself say that it hurts; the sensation of impact is distinct, but you can't seem to connect the feeling with the words. It's as though your body and mind have separated and are communicating with each other via postcards and Morse code over an ever increasing distance. Eventually the idea of getting off the unkind surface of the driveway is delivered to your feet. You veer off into the grass. It is wet with dew. You have difficulty keeping your balance. You stumble and fall.

And then you are running again. You remember falling but not regaining your feet. You have jumped ahead in time, leaving behind only a blank space where you should have information. It happens again. Several minutes are missing this time; they must be because you are now ankle-deep, squatting in Lake Yuck, surrounded by long bladed reeds. Hiding. Mud oozes between your toes. Mucky green algae stink fills your head. Any second now you are going to throw up. You have no recall of how you got here. Close by a frog is croaking out alarm. Splashing sounds bounce across the water. It is so dark here you can see nothing. And you hope nothing can see you, either.

A breeze kicks up, cutting through the reeds, tickling your sweaty skin. Your body sends an emissary to your mind advising that the outlying territories are cold and would appreciate a direct order for concerted effort back toward the warmth of the house. Your mind opens the request for debate, and while you stay very still, awaiting some sort of consensus, a new sound interrupts the proceedings. Far away, coming closer. A scratchy sliding sound of something heavy being dragged along the driveway. Drag. Stop. Drag.

You know what it is. Oh, God, you know what it is. Cover your ears. Shut your eyes. And you can't help but see what's in your head: Your father is dragging away what is left of the man in the garage. The sound drags on past the edge of the water, out toward the road. You realize how close you are to the driveway, how close you are to being seen. You need to get out of here. Now.

And then you are in the kitchen with no memory of having left the reeds. Your lungs are aching and your feet are bleeding. Your arms are scratched. You are crying for lots of reasons but mostly, right now, because your brain is messing up. You should not be losing time like this. You keep losing your place in time.

o m n i   m u t a n t u r   . . .

Greg had tried to talk me into coming back out to Swifton that night, or they would come into the city and stay with me. He thought it unwise, given the circumstances, that I spend too much time alone. I told him not to worry; I was safe in my apartment. He needed to keep reassuring the girls that although *things* might not be okay, *I* was. I'd be back out to the house as soon as I could. He said good-bye, still sounding unconvinced. I said good-bye, relieved to be finished talking to people. I wanted only silence and solitude for the next few hours.

I sat in the dark of my living room trying to perfect the boilermaker by varying the swallows of beer to shots of rye. I kept seeing Carlos, as he clambered to the top of the stairs, shouting, "Are you all right?" his boyish face as he got the answer to his question, the terror and its attendant thrill registering in his eyes.

Thanks to Carse, the bullet had only grazed Sara, gashing her scalp and nicking her skull. She would recover physically with little complication. The complicated work would come later. The search of Sara Bateson's home had inevitably moved way up on the list of police priorities. A note had been found, and after a few calls, I was able to get someone to read it to me over the phone.

To my friends and family –
   It has come to my attention that the man named Theodore Carse is most likely a threat to the safety of our children. I may not have been able to save my dearest Vanessa from those such as him, but I must do whatever I am able to prevent him from causing similar agony for other parents.
   Do not be sad for me. When this over I will be with Vanessa. Sara

It has come to my attention. I wondered if she'd hit on the plan even before she'd left my office last week. I could imagine her in the cab on the way back to her empty house, mulling over my speculation about Carse's ultimate intent until it became prophecy. I could, in fact, imagine Sara writing the note. She'd have done it at the kitchen table, the last thing she did before leaving her house for what she expected to be the last time. I'd never been to Sara's home. I'd known the woman only a matter of hours, but I could imagine her preparations: scrubbing the floors, emptying the fridge, leaving instructions for the neighbor who was to look after the cat. Sara would not have left a mess for anyone else to worry over. The furniture would be dusted and the carpets vacuumed. Down the hall, behind a closed door, would be Vanessa's bedroom. Save for the careful cleaning each day, the room would have gone unaltered since the child vanished. I imagined Vanessa's French Provincial furniture, white with gilt trim, pink gingham and eyelet lace on the canopy bed where I imagined Sara sat the whole of the night, her universe collapsing back down into the single bright speck out of which new universes explode. A purpose to her suffering. The investigation had quickly revealed that the weapon had been borrowed from a family member, a rational act of self-security in consideration of Carse's harassment of Sara. Who could have known where that would lead? Who could have imagined?

They'd cleaned Carse up, double checking him for injuries. The EMT gave him one of the squad's spare shirts to change into, offering to bag up his ruined suit as she congratulated him for his quick thinking. He'd saved Sara Bateson's life. Heroic. That's what it was. Carse stared at her mute and motionless until the EMT realized the man's state of shock might have deeper currents. She gently explained that she thought it was a good idea for him to ride along to the hospital, maybe have a doctor take a look at him. Carse let her take his arm and lead him to the ambulance.

Officer Smirk and his partner, who had returned on hearing the call come over dispatch, stood beside me on the sidewalk watching Carse being secured in the jumpseat. "Funny, isn't it?"

I glared at him. "It is?"

"Naw. Not like that. I meant the guy so obviously needed help. Probably would never have sought it for himself. Maybe he'll get some now. Along with the woman."

"Maybe. But you have to want help before you can get it."

"You have to take whatever silver lining you can find."

"Even at the risk of mercury poisoning?"

"Don't go begrudging a guy his optimism. You stop looking for the good because you're tired, that's one thing. But you stop looking for the good because you think it don't exist? That's when you go crazy."

The partner nodded and said, "I had an aunt went crazy with mercury poisoning. Turned out it was the fillings in her teeth."

"She still got her teeth?" asked Smirk.

"Every last one."

"That's what I'm saying."

"That's what the man was saying," I said, toasting my beer can with the – oops, empty again – shot glass. "Shut up," I then said to the telephone, which was ringing and ringing and ringing. Finally the answering machine kicked in and prerecorded me was apologizing for not being around to take the call but please, please, please call back, because the caller, whoever it might be, was really really important to me. Or something like that. After the long *beeeeep* that told the caller that, believe it or not, he was not the first to try to reach me this evening came the short, *talk now* beep and then some guy's voice saying a name I didn't recognize and that he was an attorney representing the management of the Reeves Building and he needed to speak with me immediately about my lease. Good-bye.

They were going to try to toss me out of the building. That's what they were going to do. I'd probably violated some kind "shooting in the public areas" clause or corollary or amendment or whatever. Well, we'd see about that, we would. Yes, sireee, Bob. We. Would. See. "Toss this, you bastards." I threw a can at the phone – or in the general direction of the phone. And then it occurred to me that I needed to call this asshole back and let him know that I wasn't going to just curtsey and make a quiet exit. I got up, and on my way to the phone in the dark, I stepped on the can I'd thrown, and as if in revenge, it caused me to stumble backward and come down on the coffee table in such a way that the corner of the table hit my kneecap. So that's the way it was going to be, huh? I picked myself up and started out for the phone again.

And then everything was hazy bright and I was looking up at the ceiling of my bedroom. I was undressed to my underwear and under the covers;

my sweater and jeans were folded over the back of the rocking chair. My head felt as though something were trying to tunnel through it with an ice pick. I slowly became aware of the smell of coffee, and then of noises in the kitchen. I moved the blankets aside and tried to sit up. My right knee throbbed. I reached down to touch the pain and found a plastic bag with the melted remains of an ice pack. Next to the bed was a big glass of water and a couple of aspirin tablets lying in wait. "Hello?" I called out as loudly as I dared.

"Good morning," came the reply.

I recognized the voice and fell back against the pillow. Great. Hungover and humiliated.

Phillip came into the room. He was trying hard not laugh. "You don't remember calling me do you?"

"I called you?"

"Hell yeah. We're suing the shit out of someone first thing this morning, that's what we're doing. Or we're baking bread. I couldn't quite make out the schedule of events."

He was wearing the old blue and white softball T-shirt and jeans he usually wore when he was up late doing research. I closed my eyes. "Sorry."

"I bet you are." He sat down at the foot of the bed. "But I heard about what happened, so you know, I'm sorry, too."

"I appreciate that" – I squinted him back into focus – "but you didn't have to come over just because I called."

"That's what ex-whatever-we-weres are for. I knew there must have been a reason I kept forgetting to send you back my key." He scratched at his cheek. "And thanks for keeping my razor."

"I meant you shouldn't have come over."

"Probably not, but you sounded in a bad way. It would have been wrong not to check up on you." He gave me a small, sad version of his asymmetrical smile. My heart upped its dirge tempo to that of a broken-down waltz: *I know you . . .*

"You still shouldn't have come. You should have called Greg."

"Oh, yes. That's who I should have called."

"Okay, maybe not, but you realize I called you because I wanted a lawyer."

"Darling, you wanted a lot of things last night – but don't panic, you didn't get any of them."

"Well, you can go now."

"Do you want me to go now?"

"Do you want to stay?"

"What do you mean by *stay?*"

"Why can't you ever just answer a question?"

"Why can't you ever just tell me what it is you want from me?"

"Christ, Mr. Hogarth, I thought I did. I told you that you could go."

"That's not the same thing as telling me you want me to go."

"My head hurts too much to be having this conversation."

"Too bad. It's the middle of the night, you're drunk and in trouble and you're not caring about right or wrong or what the neighbors will think, and you call me. That says something, Les. I want to know if it says what I think it says."

"Let's recall who told whom he couldn't take the 'ordeal' of this relationship any longer?"

"You're the only one who's allowed to have a bad day?"

"You know, I think it may be time for me to pack up my penchant for bad days and move the hell away from all of you. All I seem to do is screw up other people's lives."

"Self-pity does not become you, Leslie."

"Screw you."

He stood up. "Call me when you're feeling better and I might let you." He turned to go. "I'm keeping my key."

"I'll change the locks!"

"Right," he shouted back, laughing. He said something else, which I couldn't make out, and then I heard the apartment door bang shut. Goddamn last word on everything. We'd see about that. At the very least, I'd get my key back, even if I had to chase him down into the street. I sat up, threw the blankets aside, and stood best I could. Hobbled over to the rocker and grabbed my sweater, yanking it down over my head as my brain sent up emergency flares that exploded behind my eyes. Limping, I hurried out into the front room, only to be greeted by a sight that sent me reeling backward until I was stopped by the wall.

The Nightingale girls, the ten that I was able to see, were gathered in my living room. More substantial this time, the color coming back to them, they looked like they had walked out of hand-tinted photographs. All in their nightclothes, they were seated on the couch, standing near the window, playing with the dials on the television. As one, they turned their attention to me, as if they were waiting.

"I don't know what you want." I slid down the wall, my knee shrieking unhappiness. The girls came over, surrounding me, staring at me with some doubt, as though they were unsure I was real. Their feet, some slippered, some bare, a stubbed toe, a blister, seemed to hover on the nap of the carpet, touching it but not sinking in. Weightless. "I don't understand," I whispered. "Where is Janet?" In immediate response, a cloud of perfume closed off my throat with as much solidity of force as a rope – or a pair of hands. I clawed at my neck, trying to get it to let go. *This isn't real.* The Nightingales leaned in to observe more closely; the edges of my vision went dim. *You are not real.* They were still closing in on me when I passed out.

"You should have stayed in bed." Phillip pressed the cold washcloth against my neck.

"I wanted coffee," I lied, propping my back against the wall.

"You could have waited. I said I was just going to get a paper." He took my arm. "Come on, Self-Sufficiency Girl, let's get your heroicness off the floor."

"Be nice."

"I will if you will." He helped me get to my feet. "So what did you see? And don't argue – I can tell when you've been, ah, visited."

I allowed myself to lean against him as he guided me to the couch. "You're the only one who ever wants to know – except for my shrinks, of course."

"Of course. Stop evading the question."

I told him about the Nightingale girls, not just of that morning but also the apparitions of the past few days, which meant I had to also tell him about Molly and Lydia's party backward through my first meeting with Carse and Sara Bateson. But I didn't tell him everything. I never told anyone everything.

He sat beside me, his arms folded over his legs, listening hard. When I'd finished, he was quiet awhile. Then he asked, in his very best no-nonsense lawyer fashion, "Were you one of these Nightingales?"

"No, but honestly, at times, I wish I had been. It would have made a lot of things easier."

"You want to explain that one?"

"No."

"But you believe these girls are connected to this Carse guy and your daughter?"

"Did you ever have a kaleidoscope when you were a kid?"

"Ladies and gentlemen, the infamous Leslie Stone U-turn."

"Hear me out. The first one I ever had, well, it was really Denise's, was one of those cardboard tube deals they gave out as favors at birthday parties. I must have been five or six. Anyway, I wanted to know how those pretty patterns showed up, so I took the thing apart. Pulled the end off. Found the mirrors. Found that the bottom wasn't filled with beautiful patterns, just a spoonful of shiny bits of oddly shaped plastic. I didn't understand how it worked, only that it wasn't what I thought. So I put it back together and then, when I looked again, I couldn't see the whole of the pattern anymore. I saw only the multiple reflections of individual pieces of plastic. That's what these past few days have been like; I know I'm supposed to be seeing something larger, but as yet I can only see the parts."

He thought about that for a minute. "Which of the parts worries you most?"

"Molly. The one I can't bear to lose."

m o l l y

Mom calls again after supper on Sunday night to apologize for not being able to get right back out to Swifton, but she promises to be there in time to pick Molly up from school the next day. She wants to be there when Molly goes down to the police station so Detective Burnham can videotape her statement. Molly says okay and then puts Emma on the phone. Emma whines about her stomach and starts to cry. Molly leaves the kitchen to go back to her room. She plans what she'll wear to school tomorrow: her new black denim skirt, the red sweater, red tights, and black clogs. She'll braid her hair. Tomorrow will be the big test, the one for which she can't possibly study. She feels strangely calm, the way she's heard drowning victims feel after they finally surrender to the water. She finishes her homework and then gets ready for bed. She's dead calm, but she can't fall asleep.

The next morning, Dad says that she looks very tired, and that given everything that's been going on for the past few days, he has no problem with her staying home if she wants. Call it a mental health day, he says. Emma puts her head down next to her cereal bowl. She says that she wants to stay home, too. Dad seems distracted, he stares at Emma as though he doesn't know what to do. Molly says no thanks to the day off, she'll be fine and so will Em. She tugs at her sister until Emma gets up, and they leave for the bus stop together.

The kids at the bus stop say hi. Emma goes over to hang out with Rita and her brothers. Molly says hi to everyone but stands off by herself, happy no one is asking her questions. It's not that she doesn't feel bad for the woman who almost killed herself. She does; it's very sad. But Molly can't help but feel grateful for the cover provided by her mother's connection to the event. If Molly seems quiet or out of it, everyone will think she's worried about what happened in the city. She's worried, all right: worried that the teacher who overheard the "fight" will realize it was Molly Stone who was yelling at Lydia; worried that the teacher will talk and word will get around and no one will understand that the fight was staged, that Lydia and she planned it because it made Lydia's *memory* of the party sound more real; mostly she's worried that her mom won't be able to keep her concentration on Lydia's problem and the whole of Molly's plan will fall apart. And then both she and Lydia will be in the deep end of trouble. Molly doesn't even want to think about the consequences should Lydia start remembering or, even worse, if she figures out that if you can fake one memory, no reason you can't fake another.

When the bus arrives, Molly is the last one on. The driver smiles sweetly at her. "How you doing, honey?"

"Fine," she says, "I'm fine." Experience has taught her *fine* is what people want to hear because the more awful a person feels for you the less that person knows what to do about it. Say that you're fine, and you'll get a nod and a sigh of relief that nothing more is expected. Say it often enough and everyone starts to believe it, even you. They call you things like "brave" and "strong," admiring you for not needing them. In the end, being fine is the kindest thing you can do for everyone.

The bus nears Swifton Woods Junior High, and Molly, resting her head against the rattling bus window, sees a group of adults gathered at the edge of the entrance drive. Some of them have baby strollers. Some are carrying painted signs, cardboard stapled to pieces of wood. The signs are lettered in broad strokes: CRIMINALS BELONG IN PRISON. PROTECT OUR CHILDREN. Cars pulling into the school grounds and those driving past honk their horns and the sign carriers hoot and shake their fists in the air. As the bus passes them, the adults turn the signs away from the windows. They wave and blow kisses at the kids. Molly looks over at Emma sitting with Rita a couple rows down on the other side of the aisle. Emma and Rita – and the other kids – are leaning over trying to see what's happening. Emma catches Molly's eye. Molly, not knowing what to tell her little sister, just shakes her head. Emma misreads the gesture and shouts not to worry, she didn't break her promise. Molly raises her finger to her lips. *Hush*.

She remains seated until the last of the junior high kids files past in the aisle and then takes her place at the end of the line. She squeezes Emma's shoulder as she inches past – reassurance and warning. Out on the walkway, Molly waits to watch the bus pull out, headed for the elementary school. Even though she can't see Emma, she worries her sister might be scared again. So Molly puts a big smile on her face and waves good-bye to the bus. It's going to be a great day. Everything is fine.

She then watches the junior high kids joining up with friends and filing up the steps past Mr. Verrill, the principal, who bumps fists and laughs and good mornings everyone as they disappear into the arched entrance of the Old Building. Molly starts up the steps and notices, for the first time, that the brown bricks on the west side of Old Building are streaked with soot. The soot stains climb upward toward the top of the building, thinning and branching like the shadow of a tree. The effect is so striking that Molly slows to a stop, staring, wondering why she never noticed it before. She would probably have stood there the whole day had not Mr. Verrill interrupted her thoughts.

"How are we this morning, Miss Stone?" Mr. Verrill, the youngest principal the Swifton district has ever appointed, always uses *we*. He wants you to know he sees Swifton Woods Junior High as a team. We're in this together.

Molly straightens. Best to get this over with – if he knows, he knows. She meets his eyes, says nothing. He cocks his shaggy head, half smiles, waiting. He doesn't know. Not yet.

"We're okay."

"You don't sound so sure. Want to talk?"

She changes her intonation. "I'm fine."

He bends toward her an inch or so. "I think we can safely label the last week a rough one. More so for some than others. You need anything, we'll be around."

"Okay." Molly starts off for the door.

"I mean it, Molly," he says softly after her. "We are here. We want to help."

She picks up her pace, hurrying to get away from him, and finds herself in the lobby of the school. The main hall, banked with lockers, the corridors to the newer east and west wings, telescope away from her, impossibly long. For a second, she feels as though she's dreaming, none of this is real, and she is inside that hospital where Dad would take them to visit Mom. She dreams about the hospital a lot, dreams about trying to find Emma among all those endless corridors or dreams that she herself is being chased through them and no matter where she runs each hallway leads only to a dead end. She never finds Emma and she never gets out. She wakes from these breathless, as if the air has been knocked out of her lungs. Sucker punched, that's what they call it. It's how she feels right now. And for the flash of a second, the school around her changes. She is alone at an intersection of those antiseptic-reeking hallways; she can hear the low chattering, mumbling voices of the patients in their locked rooms. And then she's back at school, surrounded by the dull noise and sluggish motion of other arriving students. *Is that how it happens for Mom? Is that what the hallucinations are like? Is it happening to me?*

Molly decides she doesn't want the answer to that one; needing answers is what makes Mom loony. Molly makes her feet start moving, the zombie shuffle of every kid on Monday morning. She wants to run; she wants to find a dark, secret corner, cover her head and hide. It takes most of her strength to hold down the momentum. She's beginning to understand that for all the planning and second-guessing, the only thing she has succeeded in, so far, is unlocking the nightmare box so that the monsters can roam free.

. . . n o s e t
m u t a m u r i n i l l i s

When he finally saw me, Greg cut the motor on the stump grinder. The sound whirred away to silence, the blue exhaust dissipated, pulled apart and upward into the bright, cloudless sky. He lifted the safety goggles to his forehead, removed the protective earmuffs, pulled the paper filter away from his mouth. He coughed a couple times. "Howdy." He ran his gloved hand over his head and brushed out the ash-colored chips of ground oak.

"Yeah." I kicked at a drift of oak dust that had gathered in the exhaust path of the grinder. "You get to have all the fun."

"And the fun is just getting started. This thing is close to petrified." He tapped the toe of his boot against the chewed-up third of the stump. "The termite guy says we have to take this thing down four, six feet into the earth at least. Then we can fill it and lay sod."

"Ooo. Like a grave."

"Leslie – "

"What?"

He shook his head. "Never mind. You're back earlier than I expected – why are you limping?"

"Banged up my knee. No big deal. I wanted to talk to you when the girls weren't around."

"Oh." He came over – trailing oak dust – to where I was standing. "So talk." His face narrowed in preparation for bad news. I had told him on the phone that I'd called Phillip for legal advice, and although at the time Greg had said free legal advice was appreciated, he must have given the situation some thought. He seemed to sense what was coming. I saw his apprehension, and the logical, kind speech I'd rehearsed on the way back to Swifton, the speech about what was most logical and kind for every one of us, all things considered, that speech shriveled up on my tongue. "What I wanted to say first is that you've been more than patient with me, Greg. I'll never understand it, but I do appreciate it. I want you to know I realize how much I've asked of you." He didn't blink. I couldn't look him in the eye any longer, and so I focused on his hands, the stitching on his work gloves and how the seams pulled as he tightened his fists. "You know how important this family is to me. I mean, I wasn't going to do to you, to our daughters what my mother did. No matter how bad things got, I wasn't going to disappear on you. But I'm beginning to comprehend how selfish it is, using yours and the girls' lives as the battlefield for my wars. It would have been better, easier, for you, all of you, if I'd just kept going." I waited for him to say something. He didn't.

"So here it is, then. I've officially lost my lease on the Reeves place as of this morning. I have until the end of the month to clear out. I could find another office, but big picture? It seems kind of like a sign, you know. And then there's the whole Phillip dilemma . . . so I'm thinking it's time to make everything less complicated for everyone. You love me, Greg; I know that. And I do love you. But love, well, love is not an adequate defense against what my life is like, what life with me is like. You deserve peace and stability and all those things I can't deliver. I'm thinking we're long past due on the paperwork that would let us get on with it." I took a deep breath and looked up to face him.

He was staring down at his boots, vaguely nodding. At last he said, "No."

"I don't need your permission."

"But you need my signature."

"Greg, listen – "

"Leslie, I have listened. Listen is the only thing I do. I listen like I'm running the sonar search for sunken ships full of drowning men."

"And that's what I'm trying – "

He locked his eyes on mine. "No, Leslie, you don't try. You just do. You do whatever the fuck you want and you expect us to adapt because it's so damn hard being Leslie. Well, you know what? It's hard being Greg. It's even harder being Molly and Emma. We're tired of adapting. This isn't about who you love, this isn't about who you sleep with or who you don't. This is about being who you say you are. If you want to be the woman who didn't abandon her family, Les, then be the woman who didn't abandon her family." He turned and went back to the grinder. "Besides, nothing you can say will convince me that you really believe we're over," he said, raising his voice. "I was in that bed the other morning, remember?"

"And?"

"And maybe you aren't the only one who sees ghosts."

"Ghosts imply gone, Greg."

"Did you fuck Mr. Free Legal Advice?"

"Not lately."

"Then it wasn't a ghost I saw."

"Oh, come on, Greg. You can't possibly believe that because we – "

"Noise." He pulled the power cord. Blue smoke billowed and the motor sputtered itself up to a roar so that he couldn't possibly have heard me shout back at him that maybe I wasn't the only one who was crazy.

Heartsick and ego sore, I left Greg and drove over to the junior high school. It was only three o'clock, about thirty minutes before dismissal. Molly wasn't expected down at the police station until four-thirty, but I decided I wanted to spend some time with her alone before we met Greg. I wanted to make sure she was steady enough to see this through; I wanted to make sure I was steady enough, as well.

When I pulled into the drive, James Verrill, Swifton's rock-star principal, was at the curb of the entrance holding his own in an obviously heated discussion with a group of demonstrating parents. He was pointing them off school property as they talked and gestured back at him. At the sight of my car, the angered parents raised the signboards they were carrying to make sure I'd been able to read them. I had indeed; the first time being thirty years ago through the barred windows of my father's office at the station house: PROTECT OUR CHILDREN.

I parked in a visitor's space and got out of the car in time to hear Verrill loudly threaten to call in the police if the demonstrators crossed onto school property one more time, accidentally or otherwise. The windows of the school building were crowded with young faces trying to take in the commotion. One by one, shades were drawn; I could almost hear the groans of disappointment.

The school's office was quiet in that tired, end-of-day way. The air dense with the steamy aromas of cafeteria food. A skinny girl wearing an *I've been to Eden* T-shirt sat slumped in a straight-backed chair next to Verrill's office door. She held an ice bag over her left eye. She sighed loudly. At the counter, I signed Molly out while the secretary looked up her class schedule to determine which room to buzz on the PA system. She came back to tell me that Molly's science class was out in the playground area on some sort of project and that she'd go out to fetch her. I thanked the woman, who gave me a meaningful smile I didn't care to interpret. I went back out into the lobby to wait.

On the other side of the lobby was a glass door with the words "Guidance Office" painted on it. Behind the door, an older man with a round body and round glasses was speaking to a woman in a red turtleneck and plaid jumper, her arms full of books. He pushed the door open for her and held it while she exited. They spoke over each other's words, she thanking him for his help while he expressed, yet again, his, the whole school's concerns and sympathies; if she needed anything, anything at all, she should not hesitate to contact him. They turned away from each other. He let the door swing shut. The woman's polite smile faded, and her careful application of makeup could not disguise her fatigue and worry. She headed for the main doors but stopped when she saw me. After a moment's thought she said, "You're Molly's mom. Molly Stone?"

"That's me."

She shifted the armload of books and came over. "I'm Claire Zinni. Tim's mother?" We exchanged the usual oh, yesses and hellos, until they petered out into the potent silence that fills the gaps when you aren't certain how much the other person already knows. She glanced down at the books. "Tim's schoolwork," she said, looking out the main door toward the demonstrators. "We thought it would be better to keep him at home for a while. The other boys aren't coming back, either, not until this is settled."

"That's probably wise."

"I think the girls are coming back later this week. Did you see the letter the school sent home?"

"Not yet. I haven't had a chance."

"I'm sorry, that was stupid," she said, rolling her eyes. "You've had a trying few days, too."

"Word gets around."

"Doesn't it? Here, I have another copy." She fumbled through her things and pulled out the photocopied letter. "Basically, it says that the school's focus is on education and not what goes on after hours. So when the girls get back to school they are to be treated as regular students, with respect; anyone giving them problems – teasing them, laughing, even talking about what happened – will be punished with anything from detention to suspension. Zero tolerance. The kids have to sign the letter to say they understand. The parents have to sign it to say they've seen it." She handed the letter to me.

I scanned the text. "Looks like pretty standard stuff. Better to address potential problems up front."

"Except the letter doesn't say anything about the boys. What about my son? What about treating him with respect? Given the way they're defining this *crime*, Tim is as much a victim as any of the girls."

"Lydia's injuries are – "

"Tim didn't do that. Lydia says so. The others say so."

"But somebody did something."

"Something terrible, I'm sure. But my child isn't going to take the fall for it. That's why we're pleading not guilty. We're taking it to trial and make sure Timmy gets his story told."

Stories. "I'm not sure how much you know about Swifton's history – "

"Enough. That's what my husband and I believe, too. This is about Swifton and the police screwing up the Nightingale thing. They're trying to make up their failure to the Scott family, to Janet. I understand that, but this is turning into a vendetta against children. That's why my husband and I are going to the city papers. I've contacted a few columnists. They're interested."

"Are you sure you want to do that? Writers have agendas. Trust me on this one. They won't tell your version, they'll tell their version of your version."

"We have to do something. I mean, have you seen the letters to the editor in the local paper? What they're calling my son? On the talk radio shows? What they're saying about my husband and me, how we failed as parents? How it would have been better if, you know, we'd beaten the crap out of him when he was little? The legal costs of this are going to wipe us out. Tim isn't sleeping. He can't eat. We tell him, 'Tell the truth,' and he does, and now everything that he believed was in place to keep him safe has turned on him like he's the enemy – " Claire cleared her throat. "Is this Molly?"

Molly shuffled over, bent beneath the weight of her backpack. I pulled her close and kissed the top of her head before she could pull away. "You know Mrs. Zinni?"

Claire smiled. "Molly, dear, I want you to know how much your friendship has meant to Tim." She looked back to me. "Really, Molly has been wonderful to call so often. We appreciate that."

Molly glanced up. "You left your cell phone at the house."

"Oh, I did? Funny. I don't recall taking it out of my car."

Claire hefted the books in her arms. "Well, I've kept you long enough. Tim doesn't like being left alone for too long. Call whenever you like, Molly. Please." She continued on toward the main doors, her shoulders sagging.

"No one knows yet. No one knows it was me," Molly whispered. "Did you tell Mrs. Zinni?"

"No. But sweetie – "

"Okay, okay. I don't want to talk about it here. I have to go sign out, so they know you're not kidnapping me or anything." She headed for the office. I looked at the letter again, and as I was wondering if the revelation of Molly's involvement would place her inside or out of the school's protective grace, Mr. Verrill came back into building. He was clutching one of the demonstrators' PROTECT OUR CHILDREN signs. The sign itself was dented as though it had been hit – or used to hit. He saw me studying him and the sign. He shook his head. "Who's going to protect their kids from them?"

t i m

The lawyer has given him a list of things he is not to do until this is over. He is not to call any of the girls. He is not to call any of the guys. He is not to answer the phone in case it is a reporter or another threat against his parents. He is not to buy or be found in the possession of any sort of material that might be interpreted as sexual on any level. If he has any of this sort of material in his possession, he is to turn it over to his parents or the lawyer. He is not to attempt to destroy anything. He is not to watch music videos or R-rated movies. He is not to visit sites on the Internet that have sexual content or might link to sexual content or might feature pop-up advertisements of sexual content, even implied sexual content as in Web cam ads or dating service chat rooms that Tim would never have even thought of looking at when he was on-line looking, which is what he's doing now.

It was not his intention to look. He signed on when his mom left because the modem would tie up the phone line, and he wouldn't have to worry about what to do if the phone rang. He has been having a problem with loud noises, the phone in particular. The sound of the ringing startles him like a nasty static shock. He swears he can almost see blue lightning spiking out at him. But the phone is not the only hazard. When he is alone and the place is quiet, he gets antsy; he wanders from room to room as though the house is booby-trapped with firecrackers set to go off if he should stop moving. The nervous energy builds until it makes him want to break things and hurt someone and hide in his room and cry all at the same time. Not knowing what to do with any of these impulses, he does what he's been told not to do.

He's clicking through his Favorites list. There's squat at the music sites. He's seen the videos already: the guy singers promising undying love to models and the modellike girl singers promising unending nookie to guys.

The movie sites had a few trailers he'd like to see, but, based on the number of hot girls on the splash screens, the trailers are for films the lawyer would say are off limits. It would take forever to download them, anyway. He spends some time reading old movie reviews to get plot descriptions of the horror movies that would cause his parents to freak. Tim isn't sure if they're grossed out by the idea of the movies or because they have actually seen them. *Chainsaw Massacre* and *Last House* and *Spit on Your Grave* were made when Mom and Dad were kids. Tim can imagine his dad sneaking into a midnight showing of one of those classics. His mom? Never. But Dad? Definitely.

The horror movies get boring and he heads on over to the Merciless TV site to catch up on *Eden,* which he can't watch because his parents think it qualifies as too sexual because of the bikinis and night-camera bedroom action. Tim has tried to make the argument that the show is okay. You really don't see anything, and the game is based on the Bible, after all. In the original all the players were naked and really it was just a stupid game show that everyone was watching. His mother pointed out that the original had not been a game show nor were the original participants players. His parents could not be swayed, but he has the recaps, which are funnier than the show itself. He could imagine the look on her face when Jasmeena – Jasmeany, as they called her in the recaps – looked into the camera as Malcontent walked out of the clearing and said, "When you leave the garden, you leave alone. But your money, baby? That stays with me."

After reading the recap and the comments on the bulletin boards, he links over to the official *Eden* Web site where they post pictures from the show. He clicks through Jasmeena's file. She might come across as kind of an airhead, and she's supposed to be the show's official bitch, but Tim likes her. Not because she's the prettiest with that long dark hair and her huge brown eyes, but because even though she's doing really well in the game, she seems kind of sad and lonely. It's like she came into the game assuming no one would like her so she handled it by making herself unlikable up front. Tim has noticed she talks all the time, but she never smiles. He likes to imagine sitting next to her and maybe holding her hand. He could tell her jokes and make her laugh. And she'd like having him around. He'd never tell that to anyone; they'd think it was so totally gay.

Under Jasmeena's pictures is a list of fan sites dedicated to "The Most Despised Woman on Television." He's been to most of these before: single-page sites with altered pictures of Jasmeena to make her look like a vampire or sometimes one of the Viking warrior women with the horn hats. People write poems for her: There's an entire site of hate haikus for her. Tim clicks on some of the new links. One after the other, more of the same. The next to last link takes him to a site that starts dark. Letters start to fade in: GIVING THE CUNT WHAT SHE DESERVES.

Tim stares at the words as a picture starts to come into focus. The image is obviously faked. Some of it. Jasmeena's face has been Photoshopped over the face of another woman. The other woman is not fake. She is being held down by hands that belong to unseen men while another man is . . . it is awful, but he can't look away. Those hands compressing her skin, fingers digging into the muscles of her calves and thighs. His blood starts moving; his hand traces a path to the inevitable destination.

The back door slams. He's almost grateful. Tim clicks on the little x that will close the site. Instead, three more windows open, each with pictures of women held or tied up and being hurt. He tries to close one; more windows open. Advertisements for twenty-four-hour phone sex and live shows and barely legal babes. His mom his calling his name. Coming down the hall. The windows are opening on their own accord now. Pictures of fingers and legs and lips and breasts and he can't get them to stop. His mother knocks on the door. "Tim, sweetie?" He grabs the computer cord and rips it out of the wall. The screen goes black.

l y d i a

Lydia opens her eyes. She is holding a box. Silver paper. Iridescent red bow. Neil and Amanda stand back expectantly. Lydia, seated on the piano bench, has trouble seeing any more than the shadowy shape of them; their backs are to the bay window which, without the shade of the plants, is bright with sun.

"We were going to give it to you at Christmas," says her mother, "but we talked about it and thought it might be good for you to have it sooner."

"Go ahead." Neil puts his arm around Amanda's shoulder, and they become a single shadow body with two heads. "We had it made for you. In Switzerland."

Lydia pulls at the loose end of the ribbon and the bow comes undone. She rips the envelope fold in the silver paper at one end of the box, continues ripping until the paper comes free, revealing a white cardboard gift box. She sets the box on her legs and lifts the lid to find clouds of cellophane packing material. Nested in the center of the cellophane is a piano, a miniature baby grand, black and polished, about the length and breadth of her palms placed side by side.

Amanda leans closer. "It's a – "

" – music box," Neil says, doing that finish-each-other's-sentences thing they think is so cute.

"Very pretty," says Lydia and starts to put the lid back on the box. "Thank you."

"Don't you want to hear it – " Amanda.

" – play? Go on, take it out." Neil.

Lydia lifts the piano from the cellophane tufts and finds the key on the underside. She winds it but nothing happens.

"Open up the – "

189

" – cover on the keys."

She did as she was told. Mozart spindled into the air.

"*Eine kleine Nachtmusik*," says her mother. "The second movement."

"I know."

"Remember it? It was the piece you were working on when you, ah, *decided* not to play anymore."

"I know."

Neil's shadow moved away from her mother's. "If you open the lid, you can see the mechanism. That's a thirty-six-note player."

She raised the piano's lid as asked. Inside a spiked cylinder rotated and plucked at what she assumed to be thirty-six pins of graduated length. It made her think of fingers plucking other things. "Pretty."

"We liked listening to you play even better."

"Neil." Amanda sounded alarmed.

"Oh come on, Amanda. Lyddie's smart enough to understand what we're saying with this – "

"Not that we're putting any pressure on you."

"No. No pressure."

"This is only Neil and my way of saying that we believe everything is going to be all right. We'll get back to the way we used to be."

"I know."

"It will be over soon."

"I know."

"But as long as we're on the subject – "

"Neil, do we have to do this now?"

"It's too important to put off any longer. Lyddie, the boys say that the plants were still in the window on the day of the party last week."

"I know."

Neil comes closer, comes into focus so that she can see his face, his confusion. "Who moved them?"

"Neil, those boys are in enough trouble," says her mother. "We can let that go."

"You saw what they did to this room. It took us most of the night to clean it up. And that kind of destructiveness suggests they are capable of – " He looks at Lydia. "It is important that we tell Andrea Burnham everything, Lyddie. When the boys left here, were the plants still in the window?"

Lydia remembers what Molly has told her she remembers. "No plants. I'm sure of that. No plants in the window."

Neil nods and turns back to her mother. "Nothing happened here? Those little SOBs are lying."

j a n e t

"I don't understand why I still have to do this if Lydia is back." Molly slouched in the car seat, arms crossed over her chest. "It has nothing to do with me."

"I'm not going to kid with you, Mol," I said, backing out of the visitor's parking place. "This is going to be embarrassing, but embarrassment never killed anyone."

"Prove it."

"Your proof is driving this car. And you can take some solace in knowing that at least you are doing the right thing."

"Grown-ups always say that."

"Yeah, we do." I pulled out of the school drive and headed toward the business district of Swifton.

"You really believe it's that easy?" The smart-ass tone had drained from her voice.

"I want to believe it's that easy. We want it to be that easy for you. But really? In my experience, just figuring out what the ultimate right thing might be is damn close to impossible."

"Then how come you're so sure this is the right thing I'm doing now?"

"I'm not sure. The question is, would *not* telling make you feel any better?"

"Yes, very much better – but the guys might get blamed for something they didn't do."

"That's a hell of a problem you've got, then."

She quieted. I could feel her withdrawing into a deeper level of herself, thinking. "After they see this video thing I have to make, is there any chance they're going to forget about the whole thing?"

"In another town, in another time, maybe – "

"But not in Swifton. Because of the Nightingales. Because Grandpa screwed it up."

My hands tightened on the steering wheel. "You heard about that?"

"Everybody knows about it. They had the guy who did it and Grandpa lost the evidence – "

"The facts are a little more complicated than that." I couldn't look at her. "They thought they had a lead on the guy – in other words an idea of who it might be – because one of the girls had scratched him on the face, so they were looking for a man with a scratch. They had only a few days, because it would heal. Your grandpa Ben . . ." I swallowed. *Tell her the truth.* "He found a man who had a scratch, and they brought him in, but he had an alibi. You know what that is? Of course you do. Without further evidence, they had to let him go."

"Was Grandpa sure it was the guy?"

"*He* was sure."

"So why'd they let him go?"

"There are rules."

"But after they let him go, Janet Scott was – "

"Yes."

"The last Nightingale."

"Janet. Her name, you know."

"There's a game called Last Nightingale. We play it at slumber parties. You go in the bedroom and turn out the lights and say, 'Little bird, little bird, little bird, fly!' – you know, like the guy who did it said to the girls when he let them go? If you say it three times alone, in the dark, and face the mirror, Janet's ghost will appear."

"Hmmm. Well, I know nothing of the 'little bird, fly' speech. The girls all survived the assaults – "

"It's just a game, Mom." She started tapping her feet against the floorboard. Anxious. "Did you ever see her? I mean, see her like you see things?"

"No, I don't *see* her like that."

"Janet was the very last? The guy disappeared after Janet?"

"Disappeared isn't the right word. Not really. He wasn't anywhere to be found, but he never really left. He sort of became a story without an end." It was me withdrawing now, sinking into an old idea. I focused on the road and felt myself being pulled down. "Like a fairy tale. But the terrible dragon vanished before the brave knight could kill it and make the kingdom safe again. We didn't know where the dragon went; we didn't know if it was coming back. Because of that we were afraid and saw dragons everywhere – "

"Mom?"

" – and we blamed the knight."

"Mom?"

I saw her wary expression out of the corner of my eye, so I laughed, making light of the moment. "Anyway, that's why I left Swifton as soon as I was able. Just got tired of dragons I couldn't get rid of."

"Mom?"

"What, sweetie?"

"Is that why you shot that guy back in the city? Because of the Nightingales? Because you wanted an end to the story?"

I couldn't find my voice. I drove the car and nodded. I couldn't tell her that no matter what you do, some stories refuse their endings.

The Swifton Municipal Building was a U-shaped complex of 1970s architecture, functional and devoid of personality. Greg was waiting for us by the fountain in the little park that filled the open area of the U. He had changed into khakis and a sports jacket and was doing his best to look confident for his daughter's benefit. He offered her a penny to toss into the water.

"Make a wish?"

She looked at him as though there weren't enough pennies in the entire history of wishes to cover this one. He tossed the penny in himself and then wrapped his arms around her, giving her the embrace she would have declined had he merely offered it.

"Well," he said, releasing her.

Molly surveyed the area, no doubt looking for those who might recognize her. "Can we get this over with, please?"

"In a minute." He caught my eye. "We're waiting for someone."

"Who?" Molly and I asked in unison.

Greg cocked his head toward the lot where Phillip, in full designer-suit lawyer regalia, was climbing out of his red Jag. I glared at my husband, who said, "Your cell phone was at the house. He thought he was calling you. It's legal advice. It's free."

"Nothing is free," I said, watching Phillip coming toward us and trying to gauge what the hell he was up to.

Molly was bouncing on her toes in panic. "I thought you said I didn't need a lawyer."

Phillip was close enough to hear her. "You probably don't. How's it going, Molly?"

"I don't know." She wrung her hands and searched one adult face and then the next as though trying to figure out who was the most likely source of betrayal. Greg read her anxiety correctly. He drew a deep breath and extended his hand toward Phillip. "Thanks for coming out. We appreciate the help."

Molly, apparently placated in her fear of adults yelling at one another, had gone back to the original worries. "What help? Why is he here?"

"I'll tell you why." Phillip sat down on the broad ledge that circled the fountain, putting a buffer of distance between himself and Molly. "Your mom and dad want to make sure that you are being treated fairly. My only reason for coming out is to sort of referee the deal because since I know the rules, I can make sure everyone is obeying them."

Molly narrowed her eyes. "There are other lawyers. They know the rules."

"Yes." He dipped his chin. "But this lawyer knows you. This lawyer believes you are telling the truth. And this lawyer cares about what it may cost you to tell it."

"What are you going to do in there?"

"Listen to their questions, make sure they're not trying to get you to say something you don't mean – or say something that will make you look bad."

"That's it?"

"Can't think of anything else I could do. Can you?"

Molly stared at the fountain. "No. Okay. You can come in with us."

Phillip stood. "Thank you for letting me help." But Molly didn't say any more. She turned and took Greg by the hand. They started off for the entrance beneath the bronze-lettered POLICE DEPARTMENT sign.

Phillip came to stand next to me. "That was exquisitely civilized."

"Or seriously delusional. Whose idea was this?"

"Greg's. When he answered the phone, I told him exactly what had happened, well, the essence of it. You called me because you needed to talk to an attorney; you told me what was going on; I'd done a bit of research and thought it might be prudent to get some counsel in on this." He gestured toward the building and began to walk.

I caught up. "Did you tell Greg I was smashed out of my wits when I called you?"

"No." He shrugged. "What would be the point? He'd only chalk it up as your excuse for doing what you're too scared of doing otherwise."

"Too smart to do otherwise."

"You were drunk. So what? Molly needs help, and you asked for it. That's the larger consideration here."

I stopped, was stopped by the awareness of Janet's perfume, only the hint of it, as though it had traveled a great distance, like smoke from a faraway fire. Phillip was watching me. "What is it, Les?"

"Nothing," I said, only half hearing myself answer the question. The fragrance was gone, but time was slowing. My peripheral vision started to blur. "You were saying? What were you saying?"

"I was saying so what if you were drunk. The drunk are famous for calling up exlovers, estranged family members, and – Leslie, what do you see?"

Janet Scott came through the Police Department doors, leaning against the glass panels to push them open as though they were very heavy or she was very tired. Outside the doors she stopped and lifted her face to the sun, eyes closed. She wasn't in her nightclothes like the others had appeared; she was wearing clunky-heeled Mary Janes, striped tights, a pleated gray skirt, and a pink sweater set. Her hair was ruler straight, parted in the center, and her features had a nondescript prettiness in transformation of early adolescence. I began to walk toward her, away from Phillip's fading voice. Janet lowered her face, opened her eyes, looked at me. A slight smile turned up her lips.

"You're Molly's mom?"

They never speak *directly* to me. At least none of them ever had before. I wasn't certain what would happen if I spoke back. "Yes."

"I saw her inside." She folded her hands in front of her. "Why are you here?"

"You don't know?"

She shrugged. "How would I know?"

"I want to understand what is happening, Janet."

She scrunched up her face in confusion. "I'm not Janet. I have an aunt named Janet." Behind her, the door opened and a woman in a similar skirt and sweater outfit exited. She rolled her eyes in exasperation.

"Ann Marie. I've been looking for you everywhere."

"Are we finished?"

"For now." The woman turned to me, obviously perturbed by my staring at her child. "May I help you?"

"Nora?" I said, in dawning comprehension of my mistake. "Nora Scott?"

"The name is Jenkins now. And you are?"

When I didn't, couldn't answer, Ann Marie filled in for me. "She thought I was Aunt Janet."

"Do you know my sister?" Nora studied me, her expression growing increasingly suspicious. "Leslie?"

"That's Molly Stone's mom," said Ann Marie.

"That's Ben Cooper's daughter," said Nora, taking Ann Marie by the arm and hurrying her child past me.

Phillip, who had apparently moved in closer to watch this exchange, laid his hand on my shoulder. I jumped at his touch, backed away. "You all right, Les?" he asked, showing me his empty hands.

"I'm not sure." I said, hearing the trembling in my voice. "I'm not sure I can distinguish one from the other anymore."

"You're going to have to give me more than that. What did you see?"

"It doesn't matter what I see as long as I can tell the difference. I think I may be losing the ability to tell the difference between what is really there and what isn't."

"Like before?"

"I'm not going back to *before*."

"I'm not going to let you." He dropped his hands. "You can always point at things and ask me if I see them, too. Reason number six hundred and seventeen for keeping me around."

"Keep you around?" I couldn't help but laugh. "Have you ever noticed that you tend to show up in my life just as the depths of hell are about to break open?"

"Only by your invitation."

"Like the devil?"

"Yes, but at least I'm the devil you know is really here."

"Says you."

He laughed at that until he realized I wasn't joking. "What do you want from me right now, Leslie? How can I help you?"

"What I want is of no consequence right now. I need to get in there with Molly. If you can help *her*, I will be forever in your debt, but if you came here for any other of your six hundred seventeen reasons, then please leave." I didn't wait for him to reassure me or argue me down. I strode over to the doors, pulled them open, and went into the Police Department where Greg and Molly were waiting for Andrea Burnham to get off the phone. They sat on the opposite side of her desk, which was watched over by a framed portrait: the sad-eyed and grim countenance of my father.

8

You hear a pulpy splintering sound, like that of a stick of green wood forced back on itself until it snaps. It takes a second to recognize the source, but you realize it is bone. Your father has broken something in the man's face. Your father hits him again. "That one was for Kimmy. This one is for Rose." Again.

You want to believe you are dreaming. You almost think you might be. The problem is that when you are dreaming it never occurs to you to question the reality of your situation. So to think you are dreaming means you must be awake. Which means you are really here in the shadows next to the garage's side door. Which means this is really happening. The man, his mouth taped, his body tied to the chair. His eyes swollen. The bridge of his nose gashed. The orange hat on the floor. Your father, his uniform shirt wet – he is dripping sweat, heaving breath, as he picks up the length of two-by-four. The gold, gold light of the garage bulbs shining on the piece of lumber as your father hefts it, swings it, tests its potential like a baseball bat. The astringent aroma of his Old Spice mixes with a bathroom smell.

"It would be," your father says, swinging, "so much easier if I just ended it here." He cracks the wood into the metal support pillar behind the man in the chair, inches above the man's head. The man is sobbing, or making a sobbing sound. "Better knock that off or you're going to suffocate." And then he sighs, one of those long, long sighs he gives you or your sisters when he is disappointed in your behavior but not surprised. He leans in close to the man's ravaged face and says, "No one in the whole of this goddamned world would blame me if I let that happen." Then he picks up the orange hat and gently settles it on the man's head. "This is going to be my personal souvenir of our friendship. And tomorrow, I'm going out in the fields where you took poor little

Mandy and I'm going to find it there. You know why? Do you? Do you? Because when we bring you in again, tomorrow afternoon, the pattern of bloodstains on your hat is going to match up perfectly with the wound I'm about to leave in your skull, my friend. I guess Mandy fought harder than she remembers. That is if I don't let her kill you here and now." Your father straightens the hat on the man's head and then stands and readies the two-by-four, taking aim. "What goes around comes around, buddy . . ."

And then you are running.

m o l l y

ANDREA BURNHAM: We've started taping now. Don't worry about your microphone. Along with the video, a written transcript of our conversation will be prepared – just like the first time. It's important that you understand what's going on here. This is called an affidavit, in official lawspeak. It is quite possible the judge will simply accept these documents as opposed to hearing you give testimony in court. Before we start, do you have any questions?

MOLLY STONE: Is that a two-way mirror?

AB: Yes. Does it concern you?

MS: Not really. It's a little creepy. Who is back there?

AB: Only the camera operator. We want you to sort of forget the camera is there.

MS: That will be hard to do.

AB: You'd be surprised. This is part of a specific procedure for taking depositions from witnesses under fourteen years of age. The camera records the whole room, you and me talking, so that there's no question of my leading you or intimidating you in any way. That's why you couldn't have your parents or your lawyer friend –

MS: He's just a lawyer. He's not a friend.

AB: [laughs] All right. But that's why we do this with just the two of us. So you don't feel anyone is expecting you to say anything in particular.

MS: Anyone but you.

AB: Molly, I expect you only to tell me what happened. That's it.

MS: Then why didn't you believe me the first time I told you?

AB: The issue is not a matter of believing you, Molly. It is my job to question and keep questioning until I believe I have the details straight. Sometimes a witness, such as yourself, will dismiss a tiny little scrap of information that strikes her as unimportant, and yet that tiny little scrap is later revealed to be the key to understanding the whole situation. It becomes complicated when that witness is a child who feels she may have conflicting loyalties. That's what I'm trying to explain to you: that these video procedures were designed to prevent very young witnesses from being influenced by what they perceive to be good or bad responses as they are questioned. You are obviously not a very young child, but fourteen is the cutoff age and so –

MS: Here we are.

AB: Here we are. And we're clear on why I wanted to tape your statement?

MS: We're clear. Can we get this over with?

AB: Yes, we can. Please state your name and your address.

MS: Molly Stone. Box forty-seven, Jackdaw Road, Swifton Woods – do you want the zip code?

AB: That won't be necessary. Okay, Molly. It's Saturday, October fourteenth –

MS: The day of the party at Lydia's house.

AB: Right. Why don't you start by telling me what you remember of that day.

MS: Well, from what I've heard, the party started at around eleven o'clock, but I didn't get there until about two-thirty.

AB: Let's start a little earlier.

MS: Earlier?

AB: What were you doing before you went to the party?

MS: I was baby-sitting Rita and her brothers.

AB: Who is Rita?

MS: Oh. She's the daughter of one of our neighbors. Rita is my sister Emma's best friend. I baby-sit for them all the time. Emma was there with me because my dad had to work.

AB: I see. And the invitation for the party said to come after your baby-sitting job was through?

MS: No. Like I told you before, I wasn't invited. I didn't even know there was a party until after I got to Lydia's.

AB: Why did you go to Lydia's, then?

MS: I didn't know I was going to Lydia's. I didn't know where he was going.

AB: He?

MS: [pauses for a drink of water] Tim. Tim Zinni. You know this. I told you already.

AB: Then it shouldn't be too hard to tell me again. What does Tim Zinni have to do with your going to Lydia's house?

MS: When I was leaving Rita's house, I saw Tim ride by on his bike. I started following him on mine because . . . because I was sort of hoping he'd notice and stop and, you know, wait for me to catch up and talk or something.

AB: Tim is a friend of yours?

MS: Sort of. Not really. He knows who I am, but we're not, like, friends or anything. Who is going to see this tape?

AB: Only those who need to see it. So would it be fair to say Tim is a boy you'd like to know better?

MS: You could say that, but I don't think any of this is fair.

AB: I understand. So you follow Tim and where do you go?

MS: Lydia's.

AB: That would be Lydia Parrish's house on Old Quarry Road?

MS: Yeah. I didn't follow him all the way up to the house. Just to the end of the driveway. I was going to wait there until he left and then sort look like I was resting there so he'd kind of have to see me. Maybe he'd say hi or something. But after a few minutes I started to feel stupid just sitting on my bike at the side of the road, so I hid the bike in the drainage ditch and walked – well, sort of snuck up to the house, to see if I could see what he and Lydia were doing.

AB: What did you think they might be doing that would require you to have sneak up on them?

MS: I don't know. I wanted to find out if Tim liked Lydia. Lydia has guys around her all the time because, well, everyone says that she –

AB: Molly, we can't really assess what happened based on what everyone "says." In court, that's called hearsay, and since we have no way to judge hearsay's accuracy as fact, it isn't allowed as evidence. So let's keep this to what you saw with your own eyes. Does that make sense?

MS: Hearsay? Yeah, I guess it does.

AB: You reach Lydia's house and then what?

MS: I could hear music before I got halfway up the drive. It was really

205

loud. And then I saw Tim's bike and a bunch of other bikes and I guess I sort of understood that it was a party. I should have left, but . . .

AB: You didn't. Do you remember how many bikes you saw?

MS: No. I didn't count them. Is that important?

AB: Just asking. Go on.

MS: I went up to the front porch and kind of crawled over to the window and looked inside. I wanted to see who was there and what they were doing.

AB: Was it easy to see into the house?

MS: You mean about the plants?

AB: I meant generally. Were there curtains or shades?

MS: No. And although I know I told you there were no plants, I've thought about it a lot and to be honest, I can't really remember. There might have been a few plants in the window, but I'm sure there were not bunches and bunches like in that photograph.

AB: The witness is referring to a photograph of the Parrish home taken several weeks before the incident under investigation. Said photograph was volunteered by the Parrish family and is filed as PE twenty in the Parrish case folder. The witness examined the photograph as part of her preliminary interview. Is this the same photograph I showed you before, Molly?

MS: Yes. I think so.

AB: Sorry about the interruption, but this is one of those tiny details I was talking about. Do you want to study the photograph again?

MS: I don't need to. All I know is that I was able to see without any problem.

AB: What did you see?

MS: Everyone in that front room with the piano.

AB: Who is everyone?

MS: Everyone at the party. Do you want names?

AB: Yes. And if you could tell me where they were in the room.

MS: Okay. Tim, of course. He and the other guys – okay, Mark, Tyler, Chad, and Joey – they were standing kinda in a group near the window but on the other side of where I was.

AB: You weren't worried about them seeing you?

MS: Maybe a little at first, but they were busy watching the girls: Lydia,

Ann Marie, Stephie Morretty and Danielle Banks. The girls were a little harder to see because they were on the other side of the piano.

AB: That was everyone you saw?

MS: Yes.

AB: Or everyone you were able to see?

MS: I don't get what you mean.

AB: I want to clarify if these were the only people at the party or if there might have been someone else in the house whom you couldn't see. Molly? Is something wrong?

MS: No. I can't say I'm sure if these were the only people at the party. They were the only ones in the room.

AB: That's what I needed to know. What were the girls doing?

MS: Being idiots. They were drunk.

AB: How do you know that?

MS: Well, there were like beer bottles all over the room and big bottles of like vodka and those sorts of drinks lined up on the piano. And I saw Stephie and Ann Marie pour stuff from the big bottles into their glasses and drink it.

AB: Can you describe their behavior?

MS: Drunk. Like you see on TV. They were crashing into each other. Laughing. Holding each other up and shouting things at the guys. I couldn't hear because the music was so loud. The guys were laughing, too, but it was like they were watching a show or something. They looked a little freaked out.

AB: Were the boys drinking anything at all?

MS: Not that I could see. I mean there were soda cans and some two-liter bottles of stuff around as well as the beer and other junk, but really, if any of them was even holding a glass or anything, I don't remember seeing it.

AB: Do you remember what music was playing?

MS: It was a radio station. I remember hearing commercials and talking between the songs. I don't really remember the songs – just the usual radio stuff – until . . .

AB: Until?

MS: A song called "Drivin'" came on. Have you heard it?

AB: Yes. It seems to be very popular.

MS: Have you seen the video? I mean, the way they change the meaning of the words? He's singing about the kinds of cars he's driven and how much he likes to drive and it turns it around by saying he likes it best when his girlfriend drives him around? But the video makes it out like he's talking about girls he's gone out with and the reason he loves his girlfriend is because she sort of . . . you know what I mean?

AB: Even if I do, you need to say it.

MS: Okay. Well, in the video, he's driving to his girlfriend's house and he passes these cars – parked or on the freeway or whatever – and some of the cars, the ones he's singing about, have girls in thong bikinis and stuff rolling around trying to get his attention by, you know, touching themselves or touching each other, and then when he gets to his girlfriend's house, she's dressed in leather and boots and her house is full of chains and whips and it looks like she'd going to hurt him, and it kind of ends like that. You must have seen it. It's on all the time.

AB: I have seen the video.

MS: It's kind of cool. I like the music.

AB: So this song comes on at the party?

MS: Yeah. And Lydia puts her glass down and starts dancing. Then the other girls start dancing, the same dance moves the girls do in the video, and then Lydia takes off her T-shirt. Danielle points and laughs and then takes hers off, too. Lydia yells something at the other girls and they take off their tops. Lydia starts putting the girls together, I mean dragging them closer to each other. She was screaming something at them. They were still laughing, but to me they looked kinda scared, too, and then –

AB: Molly, I don't mean to interrupt you, but you're leaning a little too close to the microphone.

MS: Oh, sorry.

AB: Don't be. So the other girls look scared?

MS: Yeah, and Lydia's kind of waving her arms around. And she gets this really crazy look, her eyes got narrow, mean looking, and she takes off her jeans. I don't know what she was yelling, but the other girls took theirs off, too.

AB: So they're all in their underwear?

MS: Except Stephie. She doesn't wear a bra.

AB: What were the guys doing during this?

MS: They were watching, but they were also kind of backing up.

AB: Backing up?

MS: Yes. I noticed that because Lydia kept motioning for them to come over where the girls were and dance with them. But the more Lydia yelled at them, the more the guys backed away.

AB: And then what happened?

MS: Lydia took off . . . the rest of her . . . you know, her underwear.

AB: So Lydia was naked?

MS: Yeah. She grabbed Danielle by the arm and made her, um, put her hands on Stephie's, um, breasts. And then she dragged Ann Marie over to where Tyler was standing off to the side of the rest of the guys and forced them to kiss.

AB: Forced?

MS: Lydia kind of, well, it looked like she was smashing their faces together until Tyler shoved her away. Anne Marie was laughing really hard now. She fell over on the floor, she was laughing so hard. And Lydia stopped yelling and started to smile at Tim. It was so weird. She didn't look like herself. She comes over to him, and he's back as far as he can go up against the window seat. She says something and then starts screaming again. And I can hear her now. She's screaming at Tim to, "Do it, do it," and when Tim doesn't move, she grabs his hand and starts shoving it, you know, between her legs. And she's laughing. And then the song ended.

AB: Let me pour you some more water. So the song ended . . .

MS: Everything sort of stopped. A commercial or something came on. Lydia looked at Tim's hand and then let it go. She left. Stumbled out of the room. I don't know where she went from there. The other girls started to pick up their clothes and the guys headed toward the front door. That's when I took off for the other side of the house, away from the bikes so they wouldn't see me. After they left, I went back to the ditch and got my bike and rode home.

AB: Did Lydia leave the house?

MS: I don't know.

AB: When did the other girls leave?

MS: I'm not sure. But I figure one of them must have called her parents

. because at school they were saying that the parents knew what had happened before the police found out.

AB: How did the police find out?

MS: You know that already. Some teacher heard Lydia and me fighting about the party.

AB: Why were you fighting?

MS: She said something mean about my family, and so I called her a slut and told her that everyone knew about her party, what she had done. And that is true; everyone does know.

AB: How did everyone find out?

MS: People talk about stuff. The guys talked about it. So did the girls. But I was the only one who got overheard.

AB: And you, other than the invited guests, were the only one who had seen what happened?

MS: As far as I know.

AB: Did you go in the house, Molly?

MS: Not during the party. But I've been in the house before. Lydia and I used to play together a lot when we were little. When we were in fifth grade. That's probably why she asked to borrow my sleeping bag.

AB: Why would Lydia ask to borrow your sleeping bag if you two were fighting?

MS: I thought about that. Maybe she wanted me to feel bad, you know, guilty, for getting her in trouble – even by accident. After she disappeared, I did feel awful. That's why I went to get my mom.

AB: I see. Anything else you want to say? Anything I've forgotten to ask about?

MS: No.

AB: Then we're done?

MS: I think so.

Detective Burnham turns off the video player. "You did good, Molly. Very clear and specific. Now that you've seen it, is there anything you want to change or add?"

"No. I just want to go home." Molly lays her head on the table.

"One more piece of business, and then you can see your parents." The detective slides a piece of paper into Molly's sight.

Molly sits up and looks at it. "I thought my signature didn't count for anything since I'm only thirteen."

"I wish all my witnesses were as adept at remembering what I've said." The detective laughs and it makes her curls tumble about her face. "You're right, but this might get you what you want."

"What I want?"

"I can't promise you anything, but given the sensitive nature of the case and that A, you're Ben Cooper's granddaughter, and B, you've been so cooperative and consistent with your story, I think, if you sign off on the 'given under oath and best of your ability under penalty of perjury' statement there, I think we can get the prosecutor to submit the tape to the judge in lieu of testimony."

"I won't have to go to court?"

"The admission of your affidavit and the transcript would be read into the court record, but with all of the involved parties including Lydia telling the same story, there's a good chance we can make it so your visibility is as limited as possible."

"But I won't have to get up in front of everyone and say what I know?" Molly lets her eyes wander the fine print affirming the truth of her statement. Stalling for time to think.

"Like I said, I can't promise anything." The detective hands her a pen. "Unless of course you want to take the stand."

"Why would I want to do that?" She can barely hear herself over the crashing of collapse in her head. It's ruined. Except. Except. Maybe.

"Molly? Everything all right?"

"Yeah, sure," Molly says, as she puts the pen to paper and puts her signature to a statement for which almost every word is a lie.

invisible men

Greg brought me another paper cup of vending machine coffee. It was the third, and I'd yet to finish the first, but fetching me coffee was something to do, a useful means of pacing from the bench outside the interview room where we were waiting to the public lounge at the far end of the building. Phillip would use Greg's absence during those forays back to the lounge to wander over with the latest updates gleaned from his practiced schmoozing: The special circumstances and community disruption had mandated the invocation of the VST – Very Speedy Trial – rules for minors; the judge had issued an information that served as an indictment without having to go to a grand jury; the boys would be officially charged and enter pleas that afternoon and chances were good that preliminary hearings would start before week's end. After coffee cup number two, I learned that the prosecutors were sympathetic to the kids' situation but the district attorney was up for reelection in November and really didn't want the voters in Swifton – of all places – to see him as soft on sex crimes. The judge who had been assigned was an old hard-ass when it came to the foibles of adolescence, but the grapevine was heavy with word on how much His Honor hated the DA and his minions' tendency to use court proceedings as a platform for self-serving election speeches. The bets were on that His Honor had probably already lumped this whole mess as more preelection grandstanding. Even more to our favor, the judge, Simon Lorant, was a longtime admirer of one Benjamin Cooper and hence likely to cede in requests to buffer Cooper's granddaughter, one Molly Stone, from any undue provocations.

I stared into the murky depths of my current coffee cup. "The DA hasn't offered to plead out?"

"It was his first move from what I hear. His preferred solution." Phillip sat down beside me. "But the boys' families aren't about to have their kids cop guilty to a trumped-up sexual assault just to get it over with. They want their day on the stand. Who can blame them?"

"And Lydia?"

"Her story hasn't changed. As for the injuries the SART exam turned up, the pathologist can only estimate from the extent of the healing. Best guess is the injuries were inflicted around the time of the party. Maybe the same day, maybe a day or two earlier. But certainly not later." He lifted the coffee cup from my hands and took a long drink. "To make things even more complicated, the pathologist's report states there is reason to suspect some of the injuries may have been self-inflicted. There's other evidence of self-mutilation."

"Neil said they found bite marks."

Phillip shrugged. "I haven't seen the reports."

"Molly said it was possible – no, I don't believe it. I've seen cutters. Lydia's not one of them. Someone's been feeding on that little girl."

"This is a rough haul, isn't it? For you, I mean. Dredging up a lot of muck." He drained the cup and then crushed it in his hand. "Are you going to tell me what you saw outside?"

"It was nothing. A trick of the light. Same old lunacy."

"You aren't crazy."

"You keep telling yourself that, and I'll keep sliding over the edge."

"But you aren't. Crazy blows things up; you're trying to pull them together. It's as though you're connected to some sort of intuitive virtual reality machine – "

Whatever he said after that I couldn't hear above the gales of my own laughter. He sat unsmiling until I calmed down. "Sorry," I said, wiping my eyes. "I love how you keep trying to put a positive spin on my psycho moments."

"Why do you think I'm here, Les? Why do you think I keep coming back?"

"Well, the formal term is masochism – " I began to laugh again. "No? Then why?"

He brought his fingers to his chin as he did when he was in serious thought. "Damned if I have a clue. But I'm here, right?"

"So is my husband." I glanced down the corridor. Greg had yet to reappear. "And your being here isn't fair or good for Molly or Greg – or me, for that matter – no matter how *civilized* we are about it. It was very kind of you to rush up here, and I do appreciate the assistance, but you need to go, now."

"Oh, I get it. You think you can make it work this time?" He stood. "That *this* is the crisis will set the marriage back on even keel?"

"I don't know. Right now I need to look after my daughter, and your being here is confusing her."

"Just her?" He grinned. "I'll go. I'll be waiting for your call."

"Don't count on it."

"You'll call."

I hated it when he got that I'm-two-steps-ahead-of-you gleam in his eye, like he was about to spring surprise evidence on a prevaricating witness. I didn't wish to encourage it, so I didn't answer, hoping he'd get the hint and leave. The strategy didn't work.

"You know, Les, I get why you keep calling me back only to shove me away. Same reason you do it to Greg. He's what you're supposed to want: safe, sane, predictable. Greg knows this, and he's happy to provide it. But what I know is that you need the darkness at the end of the hallway; you need to be forever uncertain if the next move will lead to a dead end, or a door out, or yet another blind turn; you need this labyrinth you think you're trapped in. That's why you built it, Leslie. You need the mystery more than the solution. And you keep calling me back, darling, because I understand this about you."

"Oh, step off it, Clarence Darrow. You and your *understanding* high-tailed it out of my labyrinth a couple months ago."

"And yet – to risk repeating myself – here I am. You have to choose, Les. Not between Greg and me. You can't do that until you've chosen which Leslie you are going to commit to being. Until then, you'll orbit between both your lives, out of reach of anyone who would love you."

"How long have you been rehearsing that one, Counselor?" I grabbed his hand – not out of need to make him stay, more out of need to prove him wrong. "I told Greg it was time to file for the divorce."

"And he said no."

"You talked to him about this?"

"It was a guess." Phillip laughed. "I know you. If you were serious, you'd file the damn thing without the proclamation. Divorce decrees are like wedding certificates, Leslie; it's only paper. Takes the commitment of both parties to make the thing work. As I was saying, you cannot commit to anyone until – and here comes the other party now." He turned his hand over in mine, changing the grip so we were shaking hands in agreement or farewell as Greg, not trying to hide his discomfort, strolled up with yet another steaming paper cup of coffee. Phillip and I released our grip.

"They're taking such a long time." Greg offered me the cup, and I waved it off. "I hope they're not trying to twist her words. Weren't you supposed to be in there with her, Hogarth? Isn't that why you said you should come up?"

"Can't sit in on a juvenile deposition. Burnham explained that," Phillip said. "But I'd be happy to review her statement. With you. Both."

Greg nodded. "We'd hate to impose on your billable hours any more than we have."

"No imposition. I'd do anything for Molly. You know that."

"All the same, I think we can manage from here on out."

"Please don't hesitate – "

"If Molly needs representation, we'll give you a buzz. Otherwise, we don't want to keep you hanging around here just to hold our hand." Greg raised the coffee cup in toast.

Phillip scratched the side of his nose and said, "You may not be the best judge of exactly what *you* need here."

"But I'm the one holding the gavel, Hogarth."

"Other parties might object." Phillip looked at me.

"I object, all right." I stood up. "I'm going to object myself the hell away from both of you." I turned to take off down the hallway, but at that moment the door opened to the interview room. Molly exited, her expression bleak, and Phillip, Greg, and I remembered why we were there.

Molly had said she was hungry, so I told Greg we'd meet him back at the house after we picked up some burgers and fries to bring home. Molly didn't say much about the deposition except that it went fine and that it was the same thing she had said earlier to everyone. She munched on french fries and stared off into the distance. She'd been questioned enough for one day, so I left her to her thoughts and we drove home in silence. On the way down Jackdaw, we pulled over at Rita's house where Emma and Rita and Rita's brothers were gathered in the middle of their vast front yard, shouting at one another simultaneously. Rita had a basketball planted on her hip. The escalating wind snapped at their jackets and hair as though egging on the fight.

"What now?"

"Invisible men," said Molly, exhaling hard with exasperation. "They do this every single day. They try to play kickball with only five people so they have to use invisible men to take bases so they can kick again. They end up pissed off and fighting about whether their invisible men got to the next base or were tagged out. They scream at each other for ten minutes. Then they invent a new invisible man rule that they can yell about later."

"The great traditions never die." I honked the horn to get Em's attention; still shouting, she walked backward toward the car. I said to Molly, "Your aunts and I called them ghost runners. Denise once gave me a black eye over a ghost runner."

Molly gave me a sideways look of mean-spirited mischievousness. "Could you see them, too?"

"Of course I could see them." I returned the expression. "When mine crossed the plate, when theirs were out – that's how I knew when to fight."

Molly suppressed a giggle. "Yeah."

Emma hauled open the back door, frumped onto the seat, and pulled the door shut with a bang. "I hate Rita's brothers. Can I have a french fry." Molly passed a nearly empty carton over the seat. "That's all that's left? I really do hate them. Rita does, too."

"Then why do you always play with them?" Molly offered a few more fries to her sister as I pulled back on the road.

Emma, her mouth full of cold fried potato, said, "Did Dad tell you about the tent?"

I glanced at her in the rearview mirror. "What tent?"

"They're going to put a big tent over our house and fill it up with poison to kill the termites."

"On Friday." Molly was nodding. "Dad was talking to the termite guy this morning. We have to stay at a hotel or go into the city and stay at your apartment. You know what? They use tear gas first to make sure no people or pets are still inside. And if you leave like your closet door closed, the poison can collect there and kill you later next time you open the door. Dad says the tent thing is going to cost a fortune."

"And the tent has orange and yellow stripes," said Emma as we pulled into the driveway at the house. "And we have to move out all our stuff or most of it. Food and everything."

"Dad says we can move most of the stuff to the garage."

"Can I stay with Rita? Will you make sure my closet door is open?"

I didn't answer. We'd reached the house and I noticed, as the engine idled, a dull clunking that sounded like it was coming from under the hood. I was cursing the thought of another expense, when I realized it wasn't the car. Emma had already scrambled out and was running for the front door. Molly started to climb out but turned back.

"Something wrong?"

"No."

"Then why don't you turn off the motor?"

"I thought I heard something. I want to listen for a second. You go ahead. I'll be right in." Molly followed her sister – calling her, asking her to wait up a second – without closing the car door. I sat behind the wheel trying to ignore the banging sound by imagining the glory of orange-and-yellow-striped tarps draped and sashed over the porch and the dormers and the chimney, sealing in the pesticide, forcing it to seep into every crevice and crack, killing everything not fortunate enough to find escape. I could not help but warm to the idea. But then I remembered my children were in that house.

I shut off the engine. The slamming bang I was hearing came from the side of the garage. Not so much loud as insistent. I knew what that sound meant. The side door had blown open and was swinging in the wind, inching almost shut on the unbalanced hinges only to be forced back so that the doorknob struck the clapboards with each successive gust. It was a sound I knew as well as my own heartbeat, and like my heartbeat, that sound had specific meaning because it belonged to me.

7

The garage door is caught in the wind again. You know what the sound means even before you are fully awake. Denise or Joanne must have come in late and forgotten to hook the side door latch. They are always forgetting and it is always waking you up. So you have a choice. Pretend you don't hear it – which is impossible – or get up and go latch the thing. Dad says you should wake up your sisters, since it is their fault, but you can't be sure if the lapse was Denise's or Joanne's doing and whoever you choose, she's only going to mumble in her sleep that the other is to blame. It's just easier to do it yourself.

You raise the shade on your window. The garage is dark, but you can make out the shape of the door as it tries to close itself and is then blown wide once more. At the rear of the yard the grasses flatten and swell. No moon tonight, so the stars are abundant and glittery. It hasn't rained, so you don't have to bother with shoes.

Trek downstairs, through the kitchen, out the back door, yawning every few steps. In the yard, you choose your foot placement a bit more carefully, testing for pebbles and twigs before bringing your weight down. Pea gravel fills the beds at the side of the garage where your mother used to plant pole beans. The gravel is good for drainage, your father says, and it keeps down the weeds, but it hurts like hell to walk on. The unseasonably warm wind rifles through your hair and up into your pajama top. It carries the damp smoky smell of backyard incinerators. A hateful odor of burned garbage. You lift your wrist to your nose, trying to catch a whiff of the Eau de Love you sprayed on at bedtime, jasmine and lilac. Still barely there. Okay. Grab the door and force it shut, so that the dohickey of the doorknob catches in the jamb. Slip the hook of the bar latch into the metal eye. Done. You cup your hands to the window in the door and peer into the near blackness of the garage. Only one car is parked inside and the shape of it tells you it's the station wagon. The police car is gone; Dad must be at work. But he's not on nights this month. And if he got called in, you would have heard the phone. He's never out this late without telling you well in advance. You fight back a creeping sense of worry.

As though in answer to your concern, you hear car tires at the far end of the driveway and almost immediately see the headlights, hazed by the driveway dust, heading for the house. You lean against the garage door, waiting for your father, to tell him yet again of your sisters' inconsiderate disruption of your sleep. But he doesn't pull in to the garage. Strange; maybe he's planning on going out again. He cuts the engines, the lights. The driver's side door opens, and you are about to call to him, when you hear him speaking. Calm, but low, devoid of emotion, menacing like an empty room, it's his cop voice and it never fails to scare the bejeebers out of you. Something is wrong. You don't want to move, for fear he'll hear the shifting of gravel, so you squat down, pressing yourself against the door, hoping he can't see you.

You can't see much, either. Only the shape of the person he's hauled out of the back of his car. The person isn't walking right; the right leg is dragging, as though injured. The arms are bound somehow behind the body. It sounds as though he – the tone of his mumbles tells you it's a man – is trying to speak but has something in his mouth. Your father is pushing him forward, up the ramp to the entrance of the garage. You can't see them now, but hear, feel the vibrations through the building as one of the big front doors slides open a bit and then slides firmly shut. Above you, the dark panel of window in the door goes gold. The keyhole as well. Use the doorknob to pull yourself up a bit higher and put your eye to the keyhole. You aren't spying. Not really. You are curious. You are investigating. Like any good detective.

Dad has backed one of the old kitchen chairs up against the metal support post in the middle of the garage. The chair faces away from the station wagon. He forces the man, who is in a chambray work shirt and black pants, to sit. He does this by kicking the man in his hurt leg. The man kind of moans; he can't talk; his mouth is covered with a swath of silver tape – the reason you couldn't understand him earlier. His head is bleeding and it kind of lolls, his reddish hair is messed up, like he just got out of bed. Or maybe he is drunk. Dad takes a roll of tape from his jacket pocket and tapes the man's upper torso to the chair.

"Scared, huh? That's what it felt like for those little girls with the tape over their mouths so they couldn't call for help." Dad says this before he spreads an old tarp over the station wagon, the way he does when he's going to use spray paint, as though he's afraid he's going to splatter something on the car.

You remember the trip to the hardware store this afternoon – *We're out of duct tape, Princess* – and the phone call you overheard, and your stomach goes sour with understanding. Dad then reaches in his pocket again and brings out a wad of orange felt.

"Look familiar, buddy?" When the man doesn't respond, Dad grabs him by the hair and yanks his head back, slamming it into the post. "Does it?"

The man's eyes get very big and he tries to shake his head. Dad tosses the hat to the ground. He takes off his jacket, lays it on his workbench and, on his way back, stops by the bin where he keeps his scrap bits of lumber. Dad picks up a piece of two-by-four. It looks like a leftover from repairs to the tree house right before the lightning struck. He's looking at the wood one second, the next he's swinging it into the bound man's belly.

"That one was for Melissa."

The man goes as white as the wood that hit him. He can't breathe. Instead of helping him, your father smashes the wood into the man's arm. "That one was for Catherine." Blood appears on the man's sleeve, pooling fast. Your father drops the two-by-four. Thank God, thank God. It's over; he's going to help the poor man. But he doesn't. Instead he balls his fist – "This is for Jennifer" – and punches the man square in the face, and you hear a pulpy splintering sound, like that of a stick of green wood forced back on itself until it snaps.

t i m

He wears the suit his mom bought for him to wear to his grandfather's funeral. It is dark blue with a fine gray stripe in it. Even though that was less than six months ago, the pants are too short and the jacket sleeves don't cover the cuffs of his shirt. The tie, which his father knotted for him, isn't so much tight as annoying. He can feel the knot move every time he swallows. Tyler is sitting next to him on the left. He's gotten his hair cut really short since the last time Tim saw him. Chad is on his right in a jacket made out of a gray flecked fabric over a white shirt, but no tie. From where he is sitting at the long table, Tim can't see Joey or Mark, who are in the chairs next to Chad. He doesn't dare lean down the table to look or say hey. The lawyers have instructed the boys not to speak or smile or attempt to make eye contact with one another. So they sit in a row, hands folded on the table front of them on what the lawyers have called the defendant's side of the courtroom.

Tim has never been inside a courtroom before. It isn't what he expected, really. He sort of thought it would be bigger, with a high ceiling that made even whispers echo. The walls would be painted cream or deep blue and there'd be lots of dark wood, especially up front where the judge sits. He thought there'd be a statue of that blindfolded woman he always sees in movies and on television shows. Instead it's more like the multipurpose room at school when they set it up for the school board meetings. The ceiling is that white tile with the holes in it and the walls are greenish gray. The floors are scuffed up with black heel marks. The judge's seat is behind a raised podium, but he can tell from here the podium is covered in the same fake wood that they used to make the shelves in the school library. No statues, but there is the American flag and the state flag hanging from poles on either side. Next to the judge's seat is a little raised platform with a plastic chair. That, the lawyers had explained in the tour a couple of hours ago, is where the witnesses sit. Another raised platform at the side of the room holds two tiers of more of the same plastic chairs: the jury box. Behind Tim were several rows of plastic chairs, the first row being filled with his and his friends' parents. The judge has said no one else may attend. The lawyers have warned the families not to mistake the privacy as a sign that the judge is sympathetic to their case.

Way on the other side of the room, two men sit alone at an equally long table, talking quietly over a notepad. Every so often one of them laughs; Tim is certain they are laughing at him and his friends.

A woman in a uniform the same green-gray of the walls comes to the door at the back of the room. "That's the bailiff," Tim hears his father say, as though Tim hadn't caught it earlier when the lawyers explained what would happen. She asks them to rise. Tim stands, feels the room standing with him. The woman actually says "Hear ye! Hear ye!" like they do in movies. She announces that the court of honorable Simon Lorant is now in session and open to hear equally all those who have come before it. The judge comes in, long black robes sweeping, and climbs up to his seat behind the podium from where he can look down on them. He is an old guy with brown spots showing through his wispy hair. He isn't fat, but it looks like he might have been at some time because he has this wattley pouch of flesh under his chin. He has a narrow head but big lips and a long nose, so that when he gazes out at them over the top of his half lenses, he looks to Tim exactly like Percy, the old pelican that was the schoolteacher in the cartoon he used to watch when he was little: *Dingy Bay*. Yeah, and that bailiff lady with her spiky hair style kind of looks like Olivia Otter. The tall, skinny lawyers on the plaintiff's side could easily pass for the Sam and Mac, the Stork brothers, twins who were always getting themselves and each other in trouble because no one could tell them apart. One of Tim's own lawyers could be Millicent Puffin, with her sort of all-over roundness and proud kind of waddley walk.

The more Tim thinks about it, the more he is able to see everyone in the room as a character from *Dingy Bay*. Chad could be Lenny Labrador, the goofball son of the family that works the lighthouse. Tyler? He would have to be Warren Whiskers, one of the cat kids whose family owned the fishing business in the bay. And Tim himself? Well, he isn't in the show;

he's the one watching, right? Watching as Percy Pelican lectures the Stork brothers. Watching as Percy questions Millicent about some procedure. He is very polite to her. But then everyone in Dingy Bay knows that Percy has a secret crush on Millicent. Watching as Percy turns his now impatient gaze on Lenny and Warren and the other kids in his class who have played a prank or forgotten their homework. Watching as, one after the other, Percy asks the kids to stand and answer his question. And because the kids in Dingy Bay are basically good and honest, they answer old Percy truthfully: not guilty; not guilty; not guilty; not guilty.

"Timothy James Zinni?" Percy fixes his gaze on Tim, who wants to say that he's not in the show, he's just watching, but Tim says nothing. He stands as the others had. Percy sighs and says, "How do you plead?"

Because this is a show, and it's been written ahead of time. He has to say only what he's been told to say: "Not guilty." He sits down. It's all right. Everyone knows Percy will let them go with a stern warning followed by a forgiving laugh. Lessons learned. Everybody still friends. That's the way life works in Dingy Bay. The only endings are happy ones.

Millicent Puffin pats Tim on the shoulder and hands him a tissue. It is only then he realizes his face is wet. He has no idea how long he's been crying.

6

The attic is in many ways better than the tree house ever was. You can use it year-round, day and night. It is a lovely place to spend a rainy afternoon or a snowy morning, if the wind isn't blowing. Summers are harder because it gets blistering hot, but if you open the cedar chests your grandfather built, the aroma makes the space smell like a sauna. You can hang out in your bathing suit and drink cans of cold soda you keep in the cooler and listen in on your sisters' conversations about boys and sex and how much booze they drank last weekend and where they've hidden the baggies of pot. Because of the way sound travels upward in the house, amplified by the hollows between the walls, the attic is information central, the place where secrets go to keep themselves.

Which is why you are up here tonight. Listening. Something isn't right. You can almost see the air around you vibrating. At this moment you can hear Dad down in the kitchen. He's still whistling. You don't recognize the tune, it may not even be a tune, but it sounds light, happy. Dad is happy. He's been increasingly happy since early this afternoon, out in the yard, when his mood shifted. Not abruptly like turning on the lamp in a dark room, but in a steady, unmistakable brightening like scarlet dawn bleeding into the sky. That's when he started whistling. After he said he had to go to the hardware store. *We're out of duct tape, Princess.* He whistled all the way to the car.

At first you were relieved, but as the day wore on into night, you have felt weirder and weirder about it. Happy makes no sense right now. He broke up with Bethany a couple days ago; they had to release the orange hat suspect guy for lack of evidence; that magazine article calling Dad "ineffectual" was published last week – and you know people are reading it, because everyone has started calling the girls the Nightingales. Everything is bad right now, and he's downstairs washing dishes and whistling.

Over the whistling you can hear Denise and Joanne arguing about who gets to wear the red vest tonight. They both have dates or parties or whatever it is they do. You try to stay out of their line of sight as much as possible; they always have a friend of a friend or somebody's brother they want to fix you up with. They think you're strange because you're not interested in boys. Who said you weren't interested? You aren't interested in the ones around here. Most of them are chained to their families' land, their futures already written. They would fill in the blanks their fathers and uncles left behind, Swifton Woods re-creating itself for another generation. You have decided you would save yourself. Not for marriage, but for mystery. Your heart would belong to the first boy to answer a question with *I don't know* what *comes next*. And he wouldn't be in Swifton Woods, that was for damn sure. Once you finally got out of here, you'd be gone for good. Never, never, never come back. Just like your mom.

A horn beeps out in the drive. You hear Denise yell out her window that she'll be right down and then she yells at Joanne that it's Joanne's turn to fill the station wagon's gas tank. Joanne on her way down the stairs yells, "Is not!" Denise, right behind her, "Is too, witch!" Dad interrupts his whistling long enough to shout "language!" and then, "Don't stay out too late! We're going to church tomorrow." Your sisters groan and then shout good-bye and love you, Daddy. The front door bangs shut. Quiet. Dad starts whistling again.

You look through your notebook, feeling like a traitor because you put the magazine article in with the other clippings. The article is unfair. Your father is not *ineffectual*. He can only warn people of the risks; he can patrol only so many roads at once. The writer, this Margaret Wexham person, is from the city, she doesn't understand that people around here don't have air conditioners, and on hot summer nights, windows get left open, doors get left ajar, kids sleep out on screened porches. Not because they're stupid, but because they need to breathe. She made it sound like Dad was more responsible for hurting those girls than the guy who actually carried them off into the night. Bad as that was, you saw the look on your father's face when he finished reading the article, and you could tell he agreed with her.

Downstairs the phone rings in Dad's office. You hear his whistle traveling as he makes his way toward the ringing. The office door closes. You move to the part of the attic where his office comes in most clearly. Maybe it's Bethany wanting to give it another try. But no, it sounds like a business call.

"Right," he says. He doesn't say anything else for a while, only makes *hmmmm*ing sounds of listening. Then he says, "Keep buying him rounds. Keep him there. It'll take me about forty minutes tops. After midnight, probably. Damn straight I'm sure – my girls, you know? Yeah, what goes around comes around. You got that right." He laughs and then hangs up. A second later the whistling starts again.

You hear the television come on. He's watching some comedy; you can hear the television people laughing, but not him. No more phone calls come in. Denise and Joanne don't come back. You stay up in the attic reading through your notes until you are yawning. Put the things away. Go back down to your room. Change into your pajamas, wash your face, and brush your teeth. Yell good night down the stairs.

"Night, Princess."

Someone is burning garbage; the smell is seeping into your room. Old strategy, you spray your wrists and pillowcase with perfume, hope the fragrance lasts until you fall asleep. Your bed is comfortable and warm. Sleep begins to slip over you. Your mind submerges. You sink into the darkness. And then you are being pulled upward, awakened by an irritating drumming sound. Damn it. The garage door is caught in the wind again.

lydia

Tuesday morning, Lydia's mother sits at the breakfast table rubbing aromatherapy lotion into her hands. She suggests they go into the city and do some shopping. "Girls' day out," she says. Lydia asks about school. Amanda says that until these other matters are settled it would probably be best for Lydia to stay close to home. They'll hire her a tutor; she'll catch up in no time.

"I'd rather go to school, thank you."

"Junior high is hard enough on the best of days. Trust me; I remember the gossip and the teasing. Remember it well."

"But the principal said that if anyone – "

"Oh, come with me, Lyddie. Please. I thought we could buy you a few new outfits." She offers the bottle of lotion.

Lydia declines. "I don't need more new clothes. We just bought a bunch of things before school began."

"Since when have you turned down new clothes?"

"You think I need something special to wear in the courtroom."

"No." Amanda closes the nozzle on the lotion bottle and considers the label that promises a scent to relieve stress. "You've been through a lot in the past few days. I thought a little shopping might take our minds off it for a while."

"Swifton has plenty of stores. Why can't we go shopping here?"

"I want to go into the city. I want to get us both away from Swifton for little while – "

"So people won't stare at me?"

"Lydia – "

"Or stare at you? That's why you want to go into the city, isn't it?"

"There's no need to shout at me." Amanda takes Lydia's hands in her own, lotion-smooth and smelling of sage. Lydia stiffens her arms to

231

maintain the distance between them. Amanda sighs. "It breaks my heart to see you so fierce and unhappy."

"Why can't Neil go with you?"

"The vineyard. Contracts are coming due. And he's trying to get enough of our own label bottled so that we might have something to sell next year."

Lydia has heard many times of Neil's hopes for Old Quarry, the cellars, the tasting room, the small café out among the vines. He collects the catalogs of vintner supply houses and spends whole evenings at the computer designing prospective Old Quarry labels. Over dinners and brunches, he dreams out loud of gold medal awards like those announced in the magazines he reads. Lydia likes to pore through these pages where award-winning wines are described by words such as "tight" and "lush" and "muscular" and "wanton." She found an article once in which the writer theorized that Western civilization was founded on wine, the only alcoholic beverage that makes itself. Once the skin of a grape is broken, even a tiny tear, fermentation begins. The problem was that grapes take time, so early tribes of wandering hunters had to set up permanent camps to wait for the vines to grow and the fruit to ripen. Lydia thinks this theory explains much. She slides her hands free from her mother's grasp. "I'll go with you."

"Thank you." Amanda cocks her head, smiles. "We'll have fun. You'll see."

Lydia drops her shoulders and sighs. "Thank you for asking me."

"You are most welcome." She smiles even brighter. "Everyone still remarks on what lovely manners you have. That's something to be proud of, especially these days when the world is so rude."

Lydia laughs. "What are *you* proud of?"

"Oh, Lyddie." She sounds as though she might cry.

They take the train into the city. Lydia pretends to sleep the whole way, enjoying the gentle cradle rock of the car, avoiding talking to her mother. From the station, a taxi takes them to the shopping district where the better department stores anchor the ends of a row of designer boutiques, galleries, restaurants, and bookstores. Her mother steers her into the first set of revolving doors they see and then through the perfume fog of the cosmetics section, past the jewelry to the escalators. Up they go to the second floor where the juniors section awaits with mirrors and polished chrome racks hung thick with the latest trends. They mill about with the other shoppers. Amanda pulls ankle-length skirts and boxy sweaters from the racks, holds them up in suggestion. Lydia scrunches up her nose in distaste, sometimes outright laughs, as she plucks the hangers that offer more of what she has in mind and hands them to the clerk. When the clerk can carry no more, she shows them to the dressing rooms. Her mother says she will wait and seats herself in one of the wingback chairs they provide for weary shoppers near the three-way mirror. In one of the other chairs, an elderly man is either resting or waiting. Lydia sees her mother and the man exchange smiles. She follows the clerk into a spacious changing room. Alone, she takes off her jacket and the cashmere sweater and the jeans she chose to wear for this expedition. She selects her first outfit, a red dress with spaghetti straps. The fabric is stretchy, tight as an elastic bandage. She wriggles into it. The skirt barely reaches her thighs. She turns this way and that, studying herself in the mirror, before picking up the hanger to carry with her out to where her mother is waiting.

She pads barefoot back into the store. "Fashion show," says Lydia, announcing her presence. Her mother looks up, as does the old man.

"No," says Amanda upon first glance of the red dress before Lydia even reached the mirror.

"No?" Lydia echoes as she steps before the three angled reflections of herself. She spins the hanger on its hooked neck and watches the old man's face, the way his eyes are moving up and down her body. He fixes on her breasts. She's not wearing a bra. She gives him a little smile and pulls the plastic end of the hanger slowly down her body toward her crotch.

"Absolutely not." Her mother's voice seems directed at both Lydia and the man, who is watching her.

Lydia turns to face Amanda. Her back is to the mirror. "But why?" Before her mother can answer, Lydia lets the hanger slip from her hand. She bends from the waist to retrieve it, and the mirror reveals that she is not wearing panties. The old man clears his throat and gets out of his chair, hurrying away. Lydia stands up slowly and watches her mother's expression shift from shock to sorrow to anger to determination.

"Lydia. Go back to that dressing room and wait for me."

She does as she's told. Ten minutes later, Amanda knocks on the door, before opening it and depositing in Lydia's arms a selection of under-garments from the lingerie department. She closes the door. Lydia hears the hinges sigh, straining as Amanda leans against it. Lydia can see the shape of her mother in shadow against the slats.

"Why did you do this?" Amanda asks, her voice tired and sad.

"I'm sorry. I guess I forgot. You were in such a hurry."

"Lydia – "

"Are you still proud of me?"

Her mother is quiet for a long time. Lydia watches her unmoving form. At last Amanda says, very softly, "You cannot make me stop loving you."

"I'm sorry, *Maman*." She surprises herself by how much she means it.

"Go on and get dressed. We have the whole day ahead of us." Amanda straightens and the hinges on the door sigh again upon release. "I'll wait for you out front."

Lydia says that she'll be right there. She watches herself in the mirror, smiling as she begins to put on the underwear.

They are finishing up their lunch at the bistro that is one of Amanda's favorites. "It reminds me so much this little place your father and I used to love in Montmartre," she says in the same sad way she always says it, as she swirls the tip of her spoon through the foam atop her cappuccino. It is only in moments like this that Lydia sees how great her mother's grief remains. Amanda comes back to the present and gestures at the table with her spoon. "Please eat something."

Lydia shrugs and digs her thumbnail into the flesh of a pear slice that garnishes the cheese plate. "Not hungry," she says when what she really means is that she dislikes the food here, what with the edible flowers and fourteen different colors of peppercorns. She doesn't like having to sit in this place and think about her father and how sad her mother is. How can her mother be so heartsick over one man while she so obviously loves another? One of those loves is surely a betrayal. Betrayals must be redressed. The certainty of that makes Lydia feel lost and smaller than her life requires.

"Do you want to talk about it?" They are seated at a table for four, shopping bags take up the two extra chairs.

Lydia looks at the bags and can't remember a thing they hold. "Talk? About the store?"

"About the party."

"No."

"I need to talk about it." Amanda lays her spoon on the saucer and smoothes the edge of the tablecloth with her fingertips. "I thought if we were far away from Swifton, this might be easier, but I realize now it's not going to be easy anywhere." She smiles a nervous half smile. "Perhaps it is about what happened in the store, what is happening in your life that makes you need to do such things. I know your friends mean the world to you. They are good friends. I like them very much. It makes sense that you would do anything in your power to help them, and that's because you are a fine person, but what the doctors found last week – "

"The guys didn't do anything. The party happened the way we are saying it did."

Amanda leans over the table and whispers, "Fair enough, but that doesn't explain your injuries."

She snaps a pear slice in half. "I don't know how I got those."

Amanda closes her hand over Lydia's. "Baby, if somebody has hurt you – "

Lydia shakes her mother's hand free and shoves the broken pear in her mouth. "I did it, all right?"

"But what they found? Lydia, you couldn't have done *that* to yourself."

"Yes, I could. It's easy. A hairbrush. A wine bottle. The handle of your little flower trowel. Anything, really. Everything. I do it all the time. Really hard." Lydia eats the other broken half of pear. She holds her mother's gaze until Amanda, her eyes wet and brimming, has to look away. "Thanks for asking."

5

You, Denise, and Joanne try to stay out of Dad's way. Ever since George came by with the bad news, Dad's been shut down in that silent sort of rage that sucks energy into itself, draining the space around him of color and light. The air in the house now has that dead thickness that falls before a storm rolls in. And whatever is blowing in is going to be dangerous. He is the one, after all, who taught you not to watch the clouds, but to watch the birds. If the skies and lawns and telephone wires empty, if the sound of birdsong silences, it means real trouble. Silence, he said, is nature's alarm bell. He's been silent a lot lately, but the sense of absolute stillness in the house at this moment is more frightening than anything you've encountered.

He announces to the house in general that he's going out to work on the tree. That's what he does when the Nightingale problem is bothering him. In fact, the oak with its charred cracked trunk had become a project only after Melissa was taken. Before, he had only warned you off the tree house until after he'd checked out the stability of the platforms. On the morning of the first abduction, even before you – then twelve years old – had learned from neighborhood kids what had happened to Melissa, Dad told you that he thought the lightning strike had made the tree susceptible to infection and it would be best to bring it down. And sure enough, by that afternoon, he was way up in the branches with a handsaw, lopping off the smaller limbs, letting them drop. By evening the upper peaks of the oak had been butchered back to a plateau of pale stubs and the lawn beneath the tree was knolled with piles of green leaves still clinging to severed twigs.

He left it like that. Whether it was due to busyness at work or fatigue or disinterest, he seemingly abandoned the tree project for a few weeks. You thought he'd changed his mind about the whole thing until you awoke one morning to the sound of sawing outside your window. The sun hadn't completely risen and he was already out there cutting. It was only when you met your friends at the Swifton Woods Municipal Pool later in the morning that you heard about Charlotte Crowell being taken and *hurt* in the exact same way Melissa had been. You were told this while sitting on the steps in the shallow end of the pool. The water was very cold and you were shivering to the point of seeing goose bumps on your flesh. You had done fill-in baby-sitting for the Crowell kids when their regular sitter couldn't make it. You knew Charlotte. You had tucked her into bed. You looked up at the high dive, and for half a second you thought you saw Charlotte standing up there. But it was some other girl, who held her nose with one hand and then jumped, her other arm whooshing about like a useless wing.

You went home near suppertime to find that your father had already left for work. The very top platform of the tree house had been dismantled and was stacked neatly near the garage. It was then you made the guess that cutting down the tree had something to do with Melissa and Charlotte. You went up to your room and took one of the empty black scrapbooks you'd purchased at the photo supply place for pictures you'd planned to take at camp. At the top of the first page, you printed carefully CASE #1. Below that you wrote the date and time Dad started the tree, best as you could remember. Next to it you wrote *Melissa*. Then today's date and *Charlotte*. You felt kind of queasy for it, but part of you hoped something else happened so you could find out if you were right.

You *were* right. Nine times over. You go out to the yard to watch him. The trunk stands just over four feet tall now, probably nearly that wide. He's sawing off slices about a foot thick. Jagged, slablike slices of oak fan out beside him waiting to be chopped into firewood. It would be easier, faster if he'd use a chain saw, but from the beginning he had used only what he liked to call "elbow grease." He's about a third of the way through the trunk on this cut. His shoulders tense and heave with the effort of sawing. His face is red, dripping with sweat. White flakes of sawdust spray outward with each thrust and pull. He's almost finished. You wonder if he's as worried about that as you are.

He must have felt himself stared at, because he glances up from his sawing, sees you, stops, waits – as though you might have a message for him. You expect him to go back to work, but he doesn't. He releases the saw, its teeth still locked tight into the wood. He looks at you.

"You okay, Dad?"

He doesn't answer, but his posture changes as though a force uncoiling in him is allowing him to straighten fully and yet relax at the same time. A smile starts to creep over his face, a fierce sort of happiness.

"Dad?"

"I was thinking I need to get to the hardware store. We're out of duct tape, Princess."

You don't have a clue why the tree needs duct tape. "Oh. Okay. I'll be upstairs, you know, homework."

He nods and wipes his face on his shirt sleeve. "Be right back." He heads for the car, his steps at first slow, then accelerating. He starts to whistle. You head back into the house, wondering if he understands that when you say *upstairs* you mean the attic. The attic is in many ways better than the tree house ever was.

preparation

"Feather pillows, all food items, pets and plants. The wisest course of action is to remove as many of the upholstered furnishings, linens, and drapery as possible. . ." I scanned the "Preparing Your Residence" chapter in the *Tent Fumigation* booklet Bill Watson dropped off. "Wouldn't it be easier just to burn the thing to the ground and start over?"

"Yes," said Greg, "but I've already signed the contract. Watson gets paid no matter what."

"That's a pity."

"Besides, the whole burning-the-thing-to-the-ground strategy didn't work the last time, did it?"

"That depends on what you mean by *work*."

"By work, I mean what we should be doing right now."

"Yeah." But neither of us budged an inch. The girls had left for school an hour earlier. I had stood out by the cars, waving a cheery good-bye even as I was second-guessing my insistence they get out in the world and muddle through. Emma, intense even by her standards, kept turning around in the driveway to stare at me while Molly, ever vigilant and braced for the worst, forced-marched herself toward the road. I returned to the kitchen, where Greg and I still lingered over the breakfast dishes, rereading the fumigation booklet in an unbridled orgy of procrastination. It wasn't the moving of furniture we were avoiding, it was the nebulous sense that in emptying closets and lugging mattresses we were headed into the deep end of our shared past, and the currents might prove so strong we would break apart for being forced back together. Or vice versa. Either way, the idea of unloading the house held the notion that we were beginning a process that would lead to a finality of decision. Finally.

"Let's get to it," Greg said with the seductive allure of *let's lance that boil*. "We've got bugs to kill."

"Upstairs first, kitchen last," I said but not making a move. "Mattresses tomorrow morning before he gets here."

"Right."

"And then to court for the prelims."

"A dismal Friday all the way around."

"Underage sex crimes and a house full of – what is it called? – sulfuryl fluoride. We do know how to throw a party, don't we?"

He pulled the booklet away from me and closed it. "At least Molly doesn't have to get on the stand. Small blessings are still blessings."

"Blessed for the moment, maybe. Things could change. No matter what Lorant has said, I don't want anyone – especially us – promising Molly that she absolutely won't be called and then have her feel betrayed if things go south."

"What aren't you telling me, Les?"

"Nothing you don't already know. I want us to be prepared for the worst. Mol's in a tenuous position; her statement can play into the hands of either side. Sure, the defense is going to see it as corroboration of the boys' and of Lydia's own testimony, but the prosecutor, if he chooses to, can readily skew Molly's statement as only proof of what she did *not* see. You can bet that if Lydia falters, that is where the DA will have to take it. And then poor old Molly – who only wanted to protect her friends – becomes the agent of catastrophe in all these kids' lives."

"That won't happen. Life isn't that cruel."

"Gregory, old friend, what planet – "

"Don't say it. Please. Leave me the comfort of my last few illusions."

"All right. In the interest of changing the subject, then, let's go lift heavy stuff, shall we?"

"Sounds like fun," he said, nodding. Neither of us moved.

We started by unspoken agreement in what we thought of as the most neutral territory: Mom's sewing room. We stripped the bed linens and took down the curtains, rolled up the area rug, pulled old coats and bridesmaid dresses out of the closet. To the pill bugs, moths, spiders, millipedes, and earwigs we uncovered and dislodged, we wished a happy final twenty-four and let them scurry on their way.

The wooden pieces of furniture could remain in the house, but drawers had to be left open. The thought of odorless, invisible poison wafting through our accumulated chaos was troubling, not because of its presence but more for what it might leave behind. The drawers would have to be emptied. Watching me start to unload the contents of a bureau drawer into a laundry basket, Greg suggested we just take the drawers out in their entirety and carry them still crammed with their particular junk to the garage.

"Genius," I said as I began to put the plastic bags of my mother's never completed knitting projects back where they came from. "Every family should have a genius."

"But only one." He laughed. I piled three of the heavy drawers in his arms. I took the rolled rag rug under one arm and a heap of bedding and curtains in the other. We began the trek down the stairs and out the front door, which Greg had propped open. A fly buzzed in past us. "Your misfortune if you come in here," said Greg from behind me.

"We ought to put that on the welcome mat."

"I like that."

"It fits us."

"No, I meant the *we* in that statement. And that *us* thing."

I laughed. "Christ, Greg, I thought we'd have to get at least as far as the girls' rooms before this started."

"We genius types are renowned for our quick thinking."

"And for your complete denial of reality?" I was still laughing, when I semistumbled on a loose bit of asphalt at the edge of the driveway. "*We* can have two front doors, you know? One here and one in the city."

"There's that *we* – hey, a bit of warning before you stop, huh? I can't really see where I'm going. Leslie? Les?"

I could hear him, the way you hear the background music in a dentist office, at the edge of your awareness because your immediate focus is on more urgent matters. The garage doors were thrown wide and awaiting what would prove countless portage trips up and down the ramp. But right then, at the very top of the ramp, Janet Scott was waiting, blindfold in place, the ruffles on her nightgown rippling about her calves on a breeze that was not blowing where I stood. No mistake this time. It was Janet. The scent of the perfume trailed about me like a wind-blown ribbon.

Greg's voice was close to my ear. "Whatever you think you see, it isn't there. It's not real."

243

Janet started down the ramp. She moved with assurance, as though the blindfold was not a concern. Her feet were bare, and as she grew closer, I could see the little hemp anklet she always wore, the chipped-up orange nail polish on her toes and fingers. The perfume got stronger with each step she took.

I could feel Greg shaking me, hear his demand that I come back, but that sensation was far away and frail like a remembered dream. Janet was standing right in front of me, as oblivious of Greg as Greg was of her. The blindfold was a strip torn from a bedsheet that had been stolen from our clothesline on the afternoon before she'd been abducted. Janet had been the only one he blindfolded. Only my father would have recognized the significance of that gesture. My father and I. She reached up and pulled away the cloth. Janet blinked and stared up at me, studying my face. As seemingly solid as my own children – except her iris of her left eye, which, instead of holding a color, was transparent; I could see through it, past her, into the garage. See through it like a keyhole.

"I'm sorry," I said.

Her lips moved, but I could hear nothing.

"I don't understand."

She motioned me closer. I bent low. She unleashed her voice, shrill and huge as a siren: *YOU LET HIM GET AWAY.* I covered my ears, from instinct, from pain.

She was gone: Greg was in my face shouting, "Wake up, Leslie! You hear me, wake up!"

"I am awake!" I wrestled myself away from him and nearly fell backward over the pile of drawers. "I'm awake. I'm fine."

"You sure?" he said, catching his breath.

"Sure I'm sure." I started gathering up the sheets and blankets I'd dropped. "Let's get this done."

"Les, maybe you should – "

"It wasn't the first time. It won't be the last." I scooped up the rug in a wad. "It isn't real."

"Of course not." As he picked up the bureau drawers, he didn't take his eyes off of me. "Not real."

I didn't wait for him but set out for the garage, climbing the ramp as I always did, purposefully, in long, steady strides, not pausing as I crossed out of the sunlight and into the dim interior and its oily smells. The plank flooring rattled as I strode over to set the linens and the rug on top of the old washing machine that no longer worked but we held on to because we didn't know what else to do with it. The barnlike dimensions of the garage made it susceptible to the Law of Expanding Crap; if the old washer weren't taking up that corner, some other useless thing would be. The problem with the garage wasn't what was in it now but what had once been here and allowed to escape. Janet's accusation still rang in my head, but it wasn't a new one; I heard it there in the garage no more forcefully than I heard it everywhere else, all the time.

I headed out again, giving the center support post a wide margin as I passed. Greg was just coming in. His face so full of concern and fear that I wor-ried about what ghosts he had seen. I laughed softly, in hopes of reassuring him that I was no more demented than usual. "Are *we* having fun yet?"

"Oh, yeah," he said, setting the drawers down next to the center post, "these are good times."

We didn't talk about what had happened; we worked. We hauled couch cushions and quilts and toy boxes and baskets of stuffed animals and baby clothes and curtains and towels, and by the time we had finished with the obvious items, the ones on the list in the booklet, we'd hit a momentum that was irresistible. We started on books and knickknacks and then plates, glasses, flatware. Then shower curtains. Photo albums, wall hangings, file cabinets, floor mops, old sponges – I was surprised we didn't start collecting the very insects we intended to kill and ferry them out to safety. We could have kept them in the dozens of empty jars I took out of the basement. By two forty-five, when Emma was dragging her book bag back down the drive, the interior of the house was just about denuded. Em followed me from room to room, looking into the hollows of furniture where drawers belonged.

"Can I help?" She toyed with the buckles on the shoulder straps of her overalls.

"No thanks, sweetie. We're about done. You go play with Rita or something."

"Okay." But she didn't leave. She shadowed me as I swept floors and wiped off the ridges of dust that had formed behind the framed pictures we had removed. She stood in the doorways, watching me warily, as though she were waiting for me to burst into flame.

"Emma? What's the problem?"

"Nothing."

"Your tummy bothering you?"

"No."

Molly came in around four o'clock. I heard her "Wow, everything's gone" echo in the foyer, and headed downstairs, Emma in tow, for the traditional Molly post-school-day debriefing.

"So?" I asked as I tried to steer Emma around in front of me.

"Fine." Molly slipped her overstuffed backpack off her shoulders and let it drop to her feet.

"Everything?"

"Everything."

"Homework?"

"Yeah."

The answers never changed, only the subtleties of intonation. Having once spoken Thirteen-Year-Old Girl myself, however, I knew what to listen for. This afternoon what I heard was that much to her own amazement, my daughter had survived another one. "I'm glad everything is fine."

"Yeah. I guess I should start moving the stuff out of my room."

"Already done."

"What?"

"We're done. Your dad finished going through the attic. So you don't have to do a thing."

"You did my room?"

"Molly – "

"I don't believe you people!" She hefted the book bag and barged past me and Emma on the stairs. "I told you I would do it." *Stomp, stomp, stomp, stomp, slam.*

Emma looked at me and scrunched her nose. "I think Molly wanted to do it herself."

"You think?"

"She's still mad that you looked at her stuff last week."

"I suppose so. I didn't like doing it, if that counts for anything."

"You remember that day?" She turned around and glanced up the stairs before stretching up on her toes to whisper. "Remember?"

I took her little face in my hands. "What is it, Em?"

Molly's door banged open. "Where are my clothes? What am I supposed to wear tomorrow?" Before I could tell her I left things in her closet, the door slammed shut again. Emma sighed and shook her head until I released her. "Nothing, Mommy."

At suppertime, I announced we were having Garbage Night, which was a clean-out-the-refrigerator extravaganza of hot dogs and pudding cups and leftover pizza, chicken wings, half a can of peas, mandarin oranges, baby carrots, and ranch dip. When we finished, Molly disappeared to do her homework before *Eden* came on, and Greg started calling around for a hotel for us to stay in until the fumigation process was completed. I worked on getting the last of the nonperishables packed up and disposing of what wouldn't keep. Emma would come in every few minutes, stare at me, and then leave. The effect was like that of an irregularly dripping faucet in another room: The more you try to ignore it the more you become enthralled with trying to predict the next drip. At last, I couldn't take it any longer.

"Emma," I said, on what must have been her twentieth visit, "you are giving me a serious case of the heebie-jeebies. What do you want?" I was on my knees and wiping out the vegetable bin of the fridge. She shuffled a bit closer.

"You never came back."

I set down the sponge. "I never came back from where?"

"You told me to think about it and that you'd come back with dessert. I thought about it, but you never came back."

"I don't get – "

"The day you brought Molly home," she said, coming even closer, lowering her voice. "Remember Molly's secret?"

"That's what this has been . . . oh, sweetie, of course, I remember. I found out what it was."

"You did? You aren't mad? Molly was sure you'd be mad."

"Why would I be mad about her crush on Tim?"

Emma dipped her chin. "That's not the secret."

"It's not?"

"No. Everyone knows that Molly likes Tim. Everyone knows Tim likes Lydia. I meant about the secret Molly gave me money for." Em reached in the pocket of her overalls and pulled out a bill. "Twenty dollars if I promised to never tell."

My heart began to deflate. "That's a lot of money."

"I know. But I thought about it, and I think I should tell you."

"Probably a good idea."

Emma came over so that her toes were touching my knees. "The day after the party Lydia came over to borrow Molly's sleeping bag. I heard them talking. It wasn't on purpose. They didn't know I was there."

"What did they say?"

"You know how the teacher heard Lydia and Molly fighting? They planned the fight, they planned to do it in the girls' bathroom because the sound is so loud in there. They wanted someone to hear them. So it would be more believable."

"What would be more believable?"

"Lydia's story about what happened. Because – and here's the secret part – Lydia's only telling people that story because that is what Molly told her to say. Lydia doesn't remember anything at all about the party."

I felt as though the floor had dropped away beneath me. "She doesn't?"

"No, and Molly told her that if she told people she didn't remember, then Tim and the other guys would get in trouble. And Lydia running away? Molly didn't just know it was going to happen. That was Molly's idea, too."

"Even before the fight?"

"Yeah. Before the teacher heard. It was part of the plan."

"To make Lydia's saying what she had remembered more believable?"

"That's what they said. And when I told Molly I'd heard, and I was going to tell, that's when she gave me the money." She exhaled hard. "Am I in trouble?"

I pulled Emma into my arms and kissed her neck. "You did the brave, right thing, sweetie. You are not in trouble."

"Can I keep the money?"

I got to my feet. "You'll have to take up the money issue with your sister. Provided there's anything left when I've finished with her."

m o l l y

Molly, sniffling and scrubbing at her eyes with a tissue, comes into the front room where Emma is sitting on the floor, a blanket wrapped around her, watching *Eden*. Emma, seeing her sister, slides almost to the other side of the room. Molly doesn't look at her. She sits down in front of the TV, holding her knees to her chest. When the commercial comes on she asks Emma, "How much did I miss?"

Emma scoots herself a little closer to Molly. "Kevin gave Jasmeena the Want/Need card. Ten thousand dollars or a chicken barbecue dinner for everyone."

"Let me guess what she took."

"Yeah, and after she said she'd take the money, Kevin said they'd double it if she could manage to get Theresa voted out in the next Judgment Hour. So that's what Jasmeena is working on now."

"She has a plan?"

"She says she's going to make everyone think that it was Theresa who told Kevin that Sirus broke the secret ballot rules in the first show, because to prove she didn't, Theresa's going to have to admit she was the one who messed up the first set of ballots."

"Oh, that's what Jasmeena always does, makes people get voted out by forcing them to tell on each other. I wonder why they haven't figured that out about her yet?" Molly wipes her eyes again. "When they do, Jasmeena's toast."

Emma slides a little closer. "Was she really mad?"

Molly nods. "She made me tell Dad. And then she called her friend Phillip to find out what they should do. He's going to be back here tomorrow in case the judge wants to punish me for helping Lydia. He said the best thing to do is for me to tell Lydia that I was wrong, and that she needs to say she doesn't remember."

"Do you have to go over there tonight?"

"Too late for that today. Anyway, Phillip thinks it's better for me if the DA guys don't have a lot of time to think about what I've done."

"Are you going to jail for lying?"

"I didn't lie, Em. Not all of it is a lie. And no, I'm not going to jail. Probably get yelled at by lots of different people. Probably have to tell the judge what happened."

"Everyone is going to know you were there."

"Yeah."

"So you're in trouble."

"Big time."

"Do you want your money back" – Emma pulls herself right up next to Molly – "I mean, since I told on you?"

She puts her arm around Emma and hugs her close. "No. That's okay. You can keep it."

"But I don't understand. If you knew you were going to get in so much trouble, why did you *make* me tell Mom?"

Molly lays her head on her sister's shoulder. "Things change, Em."

4

He's got the game board under his arm; he wants to know if you'd like to play some chess. He's standing in the door of your bedroom. It's only eight-thirty in the morning, he hasn't been home in a day and a half. He should go and get some sleep, he says, but he's too keyed up and needs to relax. And he hasn't seen you in ages. Just come spend some time with your old man. Okay, you say, not quite awake yourself. You put on your robe and follow him downstairs.

He gets like this when he hasn't slept or he's really bugged by something at work, or both, which has been the case for three whole summers now. You watch him set up the board on the kitchen table. He then pours you a huge glass of orange juice and another mug of coffee for himself. You wonder how much he's had. On a regular day, he'll sometimes joke that his blood is now one hundred percent Colombian roast. Denise has told you that coffee is like speed and enough of it will make you crazy. Dad is looking pretty crazed this morning. He's still in his uniform, but he's taken off the tie and unbuttoned the top few buttons. His hair, over which he is more vain than you and your sisters combined, is in disarray, as though he'd been rubbing at his scalp in order to stay awake. He is so tired his expression sort of droops off his face like wet laundry on a line, but his eyes are extra bright. He's getting very thin. You ask him if you can fix him something to eat.

"No, no, Princess. Sit down." You sit down across the table from him. He's already made the first move. You shove a pawn forward; you don't really care. He stares at the board as though the fate of the free world depends upon his next decision. But he doesn't pick up a piece. Instead, he says, "We got him."

You almost ask who, but then you understand. "Really?"

He keeps staring at the board. "Yep. We got him. Bit of a fading scratch on his chin and everything. One of the seasonal laborers. Just like I always said. Right? All we need is to have Mandy Epelle ID him on voice or height or – "

"She has to go do a lineup?"

You can't be certain he's heard you. "We should have that ID any minute now. We picked him up out back of the Half Moon, sleeping one off. He had the hat with him. You know what he says to me? You know the first thing? He looks me right in the eye and says, 'I'm innocent.' Can you beat that? 'I am innocent.' Good as a confession, that is. You know why, Les? You know why?"

"Hmmm? No."

"I'll tell you. You can't be innocent and know it at the same time. Innocent is always something you used to be. It's what you were before you knew. And once you know a thing, you can never unknow, so if you start telling me you're innocent before I even begin to tell you what I think you've done, you're telling me you know enough to know you're going to be accused." He picks up his rook and sends it out into battle. "See what I'm saying?"

"Not really."

"Good. That's 'cause you're still innocent. Your move."

"What if he isn't?"

"Isn't what?"

"The guy who did this?"

"I'm not worried about that one."

"But how do you know?"

"My brain, my gut, my years of experience in this crap world. Leslie, I've never been so goddamn sure about anything. Are you going to move or what?"

Your turn to stare at the board. "I didn't mean to upset you, Dad." You make your fingers move over the pieces, faking strategy. He reaches across and grabs your hand.

"I'm sorry, Les. I'm tired. This thing has driven me up the bend and back again. I want this guy to pay for what he's done. More than that, I want it to be over. I don't want to have to see those poor little girls ever again."

You look up. "See them?"

"We have to take photographs and afterward, well, you know how a camera flash'll stay in your eye?" He shakes his head. "Can't explain it better than that."

You realize he's been working on that explanation for a while. "Maybe you should try to get some sleep now?"

He smiles. "Yeah." He rises from the table just as a car horn starts honking at the end of the drive. Coming closer. He hurries to the front door; you are right behind him. The dust cloud rises as the vehicle approaches, horn still blaring. You look though the side lights on the front door. A patrol car speeds into view. You think it's George Banyon, your dad's second in command.

Denise comes halfway down the stairs, her hair set on top of her head in orange juice can curlers. "What's going on?" Joanne stumbles out to the banister, yawning.

"Not sure," you say. Dad is already outside, loping over to meet the car. Your sisters come down and watch through the narrow windows with you as George gets out of the car. He tells Dad something and Dad kind of crumples against the hood of the vehicle. You can't hear anything, but you can tell it's very bad news. After a few minutes, George gets back in the car. Dad comes back toward the house. You and your sisters scatter. For the rest of the morning, you, Denise, and Joanne try to stay out of Dad's way.

empirical

In clearing out the kitchen, I had found a ten-pound box of just-add-water pancake mix that Greg had bought at one of the cash-and-carry discount stores he loved so dearly. The box was unopened and six months out of date. I'd set it aside because I knew I wouldn't be sleeping and bread was out of the question. So I spent the darkest hours of the night mixing up bowls of pancake batter to ladle onto the skillet in level quarter cups, flip, and then toss, golden brown disks as flat as cardboard, into the garbage. Each batch made about twenty cakes. I started counting them. I had flipped pancake number 277 when Molly stumbled in and pushed herself up to sit on the counter next to the stove – exactly where I used to sit to watch my mother cook.

"You can't sleep either, huh?" I asked as I turned another batch of cakes out of the skillet into the brown paper bag. She didn't say anything; she simply peered at me, fear and fury commingled, unblinking. I put down the spatula; I wanted to lay my hand on her cheek, bring some warmth to that icy condemnation. I moved to do so; she didn't flinch, didn't blink. I lowered my hand without touching her. "You aren't really here, are you?"

The apparition was gone before I'd finished asking. I went back to making pancakes, trying desperately to pretend that seeing Molly didn't mean what I dreaded it did: No matter the outcome of the next days' events, my daughter was now among the lost.

At seven-thirty sharp, as I was about to scoot Emma down the driveway toward school, Bill Watson and his crew arrived with a flatbed truck piled with folded striped canvas tarps, barrel-shaped fans, and sandbags. Emma immediately broke into groans of despair that she wasn't going to be able to see her house dressed up like a circus tent. Bill assured her that the tent would be in place until late the next day. She'd have all of Saturday to see it, from a safe distance, like everyone else. He gave her a couple of souvenirs: one of the metal clips they used to join the sections of tarp and a poseable plastic ant with X-ed out you've-been-clobbered eyes. Emma was charmed and skipped off to show Rita her new treasures.

"Kids sure do love bugs," said Bill as we watched her leave.

I went back into the house to make sure Molly was up and moving. Greg and I carried the mattresses out to the garage and then finished getting dressed ourselves. The three of us met in the foyer, pressed and polished and feeling fraudulent for it. We turned the house over to the Termite Guy and pulled out of the driveway in Greg's truck, Molly planted between us, as one of the crew began to hammer DANGER! TOXIC GAS! KEEP OUT! signs into the front yard.

Molly fidgeted first with the hem of her skirt and then pulled at her ponytail, tightening her hair even further. "Everyone's going to wonder why I'm there," she said.

"Let them wonder," said Greg.

We were to meet Phillip at the coffee shop down the street from the courthouse side of the Municipal Building. A waitress showed us to the booth in the back where he'd already been waiting for nearly an hour. He was on his cell phone, in the middle of what sounded like a business call, his voice raised to be heard over the din of banging and shouts from the kitchen. Molly, in what I assumed she saw as a preemptive strike against my choosing, perched on the seat beside Phillip, placing herself as far away from him as possible. Greg and I took the other side. We ordered breakfasts we weren't hungry for if only to get rid of the waitress. Phillip finished his call. He leaned his elbows on the table, looked at Molly, who tried to back away even farther without actually falling on the floor.

"How you doing, kiddo?" he said loudly enough to be heard around the table. When Molly didn't answer, he nodded as though she had. "See, this is where not being fourteen comes in handy. The court doesn't see you as a real person. You don't have the same rights. Then again, it doesn't hold you to the same rules. It expects you to screw up when it comes to understanding what it means to tell the truth."

"I did tell the truth. To Lydia. To help the guys."

He gestured for her to speak more softly. "No, you made a mistake.

That's what you're going to tell everyone. You do not say that you or Lydia lied or fabricated her memories in any way. What you say is that your telling Lydia what happened at the party was a mistake but – let me finish – the only reason you felt comfortable giving her this information is because you knew it to be true. You aren't *protecting* or *helping* the guys. The more you say that, the more it sounds like there is something from which they need to be protected. Understand?"

"Yeah." She ventured a sideways glance at him. "Do I have to get up and tell the judge that I told Lydia everything?"

Phillip leaned an inch closer. "Most likely. You are now a big old blip on the radar screen. Whether or not they take aim at you depends on how we play it. See, it would be much better for you if Lydia *decided* to tell the judge about her memory problems. And better still if no one at this table learned how that decision was made."

Molly lowered her eyes and started tapping her fingers on the sparkly spots in the laminated tabletop, crushing stars. "So it would come across more like we *chose* to change that part of the story rather than were *forced* to change it?"

"Exactly right. You two simply came to your senses at the last minute the way reasonable, honest people do. Reads much better than being trapped in a falsehood. But pay attention here, Molly, my friend – you don't have to see me as a friend for me to be one – as your friend, I'm telling you that the most imperative matter before us is how to help Lydia. So if Lydia gets on that stand and decides that *protecting* the guys is more important to her than her own well-being, then your mom and dad and I will have to volunteer what we know. Even if you catch shit for it."

"Don't worry. I'll take care of it."

"I'm sure you will."

"And, you know, thanks."

Phillip cocked his thumb in Molly's direction and winked at me. "Kid's got a future."

At the wink, Greg reached over and took my hand, holding it under his on the tabletop. Phillip searched my face for some clue toward interpretation. For Molly's benefit, I had not yanked my hand away with the immediate distaste I held for these displays of territorial possessiveness.

Instead, I made a show of shifting to stretch and yawn. Greg tried a different method of staking a claim.

"You know, Les, when *we* were hauling *our* bed out to the garage this morning, it suddenly occurred to me that it would be no big deal to fix that place up as an office for you. You'd be close enough to the city. Around for the girls. Better yet, no rent. Now that you're out of the Reeves."

"But she's not," said Phillip, indulging himself an obnoxious smirk. "That was Reeves Management I was talking to when you came in. We've reached a deal. If Les picks up the repair and cleaning fees and if she is willing to accept a three-month probationary addendum, she can keep her lease – provided nothing untoward occurs. That's what you wanted, isn't it, Leslie? That's *one* of the reasons you called me up in the middle of the night?"

I looked from Phillip to Greg and back to Phillip. I wanted to offer to dash out and buy them a tape measure but bit back on the impulse for my daughter's dignity. "Molly, sweetheart, want to walk over to the courthouse now?"

"Yes. Please." She almost leaped out of the booth.

Lydia was waiting with Neil and Amanda – all of them dressed in shades of navy blue – on a bench in the long hallway outside the courtroom where the proceedings would take place. The linoleum flooring shone with recent polishing, reflecting back the fluorescent light from the lensed panels overhead. The air was sharp with the smells of polishing compound and stale cigarette smoke that had managed to escape the designated area. When they saw us coming, Neil stood and Amanda's face tightened with concern. Only Lydia seemed unperplexed. To my eye, the child appeared beyond surprising ever again. Before anyone could ask, Molly presented her cover story.

"They wanted me to come down because Lydia had, you know, borrowed my sleeping bag, and of course Mom has to be here because she found Lydia and that stuff."

Amanda appeared to start breathing again, and Neil shook Molly's hand, offering us both a somber thanks.

Molly shrugged and pointed down the hall. "I was going down to the water fountain. Want to come with me, Lydia?"

Lydia furrowed up her brow as though this were the most complex of propositions.

Amanda nudged her. "It's all right, Lyddie. Go spend some time with Molly."

Neil furthered the cause. "We're going to be sitting most of the day. It'll do you good to get up and walk for a while."

Lydia leaned forward as if to ascertain the fact of the water fountain down by the sign that read PHONES. She sighed and said, "Let's go." The girls started off toward the big window at the far end of the hall, Molly asking if Lydia caught *Eden* last night and if she thought they were really about to get rid of Jasmeena. Lydia shook her head. No way. She's the reason people watch. Their voices faded as the distance between us and them grew. Lydia laughed about something. Amanda called after them, "Don't wander too far."

The Parrishes and I made halfhearted small talk about the weather and how Swifton really needed an updated municipal facility. We watched the shape of our daughters get smaller, less distinct as they blurred in the breeze-tossed shadows from outside. At the water fountain, they took turns bending to drink. When they finished, the Molly shape reached out and touched the Lydia shape. Molly moved into the pay phone alcove in the corner. I could no longer see Molly, only Lydia, the slight starts of her posture as Molly said whatever Molly was saying. At one point, Lydia reached up and covered her mouth and then dropped her head. She reached forward and hugged Molly, pulling her back into view. Molly did not return the embrace.

"I wonder what that's about," said Amanda, rising. "I should go see if she's upset." Amanda hurried off down the hall before I could think of an adequate reason for her not to rush to comfort her daughter.

"Molly's been a such a dear friend to Lyddie," said Neil as he lifted his glasses to rub his eyes. "We can't thank her or you enough." He set the glasses back in place on the bridge of his nose. His eyes were rimmed red, puffy with sleeplessness or tears. He realized I was studying him and turned his head, embarrassed to be caught suffering. Neil was doing what grown-ups do in a crisis; he was holding the world together by holding his emotions in check. Ashamed that I still doubted him, I ordered an end to the continuous internal debate between my desire to trust the quiet authority of empirical evidence and my need to acknowledge the clanging alarms of my intuition. Lydia's situation was too tangled in my own. I didn't have the objectivity necessary to make a valid call. My mistrust was my problem, not his.

"Neil, I'm sorry," I said, without explanation.

He chuckled. "We hear that quite often these days."

"This will end. Things will get better."

"Yes. But will Lydia?" He turned to face me, the pain in his expression more real than anything around us. Empirical.

"I don't know," I said. "I hope so." In voicing hope, I realized that the debate had, at long last, gone silent. The silence was more unnerving than any of the noise that had come before it because the silence implied trust. And if *I* could trust him, then he was most likely trustworthy at large. Which meant I'd lost the wrenchingly simple explanation of Lydia's torment. Which meant that, if not the boys at the party, someone else had ravaged the girl. Which meant that the hurtful thing walking around in human skin was still moving among us, unseen.

m o l l y

Molly sits when the judge says they can sit. Her mom smiles at her, but Molly doesn't feel much like smiling back. They are in the back of the courtroom. Molly doesn't know if the guys realize she's here. What will Tim think when he sees her? When he hears what she is going to have to say? And the girls, who are whispering together in their seats. Of course, Lydia's been really nice lately, but she's had to be because she needed Molly's help. In truth, Lydia does hate her. As do the others. They make no secret of how they feel; they tell her to her face. *No one likes you, Molly Stone.* Molly knows why. She's geeky and doesn't know how to talk to people and has stupid clothes and her mom's been in a mental hospital and the whole world knows it.

Molly looks around some more. Mr. Verrill, the principal, is here. He's sitting behind the girls. Next to him is Mrs. Domingo, the teacher who overheard the fight. Detective Burnham is in the very front. Everyone is dressed up, restless, like church feels to her since they go only on Easter and sometimes Christmas. They will all be watching her do this. It is going to be so much harder than she first thought it would.

The judge seems mean; the very first thing he does is lecture them – "the children" – about the seriousness of the situation. This is real trouble. This is not a game. *Well, that's what you think, judge guy.* He goes on about how he will not tolerate any disrespectful behavior or rude language. And then he asks that they remember the thankless lot of the stenographer who has to transcribe every word that gets spoken here, so don't mumble and try to sound reasonably intelligent. A fat woman in a purple pantsuit, who is sitting at a little black box, leans into her microphone and thanks them for their consideration. Then the judge starts talking to the lawyers and it gets very complicated and dull. Lots of stuff about motions for dismissal and evidentiary procedures. Discovery this and discovery that. It goes on forever and then, finally, the judge asks them for any opening statements. More speechifying as the DA guy says that they will prove that the defendants, although mere children, are the ones responsible for the injuries sustained by Lydia Parrish as well as the sexual assault of other girls at the party and that the DA intends to make it clear not only to these kids but to the community as a whole that such acts will not be tolerated no matter the ages of those involved. The judge interrupts him to ask if the DA sees a jury in the room. Molly looks at the vacant jury chairs and wonders if the DA has filled them with invisible men. Then a woman lawyer, who is working for the guys, stands up, and says that while the nature of Lydia's injuries suggests a horrible scenario, the guys are guilty of no more than adolescent bad judgment – blame that can be shared with the girls who were severely intoxicated at the time. The judge sighs heavily into the microphone and rubs at his forehead as though he has a headache. He looks like he wants to yell at someone, but he doesn't. He calls for the first witness, Dr. Isadora Samada.

Dr. Samada is the one who examined Lydia at the hospital. She describes bruises and bite marks. Clearly these were obtained as the result of trauma. The DA sits down. The guys' lawyer gets Dr. Samada to say that the tooth patterns of the bites match Lydia's own teeth, and then she has to admit that they can't be certain that Lydia received these injuries during the party – but she also slides in that it can't be disproved, either. Objections are yelled. Molly can't really concentrate; her mind keeps slipping to the ache the steel-winged butterflies are raising in her belly and how much her palms are sweating. She tries to keep herself calm by repeating *this is the only way* over and over in her head, but the thought keeps stumbling, startled by the shouts of *get out of this; get up and run*. But she can't. *This is the only way.*

Mrs. Domingo is called up front; she relates what she heard. Being new to the school this year – and it is such a big school – she can't say she had much hope of identifying the student with whom Lydia was fighting by voice alone, but in the end it didn't matter because by that time the events at the party were apparently common knowledge among the students. More talking. Then Mr. Verrill explains how Mrs. Domingo came to him with her concerns and how the laws demanded he report any knowledge of a crime to the proper authorities. He had no choice. He says it in such a way that you get the feeling he wasn't all that certain a crime had been committed, but then he turns it over the other way by saying that in the light of the medical evidence that's emerged, he's glad he did. Andrea Burnham gets up next to talk about what she did and why. She speaks in very crisp syllables that get even crisper, almost sharp when the guys' lawyer tries to get her to admit the case is a manufactured attempt at public relations for the police department. Mom then goes up to the stand, and they ask her a few questions about finding Lydia, her condition when she found her. She makes it sound part accident, part luck, but doesn't give them any more information than what they ask for. *Sorry, judge guy, but you're wrong; this* is *a game.* Mom comes back and sits next to Molly. Mom and Dad give each other one of those long questioning looks they use when they can't talk.

And finally, finally, they call Lydia. Molly knows why they've saved Lydia for last. By making Lydia listen to how everyone already believes something bad happened to her, it will make it easier for her to say, "Yeah, you're right, the guys did it." The rest of courtroom knows this, too, which is why, Molly figures, that as Lydia walks to the witness chair, the people in the courtroom seem as one to straighten their postures in anticipation.

Lydia sits down. Molly's dad puts his arm around Molly's shoulder. Mom reaches over and squeezes Molly's hand, doesn't let go. Normally, this would bug her, but this time Molly finds herself squeezing back, holding on.

The judge asks Lydia if she understands what it means to tell the whole truth because he expects the whole truth and nothing less. Lydia says, "Yes, sir."

The DA rises, he doesn't move from behind the table as he did with the other witnesses, and his voice is so very gentle now that he sounds like a different person.

"Did you decide to have a party?"

"Yes, sir."

"Were your parents at home?"

"No, sir. My mom was out on a piano-tuning job, and Neil was in the city ordering supplies for the vineyard."

"Did you drink alcohol?"

"Yes, sir."

"Did you get intoxicated?"

"Yes."

"Were you intoxicated when the boys – the defendants – arrived?"

"I think so. Probably."

"You're not sure?" Lydia looks at the judge and then searches the courtroom until she finds Molly.

The DA guy clears his throat. "Did you understand my question, Lydia?"

"Yes, sir. I did. I would say that yes, I was dru – intoxicated when the guys arrived, but to be really honest, I don't remember the guys arriving at all."

"You don't remember?" From the sudden, hungry edge in his voice, Molly can tell that the DA guy thinks his own luck just changed. Molly thinks that he can't possibly have any idea how much everything is about to change.

"No," says Lydia, her eyes focused downward. "I don't remember the guys getting there, or anything that happened after that. I don't remember when anyone left. I don't remember anything. I woke up in the middle of the night in my bed. What I've been saying I remembered is what someone else told me happened."

"Someone told you what happened?"

"But you have to understand that I believe it is what happened. It's what everyone who was there said happened. So just because I don't remember doesn't mean – "

"Lydia, who told you what to say your memory was?"

"I don't want to get anybody in trouble."

The judge leans over and says, with surprising kindness, "You must answer the question, Miss Parrish."

Lydia sighs. "Molly told me."

The lawyer moves his head as though trying to tune it to a different frequency. "Who is Molly?" His assistant hands him a note, but before he can read it, Lydia answers for him.

"Molly Stone. She's a friend." Lydia points, and everyone turns to look. Molly's mother squeezes her hand harder. Lydia starts to talk faster, as though the quicker she gets through it the less it will hurt. "Molly was the one who Mrs. Domingo overheard me fighting with.

264

Molly planned it. The fight? She said it would sound more like my memory if someone heard me being upset about it. Molly planned out the idea of my running away, too. For the same reason." Now Lydia's parents turn back and stare hard at Molly. A rustle of whispers moves through the room.

The judge raises his hand and says, "Quiet. Now."

The DA leans on the table. "So you have no idea what happened at the party except for what Molly Stone has told you?"

"No, sir." Lydia's voice is warming. "But that is what happened. Molly knows what happened."

"Because one of the defendants bragged to Molly when he was bragging to everyone else?"

The woman lawyer stands up. "Objection."

"Sustained." The judge appeared angry, but he kept his voice soft. He sounded sad. "What do you say, Miss Parrish? Let's make this easier for both of us, shall we? We've already had testimony that the story of what took place at the party was well circulated around school. I'm sure you must have played telephone – the whispering game, yes? – and learned how quickly information mutates. Why would you believe only Molly's version of the events well enough to claim them as your memory?"

"Why?" Lydia looks at Molly, her shoulders drop. Molly swallows, nods. And so she tells him; she tells him everything Molly told her at the end of the hallway next to the pay phones, everything about Molly following Tim and the bikes and spying through the window as though she's known about it all along. Lydia's crying because she says she feels so bad for letting Molly help her, but the crying sounds kind of fake, especially when she says that she decided it was better to tell the truth. It is clear that Lydia has figured out that she can dump this on Molly. She goes on to tell the judge everything about Molly's plans, leaving out the parts where Lydia said she thought those plans were a great idea. But then, that's what Molly expected her to do. Lydia hates her. What Lydia doesn't know is that the only truth she has told is that she can't remember anything that took place that day. She has no idea that she's just walked into a trap. Molly hates her right back, but a promise is a promise. This is the only way.

3

You can see the tree. At least where it used to be. Even in the dark. It's as though the sky were holding blank the spaces where once it was pierced by branches. Gone but still there. You lie in your bed and wait for sleep, your mind disengaging from wakeful duties. Dad says they have a lead on the orange-hat guy. Mandy scratched him. You wrote that in your notes before you went to bed. If you turn the pages of your notebook backward you can make time undo itself. Mandy is rescued from wandering lost in the dark by a monster. Her fingernail mends his face, and then he heals her wounds. He returns her to her bed where he unties the ropes from her wrists and removes the gag. She then descends into the peace of un-disturbed sleep as he slips unnoticed through her window. Her experience is the same as Jennifer's and Nicole's and Kimmy's and the others before them. If you go backward, the monster puts on his orange hat and changes the Nightingales back into their original human form leaving them no memory of the transformation.

Backward works for other things, too. Bethany and Dad fight their way out of anger into almost married; they become happier and happier until, as though unable to bear the happiness, they part in shy smiles and relief, without sorrow, their hearts full of hope. The tree itself is resurrected through Dad's hours of arduous sawing over three years. You can see him up in the branches, reattaching the smaller limbs until it is whole once more, ready for the bolt of blue-white light to zip up the charred gash in the trunk and restore the tree house with the final flick of its electric tail. The wind sucks the storm back over the horizon and the sun climbs out of the west to shine itself on what is now an ordinary summer day; backward still down into the east, into night and around again as many times as necessary to get to that one night when, quietly, your mother backs down the driveway, sneaks into the house, tiptoes up the stairs, and unpacks.

She removes the letter from the bureau and climbs back in bed next to your father to lie awake for hours until it is time to come to your room and kiss your forehead and say she's sorry as the tears roll up to dry her eyes before she smiles.

And now someone is calling your name. *Leslie?* Dad is calling to you. It's morning. He's standing in the door of your bedroom. He's got the game board under his arm; he wants to know if you'd like to play some chess.

judgment hour

Lorant called the attorneys to the bench and, after a brief conference, announced we would recess for thirty minutes. Molly was still clutching my hand, transmitting her emotions to me through a steady trembling. Greg asked her if she wanted to go out and get some air, have something to eat. She shook her head, neither looking at nor away from Lydia, the other girls, or their parents as they filed up the aisle. Amanda paused and stooped forward so that Molly could not pretend she didn't see her.

"We know you were only trying to help. And we appreciate that." She patted Molly on the knee and offered me an expression of condolence, mother to mother. "No matter how we try to convince them we're on their side, they always think they can fix things themselves. And their problems get bigger."

"Tell that to Lydia."

"Every hour of every day." Amanda bowed her head in weariness and continued on her way.

Lydia certainly was trying to get things fixed. It had not surprised me that she was attempting to scapegoat Molly. Pissed me off, but did not surprise me. She had been more than willing to use Mol one way to get out of this, why wouldn't she try to use her the other? She was a kid. That's what kids do. I leaned over and whispered into Molly's ear, "Lorant is smarter than Lydia. He knows she's been more than a willing participant in *the plan*."

She blinked at me. "Is that why you didn't tell him that you *saw* Lydia? Is that the reason you didn't tell him exactly how you found her?"

"You don't know how I found her."

"I can figure it out. I know how you find things."

"Molly, I'm not the enemy here." I held her hand tighter. "Neither is the judge."

She gave me the sort of look of pity and disgust one might offer the carcass of a recent road kill, but she didn't argue. "Whatever you say." She continued her straightforward vigil.

The boys had been taken to a holding room, but the legal types had stayed behind poring over papers, no doubt the transcript of Molly's statement. Phillip sidled into the row in front of us and took the seat in front of Molly. Greg tightened his grip on Molly's shoulder, pulling her close until he had almost lifted her off her chair.

"You're still here?" Molly rolled her shoulders until her dad released her.

"I'm here until I'm sure you don't need me." He turned sideways and leaned toward her conspiratorially. "Your friend Lydia is quite the little mistress of spin, isn't she?"

"She's not my friend. I never said she was."

"Then what's in this for you?"

Greg shook his head. "Leave her alone, Hogarth."

"I'd love to, but I can't, because *why* Molly helped is the big money question. And Molly, you should be prepared to answer it. You've gone to quite a bit of trouble for someone who isn't a friend. Why?"

"I have my reasons – "

"Unless the friend you've been trying to help is sitting on the defendant's side."

"I don't have to talk about it with you."

"No, but in a few minutes you are going to have to talk about it in front of the judge." His expression softened. "Molly, you're not the first person in the history of the world to follow someone you care about to find out what he's up to. Fact is, the need is so common that people like your mom can make a living doing it."

Molly's cheeks blushed brilliant pink. "Yeah, so?"

"So, Miss Stone," he steered his voice to that of authoritative badgering, "weren't you only telling Lydia Parrish the version of events that best served – what was his name? – Tim, a boy you have a crush on so that he would like you in return?"

"Christ, Phillip." I wanted to smack him.

"Sorry, but that question will be over the plate in the first five minutes she's up there – "

"What about the plants?" Molly almost hissed at him. "If I wanted to tell the same story as the guys, why would I change the part about the plants?"

"That's my girl." Phillip chucked her softly on the chin.

"I'm not your girl." I could feel the fury radiating off her, only amplifying what Greg was putting off.

"You're angry?" Phillip looked confused.

"Yes, I'm angry."

"Good. Stay that way." He gave her one of his ingratiating grins. "I'll be in the back if you need anything."

Thirty minutes to the second, Lorant was back on the bench, gaveling the court into session. Molly was called. After one last squeeze, I let go of her hand. She stood and inched past me to walk to the front of the courtroom, her head up, her eyes on Lorant. Molly stood in the witness box until Lorant invited her to be seated and state her full name and address. She spoke quietly but clearly. Eerily composed as though she'd done this hundreds of times before. Why is it that we are most aware of our children's vulnerability at the same moment they seem most certain of their self-sufficiency and strength? Suddenly terrified that I'd lost her, I reached out physically to stop the sense of weightlessness and found Greg, who had apparently been reaching out for the same reason. We clasped hands, and smiled, too big, over the empty seat between us, each pretending faith for the other's benefit.

Lorant was studying Molly over the top of his glasses. "Well, Miss Stone," he said with a hint of remorse, "if getting to the facts of a matter were easy or fun, I and the rest of the good people in this courtroom would be out of our jobs. But I do wish most sincerely that my job were more pleasant than it occasionally is. I find myself now in a far more complicated situation than what I thought I was sitting down to when we began this morning, and the court is depending on you to help us sort things out again. Do you understand me?"

Molly nodded. "You want me to tell what happened and what I did."

"Very good. And I am aware that it may be disconcerting to have to present this information in the presence of your peers. Old man that I may be, I am not so old that I can't remember the cost of perceived disloyalties in the schoolyard, but for the time you are on this witness stand, your first loyalty must be to the facts themselves and not to any individual who may be embroiled therein. You will tell this court the truth in its entirety and worry about the cost later. Are we clear on that?"

"Yes. Sir."

Lorant waved the DA onward. He stayed behind the table, as the rules for examining children said he must, but he reached out across the room in a let's-be-pals tone of voice that made me feel sick to my stomach.

"So Molly, you don't mind if I call you Molly? Let's see if we can get to the bottom of what really went on at Lydia's party, okay?"

"Okay."

"I just want to walk you through your statement as you gave it to Detective Burnham earlier this week. Do you remember that?"

"Of course," Molly said and then amended her snarkiness. "I mean, yes, I remember it."

"Try to bear with me here. Going over these points again and again is tedious, I'm sure, but we find ourselves in a bit of jumble all of a sudden. So according to your statement, you were baby-sitting at your neighbor's house."

"Yes."

"And can you tell us what occurred when you finished your baby-sitting job?"

Molly bit her lip and then looked up at Lorant. "I have to tell?"

" 'Fraid so."

She turned back to the DA. Her posture shifted, straightened, elongating in the chair, as though she were being filled with quick-setting cement. She lifted her chin. "I went home, back to my house."

The DA scratched his head and shuffled his notes. "Maybe you misunderstood me, Molly. What happened as you were leaving your neighbor's house?"

"I rode my bike back home."

"But in your statement – in both your statements – you say that as you were leaving your neighbor's house, you saw one of the defendants, Tim Zinni, ride by on his bike."

"Yes. That's what I said."

"Are you changing your testimony here? Are you saying now that it didn't happen that way?"

Andrea Burnham looked back at us with an I-told-you-so smirk. Greg and I exchanged a quick glance of panic. I turned back in time to see Molly nodding.

"You'll have to answer me out loud, Molly."

"No. It didn't happen that way. Nothing I told Detective Burnham happened. Not the way I told it. Except about the plants. When I got there the plants were gone from the window; they were all over the floor and the piano. But by then the party was over."

I remembered the potting soil smell and grit from the piano the night I went out to the Parrishes'. Amanda and Neil were staring straight ahead, but not at Molly. Lydia was sitting forward, her expression worried. I looked again at my daughter's warrior bearing, the combative glint in her eye. She had been one step ahead of us from the beginning. We'd been played.

The defense made a motion to recess in order to allow Molly to make her statement in such a manner that it might be reviewed before entered into testimony. Lorant shook his head. "For the first time since this mess started, I feel like I'm getting a version that didn't come out of a committee. I think Miss Stone here is on a roll. You can cover any concerns in redirect. Let's keep going."

The DA looked at his notes. "You weren't at Lydia's until after the party was over?" He was choosing his words as though they might be wired with explosives.

"I had no reason to be at Lydia's. We haven't been friends for a long time. But when she called, she said she was really sick and she didn't want to be by herself. I asked her if I should call someone. She got really upset and said no, that she was in a bunch of trouble. She sounded awful, so I rode out to her house to, you know, make sure she was okay."

"When did she call?"

"I'd just gotten home from the baby-sitting job when Lydia called. I didn't go right away. But the more I thought about it, the more I got scared. So I decided to ride out there to check on her."

"Was there anyone else at the house when you got there?"

"No. In fact, I thought Lydia had played a joke on me, because I knocked for a long time but no one came to the door. Then I tried the handle and found out it was open. So I went inside and found Lydia sitting in the middle of all these spilled plants. There was dirt and roots and leaves everywhere. Like she'd torn them apart. It looked like she'd thrown up on the carpet a couple times. She didn't have any clothes on and she'd been, well, like rolling around in the dirt and gunk. When she saw me, she asked me if I liked piano music and then she picked up a handful of dirt and threw it at the piano and screamed. There was a lot of dirt and broken plant stuff all over the piano." Molly had focused her attention on Lydia, leaning into her answers, enunciating her words as though she meant to prompt some response from the girl who now had her head down.

"What did you do then?" The DA, in audibly growing confidence that Molly was about to make his case against the boys, sat on the edge of the table.

"I kind of finally understood that she was drunk. There were bottles all over the place. It was a huge mess. I asked Lydia if she'd like to go lie down up in her room. But she said she felt gross and wanted to take a shower but getting up the stairs was too hard. So I helped her. I almost had to carry her; she nearly knocked me down the stairs a couple of times. But I finally got her in the shower. She wouldn't stand up. I was afraid to leave her because I thought she might go to sleep and drown or something. So I sat in the bathroom with her while she crawled around in the tub with the water pouring down on her. She was singing parts of the song 'Drivin'' – I don't know if you know that song? – and she'd start crying and then she'd start laughing. It was really scary. I didn't know if I should call nine-one-one or what. And then she just snaps out of it and sits up, very calm and normal, like she's not even drunk, and asks if I had been at the party. I said what party? That's when she told me everything that I've said I saw happen."

"Hold up a second, Miss Stone." Lorant took off his glasses. "Miss Parrish told you everything you know about the party that Miss Parrish now says she can't remember?"

"Yes, sir. She told me something else, too."

Lorant's years of experience solidified his expression into one of pragmatic expectation. "Oh, I bet she did. Mr. DA, sir, do you wish to continue?"

The DA pursed his lips and looked over at the boys, who, along with their parents and lawyers, had adopted collective expression of dreadful curiosity. "You understand, Molly, that all any of us wants is to get a picture of exactly what transpired in terms of the people in this courtroom?"

"Yes, I understand that. This is only about what happened at the party."

"That's right. So what did Lydia tell you?"

Molly swallowed and leaned closer to the microphone. She closed her eyes. "Lydia said that the guys at the party had been stupid, useless jerks. That they were scared little babies who didn't know how to do anything with girls. That she had to make Tim touch her where she wanted him to touch her. She, ah, showed me what she meant. She kept saying she shouldn't have to make men touch her; she shouldn't have to make Neil – "

"Shut up!" Lydia was standing, her fists clenched. "Molly! I never said that! Shut up!" Amanda pulled Lydia back into her chair, shushing her. Neil Parrish buried his head in his hands. Lorant pounded the gavel. "Silence. All of you. No one moves. Miss Stone, you were saying . . ."

"Oh." Molly opened her eyes, shook herself as though she'd been dozing and just that second jerked out of a dream. "That was everything, really. Lydia kept saying the boys were useless and scared, like Neil. She had to make them touch her. Then she made me promise over and over that I'd never tell about the party. I finally got her out of the shower and into a nightgown. She was asleep before she got into bed. It didn't seem like I could do anything more, so I just, you know, went home. The next afternoon I called to check on her. She had no idea why I was calling. She didn't remember me coming over. I asked her what she did remember and then she started to cry. She said she couldn't remember anything. That's when I told her what she had told me – but only about the party, I didn't want to, you know, think about the rest of it." Molly sat back in the chair and exhaled.

Lorant held up his hand to stop the DA's next question. "I want this one. Why now, Miss Stone? Why not in the two previous statements?"

"Why?" Molly squirmed in her chair. "Because I had promised Lydia I wouldn't say anything, and I thought that the way we had worked it out, that everyone would understand that the guys hadn't done anything bad. It wasn't a lie. But this morning I realized that not telling would be a mistake worse than breaking the promise. So I told Lydia to go ahead and tell the truth about not remembering, and I'd tell my side of what happened, and you would still see that the guys didn't do anything."

"And you would be telling on Mr. Parrish over there so Lydia wouldn't have to?"

"That's what happened. I know she doesn't remember any of this, but that's what Lydia told me. It's the same thing, right? I'm telling the truth this time."

"*This* time." Lorant massaged his forehead. "Would the district attorney care to instruct Miss Stone on the concept of hearsay evidence?"

Molly didn't wait for the lecture. "I know what hearsay is. Detective Burnham told me. It's when you talk about what someone else said to you and the problem of . . ." Her face went slack as the futility of her efforts began to sink in. "You can't use anything I told you about what Lydia said?"

"Nope," the DA said. "For the record: Move to strike the preceding as inadmissible – not to mention the witness has admitted to perjuring herself."

Lorant rested his chin in his hand. "Motion granted. But I will ask the bailiff to put a call into Social Services and have them send someone down here, *tout de suite*. Mr. Parrish and Mrs. Parrish, I trust you will not leave the building?"

"No, Your Honor." Neil almost laughed. "We know the drill."

when you leave the garden, you leave alone

Lorant announced we were recessing until the next morning. Andrea Burnham herded us into a conference room to await further instructions, and Greg made it clear to Phillip that *us* did not include him. We would contact him later if Molly's need for an attorney changed. Phillip informed Greg it had already changed, and he was going to see if he could find out by how much.

The conference room was one of those cubical spaces they set aside for lawyers to consult with their clients. The walls were painted a turnipy beige and the miniblinds on the windows were bent and dusty. Decades of cigarette smoke, coffee, and nerves flattened the air to a permanent staleness that could not be cloaked by the solitary air freshener someone had hopefully fastened above the light switch. Too anxious to stay seated in the worn vinyl chairs, Greg and I stood on opposite sides of the conference table and watched Molly pace the perimeter of the room. Unsure of even where to begin with our questions, neither Greg nor I spoke. Molly's testimony had jolted me out of the temporary lull of trusting Neil or Amanda or anyone – including my daughter. Asking her anything at this point would only lead to more confusion. The needle in my mind was already dangerously into the red zone of self-accusation, although I could not begin to define my failing beyond the certainty that I had missed a crucial detail.

Burnham came back into the room, closing the door behind her. "I spoke to the court clerk."

Molly stopped by the window and toyed with the strings of the miniblinds. "The judge doesn't believe me."

"Lorant believes you enough to call in a caseworker." Burnham sat on the edge of the table, arms crossed over her chest, more concerned than angered. "Why didn't you tell me any of this?"

277

She looked to her father and me for intercession. Greg shook his head. "Answer the woman."

"I wanted to." Molly pulled at the strings and the slats of the blinds raised unevenly until they jammed. "But I thought if I waited until I got up in the courtroom, then Neil wouldn't have a chance to make up an excuse and get away with it."

Burnham caught my eye. "If you *waited*? Molly, were you trying to get up there? You were, weren't you? And that's why Lydia is admitting she can't remember. You told her to tell the truth this morning because you knew they'd have to call you to the stand."

Molly shrugged and walked a few steps forward, seemingly drawn by a buckled patch in the paint on the wall. "Maybe," she said.

"No, that can't be right," I said. "None of us would have known about Lydia's memory if Emma had not . . ." *Aw, crap.* "You got Emma involved with this?"

"Not on purpose. But after we did the videotape *she*" – Molly pointed at Burnham – "said I wouldn't have to be in court. I *had* to be in court. Emma telling you what she heard was the only way I could think to make it happen. It wasn't supposed to go like this."

"I'd guess not," said Burnham. A knock sounded at the door, and Burnham went to open it. Amanda Parrish was on the other side, quite a distance from the door, as though she'd knocked and then backed away.

"This has been a terribly long day, hasn't it?" she asked of the room as though she were seeking a guarantee things wouldn't get any worse. When it became clear we couldn't offer such a comfort, she said, "I was wondering whether I might talk to Molly?"

"If you talk to her here," said Greg.

"Of course." Amanda took that as an invitation and entered the room. She took the chair closest to the door, gave us a little smile, and smoothed her dress. "Will you come talk with me, Molly?"

"I'd rather stay over here."

Amanda nodded. She held herself very still and straight. "I wanted to tell you that no one in our family is angry with you."

"Lydia is."

"Yes, but there are things about Lyddie you could not know. You are not the first person to whom Lydia has told tales of horror suffered at the hands of her parents. She has a history of making up stories that turn out to be patently false. I want you to know that these accusations are always taken seriously. This is not easy for me to talk about, but we – Neil and I – have been investigated and observed and questioned. We've taken lie detector tests. Each time she does this, after the crisis has gone on long enough to suit her purposes, Lydia will simply laugh and tell everyone she was making a joke."

Molly narrowed her eyes. "You're saying Lydia is lying?"

"It's not as straightforward as that. I think my child has difficulties distinguishing where her imagination ends and the real world begins. If she doesn't know the difference, it's not exactly lying, is it? I really don't think she cares about the difference. She cares about the attention her stories get her. She loves the chaos she's able to create. The pain she causes. Sometimes – " Amanda's voice broke. She calmed herself before continuing. "Sometimes, it seems to me that she wants to punish us or anyone else for loving her. Look at how miserably she's treated you. What have you ever been to her but a friend?"

"I don't believe she can't tell the difference," Molly said, picking at the cracking paint with her nail. "She can tell."

"I have trouble believing it, too. But you do know the difference, Molly. Neil and I wanted you to know we trust the truth in every word you spoke up on that stand. I'm the one who cleaned up the plants she dumped in the piano, what I thought was just more aftermath from the party. Yes, I know, Detective Burnham, I should have told you, but the last thing these children needed was another strike against them."

Burnham wrapped one of her curls around her finger. Unwrapped it. "You don't buy Lydia's memory problem here, do you?"

"No," said Amanda. "She gave herself away in court. Lydia claims she doesn't remember telling Molly any of what happened at the party. Don't you think it's funny, however, that she is able to remember with perfect precision the promise Molly made not to tell?"

"But – "

"She remembers, Molly. She remembers all of it. Or enough of it. She's admitted as much to the poor young man from Social Services. She's known exactly what she was doing from the start. I'm so sorry, Molly. You took a huge risk on Lydia's behalf. You said in the courtroom that you thought at first she might be playing a joke on you? Well, she was, but only she finds any humor in it. That's why we're shutting this ordeal down right now. I've talked to the other parents. We're withdrawing the charges."

"You can't do that," Burnham said, nearly guffawing in disbelief.

"Certainly we can. Based on Lydia's confusion, her dishonesty. My daughter cannot be trusted except to disrupt as many lives as she is able. This has already gotten too huge and ugly. The other children don't deserve to be dragged through her little game. We'll deal with the drinking aspect of the party by any means the court wishes. Lyddie was no doubt the instigator there as well."

Burnham turned her outraged glare to Greg and me. "Does this make any sense to you?"

"When has any of this made sense?" Greg dropped into a chair.

"Amanda, what about Lydia's injuries? Are you going to close the book on those as well?"

"She says that she gave them to herself. The doctor supports that as a distinct possibility."

"Which means other *possibilities* may be out there. Don't you think it would be wise to pursue –"

"Molly?" Amanda took a deep breath. "You said that Lyddie 'showed' you what she wanted from Tim? How did she show you?"

Molly rested her head against the wall. "A bottle of bubble bath. It was made of glass. She was . . . I was afraid the bottle would break. I tried to make her stop."

"Oh, baby." Amanda surrendered her attempt to remain above her sorrow. "I'm so, so sorry. But that would account for some of the more recent bruises, wouldn't it. She probably guessed that by letting Molly witness that little scene, Molly would feel compelled to play along. The child needs more help than I can give her. I'm beginning to believe it would be best to separate her from rest of us before she does serious harm." Amanda seemed to realize that her thoughts had drifted out of conscious control. "I suppose I should get back out there with my family, such as we are. Social Services cleared Neil, of course; they always do. So we'll be heading home. Again, Molly, you tried to do good for Lydia, and we're heartbroken for any pain she's brought into your life." With that Amanda left.

"So is this over?" said Molly, after the door had closed.

Andrea Burnham and I exchanged a look of *I don't think so*. Burnham clucked her tongue. "Hang on. Let me go see what I can find out." She took off, leaving the three of us alone.

"For a second there I forgot you weren't a cop," said Greg, without joking.

"As if the world doesn't have enough problems. You okay, Mol?"

"Yeah." She went back to picking at the flaw in the paint. "Do you guys think Lydia is making this up? That she really does remember?"

Greg gestured that this one was mine. "I'm not sure," I said, going over to her so I could see her eyes, read the severity of the explosions she must be enduring. "Amanda does have a point with Lydia remembering that you made her a promise."

"Maybe it wasn't the same promise."

"Not the same promise?" The dissonance of unordered information in my head started to align into a faint, clear signal. A high-pitched buzzing. An alert from the Emergency Broadcast Center. "Molly?"

She kept picking at the paint. "I've made other promises to Lydia."

"What sort of promises?"

She didn't answer, and out of the emergency buzzing the first fine tentacles of a horrible notion began to worm into the open silence between me and my daughter. A question. A simple question. One that I'd never asked because they were kids, right? I'd never asked because I thought I already knew. "Molly, you and Lydia were best friends. What happened? Why did you stop wanting to go play over at Lydia's house?"

"She stopped liking me."

"Why?"

She shrugged. I watched as she finally dislodged a good-sized flake of paint. She put it in the palm of her hand and then glanced up at me, sad, fearful, but determined all the same. "Bad stuff happened."

Greg was on his feet. "What sort of 'bad stuff'?"

I held up my hand to quiet him. Or maybe to forestall my own question. I asked anyway. "Did bad stuff happen to you?"

She sucked in her breath and looked down at her shoes. "He wasn't supposed to get away with it."

Molly's words were almost an exact echo of Janet's the day before. The present running headlong into the past and in the resulting collision, I finally understood. The connection wasn't between Lydia and the Nightingales; it was between Lydia and me, the daughters of men who do secret, unimaginable deeds. That's what they'd been trying to tell me. "You stay here with your dad, sweetheart," I said, trying to keep the shaking out of my words. "I need to go talk to Detective Burnham."

As I left the room, I looked at Greg. His always tired eyes were widening with the emergent knowledge he would have given his very soul to have remained blind to: For all the rules enforced and handholding maintained, for all the checking on her in slumber and making certain she'd eaten enough vegetables, for all the dentist appointments and immunizations, math tutors hired, dance recitals attended, library cards renewed, for all the superstitions and rituals and second chances begged from heaven, his child had still fallen under the wheels of the world.

Andrea Burnham was seated at her desk, on the phone, the stem of her glasses clamped in her teeth. When she saw me, she asked the caller to hold for a second; she looked again and told the caller she'd have to call back. "Social Services backs Amanda Parrish's version. Lydia's got a file thick as . . . what is it?"

"I can give you the Nightingale perp."

"Beg your pardon?"

I glanced up at my father's portrait before lowering my head and speaking just above a whisper. "You said you've been working the evidence. You have the DNA. Do you have Janet Scott's?"

"You kidding? We pretty much have a shrine built around the evidence from those girls. Every so often we run the charts through the agencies to see if we hit a match. Nothing yet."

"Janet's was the same as the others'?"

"Yeah, but thirty years ago Swifton was such a backwater burg – all due respect – they didn't think, couldn't have guessed where the technology was headed. They didn't get specimens on the one suspect they had. They let him go so quick." She was watching me clench and unclench my hands.

"No, they didn't. Let him go. Look, Burnham, I can get you that sample. You may be able to close this thing down once and for all, but in return, I want a favor."

Color came up fast behind her freckles. "Name it."

"Come out to the Parrish house with me and make sure I don't kill this guy."

2

The birds are gone. You can't tell if they disappeared rapidly over the past few minutes or if their numbers have diminished little by little over the hour that you've been out walking with Dad. You haven't really been paying attention. Until now. You check the sky above you again. The clouds are moving in layers, as though they are running on three different clocks; wispy sheets of mist sweep along beneath chunks of thick gray wadding. The wadding crawls, seemingly pulls itself along the iron-colored plane that has blocked out the June sun. The sky has gone dark as the cusp of night. The air has stilled – nature holding its breath.

"We'd better get moving," Dad says and licks the dripping ice cream off the side of the cone.

You poke the pink plastic spoon into the soupy remains of the sundae he bought you at the Dairy. Lightning whipsaws the horizon. "I'm not hungry anymore."

"We're okay, Les. That's just the fireworks I ordered up for your birthday. Big number twelve."

"My birthday was last week." Thunder lumbers over you. You step closer to him.

"Better late than never." He laughs. "Eleven more. I bought you one for each year." Lightning triple strikes, bars of fire like an electric cage. Thunder falls about you like an avalanche of invisible boulders. The stillness sighs and the sigh grows into a gust that rips through your hair and stings your eyes. The rain starts, a billion-footed army of steel-armored droplets charging after the wind.

"This is where we run," Dad says, tossing aside his ice cream. He's still laughing, but he's running like he means it. You run alongside of him. You reach your driveway, already mud and puddles. You can see the lights in the front room of the house. You are just passing Lake Yuck, the velvety green surface churning with tiny waves, when a tingling buzz runs past your soaked skin, plucking at you. The hair on your arms, the back of your neck, rises.

"Christ Almighty," Dad says, and you can't tell if it's a call for assistance or a curse; at that instant the sky above your house goes bright like the center of the sun and a spindly white claw reaches out for the oak tree. Your eyes snap shut in defense as an explosion that sounds like the sun cracking open splits the world in two.

Dad has his arm around you, his voice barely audible above the humming in your ears. "You all right, Les?" You open your eyes. The rain distorts your vision, but you can see smoke rising through the branches of the oak tree, being sucked upward, feeding the clouds. Dad points at the house where the windows are now dark. "Run, Leslie! Make sure your sisters are okay." He takes off down the driveway.

"Where are you going?" you shout after him. He either doesn't hear you or you don't hear him answer. "Where are you going?" you shout again into the storm. He disappears around the side of the garage. You start running for the house. You can no longer see Dad, but you can see the tree.

l y d i a

They ask if she is hungry. They ask if she'd like to go away for a while. Neil watches her in the rearview mirror as he drives. Amanda is turned in the front seat so that she can watch Lydia straight on. They ask if she's tired. Angry? Sad? Does she miss her father? Does she miss her friends back in France? Is school challenging enough? Does she want to try a private school? They ask if she gets headaches. Stomachaches? Cramps? Does she sleep enough? What about her dreams? Good? Bad? Scary? Perhaps she does have allergies. Perhaps they should see an allergist and have tests. Those scratch tests are a chore, they hear. Perhaps they should try a counselor again. The same one? A new one? A psychiatrist, maybe? They read of new medications all the time. They ask about drugs. Pot? Ecstasy? Because they know those are readily available everywhere. What about the drinking? Does she do that often? Get that drunk? Really, she can tell them, they won't be upset. They'll put a lock on the bar if they have to. Television, they say, it's the damn TV. Perhaps they should limit the number of hours even more? The channels? Perhaps they should get rid of the thing. And the messages young girls get from the media in general. Does she worry about being pretty enough? Because she is a truly beautiful girl. Does she worry about being thin enough? Is she making herself throw up? Is she exercising too much? They ask about her hopes for the future. What does she want to be? Where would she like to live? If she could have anything, if they could give her anything at all, what would it be? What would it take to make her happy? Because really all they've ever wanted is for Lydia to be happy.

what goes around comes around

Burnham drove. She tried to get more information out of me as we sped, bumping and jostling, along Old Quarry toward the Parrish place. Questions about what Molly might have told me, questions about the Nightingales. I said nothing. I intended to have her keep her half of the bargain because I was terrified of what impulse might overtake me when I saw Neil.

We pulled into the Parrish place. They must have arrived only a few minutes ahead of us. Amanda and Lydia were at the front door, grocery bags in their arms. Neil had removed his jacket, the sleeves of his blue shirt rolled up his forearms. He was unloading wooden crates from the back of their SUV. I was startled by the sudden sense of loss that tugged at my outrage. It was the first time I'd been aware of how much I'd actually liked the man. My decision to trust him, made only hours earlier in a completely different universe, had been based not so much on careful analysis but on affection. He had been a friend, and I needed friends. The sadness doubled back on itself in the understanding that he'd probably cultivated that friendship as cover. If he could fool me and my tripwire paranoia, he could fool anyone. I had been fooled. Wouldn't happen again.

They appeared perplexed to see us but not overly so. Neil motioned to Amanda, and they headed over to where Burnham had parked the car at a diagonal so that it blocked the driveway from exit. I was keeping my eyes on Lydia. She must have sensed what was coming; she had flattened herself against the front door, trying to get it open, looking for a way to escape. Betrayed as I felt for Molly, the first priority at this instant was to protect Lydia from further hurt. For her sake, I tightened the bolts on what little restraint I had left.

Burnham got out of the car first, she pointed at the boxes. "The work never ends, does it?"

Neil laughed. "Never."

Amanda smiled, no disguising her pride. "Those are the bottles for our first vintage."

"How nice," said Burnham. "I brought Leslie on out because – "

"Because," I said, as I climbed out of the car, "we wanted to talk to you again about not dropping the charges. I know I'm being pushy, but I have seen too many cases like this. I have to wonder if you've considered the full implications where Lydia is concerned. Is this a bad time?"

They shook their heads and gestured to each other, talking over each other's voices. *Of course not. No.* Amanda invited us toward the house. "Please, come in. Let's talk."

When we reached the porch, Lydia was still trying to get the door open, pounding on the knob, pushing. Neil gently took her hands away. "It's locked, Lyddie."

"Sorry. Sorry." Amanda hurried to her daughter's side with the keys, unlocked and pushed the door open, but Lydia, so intent on getting inside, did not move. Neil regarded her quizzically before giving up and going inside. Burnham followed. Amanda held the storm door for me, but as I passed Lydia, I stopped and rapped myself on the forehead, making a show of my forgetfulness.

"Molly wrote a note she wanted me to give to you; I left it in the car. You want to come with me to get it?"

"No. Thank you. I don't want to hear anything from Molly ever again."

Amanda gave her a stern look. "You will not hold Molly responsible for this. Molly is very kind to want to have anything to do with you at this point. Now, go with Mrs. Stone as she has asked you to."

Amanda let the storm door close. Lydia rolled her eyes and headed off toward Burnham's sedan. I hurried to catch up to her. When we reached the car, I opened the passenger door and said, "Get in."

"Why?"

"Get in. Lock the doors. Lie down in the backseat. Do not sit up; do not unlock the doors for anyone but me or Detective Burnham. Do you understand?"

"What is happening?" She suddenly looked very afraid.

"It's over, sweetheart. Get in the car and stay down." The fear drained from her eyes leaving nothing behind it. Trance bound, she nodded but did not move.

"Now, Lydia." She started to climb in, but paused for a moment, her gaze fixed on the open crates of wine bottles. I laid my hand on her shoulder to urge her to keep moving; she continued down into the car seat. I closed the door, waited until I heard the click of the locks engaging, saw her slide down out of view.

I went back to the house and let myself in. They were in the front room. Amanda seated on the end of the piano bench, her back to the window. Neil was by the fireplace, leaning with his right elbow resting on the mantel. Burnham had positioned herself in the archway so that she was nonchalantly blocking any chance of either of them leaving. She was in the midst of listing the costs in time, manpower, and tax dollars already invested in the case, selling hard the point that given these costs, given Lydia's injuries and uncertain story line, it made more sense to keep going than it did to quit now.

"Where's Lyddie?" Amanda asked as I came into the room and strode past her toward the fireplace.

"She's reading Molly's note." I went over to Neil, stood by his side. He shifted his stance, obviously unnerved by my closeness. Probably more unnerved by my staring at his hand. He made a fist and relaxed his fingers, and then moved his elbow in a casual attempt to back away from me.

When this didn't break my gaze, he said, "Is there a problem, Leslie?"

"Maybe. Do you mind?" Before he could answer, I reached out and carefully took his right hand in mine, pulling his elbow from its perch on the mantel. I turned his palm one way and then the other, studying the calluses, the spaded end of his fingers, the short trimmed nails, ending the inspection when I had his arm in an awkward, uncomfortable contortion. "You have strong hands."

He smiled at me the way people smile at those they fear are unstable, but I felt the tension ease out of him. He laughed. "Yes, well, work gets the credit for that."

"You work very hard, don't you?"

He bobbed his head. "Yes, but then who doesn't?"

"Did you touch my daughter?"

"I beg your pardon?"

I closed my hand over his, slid my grip down to his wrist, tightened. "Did. You. Touch. Molly?"

Neil shook his head as though I'd struck him. He moved away from the fireplace, trying to straighten his arm. I wouldn't let him. "Leslie? I don't understand."

"I can make it clearer." I used his surprise and my fury to yank him around so that he was facing the fireplace. I had his arm up behind him. I slammed my foot into the back of his knees and he went down, almost hitting his head on the mantel, his glasses sliding halfway off his face. "Do you understand that any better?"

Amanda was on her feet and pleading for me to come to my senses, to let Neil go. Burnham got in between us. "I think, Mrs. Parrish, we ought to see where this goes."

Neil was breathing heavily. "What are you talking about, Leslie?" I could hear how much he was hurting. I won't pretend that caused me too much unhappiness. Neil shot a sideways glance to Burnham. "Do something," he said, spitting out the words. "Get her off me."

Burnham put her fingers to her lips. "*Shhh*. I'm picking up pointers on technique."

"What is this about?" Amanda shrieked at us.

"I never touched Molly. I never touched Lyddie, either."

Burnham caught my eye. I leaned into Neil's ear. "I don't recall saying anything about Lydia."

"But that's where you're heading, right? That is why you are here?"

Amanda was begging us to listen. "He's been tested. He's been – "

"Yeah, yeah, I know, polygraphed." I applied more upward pressure to Neil's wrist; he yelped. "See, the problem with the polygraph, Amanda, is that it picks up distress only in those who feel on some level guilty about what they've done or at the very least worry about getting caught. If you don't feel bad about what you're doing, the machine won't feel bad about it, either." I leaned into the pressure a bit. A little more and I'd snap his shoulder right out of the socket. I wanted to do that. I really did. Instead, I shunted the need to brutalize him into words. "And why, Amanda, I have

290

to ask, would you believe a fucking machine over your own bruised little girl?"

Point-blank, straight to her heart. "I," she said and sank to the piano bench. I turned back to Neil. "Guess who I believe? I believe Molly."

"Molly? How could you believe a single – "

I jerked his arm. "I'm sure you've heard how I tend to handle these situations when I'm distressed, and I'm very distressed at the moment. So don't be giving me reasons."

"Please."

"When Burnham ordered the SART exam you realized you'd been caught. And then you figured out you could let those boys take the blame. It was perfect, right? The party provided the perfect cover – "

"I have never touched Molly." He spoke slowly, trying to keep his voice level. "I have never touched Lydia. If you can't accept the polygraph machines, then what about the doctors and social workers and cops I've had to talk to? Don't they count?"

"They have to count," said Amanda, reasserting her defense of her husband. "The doctors have said, several times, that Lydia has trouble discerning what is real." I could hear her faltering. She'd begun to work the arithmetic of reconciling what she'd seen with what she wanted to believe. "Molly even admits that she has been fabricating almost everything she's told us."

I thought of poor Molly up on that stand having to relate her awful vision of Lydia's pain: *I shouldn't have to make men touch me; I shouldn't have to make Neil.* And Lydia when I found her: *Nobody touches me.* And there it was. I'd finally seen beyond the pieces of the pattern to the whole. "You're not lying, are you? That's why no one picks up on it. You are always telling the absolute, cold, incontrovertible truth. You never do touch her. You make her do the touching and you watch. That's it, isn't it?" As the reality of the situation clarified, it was all I could do to keep myself from slamming his skull into the fireplace brick. "So you're doing nothing wrong. You're not *touching* anything. Right? Is that right?"

"If I say you're right, if I confess, will you let me up? The detective can go ahead and arrest me."

Burnham chuckled. "So that you can claim duress? A, I don't think so, and B, I'll arrest who I want when I'm damn good and ready, okay?"

I was, at that moment, very tired. "You don't have to confess, Neil. Lydia will talk now that we know how to ask the questions." I gave his wrist a final wrench and then shoved him forward, letting him fall free to the floor. "Not to mention what we'll have you on when Molly gets through talking."

He pulled himself up on all fours and crawled haltingly toward the piano. "I don't know what Molly's told you. I have never been alone in the same room with Molly – I don't understand why she's making up such terrible lies." He reached upward with his working hand, grabbed the edge of the piano, and hauled himself up on his uninjured knee, adjusted his glasses so that he could see Amanda. "The child is lying," he said.

Amanda leaned forward and stroked his hair. "What about Lyddie?"

They held each other's gaze. Neil, barely audible, said, "You know how she is." Then he dropped back against the piano, laid his head against the frame, and began to quietly sob. Amanda exhaled heavily and stood. She moved closer to her husband and squatted down beside him. She stroked his back. He leaned into her as she hushed him and helped him get his sore arm up so that he could balance better with both hands grasping the open piano frame. He began to bang his head softly against the ebony case. Burnham stepped toward him, but Amanda, dry-eyed and determined, told the detective to wait a few minutes, give the man a second to get control of himself. Amanda stroked his head, patted him gently on the shoulder. She stood again and then shoved the post supporting the open piano lid, sending the lid to crash heavily onto Neil's hands.

Neil grunted with the impact and then began a low moan of pain. Amanda went back to stroking his head. "Bastard," she said with an otherworldly tenderness. She looked up at us. "I didn't know." Her eyes grew big. She started to cry. I turned to see Lydia watching through the window.

t i m

They have been waiting in this room for hours – the other guys, some parents, and a guard – to find out what the judge wants to do about Molly and her new version of things. Tim wonders if he should ever tell Molly that he too had been so worried about Lydia, that halfway home he decided to turn his bike around and go back to check on her. He'd found her sprawled in the entryway, still naked, covered in dirt. The plants had been trashed, and Lydia had puked on the carpet, like Molly had said. It seems important that Molly know that Tim did try, but telling that would mean he'd have to tell it all. He'd only told it all to Tyler and Joey later at school. Tyler said they were lucky she didn't choke to death on her own puke. Because that does happen. After the police got involved, Joey said that none of them should say anything about Tim's going back to the Parrish house. They might think he'd gone back to do stuff to Lydia. Joey and Tyler also didn't want to say anything, as far as Tim could tell, because they didn't want to look like assholes for not even considering Lydia might need help. He might be able to tell Molly that, but he couldn't tell her what he did. He hadn't told anyone about what he did when he found Lydia. He'd done nothing. Instead of helping her up or calling an adult or even getting her a blanket, he'd just left her there. Naked and sick in the dirt. He'd gone home without doing a thing. That memory was the worst. Fortunately, Lydia had called Molly, and Molly had come, and Lydia had not choked trying to throw up all the crap she'd drunk. But he'd walked away when he knows he should have done something. How could he ever tell anyone about that?

A commotion of voices churns past the door. The adults seem to tense in anticipation. The door opens and the lawyer Tim's been working with comes into the room. She seems excited. "Lorant wants to see the boys in chambers. Something's going down." She gives them tiniest of smiles, and the air around the room seems, at that instant, lighter. It is easier to breathe. His body feels buoyant as though he might float off the chair. Worry is gone. Fear is gone. He's on that ride at the amusement park again, and whatever is about to happen can go ahead and happen because Tim isn't here.

"When I was a boy," the judge begins, his tall-backed chair swiveled away from them so they cannot see him, "a boy not even your age, I had a friend named Frieda Stubbs. Frieda was not a pretty girl, not by any stretch of the kindest imagination. Always smelled like a cow barn. We called her Tubbs because she was a big girl. She didn't seem to mind that much, or maybe she did, but she never mentioned it. Quiet girl. Not much to say. She was one heck of a pal, though. Big as she was she could scramble up trees better than any of us. Go higher than any of us dared. And she could run – she wasn't fast, but she could run forever. She was great to go fishing with – the girl had this sixth sense about the exact spot in the creek to drop our lines. One evening, after supper and chores, Frieda and I were digging for worms before heading out to try to hook a few trout. We were on our knees, trawling through the mud, pulling worms out and adding them to the cigar box we used for bait.

"Frieda stopped digging, looked at me, and said, 'Do you want to kiss?' She went on to explain that she'd been to the picture show, and the picture seemed to be a story about nothing but kissing. We were farm kids; we knew how the calves and the piglets came to be, but cows and pigs don't kiss. She didn't get what was so important about kissing, so she thought maybe she should try it and find out. I, often annoyed by how the whole kissing craziness got in the way of a good cowboy movie, said I'd like to know what the big deal was as well. So we puckered up and held our lips together for what seemed like the eternity most movie kisses were. When we'd had enough, we separated and stared at each other, until Frieda said, 'Still don't get it.' I didn't say anything. We went back to digging worms. Since then, I've shared much better kisses with much prettier individuals, none of whom smelled of cow flop, but that kiss with Frieda is the one that changed everything, because it was the first time I was made consciously aware that I was on the wrong side of knowledge."

Lorant turns his chair to face them. He's taken off his judge's robe and

294

now looks to Tim like anybody's grandfather on his way to play a round of golf. "The point? Even though you may be prodding, poking, tonguing one another's anatomy with pornographic expertise, I'm here to tell you that you, being children, are still on the wrong side of knowledge. And I, for one, am frightened for you." He looks down at the papers on his desk. "The DA is going to want to withdraw the charges against all of you. Not because he can't make them stick, but because new information has come to light in the past few hours that makes winning a conviction here politically to his disadvantage. I do not care for the DA, so I've beaten him to the punch and dismissed the case due to insufficient, not to mention inadmissible evidence. I'm doing this not because I'm okay with what occurred at your party, but to make it clear to the voters that this is a man whose ambitions lead him to trumping up a case against children, whose sole crime is, in the eyes of this court, being young and, therefore, stupid. We'll have to formalize matters in court this evening, but by the time you go home tonight, you will be innocent once more in the eyes of the law."

Tim's mom, the others moms begin to cry. The dads shake hands and grab one another by the shoulders. Everyone talks at once, thanking the judge, who glares at them like he very much wants them to clear out of his office. The floating feeling inside Tim begins to collapse. His stomach clenches as though he's going to vomit and his heart is revving and then it comes to a thudding halt and he realizes that he is still here and he's made it to the bottom, and really all he wants is to get away from this thing because he knows, just knows, it's going to start up again.

the path of
least resistance

Once we assured her that Neil Parrish was in custody, Molly agreed to talk to Burnham – as long as Greg and I were kept out of the room. Certain words could be spoken only to strangers who could not measure or guess what speaking had cost and, therefore, could not judge. We waited, and when Molly came out of the conference room her face was pale and her expression rigid. Telling was never the relief you hoped it would be. Molly marched past us without acknowledgment. Greg trotted after her, so she could be alone without being alone. Burnham came out of the conference room, wrapping the microphone cord around the tape recorder.

"I'll get this typed up ASAP. You can see it in a hour, max."

"I'm not sure I want to."

"Yes, but Molly needs you to – "

"I know. How bad?"

"All I've gotten out of her to this point is that on an overnight visit a couple years ago, she walked in on Neil and Lydia in the bathroom. Lydia was, as Molly describes it, *performing*. Your daughter seems very suspicious of her own experience. Fears her mind is playing tricks on her."

"Runs in the family," I said.

"Anyway, later that night, Lydia told her that the same thing had happened in France, that her father had 'caught' the two of them and it had killed the man. Neil had convinced her of that, and if Molly didn't believe this about Neil, she could come and ask him herself."

"And the threat extended: If other people were to find out, if *Amanda* were to find out – "

"That's what Lydia told Molly she believed would occur, so Molly had to keep the secret as well, or it would kill her mother. Or people would think Lydia was crazy. You know, basic Creepspeak One-oh-one. Molly, of course, didn't really buy into the logic of that. But she wasn't certain of what she had seen, so she went ahead and made the promise. If this party had not happened, if her other friends had not been put at risk, she might not ever have said anything. Your daughter takes her promises very seriously."

"That's because she's seen so many of them broken." The enormity of Molly having to trudge through the war zone that was already her life while trying to manage so huge a burden wracked my heart with shame for my failure to sense it earlier.

Burnham must have seen the recrimination on my face. "Molly's going to be fine. Lydia, maybe not so, but Molly, she'll get through it. The hard part is over."

"The hard part is never over," I said. "You know that."

She dropped her shoulders and nodded. "I'll let you go find your kid, and as soon as these are ready, I'll track you down." She stopped midstep. "You were quite competent out at the Parrish place this afternoon. I thought I'd mention that we're hiring. In case you might be interested." She continued on down the hall.

That almost made me laugh. Why did the path of least resistance always lead back to the sites of the old disasters? I, no, we, Greg and I, needed to start over or start again in a direction we'd never tried, choose the resistant road that would force us to fight for every inch, to think through the consequences of each potential step. *We.*

I headed off to locate Greg and Molly. I wanted to hold my daughter and apologize for the world she was born into. I wanted to tell Greg that refurbishing the garage into an office was out of the question, but Swifton was brimming with available space. I wanted to tell them both and then tell them again later, after we'd collected Emma, that I was tired of being the missing piece in *us*, and if they would have me, I wanted, very much, for us to rebuild. No, that would lead to the same old mistakes; we should build new, for the first time, from the foundation up, timber by timber, the family we had always wanted to be. I was so suddenly sure of the correctness of this plan that I was almost panicking to find Greg, and before I was derailed or distracted, tell him that yes, I knew that I'd promised this before, but I really could do it this time, I could make us okay again. It was what he wanted, after all, and I rounded a corner, knowing, of course, they must be in the visitors' lounge, that's where they'd go, I knew them at least that well, and I sped through the door marked LOUNGE and ran into, physically collided with, Phillip.

"Whoa," he said, laughing, as he caught my arm to keep me from falling over backward. "I was looking for you."

"And I'm looking for Greg." I righted myself and tried to see over his shoulder.

"He's not in here. How's Molly?"

"Not sure. That's why I'm trying to find them." I tried to step around him.

He blocked my way. "Oh. I see. You still think you're staying in Swifton, don't you?"

"Of course I'm staying. I can't go off and leave Molly after today. And we have to get the house put back together. I'm going to be here at least another week."

"No, I meant you think you are staying for good." He fixed his eyes on mine, and my body gathered its far-flung awareness and focused center, attuning itself to his presence.

"If they'll have me," I said too loudly, trying to drown out the humming in my bones.

"Ah," he said, laughing even harder. "Here we go again."

"So you think you know what's going to happen here?"

He stopped laughing. "No." He placed his finger under my chin and lifted my mouth to meet his. We moved no closer but kissed across the distance. He let me go and said, "But I know you." He smiled and then pressed on past me. "What do you want to tell the Reeves?"

"Tell them I said thank you but no thank you," I said without turning around. He didn't say any more. The room before me was empty except for a few crumb-strewn tables and a scattering of chairs. Quiet except for the tinny music piped in through a single speaker. It was a love song like every other love song in the world. Interchangeable. Disposable. Un- moved, I realized that my heart and my conscience had just parted company. If I were to make this work, my heart had to be disowned. Love did not matter. Could not. What I wanted was insignificant when held to what was needed from me. I could adapt for their sake. I could be someone else. So resolved, I set out once more to find my family. With each step the resolve felt increasingly familiar and with that familiarity came the aching sorrow of recognition. This was how it always started. Phillip was right. *Here we go again.*

Emma and Molly spent an hour in the hotel's indoor pool. Greg brought in deli. We sat on separate beds, eating bread and slices of cheese and pasta salad out of plastic cartons. Em and Molly sat on the floor and watched a television show about television shows. They screamed "No-o-o!" in unison when the *Sneak Peeks* reporter announced that, although they had no official confirmation, inside sources claimed that this week's episode of *Eden* would indeed begin with the banishment of Jasmeena.

Greg insisted that they switch it to the *real* news for a while. I curled up on the bedspread and fell deeply asleep, waking in the dim light of the next morning to find both Emma and Molly in bed with me. I pulled Emma closer, snuggling into her warmth and swimming pool scent. She roused a bit and said, "Daddy snores."

On the other side of her Molly yawned. "So do you." Outside, trucks rumbled past on the highway. In the quiet seconds between their passing, I could hear a few, full-throated bird calls. Crows, mostly, no doubt scavenging the night's road kill, but every now and then I could make out the warble and trill of song. It occurred to me as I was settling back into sleep that I had never heard an actual nightingale sing.

m o l l y

Over breakfast at the waffle place, Mom and Dad watch her not eat. She tries to ignore them by filling each square of her waffle exactly to the brim with a dollop of syrup from the dispenser. The rest of them have already finished. Emma is whining about being bored and wanting to go see the house while it's still under the tent. It finally gets to be more than Molly can stand; she slams down her fork and leaves the table – keeping her head down – and makes for the noisy serenity and space of the parking lot.

She stops at the curb of the road, a step away from walking into traffic, and backs up until she's beneath one of the parking lot lampposts. She doesn't have to turn around to know Mom is right behind her.

"Hey, Molly."

"I don't want to talk about it."

"Talk about what?"

"I'm not ready to talk about it."

"All right, sweetheart."

"Yeah, well, I don't want to talk about you moving back here, either."

"We're going to take that very slowly." She sounds sad. "I spoke with Amanda Parrish this morning. Lydia is starting to open up. Talking. That's how these things get better."

"You think I should have said something earlier."

"I think you did the best you could. You were trying to be a good friend."

"And that's why she hates me?"

Mom moves around to the other side of the lamppost so she can see Molly. "I can't speak for Lydia, but she may have needed to hate you in order to keep you safe."

Molly squints and shakes her head. "What does that mean?"

"Lydia believed that anyone who found out about Neil would die. You found out. The only way to protect you was to get you as far away from herself as she could."

"Why would she believe such a stupid idea?"

"She couldn't afford to lose anyone else. And Neil used that threat to keep her quiet."

"Oh." Molly looks at her feet. She tries to wiggle her toes, but her shoes are too small. And this is the last pair that are good enough for school. She'll have to get somebody to take her to the mall. She starts to ask Mom but says instead, "I liked him. I liked Neil, a lot."

"Yes," says Mom, "I liked him, too." And then Molly is crying, holding her head against the lamppost, resisting the tugging at her shoulders as long as she is able before giving in to her mother's embrace.

the other side
of knowledge

The tarps were down and folded again on the back of the flatbed. The house was still there, where we had left it. One of the crew informed us that Bill was walking the interior with a device for measuring contaminants in the air. We'd have to wait for him to finish. Eventually, Bill came outside, removed his mask, and gave us a thumbs-up. Greg and the girls went into look around.

"All clear, ma'am. But watch for falling rodents. If we got any mice or rats, their little corpses may turn up in the oddest spots."

"Thanks for the heads-up," I said, envisioning a rain of tiny gray bodies. "We're okay to sleep here tonight?"

"Aw, sure. Probably be the first night you ever slept here completely critter free. Not that it will last." He wound up the cord on the meter. "No way of keeping them out. Left your invoice on the kitchen counter." He gave me another thumbs-up and headed for his van, just as Andrea Burnham came hiking up the drive. She was wearing corduroy trousers and a leather jacket. Her curls were clipped back behind her ears and she looked even younger than she had at work. She lowered her glasses to check out the big metal ants on Watson's bug van.

"Groovy," she said and pushed the frames back into place to look at me. "I'm here."

"Indeed. I need to grab something from out back first."

She walked with me out to the garage. "Parrish is on a suicide watch. Why is that always the last idea they come up with?"

"Oh, I think it's probably their first idea and their middle idea, too. They're too scared to go alone." I took the crowbar from the pegboard above Greg's workbench, used it to point back at the house.

Andrea lifted an eyebrow. "This is going to be good." She took a pair of latex gloves out of her pocket and began to work her hands into them. "Lead on."

We went in the back door, through the kitchen, up the stairs. I could hear Greg in the front yard, yelling at Emma to come help move stuff back inside. At the top of the stairs, I stopped and looked up at the attic panel. The rope pull was swinging.

"Something wrong?" Burnham was looking up at the panel with me.

"A few years ago, when I was close to losing it completely and forever, I couldn't tell, from moment to moment, what was real and what was only in my head. What saved me, in the end, was realizing that it didn't matter if the net was real or not, what mattered is that I got out of the tower. The only thing that needed to be real was me."

Her expression shifted to one of professional skepticism. "May I ask you what you mean by that?"

"Oh, you may ask." I wrapped my hand in the rope and tugged. The panel glided open and the stairs slid down. Burnham helped me guide the stairs to the floor.

"After you," I said, and she trotted up the stairs. She found the pull for the light. The shadows were instantly pushed aside by the white-gold of the incandescent bulb.

I pressed the crowbar against my sternum, trying to reinforce my heart from the exterior. *Forgive me.* I started up.

It was only an attic. The same attic it had always been. Still, I had to stop and get my bearings. Burnham was poking around the few things Greg had left in place for the fumigation. Some pieces of furniture. My mother's old vanity. Burnham peered in at the photograph tucked in the mirror.

"Is this you?"

"No, that's my mother. Ellie."

"So this is the infamous Eleanor Cooper – that was thoughtless. I'm sorry."

"It was a long time ago."

"Wow, you look just like her."

"I've been told. Funny to hear her name like that. My father was the only one I ever heard call her Eleanor. To everyone else she was always plain old Ellie."

Burnham looked around a bit more. "You owe me some evidence."

"Yes. I do." I went to the end of the attic. The carved letters in the board were clean, as though a box or chest had been resting on it, hiding my name until the termite fumigation had necessitated uncovering it. I set to work.

"It was so hard that first time," I said as I pried the crowbar into place and the board loosened. "But I was so scared. I was only fifteen. I thought my father had killed him; from what I saw out in the garage, it sure looked like he killed him. I don't believe that was Dad's intent; everything just got away from him and he lost control."

"Oh, my God, Leslie," Burnham said as she came closer. "What did you see?"

"I was terrified that if someone found this, they'd think my father was a murderer. To this day, I believe that Dad probably feared the same thing because if the guy wasn't dead when Dad finished with him – well, I heard him dragging the body off somewhere toward the road. And then a couple of weeks later? Janet was abducted. I'll never ever forget the look on Dad's face when that call came in. He kept staring out the front window saying, 'Impossible.' And of course, Janet was the only Nightingale to have been blindfolded. She couldn't ID anything by sight, and the *evidence* Dad thought he had was gone, courtesy of me. We waited for the next abduction. Nothing happened. The perp disappeared and Janet had been assaulted and it was my fault because I'd hidden the one thing that might have taken him out of circulation." The board came up. I got down on my knees and, careful of the exposed points of pried-up nails, I slipped my hand into the void I'd opened, feeling around in the spongy insulation. "I've spent a lifetime trying to make up for that night, for what I did. And stupid me, it wasn't until I was in the academy, and we were studying crime scene investigation, that it dawned on me that Dad knew. When he found the substitute, he would have had it dusted. If he needed to do even that." My fingers hit the corner of a plastic bag. I pinched at it, pulling upward, tugging it back through the opening into the light. The shoe store bag was intact. "I was expecting mice. After thirty years. Mice eat everything."

"Perhaps you wanted him to know?"

"Perhaps." I tore open the plastic and laughed at the towel as I unfolded it. "Bugs Bunny. Anyway, I have to assume now that he realized I'd been watching, that it was I who switched the hats, but he never said anything about it. Neither did I. We never really talked again. What could we say? I left Swifton the weekend after I finished high school. Didn't even hang around for the cap and gown deal."

The masking tape around the book had become brittle and the adhesive had dried up. It fell away from the book's cover in sheets. The smell of Old Spice was still detectable, at least to me. I pulled the plastic bag out from the pages. Matted, black with ancient blood and mildew, the hat still showed areas of bright orange. I tossed the bag to Burnham. "You've got hair, blood, perspiration. Both the perp's and my dad's. I hope the DNA matches, that Dad was at least right about the guy's ID."

She turned the bag over in her gloved hands. "It would make Janet's blindfold make sense. The girl wouldn't be able to describe his injuries." Burnham affected an expression of genuine sympathy. "When they ask how I came into possession of this?"

"The truth."

"What I know of the truth at this point is that in cleaning out your attic, you found something interesting." Burnham studied the contents of the bag, holding it up to the light. "You know, this may not be a match. Even if it is, no guarantee we can find him. If he's still alive."

"But if you do and he is – "

"Ben Cooper was a decent man. That's part of the truth, too." She took a folded evidence envelope from her jacket pocket, flattened it before sliding the plastic bag inside. "I was serious about that job offer, Leslie." She stood. "Think about it." She left me alone.

I sat there a long time before I could even open the book. At last, I began paging through the bad memories, reading through some of my notes, studying the photographs of the girls that I had cut out of class photographs. It was so long ago. I came to the Nightingale article and decided I'd had enough. I closed the notebook and looked out into the yard as the last of daylight drained from the sky. Greg had planted the first of his orchard in the place the oak had stood, the spindly trunk of a young pear tree surrounded by a broad patch of topsoil and peat. I could hear Greg and the girls coming in and out, putting our lives back in their proper places. They needed help. I replaced the floorboard, realigning the nails as

I had done thirty years ago. I got up to leave, old notebook still in my arms, and glanced once more out at the yard. Janet, in her nightgown, blindfolded again, was sitting under the pear tree. Her head was tilted so that if she could see, she would have been looking at the attic. I sensed that she would be sitting there tomorrow, and the next day, and the day after. She would sit there until the sun itself burned out and the world was gone. This was the past. It alone never changed.

I had to get downstairs and be with my family, be the Leslie they needed me to be. As I was going, I caught my reflection in the broken vanity mirror. Thirty years ago, I had wondered if I looked as my mother had when she was fifteen. Now I wondered if this is what Molly would look like after dealing with the memories of her life with me. Could I do that to her? I had inherited more than my mother's features, I'd inherited her dilemma: She couldn't stay and she couldn't leave. Trapped by love, expectation, and despair, the impossibility of choosing had driven her to the only thing she could do. She had vanished. Her path of least resistance.

But I couldn't just vanish on them. Not again. Maybe the path toward the certainty I wanted for them was not mapped into the future, but rather directly through the past. Phillip had been right. I needed mystery, and the biggest mystery before me was Greg and the girls, how to invent the family I wanted but had never seen. It was then I knew I'd already chosen years ago on the morning I awoke to find my father in the kitchen, clutching the farewell note from my mother to his chest. I had stayed on the periphery of Greg and Molly and Emma's lives not because they had needed me, but because even as screwed up and unsteady as we were together, I needed them. Would continue to need them. It wasn't mystery pulling me away, but pulling me back. I owed Phillip my gratitude. Gratitude and a proper good-bye.

As though on cue, downstairs, the phone rang. I heard Molly in the front room pick up and say hello. Sound in this house was so strange. I moved closer to the spot where the front room came in strongest, until I could hear her with unmistakable clarity, even though she was trying to keep her voice low. It took but a second to figure out it wasn't Phillip calling.

"Are you okay? Where are you? Lydia, why are you yelling – I did not! I did not do that, Lydia. Yeah, well, I couldn't let everyone think the guys did something terrible, either. Why do you think I did this? No. The whole school knows what happened at the party, anyway. You were telling everyone that you couldn't remember, or were you just saying that, too? Why should it matter if I was ever there or not? No, I didn't lie to you or anyone else. Yeah. Of course I didn't tell you the whole plan because you would have – I don't care – fine. I hate you, too. I did not break my promise, Lydia. The promise was not to tell the secret, and I never told anyone what you told me. Never. I made *him* tell. Because it was the only way to make him stop. You wanted it to stop, didn't you? Didn't you?"

My mind went blank in the instant before full understanding hit. I tossed the notebook down on the vanity, and ran, nearly falling down the attic stairs. I was halfway down to the foyer when Molly came out of the front room. Her face was flushed, and she started when she saw me. "Something wrong, Mom?"

I held on to the banister. "When you were in court yesterday, those things you said on the stand, what you told the judge and all of us about Lydia calling you over to the house and what she said, what she did in the shower – "

"Yeah?"

I came down the rest of the stairs and took her by the shoulders. "Molly, was that true? Did that actually happen?"

She turned her eyes to the floor. "It was hearsay, they couldn't use it."

"Molly, you were never at the Parrish house that day, were you? You didn't go to spy on Tim at the party. Lydia never called you for help. None of it happened, did it? Did it?"

She shrugged. "Everything I said was true, Mom." She raised her eyes to meet mine. "Well, you know, true enough."

1

"Checkmate," Dad says, trying not to smile. He clamps his hands onto the board in case you're mad enough to throw it.

"I'm not playing this stupid game anymore. Ever again." You sit back in the chair, arms crossed over your chest.

"Leslie, you're twelve years old now. You can't sulk like a baby every time you lose. Besides, you're not going to get any better if I just let you win." He sweeps the remaining pieces off the board with the side of his hand. They tumble into the box. "It's going to storm pretty soon. Let's go for a walk."

"I don't feel like it."

"We'll stop at the Dairy for ice cream." He singsongs this in such a silly voice you can't help but laugh. He grabs his jacket. You pull on your mother's old sweatshirt.

You walk a couple miles out Swifton-Brank. He asks how you spent your day, seeing as your chores are still not completed. You tell him instead that Joanne and Denise went to the city – without his knowing – to see *The Exorcist*. You tried to stop them. He frowns at this but says that you should deal with your chores and he'll deal with your sisters.

The road ahead of you is dimming as thunderheads advance on their broad flat bases. The anvil-topped clouds look like floating fortress walls from behind which even larger clouds seem to be trying to escape. Lightning flashes on the horizon and thunder rolls in a few seconds later. The sun is still bright, but the air is starting to cool. The breeze stiffens. Swifts and starlings whirl and dive high overhead. Your father's steady pace slows. He looks up at the birds. "We should be heading back."

By the time you've reached the Dairy, the sky is as gray as wet granite. The sound of cars and voices in the parking lot have a pushed-down quality. One of the cars is blasting "Crocodile Rock" from the radio. Your face begins to ache under your eyes, in your forehead. Dad waits for your order at the pickup window. You walk out to the edge of the parking lot, better to see the oncoming storm. The wind has kicked up a bit. You know the air is being pulled backward. Dad says it's like when a tidal wave pulls the water away from the shore in the seconds before it crashes down. Cars are putting on their headlights. People are leaving the Dairy. Melissa Shapiro, who had been sitting at one of the picnic tables with her friends, roller-skates past you. She waves.

"Hi, Leslie!" She almost falls for trying to move forward and talk to you at the same time. Thunder sounds closer. She makes a scary face and says, "Yikes!" before she waves again and starts to skate faster down Old Quarry. She doesn't live too far. She'll be all right. You wonder about the man who is walking on the other side of the road in the same direction as Melissa, if he has far to go. This is not the sort of storm you want to be out in for long. As if to prove your point the wind gusts suddenly and yanks the hat right off his head. The hat tumbles down the middle of the road toward you. You check for cars and then run out to grab it.

"Hey!" you yell, waving the hat to show you have it. But he doesn't turn around. It's like he didn't even notice it was gone. He keeps walking. Oh, well, it's just a stupid hat. No biggie. You don't know what to do with it, so you stick it in the kangaroo pocket of your sweatshirt. Dad brings over your sundae. He is scanning the sky.

"Let's head for home." He's trying not to sound worried, but you can tell he is. You look above you and see what he sees. The birds are gone.

KEEP READING!

Turn the page for a sneak peek
at the dark and thrilling new entry in the Leslie Stone series,

THE WILDERNESS

When the body of an elderly man is found naked, frozen to death on the grounds of an abandoned petting zoo near where private investigator Leslie Stone lives with her family, the discovery triggers what Leslie calls the "haunted amusement park" of her mind. Voices and apparitions she knows to be hallucinatory disrupt her waking world. And she is unable to forget that the old man has left behind what seems like a riddle to be solved: a strange drawing and a children's poem with a shifting meaning, titled "The Wilderness."

Compelled to find out what happened, Leslie finds her search interlacing with that of investigative journalist Sophia Mallory, who is tracing a personal path through the historical tragedy of slavery and its aftermath. Together they uncover a pattern of institutionalized violence so brutal, so inexplicable, that it resembles a curse. As "The Wilderness" leads each woman deeper into the past, it also leads them deeper into their own psyches, forcing them to question their motives for solving a mystery which threatens to destroy the lives of everyone they love.

The new novel by Karen Novak

THE WILDERNESS

Paperback $14.95
Bloomsbury Publishing
Available wherever books are sold

s o l s t i c e

I had been thinking about the body since morning. More accurately, I had been trying not to think about the body and its former inhabitant, how his last hours had been spent alone in the cold night. The story—DEAD MAN IDENTIFIED—had been boxed on the second page of the local paper, lower corner, near the fold. When measured against the headlines that the discovery of his body had rated earlier in the week, I took the placement as an indication of diminishing interest. It wasn't a murder, after all. Nothing remarkable. He had been no one.

Skiers trekking the fields around Willet had stumbled upon the body, frozen, beneath a knoll of heavy snowfall. Authorities determined that he had been an itinerant trying to ride out the cold snap at Happy Andy's, the abandoned petting zoo and defunct cut-it-yourself tree farm. Preliminary coroner reports estimated the victim to be in his late eighties or older; this advanced age had only hastened the effect of the below zero temperatures. The body showed no indication of foul play. No alcohol or drugs in his system. That blankets, clothing, cans of food had been scattered around Happy Andy's empty caretaker's house, that the woodstove there had been stocked with kindling but gone unlit, that the body was naked, curled fetal several hundred feet from any structure implied he had wandered away from his shelter. Whether this was due to confusion, dementia, or the outright courting of his end was not pertinent. Officials were calling the death an unintentional suicide.

The unintentional now had a name. He was—had been—one James Kendrick, this according to a homeless shelter ID card found among other papers squirreled away near a "graffiti-covered wall" in the caretaker's house. It was hoped that someone would recognize the name and aid authorities trying to locate the man's family. The paper again offered a brief description of the lanky, toothless remains and noted a forearm tattoo that was not described in detail beyond "unusual." Kendrick's name was familiar to me in the way that names in newspapers always seem familiar, but it was the details—the cold, the aloneness, the naked body beneath the snow; these nagged at my thoughts. Poor old man.

Not counting a few mean-spirited spates of wind-driven slivers, it had not snowed since Kendrick had been found. The snow we had was now hard, icy, and dulled under grime. We wouldn't be getting any more soon. Too cold. The forecast in the paper had arctic air slicing south for the holidays; we would be hovering at the zero mark through New Year's, and it was only the twenty-first. Outside the clock of the northern sky was striking nadir: longest night, first of winter, the climatic shimmer on our tambourine panic that the sun's attentions might have drifted beyond recall.

I carried the paper with me all that morning into the afternoon, feeling pursued. The shadows stretching across the windows and floors had taken on a sense of hunger. This was how my illness announced its return, unease percolating through reality, investing even inanimate motion with a palpable intent to grab and swallow. The illness had a name of multiple syllables that came no closer to describing it than I could beyond this sensation of exterior hunger. Like any prey, I did my best to keep moving. To stop would mean I had admitted that I could not outrun the appetites of my madness, and would have no choice but to admit that sense of encroaching menace to my husband, Greg. That was my half of our reconciliation bargain. I was not to harbor ghosts in secret. If *it* started up again, he was to be told. His half of the bargain was that until told otherwise, he was going to believe everything to be fine.

My bargain keeping leaned more toward the spirit rather than the letter of our deal. It was our first Christmas back together after a four-year separation that had not worked out any better than the marriage. Forces beyond logic joined Greg and me, our essential selves melded on the molecular level so that we were just as unstable apart as together. We were each other's irresolvable, the *why?* that pride and stubbornness could not leave alone. There was love here, without question, but for Greg and me, love without question was not to be trusted. We poked, prodded, split up, and fused back together if only to keep proving love's existence to our own satisfaction. We were one of those couples with a half-life, more interested in the glow we gave off than in the long-term implications for the health of those around us.

This year, however, was going to be different. This Christmas was to be the demarcation line, the moment we could point to from a vantage in the happy future and say, "That was the beginning of better." In deference to our agreement, in hope for that future, I waved the newspaper in Greg's general direction while he, on the other side of the room, was trying to find which of the tiny twinkle lights had burned out on the decidedly nontwinkling Christmas tree.

"Do we know anybody named Kendrick?"

"Who?" He pulled his hand from deep inside the stiff-branched pine and lifted it to his mouth to suck on a bleeding scratch. "It would be a big help if someone actually checked these lights *before* I put them on the tree."

We went through this every year. Greg, not remembering the ordeal from one year to the next, saw the tree lights as just another annoyance to cross off his current to-do list. I saw the whole exercise, from finding the unmarked box that held the lights to the moment we finally had twinkle, as a tradition as vile and nutty as the fruitcake I was obliged to make but no one ever ate. Even during our separation, when we only pantomimed our way through a semblance of a family holiday for Molly's and Emma's sake, we had had this fight. We had to have this fight or it simply was not Christmas.

"Greg, I *did* check those before you started—"

"All of them?"

"No. I only checked every other—of course, I checked all of them. I always do, don't I? They were working."

"Well, they are not working now."

"Maybe one of them got knocked loose when you—"

"It's all right, Leslie. I've got it under control."

"No one said you didn't."

"Why do we hold on to this cheap crap? Next year we're getting brand-new everything. I'm amazed we haven't burned the house down."

"You say that every year—"

"So why do we still have these?"

"—And then you hold me responsible. Every year."

"If you're so up on what happens *every year* then maybe you could have bought the damn new lights?"

"See? Why is it my responsibility? You put them up. You take them down. If *you* want the damn new lights shouldn't *you* be the one to go buy the damn new lights?"

This was my traditional ploy of trying to end the discussion with a persuasive mix of the obvious tinged with just enough sarcasm to come across as both insult and threat. Anger thus ignited, he'd shut down, shut up for fear of setting off something larger.

Determined, willfully silent, he would go back to twisting bulbs in and out of sockets. I'd grouse under my breath about how he had to stop treating me like an open keg of nitro; if he was pissed at me, he should say so; it was the quiet that made me crazy. He'd continue as though I were not there, inches away from his ear, yelling at him in whispers. The tree would not light. Greg's movements would intensify, his body bending away from me; my complaints would grow louder. Our daughters would hightail it to their rooms, taking cover before the inevitable combustion of my superheated frustration met their father's airless nonresponse. Hark! The herald angels sing . . . *Kaboom.*

But this year *was* going to be different. We had promised each other we would do whatever we could to try to be different. In the name of trying, I clamped my mouth tight. Our eyes locked in mutual pleading to not go where the ritual demanded. Greg broke the gaze first to examine his scratched knuckles. "Yeah, you're right. I should have taken care of it."

"No, you're right. I'm the one who remembers. I should have done it. Still can. The stores—"

"Don't bother. More of a pain to take them off at this point. I'll find the uncooperative bastard—" he noticed the paper "—you wanted something?"

"Never mind." I crumpled the newsprint in both hands, twisting it, the ink smearing on my damp plams.

"You asked me if I knew someone?"

"No. It was nothing."

"New lights next year, then?"

"Absolutely. Next year." I tossed the paper into the fireplace where it caught on the lazily flaming logs and was gone, flared to ash in an instant.

Nothing burns that fast. I had blanked out and come back. Flames clutched at the charred bits of paper caught in the updraft. How much time had I lost? Ten, fifteen seconds?

"Leslie?"

I should have told him what had happened. But how could I explain it? That time was getting as unreliable as light? Anyway, when this sort of thing started happening, it was too late to do much about it. I smiled at my husband. "It was nothing."

Night came on thin and quick, edged by a shrill icy wind. The tree was dark still; Greg still checking bulb after bulb and swearing softly in time, in tune to the carols lilting from the stereo, both refrains drowned out by the occasional shriek of wind in the chimney. Molly knelt at the coffee table in front of the fireplace, book open before her, reading, her face flushed from the heat of the now-dying flames. Emma was in the kitchen giving gingerbread men fashion statements of colored icing. I, who had been growing increasingly restless, was wandering the house, unable to settle my body, let alone my concentration for having to admit to the sense of whispers just beyond my hearing. I shuffled about in my bedroom slippers, annoying my family with cheery inquiries as to whether they were hungry, if maybe they wanted cocoa or cider or anything at all.

Greg kept eyeing me as I passed him in my anxiety-driven circuit. "Les?" he finally said. "Why don't you sit down?"

"I'm fine." *Fine* was what he wanted to hear; *fine* was what I wanted to be true. I could not tell him, could barely tell myself, that since burning the Kendrick story, *it* had been getting worse: time was hiccuping fast, slow, skipping moments in which I, outside of time, was seeing the shimmer of movement, quicksilver running through rooms I knew to be empty.

Even if I could have told Greg, what would I have told our daughters? The scary stuff is back but don't be scared? They'd heard that one before. My selfish insisting that they endure my uncertain presence often appalled me; it would have been more selfish to explain to them why I needed it so.

An ember in the fire snapped. I startled as though it had been a gunshot. *Run.* "Going out to get wood," I announced to no one, turned, and headed for the kitchen. I thought to grab my gloves but not my boots or coat before dashing out the door, down the back porch, and into the trench of a path we'd worn through the snow trekking back and forth to the woodpile. The wind hit sideways, thrusting into the collar of my shirt, under and up the hem of my sweater. My feet, bare in thin flannel slippers, ached with the insult of the cold. Pointless to turn back, I was already halfway to where I was headed; I pulled the collar closed around my throat and hurried on to the side of the garage where the wood was stacked. The motion sensor of the light fixture had already been tripped by the wind. Sparkling filaments of powdery snow danced tornado ballets through the spotlight. I quickly filled my arms with a bunch of hardy branches and wheeled about to run back for the warmth of the house.

The wind built, gusted. I tried to hunker into myself, make the thump of my footfall thump faster. The floodlights Greg had installed over the girls' basketball hoop were blazing, the sensors there tripped, too. Into the light swirled a sheet of newspaper. I would have ignored it as an errant piece of litter, but it was followed by another sheet and then another. I stopped to watch them—dozens now—tumbling and twirling toward me, giant curling planes of translucence just above my head. I dropped the branches and tore off my gloves so that I could better grab at the sheets when they passed, but the wind attenuated, wilted like a dying breath; the sheets fell, not far away, and slid in a lazy jumble on the ice crust. I took off after them, my numb feet punching knee-deep shafts in the snow, moving farther and farther from the shelter of the light. Aware of nothing but the repeated crunch of punctured ice and the throb of my breathing, I did not feel myself fall out of time. I reached the pages, began gathering the ones I could. I heard Greg shouting from behind me: *Leslie, what are you doing?* I was about to shout back, but when I turned to show him the papers, my voice retreated. In front of the woodpile stood a peacock. The bird's thickly clawed toes ticked on the icy crust; his broad, night-blue breast heaved. The tail draped out heavily behind him in a massive train of plumes twelve, maybe fifteen feet long. He took no notice of me at first, but in a moment his head bobbed about, sending a vibration through his crown of spurred frills. He turned toward me, and with a flourishing snap, he fanned his tail upright, an arc of a hundred blind, burning eyes, staring out red and gold, unblinking, still, even in the once-more-building wind. All those eyes directed at me. It was an accusation.

Greg called my name. At least, I thought it was Greg. The moment was disrupted; the bird vanished and the world resumed. I looked down at my hands clutched tightly around nothing. The paper had been unreal as well.

Greg met me on the path and helped me collect the wood to carry back to the house. He asked if I was all right, and I told him that I was fine, that I had chased off a raccoon or bear or something. He wrapped his arm hard around my shoulder, pulling me against him, saying we should get me inside where it was warm. I told him I wasn't looking forward to that. He noted my snow-clogged slippers and said something in my ear, his breath hot where I could feel it. I lost the sound of his words in the whine of the gathering wind. Greg urged me toward the house. I kept shifting my gaze, turning my head to look behind me where the peacock had been, turning back to where I could see the shifting patterns of tree lights now in play as patterns on the windowpanes.

The next morning, in full sun, I went out to check the woodpile. Maybe I was hoping to find one page escaped from the girls' school bags or a newspaper insert, a single fragment from my current willed-to-center life that could have triggered the hallucination. I found none, of course. The trigger had been that reference to *papers* in the Kendrick story. The part of my mind too slippery for words had wanted to see those papers and so had made its request in dream-speak. Until I saw them, I wouldn't know why the pages were important to me. Or what the hell that peacock was supposed to mean. I might not even know then. But until I saw them, the hallucinations would continue, intensify. My subconscious, having no self-awareness, had no self-control either. What the illness wanted, it got. Better to surrender up front.

I stood in the snow and considered the windless sky scoured to a gleam by the cold that was now steeling itself in my head as a too-bright idea. I could call Andrea Burnham, my detective friend on the Swifton police force, to see if she might call up to Willet and finagle copies for me. Apply police logic to uncertainty, isn't that what I always did? As a child, I had assessed the forces of the world as oppositions embodied by the quiet constants of the resolve of my father, the police chief, and the continually dissolving variables of my mother's carnival impulses. My mother ended up lost inside the violence of herself and left us to avoid hurting anyone. We never heard from or of her again. My father lost himself in the violence of the world and tried to will peace through his fists and a two-by-four. I had watched him try to kill a man he feared might kill us. And so I was lost, although I did not know that yet.

I ran away to the city where I joined the police force. I thought that being able to name chaos was the same thing as creating order. It wasn't until I was talking to shrinks, bleary between dosages in the day room of the institution and going all third-rate Lady Macbeth about the blood on my hands, that I started to understand everyone in my family was running different frequencies on the spectrograph of crazy. I, the introspective cop, the family mediator, had lost it completely and, like my father, killed a man; like my mother, abandoned my daughters. Because I was scared. See? My madness was nothing if not reasonable.

For obvious reasons, I had to call Andrea, and appeal to the hierarchies of law to graft order into my thoughts. The simple imagining of the chain of events this might set in motion sent a wave of warmth though my chest, as though a deep breath had at long last reached my lungs. My posture straightened, the curl of a genuine smile tensed the muscles of my face for the first time in days. Maybe I could be of use tracking down Kendrick's family? Calling Andrea might lead to work. That was what I needed. I needed work, a purpose other than proving myself sane.

The nature of my work, however, would only accelerate the illness. Tracing effect back to cause necessitated imaginative thinking, and my imagination was a dangerous place. I longed to have my husband and our daughters see me as safe. The effort had failed. It always failed.

The initial glow of happiness cooled; icy air replaced the warmth around my heart. To even contemplate returning to a search for the missing was an untenable risk to my family's security. To pursue this Kendrick fixation, which had already put my mind in jeopardy, was selfish and foolhardy. I knew that. I also knew I had to see Kendrick's papers, that if I did not see them my waking mind would be overtaken by the depths of shadows spilling out from beneath it. I had no choice.

Before heading back to the house and the telephone and the call, I scanned the yard one more time. Maybe, just maybe, I was hoping to find traces of peacock claw in the snow. If it had been real, I could forget it, leave it behind the way real things get left. I didn't find anything, no scratch nor puncture in crusted snow. Nor could I seem to find those gloves.

A NOTE ON THE TYPE

The text of this book is set in Linotype Sabon, named after
the type founder, Jacques Sabon. It was designed by Jan
Tschichold and jointly developed by Linotype, Monotype,
and Stempel, in response to a need for a typeface to be
available in identical form for mechanical hot metal
composition and hand composition using foundry type.

Tschichold based his design for Sabon roman on a font
engraved by Garamond, and Sabon italic on a font by
Granjon. It was first used in 1966 and has proved
an enduring modern classic.